The Underland Tarot

XIII: Stories of Transformation
XVIII: Stories of Mischief & Mayhem

Underland Arcana Deck One

UNDERLAND ARCANA DECK ONE

This book is published by Underland Press, which is part of Firebird Creative, LLC (Clackamas, OR).

First, the Querent forms a question . . .

Edited by Mark Teppo
Book Design and Layout by Firebird Creative
Sigil art by Andrew Penn Romine
Cover art by warmtail/stock.adobe.com

This Underland Press trade edition of the first year of *Underland Arcana* has been released in conjunction with the ending of one cycle and the beginnng of the next.

It has an ISBN of 978-1-63023-077-7.

Underland Press
www.underlandpress.com

UNDERLAND ARCANA
DECK ONE

To B, eternally wreathed in roses.

Family Dinner

~ A. P. Howell

Margot's mother still sets a place for him at the dinner table.

It has been two years, or three. Long enough that there are no expectations of mourning, no more messages of condolence. The logistics of death have been resolved: the will read, the legalities settled, the funeral paid for, the stone memorial to Margot's father raised.

Margot's mother still serves his favorite foods.

It took some time for Margot to notice. But some nights she picked at her plate, finding the meal unappetizing, and looked up to see her mother doing the same. It occurred to Margot that they could eat other foods, foods that they enjoyed. After more time, it occurred to Margot that she could share this revelation with her mother. After yet more time, Margot wondered why she had not done so.

Each day, she watches her mother repeat the routines of decades. Each day, she feels her father's presence looming over the household.

Margot eats little. Her mother eats less.

Her father would eat so much. Instead, it is his memory that consumes them.

It is exhausting. It is ghoulish. They are starving, and for no reason.

But Margot is starving less quickly and cannot bring herself to speak.

Bloodletting

~ *Vera Hadzic*

After my husband's funeral, I went home and took my own blood, just as I had every Sunday for the past three years. The funeral had been dismal. I'd stood there, draped in black satin and gauze, like I was made of wax —like each passing second melted another inch of my flesh. The heat was heavy as lead, and humid. Just as his coffin thumped into his grave, the clouds had split open. His family had grumbled. They weren't used to Louisiana's afternoon thunderstorms. But I was grateful for the rain, even though it made me melt faster.

"You did the right thing," Michael, my husband's friend, had told me at the reception. "Keeping his body here. His home."

By now, I was so used to drawing my own blood that I could have found a vein with my eyes closed. The needle pinched as I slid it under my skin. The thin, plastic tube slithered down my arm. As it filled with blood, I felt it sigh. The bag swelled red. Through the window, the storm's breath gathered under my ears. The hulking, twisted oak on the edge of our property sucked the rain into its dark wood.

The day after the funeral, Michael visited. He brought another of my husband's friends, someone whose name I couldn't hear. I heard only the rushing of blood in my ears.

I took them to the living room. Made them something —tea, or lemonade, or coffee. I wasn't sure which. My gaze stuck on Michael's face, in its creases and its curves like sap. Today, he seemed so much more alive than my husband had been, but I could see the coldness in him—the pallor of his cheeks, the gauntness under his eye. My husband had, on his worst days, seemed a sheet of paper: like if you shone a flashlight on his forehead, you'd see into his skull.

"Was it really a car crash?" said the second man. "He was getting enough—you know? And it was good?"

"You can speak plainly here," Michael said. "We're all—friends."

Still, he looked out the window, at the oak tree as though its leaves were ears. As though the sunlight fermenting on the window could listen. Or as though the woodpeckers on the lawn wore wires.

"No." I was firm. I eyed my cup. Something brown—tea. Or coffee, with cream.

"But, if the source was contaminated—"

"It wasn't," I said. I put my right hand over my forearm, where the Band-Aid from yesterday kissed my skin. "He crashed into a tree. Branch went straight through his heart."

A week after the funeral, I took my blood again. A woodpecker ducked its head under the open window. Its feathered gladiator's crest was the same color as the plastic snake crawling over my arm. The bird tilted its head: *Where are you going to put it?*

My husband and I had met in New Orleans. The sun gave him headaches, so he slept all day in a dusky hotel room, blinds drawn tight. I'd had insomnia. At night, New Orleans glittered like a cracked kaleidoscope. The balconies' ironwork laced with light and color. Music, even. The stones vibrating under our feet had a heartbeat. Funny that a city's heart could beat louder than his.

I hadn't felt warm, or sexy, the first time he bit me. It hadn't even happened in bed. He had carefully laid his fingers over my neck, had felt for the veins. When I replayed the moment, I always imagined an open window, whispers of blues music bubbling into our hotel room. But when his teeth broke my skin, it was something like getting a flu shot.

In our bedroom, we'd turn on all the lights. Two weeks after the funeral, the room was still cluttered with the lamps we'd bought. We had chosen the yellowest, the orangest and warmest lamps. We had a ritual, racing upstairs, twisting each knob or button, watching the lights meld into a web of gold. We pretended we were in the sun, pretended it was the sun leaking into the pores of his skin, lighting up the shadows in his eyes. He'd hold me in his arms and tell me he loved seeing me with the sun braided through my hair. I was floating, he said. The second week after the funeral, when I climbed into bed after taking my blood, I left the lights off. It seemed wrong to enjoy our false sun without him.

Three weeks after the funeral, I heard from my husband's family. I was standing in front of the fridge when the phone rang.

"Fine," I told his mother. "I'm doing okay."

"That's good to hear." Her teeth worried her lip. "Would you like someone to come and be with you?"

She was relieved when I turned her down. I let her talk about how sorry she was while I rearranged the tiny glass bottles in the fridge doors. Whenever I moved one, the blood inside swirled into a red vortex. I poured today's blood bag into another bottle, stoppered it gently, put it in the place of the Tabasco sauce. I was running out of space. The peaches Michael sometimes brought me had rotted. I'd left the bowl on the windowsill and watched the woodpeckers' beaks tear the browning flesh into strips.

When Michael came next, he found me under the oak tree. His wide-brimmed hat shielded his face from the sun. It was five weeks after the funeral. The tree's branches, thick and oiled with moss, arched low over the ground, wooden snakes. It was a tree of spaces, each branch a basket of sky. The sparse green leaves offered little shade.

"We used to have picnics out here," I told Michael. "After dusk."

"What about the bugs?"

"Hell," I said.

He laughed, handed me another plastic bag. The fruit strained against it. Under this oak tree, I had first offered to draw blood for my husband. Right then, he would have become as translucent and sickly as stars behind smog, if he could have become any paler. But this had been a clear night, and the oak had buckled under the weight of the starlight. He'd agreed.

By six weeks, I was leaving the house more and more often. I took walks in the woods that curled around the property, waved a stick in front of me to tear down the spiderwebs that fizzle across gray-barked branches. I went alone. Spoke little if I passed any neighbors. Michael said he was glad to see me getting better. If anything, I was desperate to get out of the house. I'd stopped sleeping in our bedroom with all its lamps.

On my walks, I watched the birds coast low over the bayou, their red bellies warped by the gray-green waters. Heat cushioned my armpits. If a summer thunderstorm caught me, as it often did, I imagined that the mud suctioned a piece of me away with each step. When I got home, I drew my blood. Struggled to find a place for it in the fridge.

Eventually, Michael figured it out. It was the eighth Sunday since the funeral. At this point, the sacks of blood I filled, emptied, and refilled had become my timekeepers. The hands of a clock, a clock I couldn't properly read.

Michael found me by the window, plastic tube whispering along my forearm. Didn't say a word as we watched the red dribble into the fleshy sack. The woodpeckers thundered at the oak tree. I pressed a pale pink Band-Aid to my forearm.

"Didn't know you did that for him," Michael said finally.

I didn't answer. Didn't know how.

"He put you up to it?"

I shook my head. Offered him tea—I was pretty sure he preferred it to coffee. For a second, I wondered if I should offer him the blood I had just drawn. Or one of the chilled vials, one of the countless tiny bottles swaying in the fridge. Most of them, especially the ones in the back—filled before the funeral, or even before the crash—had darkened with time, turned earth-red or even black.

Michael took the tea. Slowly, he said, "I thought you were doing better. But this . . . isn't healthy."

"I can't stop." I swirled my tea.

"Can't stop?" He tilted his head. The shadow of his hat dripped into the lines of his face. "Or can't let go?"

He wanted me to talk to someone. *A friend. Family. Therapist. Anyone*, he said as he left.

I started filling the freezer with vials. I had already cut down on food to make room in the fridge. Let the fruit that Michael brought me rot. Thrown out meat. I couldn't stop, but seeing all the vials infuriated me. They spat in my face when I opened the freezer. Reminders that there was no one to drink them all.

I took my longest walks on Sundays, after I'd poured fresh blood into vials. These walks were free from memories. What I'd cherished in the first weeks since the funeral, the warm, tingly thoughts of our meeting in New Orleans, of our hotel room, our bedroom with its fake suns, were now difficult. I stripped the memories to pieces as my stick tore down spiderwebs in the woods.

I was at my weakest after taking blood, but I relished the buzzing in my head, the way my limbs felt light and wasted in the sun. Sitting by the bank of the bayou, watching the woodpeckers skim its sun-eating surface, was a kind of peace. The bugs that took to my arms made me feel better. Someone, at least, was using the blood in my veins.

At ten weeks, I slept in the kitchen every night. Sometimes I never bothered to get out of the chair by the window, where I could see the oak tree and let the woodpeckers drum me to sleep. I dreamed of my husband. Of our midnight picnics, our made-up sunlight. The precision when he sought out my veins. The softness in his voice, its warmth and richness.

Sometimes, I dreamed of the funeral. In those dreams, I really did melt away like a wax candle, turned into a puddle by a scorching thunderstorm. His family's lips curled in distaste, disgust. My thick, viscous self saturated the soil, absorbed by the earth: I pooled into my husband's coffin. The steaming hot wax, all that was left of my body, was acid to his corpse. Despite my best efforts, he dissolved at my touch.

Michael no longer came alone. He always brought someone new for me to meet—people who had never met me or my husband before. Sometimes they were his relatives, people with sunny eyes and tender handshakes. Or friends who thought I should come spend a weekend with them in New Orleans. I always said no. But I started to drink more water, to speak in longer sentences. When I had trouble remembering if it was week twelve or week thirteen since the funeral, I realized Michael's plan was working.

The fridge had been threatening to burst from all the vials I'd stuffed in. There truly was no more space. But it was my dreams that finally pushed me to empty it. After my husband's body flaked into nothingness, it was just me in the coffin. A puddle of wax, I could hear the rain punching the ground, could hear his family's footsteps echo as they trudged to their cars. Then, silence. As I cooled, I reformed. The coffin shrank around me—its walls resisted the push of my palms, stood fast against the beating of my feet. I wasn't dead. I screamed I wasn't dead.

My husband's dead, I said to the coffin. *Not me.*

But the earth had swallowed me up.

When I woke, it was the first Sunday since the funeral that I didn't take my blood. I piled the vials into cardboard boxes, loaded them into the back of my car. Trundled up the sun-beat, dead-beat road to my favorite curve in the bayou, where I usually sat with mosquitoes and watched the red-bellied woodpeckers. I was tempted to throw each box into the water, to watch the vials sink. Instead, I opened them up, uncorked each bottle, and spilled its dark, shining liquid into the bayou.

It must have taken me hours, but I didn't feel the time. I heard my own pulse as thick red liquid clouded the water, bent into itself in sleepy, heavy curls. Soon, the bayou started sounding like my husband's voice. Viscous and slow, he said, *I love you, I love you, I love you.* He said, *I'm coming back.* He said, *Wait for me.*

Hours and hours must have passed because the sun had softened to molten orange, clinging to the tops of trees like globules of juice. And the water—I wondered if I was hallucinating. The slow current inched quietly along, all of it blood-red. All of it. As red as the plastic tube that meandered so often down my forearm. As red as an artery in my own neck. I couldn't look away.

The woodpeckers spiraled down from the trees, perched on the lower branches that twisted above the water, or by the bank. Their beaks shone, golden scythes in the fading sun.

Down cut the scythes, into the red water. Again and again, drinking up the blood, my blood.

Some of them were red-feathered already—the others matched before long. They descended upon the bayou in droves. For the first time, I couldn't hear a single one pecking against the tree.

I drove home. My fingers left luminous, sweaty prints against the steering wheel. First, it was only a couple, fluttering in the darkening sky, flitting by my mirrors. By the time I pulled into our long, sandy driveway, the oak tree was groaning under their weight. They fell silent when I stepped out of the car. Not even their red-soaked feathers rustled as I ran inside.

I slept fitfully, curled up and tangled in my own limbs on the chair by the kitchen window, the chair where I sat every Sunday to draw my blood. When I lay in my husband's coffin, I heard his voice inside my head. Felt it trickle through my bloodstream. Mingle with the wax of my flesh.

Why have you stopped? he would ask. *Don't you know I need it?*

Awake, I was chilled with sweat. I wore it as a blanket, a film over my body. Colder than his touch had ever been. As the night went on, the woodpeckers swarmed the oak tree, lined the windowsill. Their beaks clacked against the glass. Their talons clamored against the wood. Their feathers whispered in my husband's voice.

They were here for my blood. Didn't they have a right to it? I began to think they were some part of him, some leftover part of my husband that had peeled away from his body when he'd been impaled.

I couldn't force myself to cry. I could hardly force warmth into my fingers and toes as I limped to the door, threw myself onto the porch. The simultaneous beat of hundreds of wings made a cylinder of sound around me. They tussled for space on the railing, hooked their claws to the beams above my head, hopped boldly on the deck. My knees dug into the wooden boards. My arms were as contorted and gnarled and aged as the oak tree, the one in the edge of my vision. I felt I might burst from all the blood in me, all the blood straining against my skin, begging to go out. A single prick from one woodpecker's beak might split me open.

But in all that time, the night had bled away. That was the sun rising, crawling along the spines of the trees ahead, flooding the gaps between them. The sunrise ate up the grass like fire, pooled into my palms like wax, like honey, and held me tight. It was red, redder than blood, redder than the woodpeckers' bellies, redder than how I'd felt when I heard how my husband had died. I had a redness in me, too. A redness just as burning, just as powerful, just as alive. A redness that belonged to me. I wanted to keep it.

The birds didn't make a move, or a sound, as I stumbled to my feet and leaned against my doorway. I let the sun, the real one, wipe away the gray in my face.

I boxed up the lamps in my bedroom and left them in the attic. My memories of my husband still ached, and I still loved them. But the weeks gained meaning again. I donated the equipment I'd used for drawing blood.

Some days, I went for walks in the woods—alone, or with friends. Often, I had lunch with Michael. And some weekends, I went to town, or to New Orleans, and let the city unravel me as it had before. Let its streets beat in tandem with my own pulse. The woodpeckers would never be far behind. They would caper on the filigree balconies, or hammer at the trees when I passed underneath them. Sometimes, they flew overhead, circling. Waiting for something I wouldn't give.

Occasionally, I left peaches for them on the windowsill.

Occasionally, I watched the sun rise.

A Pamphlet Found Among Broken Glass
Near the East Wing Entrance

~Jonathan Raab

The Orford Parish Historical Society welcomes you to the Marvel Whiteside Parsons Memorial Mall and Food Court! This pamphlet's production and printing costs are generously funded by a partnership between the Historical Society, the Orford Parish Downtown Improvement District, and mall property owner, Malthus Retail and Correctional Services, Inc.

Since being built in 1972 by local labor—just like Revenant's Finger Middle School slogan says: "Orford Parish Breeds for the Labor Pits!"—and designed by an architect and suspected occultist whose name was struck from the blueprints, the Parsons Memorial Mall has been a center of commerce, culture, and alternative aerospace research for almost 50 years.

Upon first glance, Parsons Memorial Mall may seem like it has seen better days—what with the majority of its storefront units rendered abandoned by the predations of global capital, the rats, the imminent structural failure of a large portion of its roof system, the ever-present blood in the central fountain, the rats that *crawl and squeak like human babies*, the theft of the Moroni the Angel mannequin from the tableau depicting various secret and nefarious Masonic rituals brought out every Lenten season, the strange and malignant whispers that only cancer survivors working the closing shift can hear, the rats that *think* and *talk* and *parlay with the goat-legged sorcerer who appears nightly at the edge of the wood*, and the ominous radiological phenomena around the second floor men's bathroom (mentioned in FOIA-acquired and heavily redacted Air Force documents from Project WILL-O-WISP)—despite all this and more, we can assure you that the mall's best days are yet to come!

That's why we have authored this one-of-a-kind pamphlet and tour guide to this historic and beloved community institution. As part of a mysterious and generous state grant offered by a bureaucrat from Away whose face and voice none could recall save through their inexplicable and invasive presence in traumatic memories of car accidents that never occurred, this pamphlet and guide was commissioned to bring a little of the Mall's history to life for shoppers, local history buffs, and wayward tourists who pulled off the highway for gas and have found themselves unable to navigate the labyrinthine roads to find an escape. No matter how many maps they consult or how loud they scream and beg with the invisible, indifferent idiot-god that has made their lives a living hell, they will not be permitted to leave until the *Proper Time.*

If you happen to be one of those unlucky souls trapped in a space-time loop that refuses to release you from our quirky and historic city—welcome to your new home! Please contact the Historical Society to get recommendations on our many affordable abandoned home properties scattered throughout the hollowed out remains of our once-vibrant municipality. It's a buyer's market!

Although built in the early 1970s over the razed remains of an impoverished and largely ethnic neighborhood colloquially referred to as "the Mick Warrens," the history of the site goes far beyond the cyclical displacement and disenfranchisement of minority groups that define Orford Parish's Nietzschean gyre through dead and haunted time. In a collection of documents housed in one of our beloved Historical Society's many FORBIDDEN ROOMS there are accounts of hometown Revolutionary War hero and accomplished serial murderer Eli Elderkin himself negotiating for the town's purchase of the land from a local American Indian tribe that refused to have its name written on "cursed Orford parchment, lest we find our souls drawn to one of the white man's deranged hells."

Elderkin had made a study of the ley lines intersecting throughout Orford Parish and identified the low hill where the mall now sits as a "confluense of forces malign and untapped." The anonymous tribe had been using it as a burial ground, but were eager to quit the land surrounding Orford Parish and happily took Elderkin's meager initial offer and departed for Canada. According to tradition, they cautioned Elderkin to "mind the cairns and see that water is never drawn from that blighted hill."

Eli, emboldened against curse-work by his pact with some foul pig-headed devil of the lowland hills, promptly secured town funds to hire local laborers (read: the Irish) to clear the stacked rocks and piled deer antlers marking the hill's many graves, but left the bodies of the tribesmen buried beneath, "that their bones might be the pillars upon which our white man's imperial domain is built." Now you know where the mall's motto comes from!

As for the water. Management tore out all of the drinking fountains in 1974, yes, but that was part of a boarder, city-wide project to discourage feckless hydration among the city's ill-constitutioned youth. It had nothing to do with the appearances of a stone statue of dog-headed St. Christopher the Cynocephalic throughout the property the year prior. That was most likely due to the personal moral failings of our city council, not to contaminated water, although the symbolic synchronicities are not lost on this committee.

Elderkin led the parish's efforts to construct what his blood-encrusted personal papers refer to as "The Black Longhouse," but his death in 1793 halted construction. For several decades later, as the village limits grew closer and closer to that sloped and damnable hill, drunks and impure Catholic children reported seeing processions of "befoul'd emerald fairie lites" at certain unholy times of year, often appearing with dwarven, blue-faced hooded figures gathered to commune with witches and syphilitics among the abandoned pillars of Elderkin's unfinished dread longhouse.

Parish records resume mentions of the site again in 1837, when the deed was purchased by one Genesee Dryden of Rochester, who, having quit the Empire State and his failed career as a human taxidermist, decided to seek his fortune in Orford Parish as an amateur apothecarist and whoremonger. Dryden oversaw the clearing of the ruins and built his cathouse-of-medicine upon the very same diseased earth. He is credited with the precursor to Orford Parish's first public housing projects, having built a series of rowhouses for his female employees for when they were off-duty and in the blissful embrace of high-potency opium. The Whore's Hill Recreation Center gets its name from this industrious chapter of Parish history!

Our beloved Parish's growth, spurred on by the licentiousness of its vaguely European doggerel ethnics, soon reached and subsumed the outpost. From the latter half of the 19th century to that of the 20th, the hill was, at various times: home to multiple disenfranchised immigrant communities driven to American shores by an imperial war machine that blindly drinks blood and sows chaos; a hotbed of fringe religious and political activity; the site of ghastly exsanguinations occurring off and on over a thirty-year period that continues to drive troubled police detectives to madness; ground-zero for an anti-natalist plot to overthrow the government of these United States; selected to host the American Eugenics Movement Conference of 1967; home to the First, True, and Ever-Present Mall; and was prominently featured in a number of unaired UFO documentaries produced by disgraced quack and noted promise-breaker "Doctor" Jacques Vallee.

"The entire city is an open sewer of satanic ufological phenomena," Jacques? Really?

The construction and opening of the Marvel Whiteside Parsons Memorial Mall and Food Court in 1972 is perhaps the damnable hill's proudest hour. The multi-winged, multi-storied monstrosity has been studied in architectural programs the world over as a cautionary tale of the hubris of man, and has been home to a number of great retail outlets over the years, including Sears, K-Mart, Target, Macy's, Electronics Boutique, Suncoast Motion Picture Company, Media Play, Spencer's Gifts, Victoria's Secret, Foot Locker, and the best fast food restaurants that can be found wherever our brave boys and gals in uniform bring democracy and freedom.

Occupancy rates are down 70% since the self-implosion of American industry during the decades-long death crawl of post-war capitalism, of course, but many fine stores still remain open for your shopping pleasure! Here's just a few of the great establishments ready to serve you here at the Parsons Memorial Mall!

Polygonal Dreamwares

Owned and operated by Barret Carmile—a local man inexplicably still interested in electronic distractions for small children and the mentally deficient, and who is therefore disqualified from other fields of employment reserved for virile and self-sufficient men—Polygonal Dreamwares is Orford Parish's premiere one-stop shop for all of the latest video games and systems. In addition to the hottest titles and big releases, Mr. Carmile's public shrine to his own masculine inadequacies features a wide variety of "retro" games and consoles from generations past. The back room features a number of unique and rare items for those unfortunate degenerates self-identifying as video game "collectors." Working prototypes, homebrew carts, and copies of banned, satanic, heretical, illegal, madness-infused, and reality-breaking collections of forbidden code occupy these shelves, waiting to corrupt and metastasize human brains with waves of paranoia-inducing graphics, flashing lights, and horrific electronic sound effects tuned to the frequencies of dying pulsars in deep space.

Anne Gare's Rare Books & Ephemera II

The first (and only, to date!) expansion location of our sister city Leeds' original shop, founded in an abortive effort to cash in on the hot retail-chain-bookstore craze of 2009, Anne Gare's Rare Books & Ephemera II is the best place this side of the Ron Paul School of Medicine on 5th Street to find a summer potboiler, the latest pathetic self-help bestseller, or a moldering tome writ in blood describing the true occult history of the United States. Here you can find rare and out-of-print titles such as a first edition of the infamous proto-Gothic horror novel *The Crypt of Blood* by Countess Blair Oscar Wilflame, an original, fire-damaged screenplay of *Behold the Undead of Dracula* pulled straight from the smoking ruins of Camlough Studios in Northern Ireland, and the flesh-bound *A Grimoire of Dark Magic as Revealed by the Lesser Swamp Gods of Little Dixie*. The owner is a bit old-fashioned—dressed as he/she is in limitless, flowing purple robes, face hidden behind impenetrable folds of darkness, her/his voice the tenor of repressed childhood traumas—so be sure to bring your standard American Petrodollars, as this nightmare-made-flesh only accepts cash! (Or Innsmouth gold.)

The Media Graveyard

An eclectic, solitary boutique housed in the otherwise-abandoned east wing, the Media Graveyard features row upon row of vinyl records which, this Society has learned, have come back "in style" once more, yet again proving the infallible thesis of mathematician and misunderstood genius Dr. Gene Ray's (PBUH) Time Cube theory. Used DVDs and Blu-Rays, paperback pulp novels, stacks of VHS tapes, vintage board games, and more are piled high to the water-damaged ceilings, forming what the regulars refer to as THE IMPOSSIBLE LABYRINTH, into which more than our fair share of missing pets, children, and the elderly have wandered into, only to return days, weeks, months, or even years later, possessed of some nightmarish intelligence that accurately predicts the geometric dispositions of the crop circles appearing in the fields of frustrated local farmers every fall. There's also an espresso machine.

The Food Court

A selection of local and chain stores so vast and terrible that none born of woman may know its true limits or majesty. Behold, in flashing neon signage and blinking electronic screens, *behold*, in the rising steam of frying meats and meat byproducts, *behold*, in the sugary embrace of death hidden in each gulp of corn syrup-laced drink, behold, in the capitalist illusion of upward mobility flickering in the dead-eyed stares of middle aged adults working dead-end fast food jobs, **BEHOLD**, in the horrors of our class system, of our Mammon-worshipping business caste's indifference to the quality and quantity of food produced through an inhumane (but truly human) agricultural system that destroys the earth, the animals, the plants, and the very people who produce and consume it, **B E H O L D** America itself, laid bare and spread-legged for all to see her shame, her nakedness, her rotten and pestilence-ridden touch upon a holy earth created and consecrated by God Himself for our failed stewardship. Woe, woe unto man! Who in his hubris and lust might produce such soul-rending terrors, who might visit such violence against the birds of the air and the beasts of the earth and the creatures of the sea, all in the name of the demon-gods Convenience and Quarterly Profits. Woe! Woe, unto thee, dear visitor, for the cabal of goblins that infest this satanic charnel house seek to slake your thirst and satiate your hunger through their Value Menu delights! Frolic in pink slime, chicken nuggets be thine!

The Store That Has No Name but That Will Appear in the Dreams of Those Touched by the Gods of Dust
(You struggle to focus on the text but find it unreadable, the letters and words jumbled and twisting just out of sight. You can't read this section of the pamphlet yet. But you will. When the time is right.)

The Orford Parish Outdoors Superstore
Need supplies for hiking, camping, fishing, or hunting? The OP Outdoors Superstore has you covered! Featuring high-quality gear at reasonable prices, you can stock up on supplies before hitting the woods this weekend. Considering the per capita rate of disappearances in the unmapped wilderness surrounding Orford Parish is the highest in the nation (outside of our terrifying National Park system, of course), having a few extra supplies and the right equipment is a good idea for regional outdoor recreators! The superstore also features the largest selection of for-sale firearms in the state, rivaled only by the militia encampment and open-air weapons market outside of town. We've even gone so far as to beg for assistance from the state police for help with them, but it turns out many such officers are members of the American Templar Sovereign State themselves and are quite unwilling to dislodge their fellow armed racists from their fortified redoubt.

Malthus Alternative Aerospace Research Labs and Anomalous Atmospheric Phenomena Data Collection Station 6

Remote Viewer: MB
Interviewer: TB
Observers: JR, SMT, JP, SJB, TC
Date: 08/23/19
Starting Time: 1143 hours, local
Site #: MAARLAAP DCS6
Site Acquisit.: PVD RI
Working Mode: OG
Ending time: 1151 hours, local
Highest Stage: 8
Actual Site: Arapaho National Forest, CO. SECOND SITE UNKNOWN
RV Summary: WENDIGO 4

TRANSCRIPT BEGINS AS FOLLOWS

TB: We have given you the coordinates. Please go to that location.

MB: Okay.

TB: What do you see?

MB: It's sort of a large space. Big, but full of something. Maybe half-empty?

TB: Please affix yourself to these coordinates, and these coordinates specifically, and describe what you see from that location.

MB: I'm sorry, it's like there's a current here. Is this—moving water? Like a river? No, that doesn't—there are tall—okay, trees? I get the impression that I'm very tiny. Like I'm small, and everything around me is—trees. Okay, this is a forest. I see a hill, across—across a road. The reason I didn't realize they were all trees at first is because they're skeletal. Grey. A fire's been through here. I don't know much about forest fires, but it looks like some trees are okay and some are knocked over but there's a lot of grey ones, burnt up.

TB: Please sketch out what you see from your perspective. Build a terrain map as best as you can.
MB: Yeah, I'd like to, but I get the feeling I'm in that river—that I'm being pulled—[INCOMPREHENSIBLE]. Jesus Christ. Jesus Christ.

TB: What's happening?

MB: I'm moving. Going somewhere else.

TB: Please remain at these coordinates.

MB: I can't. Please. I can't. I don't want to go.

TB: Remember your breathing techniques.

MB: They're not—they're not letting me. They know I'm here. They saw me immediately. I couldn't get—

TB: Please return to the coordinates.

MB: Saw me before I even went to the forest. Felt me. They've taken me someplace else. Said there's something I should see.

[Cross-talk. A third voice speaks inaudibly from the control room.]

TB: Okay, we want you to go with it now.

MB: Go with them.
TB: Okay. Where are they taking you? What can you see?

MB: It's . . . red, here, brown. Rust-colored. Rust everywhere. Like a desert, but deeper than that, you know?

TB: What do you see? Can you generate any numbers for coordinate sequencing?

MB: I can, yes, but it's not in USGS format. The alphanumeric strings are—

[An unidentified voice from the control room says the phrase "off world."]

MB: Right, that's what I was—the sense I was getting. I'm on a plateau. There's a canyon below. They're pointing toward the canyon.

TB: What do they look like?

MB: They won't let me see. I try to look at them but they get angry. I get the impression of teeth. I don't know if they have teeth, or if they are using the image of teeth to communicate threat or displeasure. I can't tell.

TB: Try.

MB: They're going to hurt me. They're going to hurt me if I don't do as they say. They want me to look into the canyon. There's something there they're trying to show me.

TB: I need you to look at them. We need a description.

MB: They're saying that they will not let you see [REDACTED]. They'll never let you see. They will show you what they have to show you.

TB: Don't break the connection. Okay, look into the canyon, but try to—

UNKNOWN SPEAKER: Your walls of concrete cannot protect you. Your plutonium cannot protect you. Your procedures and your rituals are inadequate. They are merely vectors for our emergence.

TB: Terminate connection, remove the DMT drip.

[Metallic sounds, a low hum, a grinding noise. The sound of a pistol cocking.]

END TRANSCRIPT.

Bethy's Pretzel Stand and Cell Phone Kiosk

The scent of cinnamon, butter, and baking dough can be smelled all throughout the north wing of the mall—and that's thanks to Bethy's Pretzel Stand and Cell Phone Kiosk! Grab a quick snack or an untraceable burner phone from a man who speaks with an incomprehensible guttural accent, and who is constantly shouting at someone on his own phone when not engaged with a customer. The wall you can see behind him is home to a door. A door that opens to a large, empty white room, where all of your personal failings, embarrassments, and sexual frustrations are projected onto the walls and ceiling. A sitcom audience laugh track groans and boos and chuckles in concert with your many inescapable shames.

Gustav's Surveillance and Home Security Emporium

What home in Orford Parish is complete without a series of byzantine and impenetrable locks on the door that leads to the Tunnels? How does one feel safe without a grainy, closed-circuit television system installed in the secret reaches of their house or apartment? Need porch cameras to capture footage of the strange, string-like beings that stalk through your lawn at night? What about audio equipment to record the secret whispers in the ventilation system spoken in the voice of your dead grandmother? Gustav, ex-Spetsnaz paratrooper, has you covered! Top-shelf military- and police-grade surveillance equipment is flooding the market and cheaper than ever, thanks to our society's horrific police state apparatus. Also available are Gustav's signature gold-foil plated helmets, designed to prevent extraterrestrial mind-wave interference and decrease the rate of those nightmarish abduction experiences so many of us in the Parish have been suffering since puberty. He's only sold a few so far, and the reviews have been mixed—but every purchase helps fund further research. Keep tinkering away, Gus!

We hope you'll enjoy your time here at the Marvel Whiteside Parsons Memorial Mall and Food Court. You have of course by now realized that while the exits from the mall are all clearly marked, leaving Orford Parish itself is another thing altogether. The roads may yet disentangle and let you leave—as they have been known to on nights like tonight, when the ley lines' terrible occult energies wane—but the mall itself will remain lodged in your memory, a siren calling you back in thought and dream. And call you back it will, to this time, to this place, over and over again.

The Eurasian swastika shape of the mall's design was meant to be a defense against the malignant forces at work deep beneath the soil of our beloved Parish. But even unenlightened outsiders From Away eventually realize that symbols of light-aligned forces are meager defense against the seething will of That Which Dreams Beneath. You must see now that, even if you do leave and somehow manage to carve out a full and meaningful life somewhere else in this hellscape of a rotting empire, a piece of you will always be here. With us. With all that breathes and slinks and sucks and shambles in the darkest reaches of our beloved mall, when the lights go out and the shadows grow long and the smell of Bethy's Pretzels permeates your very soul.

Thanks for visiting the mall! If you enjoyed this pamphlet, please consider making a small contribution to the Orford Parish Historical Society. We keep local history alive!

(Donations are not tax deductible.)

Scorched Planet School of the Arts Course Catalog Fall Semester 2120

~Lorraine Schein

Degree Offered: B.A. (Bachelor of Apocalypse-Terminal Degree)
The goal of our school is to prepare students to be able to exchange their artwork for food or shelter in a dying ecosystem. Upon graduation our students have found freelance work for private clients or jobs in the corporate death field.

All students must choose one required major concentration and two minor electives from the following:

DESIGN CONCENTRATION
Portfolio required and a score of 850 or above on the SAAAT (Scholastic Apocalyptic Arts Aptitude Test).

FASHION
Prereq: Design 1, Sewing Techniques, Microbiology
Students will design full hazmat suits that are flame-proof, virus-proof and have attached gas masks. Workshops cover creation of clothing that converts to a house, submersible boat or teepee.
Successful fashion major graduates have been commissioned to design face and body masks for private and corporate clients.

BODY ART
Prereq: Needle Techniques 1 & 2, Art History
Students will learn how to create and apply original designs using ink and laser techniques for applying tattoos on irises and construct migrating nanotattoos on a variety of bodies.

HABITAT
Prereq: Oceanography 1, Physics, Architecture 1, Materials 1, Shop Class
Prospective architects will design house pods with legs or flying houses that will avoid floods, expandable houses, and immersible submarine dwellings.

WEATHER CONCENTRATION
Prereq: Astronomy, Anemology, Chemistry, Meteorology, Flight School 1
NOTE: Students with a current pilot license are exempt from the Flight School requirement.

SKY ART
Prereq: Heliology, Color Theory 1
Students majoring in Sky Art will manipulate sunlight to create unique sunsets and sunrises that stay up all day or night and are moveable to any location. Graduates have found freelance work in both the private and corporate sectors.

RAINWATER ART
Open to Weather majors only by permission of Professor Roy G. Biv.
Prereq.: Color Theory 1, Meteorology, Psychology 1, Pluviology
This course will teach seeding of clouds with color-infused droplets to create varied shades such as iridescent and rainbow spectrum rainfall. Graduates have found employment in both the private and corporate sectors.

RAIN MUSIC
Prereq.: Harmony 1, Meteorology, Audiology, Pluviology, Roofology
Students will create original musical compositions using directed rainfall, orchestrating rainstorms and rainfall into musical compositions. Graduates have been commissioned to compose orchestral pieces for private and international clients.

RAIN SCENTING
Special Topic. Open only to students who have completed Rain Music and Rain Art and permission of advisor.
Prereq: Aromachology, Osmology, Neuroscience.
Students will learn to create scented rainfall.

CLOUD SCULPTURE
Advanced Seminar Prereq.: Art History 1, Nephology, Portfolio Review
Learn techniques for carving cirrus and cumulus into portraits and landscapes.

DISASTER ART CONCENTRATION
Our graduate Disaster Artists have found employment with regional warlords, career military, and major corporations. Eligibility Requirements: Open to students with a criminal record and/or a portfolio evidencing psychopathology and interview by a former advisor on probation from Arkham Asylum.

WILDFIRE ART
Prereq.: Pyrology 1, Printmaking, Explosives 1, Flight School 1, Pyrotechnics 1 and 2 (Preference given to students with high SAAAT scores on pyromania.)
Wildfire students will design and selectively burn areas of forests to create aesthetically pleasing patterns using foam retardant and explosives dropped from a plane to form control lines.

HURRICANE PERFORMANCE ART (Independent Study)
Students must have an interview with department head Professor Marvel and obtain permission of instructor, staff psychiatrist, and next of kin.
Prereq: Photography, Videography, Sky Diving, Aerial Stunts and minimum 4.3 grade-point average in prior Weather courses.
Under faculty supervision, students will design, choreograph and write the script for a special interactive performance to be performed within a hurricane of their own creation. They will then photograph themselves inside it as well as document the wreckage below.

BLIZZARD PERFORMANCE ART (Honors Project)
This advanced course is only open to surviving Hurricane students with a grade-point of average of 3.5 or above and permission of advisor.
Prereq.: Cross-Country Skiing, Snowboarding, History of Antarctica
See Hurricane Performance Art above for course description, but colder and snowy.

POLLUTION ART
Prereq.: Oceanography, Intro to Questionable Business Practices, Urban Non-planning

Students will learn to create a variety of artistic pollution such as smog, particulate matter, and nonrecyclable plastics. They will measure and document the effects of environmental degradation on animal and human health in their chosen environments using such indicators as exceeding the Air Quality Index standards, the creation of plastic islands in the sea and rates of coral death.

DEATH CONCENTRATION
Prereq.: Biology, Abnormal Psychology, Morbidity 2, and permission of Professor H. Lecter.

DEATH DRAWING STUDIO
Prereq.: Art History, Anatomy 2, Taxidermy 1, Decomposition 1 & 2, Forensics Pathology

Students will draw portraits from expiring models and photographs of extinct and endangered species.
Formaldehyde tolerance test required.

DEATH LITERATURE (Work/Study)
Prereq: English 2.6 (Shakespeare's Tragedies), Japanese Literature, Gravestones 1, Journalism, Videography, Snuff Cinematology 1

Students will learn to create and write deathbed poems and narratives for dying and suicidal people and document their deaths by posting on the web, Facebook and TikTok. Graduates have been hired by gang lords and employed by major political parties.

VIRUS ARTS
Prereq: Virology, Biology, Genetics 1 & 2, Pathology, History of Germ Warfare, Culinary Contamination Skills

Students will learn to design and infect populations with new viruses using recombinant DNA and devise their possible cures. Fall Semester: Designing Viruses. Spring Semester: Reverse Engineering for Antidote Vaccines

QUARANTINE TECH
Prereq.: Virus Arts, Information Technology, Network Administration, Sexology

Students will explore advanced 5 Senses Zoom techniques such as Lurid Imaging with Realtouch™ peripherals that allow online self-pleasuring or group orgasms. Topics covered include the synchronization of lucid dreams to simulate the experience of pre-pandemic socializing.

BODY DEFORMATION
Prereq.: Genetics 1 & 2, Anatomy, Biology, Mutation Surgery, Abnormal Psychiatry, German History 2

Using directed mutilation techniques and plastic surgery, students self-sculpt and sculpt others to create malformed designer bodies. Techniques studied may include cloning, Botox augmentation, abdominal fat redirection, feather transplants. Includes off-campus field trips to mental hospitals and prisons to select subjects for operations and visiting guest lecturers from the Moreau Institute of Body Hybridity. Successful graduates have found work in the entertainment industry and for international clients.

Whatever Lives in Them Mountains

~ W. T. Paterson

Sometimes the hiss of the diner's grill while cooking eggs sounded to Davey Spence like the walls of rain in the Mekong Delta, and sometimes he would stare as the yolk turned white remembering the day the orders came through. The thing that scared him the most was joy he felt back then, a twenty-year old with a gun and grenades, tromping through jungle hungry for blood.

"Still no sign of that boy," Maryanne said, folding forks and knives inside of washable napkins behind the counter. She paused to rub her fingers and stretch her trick hip. The Virginia Slim tucked behind her left ear didn't budge. "Every year, them mountains claim another one. It's cursed, you know."

Their only patron, a middle-aged woman named Kathy with long, delicate fingers, sat at the diner's bar slow sipping a coffee happy to have the company. Living in the mountain town of Penny Bridge along West Virginia's Appalachian hills was a lonely existence, but that was kind of the point. People went there to escape. They went there to disappear. Filled with the likes of self-proclaimed sovereign citizens, anti-government militia, smugglers, day laborers from the Mohawk and Seneca tribes, and remnants of the old mining ghost towns, when city folk drove through Penny Bridge, they just kept going.

"Y'all have a name for it, don't you?" Kathy asked.

"The Ba'hari," Maryanne said, and winked. "You can't be tempting the Ba'hari."

Davey sliced through the eggs with two spatulas and watched their perfect form shrivel into popcorned yellow scramble. He placed two pieces of thawed, pale bacon on the hot surface beside them and listened to meat pop and bleed. Sometimes, it sounded like distant gunfire.

"It ain't no monster," Davey said through the order window. Kathy and Maryanne looked up together. "Just tales to keep people out of them woods.

"The Ba'hari is real. Ken Taima saw it once," Maryanne said. After working side by side with Davey for the past thirty years, she knew exactly how to poke the bear without getting bit

"Ken Taima comes from a line of Iriquois but don't know a shop-lifter from a good Samaritan. How he ever became sheriff is beyond me," Davey said. He flipped the bacon. Grease sizzled across the smooth surface trying to flee the heat like half-dead bodies pulling themselves into the jungle to find a peaceful spot to die.

"So tell me more about this Ba'hari," Kathy said. "Now that I'm a townie, and all."

Maryanne pushed a lock of silver hair away from her eyes and tapped the Virginia Slim to make sure it was still there. It was. She bent elbows-first onto the diner's bar and looked through the plate glass window near the booths where yellow and pink painted letters advertised $2.99 breakfast specials. Beyond that, the shallow grey day took hostage the tall pines and evergreens.

"They say no man kill it, only a monster can, and if you go huntin' for the Ba'hari, the Ba'hari hunts you. And if it catches ya, it turns your soul black as tar. Makes you only want the things that hurt ya."

"Must be why I keep thinking of my ex-husband," Kathy said, and an unnamed longing flashed in her eyes. She smiled a plastic, practiced smile that only engaged the lips.

"I lost my husband to lung cancer. Smoker, packs on packs a day," Maryanne said, and pinched the cigarette out from behind her ear. She sniffed the white paper. The scent brought memories of her younger years when she felt whole, a harkening to another life a world away. "Even though I watched him go, some days I still miss the pull of these ladies. I blame them mountains and whatever lives in'em. The curse of the Ba'hari."

Sometimes, the smells of the diner rocketed Davey into memories from his past. Something about the burning coffee in Maryanne's pot that blackened on the burner while she spoke with Kathy put him in dead smack in the middle of those meetings in the basement of the church. They came recommended by a patron after the nightmares robbed him of sleep, a place to go where men like him could unload their baggage and find forgiveness. Davey, after a cycle of night terrors got the better of him, decided to give it a go and after the first night, it became a regular thing.

The organizers set up folding tables with coffee and pastries from the local store. It wasn't for a meal, just something to keep nervous hands occupied. Chairs pushed into a circle, the wide-open room felt vast and unexplored. It felt hesitant. The man who ran the meetings had a well-trimmed beard and wore thick sweaters. Compared to the hardened men with leathered faces frozen into scowls, he seemed soft, but he opened each meeting the same way.

"Y'all must be wrestling with the nature of good and evil," he said, and the group tilted their heads. "How does good triumph over evil? What does it realistically take? And at what cost?"

Davey rarely spoke at the meetings, he mostly listened. There was something sermon-like in those lectures there in the basement of a church, something peaceful and connective. In the dark shadow of the mountains, that room felt guarded, safe.

"Evil is not overthrown by good," the man said. "Evil is overthrown by the blood of the poisoned and obsessed who have lost to evil before and have thus learned the same evil to properly battle evil. And in doing so, evil is vanquished, and these men are redeemed, and as a reward they are exiled because good an un-poisoned people devoid of evil will never understand them. And then the nightmares come, and we wonder if evil has seeped into our souls, and maybe we wonder if evil exists, or if it's just a word people use to bucket the things in which they cannot understand. Would anyone like to speak tonight?"

Davey wasn't sure why, but he raised his hand one night. The man in the sweater smiled and nodded. Davey had the floor.

"I didn't know what I was doing," he said. "I was young. Too young. Did horrible things following them orders, but never saw myself as evil 'til ten, fifteen years out. Then the nightmares started and I can't seem to reconcile."

"It often comes as an echo" the man said. "What do you do for work?"

"I run a diner," Davey said. "Furthest thing from being a soldier."

"Orders come in, orders go out," the man said. "Always following orders."

"Nah, that ain't it," Davey said sitting back, and that was the last he spoke.

Now, behind the grill, Davey scooped the yellow and fluffy eggs onto a plate and flipped the crispy bacon on top. He placed the dish on the lip of the order window and dinged the bell.

"Order up," he said.

"All business, this one is," Maryanne said as she limped to the plate and twisted to give it to Kathy when all at once she froze. A man sat in booth three. She hadn't even heard him come in, let alone seen his approach through the plate glass window. Though he was across the room, Maryanne saw the man was bleeding from face and hands.

The tented table sign said NO SMOKING, but the burnt stench of nicotine cut into the stale air of the diner as the bleeding man in booth three let the cherry burn the cigarette to ash. His left eye, purple and swollen shut, twitched as his large chest rose and fell. The fluorescent lights made the streaks of deep red running nose to chin shine like ribbons of fresh ink, their story screaming to be told. His large hands quivered barely holding onto the cigarette, his knuckles torn with fresh wounds.

Then, the bathroom door opened and a child walked out with matted hair, no more than six years old. He wiped his hands on dirty pants and sat across from the man. The child picked up a laminated menu and tried to sound out words. The man didn't move.

"Bay-con, ham, and ca-heese, ca . . . cha-heese, cheese, omuh-omuhlee," the boy said.

"Sound it out," the man said, his voice deep and steady like campfire smoke.

"Oh-ma-leet-te . . . om . . . omlette! Bacon, ham, and cheese omlette!" the child said.

"Very good," the bleeding man said.

Sometimes, Davey thought he saw things that weren't there. Every now and then after closing, he'd drive the long way home and on those winding mountain roads in the pitch dark, sometimes he'd see a small Vietnamese boy on the side of the road. He'd clamp on the brakes and roll down the window to ask if the boy needed help, but whenever he reversed, the boy was never there.

And sometimes, he could have sworn the boy was bleeding from the head.

But this wasn't one of his visions. Maryanne and Kathy saw it too. This bleeding man in booth three, and the small feral boy sitting across from him.

The enormous fan kicked on in the kitchen like a jet engine roaring across the sky to rain fire on Charlie.

"Should he be . . . " Kathy asked in a cotton soft voice.

"He shouldn't be," Maryanne whispered, and her eyes went to slits. "Davey, we got a problem," she said into the kitchen.

"That's the boy . . . " Kathy said. "The missing one."

"Go take their order. Now," Davey said. Maryanne looked at Davey and something silent passed between them. She wasn't a soldier, wasn't one of Davey's war buddies that showed up after hours on Thursday nights to trade stories until the sun rose. She was a server for heaven's sake, a widow, and that man looked dangerous. Her seen-it-all-eyes loosened as she realized that not taking their order might trigger that deep, mountain anger living in the folks of Penny Bridge.

"Mornin' boys," Maryanne said, limping to the booth. She tapped the cigarette tucked behind her ear and pulled a pen and green flip pad from her apron. "What'll it be?"

"Tell her," the bleeding man said, still as stone.

"Bacon, ham, and cheese omlette," the boy said.

"Bacon, ham, and cheese omlette what?" the man said.

"Please," the boy said.

"And for you?" Maryanne asked.

"Ain't hungry," the man said.

"Toast? Muffin?"

"Muffin," the man said. "Blueberry muffin."

The cigarette burned out, hissing against the man's thick and bloodied fingers. He didn't flinch. Outside, small flecks of rain tapped on the glass like small knuckles trying to alert anyone who would listen.

Maryanne wrote down the order. She brought it all the way back into the kitchen and handed it to Davey who took one look and got started on cooking.

"You're gonna feed'em?!" Maryanne asked.

"Yes, I'm gon' feed'em," he said. "And you ain't gon' charge them neither."

"What's gotten into you?!" Maryanne hissed, and stole a peek through the kitchen window at the boy pointing to new words on the menu as though the bleeding man across from him wasn't bleeding at all. The child's clothes seemed too loose.

Sometimes Davey had these feelings like he knew people, even if he didn't. Working at the diner for the past thirty years, he'd met all types and sizes, but every now and then he could sense in people the same thing he sensed in himself – that unspoken pain of regret, the violence of time's stranglehold, the anguish of having no choice but to move forward. He never charged those people and even though not one of them ever thanked him, he felt connected to their darkness in a way that no one else would ever understand.

The bleeding man had his eyes closed and head tilted forward breathing like he might be asleep. Then, as though jolted by an electric shock, he snapped straight up and spit a glob of bloody phlegm onto the diner's tiled floor. The boy pulled out a napkin and handed it to the man who took it with quivering fingers and dabbed the side of his mouth.

Maryanne almost lost her nerve at the sight and silently cursed Davey for even allowing them to stay. After a lifetime of working in a mountain-town diner, she'd seen her fair share of disrespect. She'd tossed men twice her side out into the cold, told women to shove it, even broken up a fight or two. But something about this man gave her pause.

She filled up two glasses of water and a small plastic cup of chocolate milk. Balanced on a tray, she walked over and set the drinks down.

"For me?" the boy asked, wide eyed.

"Of course, sweet'ums," Maryanne said. She had the urge to reach out and touch the child's dirty hair, to silently let him know that he was safe so as long as he was in the diner. Once out the door, who knew what the night would do once it sunk its teeth into the tall pines and evergreens.

"What do you say?" the man said to the boy.

"Thank you," the boy said, and knelt on the plush plastic cushion to hover over the glass and sip through a bendy straw.

From the kitchen, Davey dinged the order bell and put two plates on the sill. It was far more food than what had been ordered. Hash browns, extra strips of bacon, a muffin, toast, sausages, pancakes, the works.

Maryanne limped back and loaded up her arms.

"I can't sit here and do nothing," Kathy whispered. She forced eye contact with Davey to demand action and slid a phone from her purse.

"You're gonna sit here and do nothing," Davey growled from the kitchen. "Put that goddamn phone away, you hear?!"

"That's the missing boy!" the woman hissed.

"Either way, that boy's gotta eat," Maryanne said. For a brief moment, she understood Davey's move. "There's a whole lot I don't know, but that's what I do know. That boy's gotta eat."

"And I just sit here?" Kathy said. "I do nothing and I'm just as guilty."

"You'll do nothing, and doing nothing keeps that boy in his seat eatin' my cooking," Davey said.

The woman pinched her face into a tight knot and turned in the stool to watch Maryanne drop off the plates. As soon as the food hit the table, the boy dug in like he hadn't eaten in weeks. The bleeding man plucked at the edges of the muffin, but never took a bite.

"Someone's hungry!" Maryanne said. The boy made animal noises and chomped.

The bleeding man took a trembling hand to his lips with a new cigarette and tried to light.

Maryanne's insides clenched. She wanted to rip that poisonous stick from his lips and scream in his busted face that he can't smoke in here, can't he read? This was a fine establishment with proper rules and didn't he know that smoking could kill a man and destroy his wife?

"Do you mind?" the bleeding man asked and offered up the lighter. Maryanne took it and a distant, familiar comfort returned. She wasn't sure why, but she took it, flicked it on, and bent forward. The tip caught and the bleeding man inhaled.

"What else can I get'cha?" Maryanne asked, and placed the lighter on the table. The bleeding man looked off into the tall pines and evergreens, his eyes like rivers running through painful memories of something he'd rather forget. Maryanne recognized the look. She wore something similar when her husband was on his way out and she had to sit by and watch. She saw it on Davey's face when the stove made clanging sounds and said he needed to close early.

"We'll get out of your hair soon," the bleeding man said.

At the bar, Kathy twisted in her stool like she was itching to leave. Maryanne approached at a half-steady clip.

"Don't be foolish," she whispered.

"I will not sit by and let society crumble just 'cause you're too scared to take action," Kathy said.

"Hey," Davey said from the kitchen. "You take action because there's action to be had, you live with the consequences forever. Same as giving twenty-year-olds guns and tellin'em to wipe out a peaceful farming village so the enemy can't eat. It's pulling the trigger and feeling alive by causing death without understanding what makes life fragile."

"This isn't the war, Davey," Kathy said.

"All's the war," he said. "And this is my joint. I'm tellin' you to stand down."

"Can we please?" Maryanne said, waving her wrists.

Outside, the sheriff's police car crunched into the gravel lot and the fog surrounding Penny Bridge thickened. Ken Taima stepped out with aviator sunglasses and long black ponytail pulled tight running between his shoulder blades. He read the writing on the window in front of booth three and said something into the radio on his shoulder.

"Good god . . . " Kathy said. "What if this gets ugly?"

Maryanne held her breath as Sheriff Taima stepped inside. He spotted the bleeding man and the boy and flipped the OPEN sign to CLOSED. He locked the door and approached the table.

"Billy?"

The boy looked up mid-chew. The sheriff nodded and looked back to find Maryanne and Kathy frozen in place. He radioed something into his shoulder. The bleeding man put the lit cigarette between his swollen lips.

"Billy, I would love to hear about your adventure if that's ok with you," Taima said, and the boy looked to the bleeding man. The bleeding man gave a small nod in acknowledgement, and the boy put down his fork. They went to the far corner of the diner and sat in booth seven.

"Do you believe in monsters?" the boy asked.

Taima nodded his head and whispered, "I've *seen* them."

Davey took a magnetic carving knife from the metal hanging strip in the kitchen and wrapped his fingers around the hilt. He walked out with his hands behind his back and felt the air go still as Maryanne and Kathy held their breath at the flash of hidden metal. He sat down across the bleeding man.

"I ain't gon' charge ya," Davey said. The bleeding man nodded. "Obliged."

They sat in the booth together, but the distance between them was both enormous and somehow non-existent.

"That boy," Davey said. "You take him?"

"Not the way you think," the bleeding man said. Davey squeezed the hilt of the knife and felt that flash of red he felt all those years ago in the Mekong Delta.

"Y'either did, or you didn't," he growled.

"You believe in the Ba'hari?" the bleeding man asked.

"I think you're the Ba'hari to that child."

For the first time, the bleeding man smiled from the corner of his mouth and took a slow drag. He exhaled smoke as thick and blinding as the fog outside.

"I killed the Ba'hari," the man said, and in the small seconds that passed between thought and understanding Davey felt a completeness that the meetings had often referred to as a moment of clarity.

This man didn't take the boy, and like all echoes, what existed in the present was a backwards re-examination of everything that came before.

"Farming village. Now I cook," he said to himself, stunned.

"I was a younger man when my little girl . . . " the bleeding man said, and he stopped to take a drag. "Never found."

"So now you bring'em home," Davey said. He loosened the grip on the knife.

Taima and the boy named Billy rose from their booth and walked over to Davey and the bleeding man.

"He's ready to go," the sheriff said, and the bleeding man tilted his head in acknowledgment. He stood up, touched the boy on the shoulder with shaking fingers, and unlocked the door as wisps of smoke trailed behind. Inside of a dozen steps, the fog swallowed the man whole. Taima turned toward Kathy.

"He was never here. This never happened."

"You're gonna let him go?!" Kathy said.

"Only a monster can kill a monster," Taima said. "And our town is full of 'em. Pain does funny things to a person. People like you will never understand. You be careful now."

He left with Billy and the three inside watched the small boy climb into the backseat as Sheriff Taima pulled off and drove away.

Sometimes the thick fog of memory played tricks on poor Davey and he wondered if anything would ever make sense. He wondered if he'd ever find peace. He watched as Maryanne sat in booth three and closed her eyes to breathe the thin remains of cigarette smoke and re-live those moments where she felt happy, and alive, and whole, before the world took from her something it could never give back. The lighter still on the table, she pulled the Virginia Slim from behind her ear, put it to her lips, and flicked the flame after years of cold turkey.

Kathy put on her jacket and counted out five singles with her long, delicate fingers. Davey walked to the door, flipped the sign back to OPEN, and headed into the kitchen to prep the grill in for lunch. Whatever lived in them mountains, when it awoke, it would be hungry, and need to eat.

The Continuing (Superpositional) Adventures of Schrödinger's Cat

~ *David Hewitt*

Erwin Schrödinger's famous feline thought experiment on quantum uncertainty should require no introduction. As a quick refresher, Schrödinger himself expounded it thus:

> . . . *A cat is penned up in a steel chamber, along with the following device . . . in a Geiger counter, there is a tiny bit of radioactive substance, so small, that perhaps in the course of the hour one of the atoms decays, but also, with equal probability, perhaps none; if it happens, the counter tube . . . releases a hammer that shatters a small flask of hydrocyanic acid. If one has left this entire system to itself for an hour, one would say that the cat still lives if meanwhile no atom has decayed. [Until an observer opens the chamber] the psi-function of the entire system would express this by having in it the living and dead cat (pardon the expression) mixed or smeared out in equal parts.*

Recent theoreticians, however, consider Schrödinger's formulation over-simplistic. Before the box is opened, the cat cannot be said to exist "smeared out" over only the two states—alive and dead. Rather, this daring hypothetical adventurer simultaneously exists, with varying statistical likelihood, in every conceivable state of its own wave function. What follows is a by-no-means-exhaustive summary of possible outcomes, and hence co-existing states of being, revealed by continuing analyses of "the cat problem":

• An atom decays; the hammer strikes the flask of hydrocyanic acid; the cat dies of cyanide-induced histotoxic hypoxia.

• An atom does not decay; the hammer does not strike the flask of hydrocyanic acid; the cat does not die of cyanide-induced histotoxic hypoxia and lives happily and healthily to a ripe old age.

• An atom does not decay during the one hour; but in the name of thoroughness and replicability, the scientist repeats the experiment the next day. This time, an atom does decay and—hammer, cyanide—the cat dies.

• An atom does not decay on the first day, nor when the experiment is repeated on the second, nor even on the third; but on the fourth day, though the clear and present odds are still a simple 50/50 coin toss, the cumulative 15-to-1 odds against surviving four such coin tosses in sequence finally catch up with the cat and . . . hammer, cyanide—dead.

• The cat survives the first, the second, the third, and even the fourth day. On the fifth day, the scientist, who originally intended an even five experimental trials, has a change of heart. Just as the atom is decaying, she hurls open the door of the steel chamber and, as the hammer is falling, yanks the subject out and tumbles to the floor with cat cradled in her arms, saved in the nick of time from the grim clutches of cyanide-induced histotoxic hypoxia. The scientist takes the cat home, names her Princess Purrsnickitty, and the two live happily ever after.

• The scientist experiences no change of heart, but just as the cat is being placed in the steel chamber, a joint PETA/Animal Liberation Front strike team armed with crowbars bursts into the laboratory, and liberates the cat into the uncertainties and vast open spaces of the suburban wilds.

• Just as the cat is being placed in the steel chamber, not animal-rights commandos but an ASPCA lawyer sporting a stodgy suit, a questionable comb-over, and a restraining order bursts into the laboratory, and liberates the cat into the uncertain and vastly time-consuming and expensive vagaries of the United States judicial system.

• Just as the cat is being placed in the steel chamber, neither PETA/ALF commandos nor ASPCA advocate but rather two blue-tufty-haired, red-jumpsuited individuals burst into the laboratory. Running full tilt and wreaking general havoc by toppling sensitive equipment, a coffee maker, and even a fish bowl, they free the cat through happenstance from the steel chamber and flee. Because of the suspects' breakneck speed, blurry security footage provides only one lead: a single frame in which the cryptic letters -*ing 1* and -*ing 2* can be discerned on the backs of the jumpsuits.

• Just as an atom is about to decay, the cat reaches into a magic fourth-dimensional pocket on his belly and extracts an "Anywhere Door"; he transports himself out of the steel chamber and into the bedroom of a young Japanese boy who, though receptive to the cat's aid and tutelage, never masters the important life lessons the cat endlessly strives to impart.

• The atom does not decay; the cat will live another day, it seems—but wait! Just as the chamber is opened, a gleeful-looking Maya-blue mouse rushes into the laboratory, carrying a giant drill and a hose with a suction cup at one end. The mouse drills his way into the steel chamber, slaps the suction cup onto the cat's muzzle, squeezes cartoonishly through a hole into the perforated box where the flask of cyanide sits, screws the other end of the hose to the mouth of the cyanide flask, and flips the hammer's trigger with a white-gloved hand. The hammer smushes the flask, squeezing all the cyanide out as a visible bulge which travels up the hose, through the suction cup, and into the cat. The cat turns a grotesque shade of green and its eyes a jaundiced yellow, then its fur and skin melt from its bones, and the bones themselves dissolve into a steaming puddle of acid with a pair of yellow eyes lolling on top. The mouse kicks one then the other eye, shot-on-goal style, and scampers off in the height of good cheer.

• An atom decays; somebody erred, however, and, in place of hydrocyanic acid, filled the flask with rye whiskey. When the hammer strikes the flask, the cat, goaded by the stress of its captivity, laps up the rye. Outside the sealed steel chamber, the scientist, who can know nothing of all this, takes a glass flask from his pocket and sips. He could swear he'd filled it with rye this morning, but the mouthful he sips has a distinctly non-whiskey, almond-like flavor.

• An atom decays, but rather than triggering the hammer, the ionizing radiation flies in another direction and collides with a spider which, unbeknownst to anyone, crept into the steel chamber before the experiment began. Bitten by this spider, said cat gains the spider's proportional strength and agility (the latter resulting—since arachnid agility rates much lower than that of family *felidae*—in a net agility loss). The cat uses this super-strength to break free from its captivity, and goes on to fight for cat-truth, cat-justice, and the Siamese way.

• An atom decays; the cat is poisoned and dies, and is buried unceremoniously under a rock. On the third day, though, the rock is miraculously rolled aside—the cat, licking itself, rises from the grave as savior to all catkind, having paid with its suffering for the original sin of the first cat-ancestors, Muffin and Max, who selfishly tasted of the catnip of the Tree of Sloth and Hyperactivity.

• An atom does not decay, but neither does the cat live to a ripe old age. Instead, loose in the neighborhood, it is run over by a car the very next day—but the bereft scientist inters it in an ancient Native American burial ground. Two days later, the scientist hears a scratching at his door, and either does or does not open it; in either case, his own story ends in a manner that may with 93.2% probability be described as "bloodcurdling."

• Just as the cat is being placed in the steel chamber, not PETA/ALF commandos, not ASPCA advocates, not red-jumpsuited hooligans, but rather a wealthy private benefactor arrives at the laboratory to rescue the feline, offering a generous research stipend in compensation. This benefactor, an older gentleman in tweed jacket and wrinkled trousers, brings the cat home. Soon after, a meeting is arranged with an editor from a major publishing house. The result is *Eight More Lives: My Journey Through the Steel Chamber* (ghostwritten). The hardcover release hits #6 on *The New York Times* Best Seller list and paves the way to the cat's starring on the popular but horribly ill-conceived reality show *Pussies and Pitbulls*. Against all odds, our hypothetical feline hero emerges victorious, leaving a trail of savaged canine bodies in her wake. But she is a changed cat—hardened, unstoppable, eyes blazing with plutonium potency and heart hell-bent on revenge. Against all her benefactor's protestations, the cat gives herself over once again to science, this time volunteering for a ludicrously improbable time-travel experiment. The experiment succeeds, transporting the cat a century into the past. Through hard-won cunning and craft, this survivor among survivors, this titanium-willed tiger among tabbies, makes her way to her target. The next morning, a young Erwin Schrödinger is found dead in his bed—of histotoxic hypoxia. No evidence of forced entry or a struggle is found. In fact, Schrödinger's demise, mere days before he formulated his famous paradox, renders the existence of the thought experiment, the cat, and this story alike—

(With a 99.967% probability, very likely) The End

Another Night on Earth

~ J. A. W. McCarthy

The thing that gets me is the silence. No owl calls or cricket chirps puncturing the folds of night draped loosely overhead. No rustle of small creatures in the bushes, scattering from the vibrations of my footsteps. Not even an abrupt breath of wind to rattle the air around me.

And certainly no cars. Though paved, I get the feeling this narrow road has been unkind to many vehicles before mine.

I adjust the leather strap of my bag where it cuts across my chest and glance back at my car. My eighteen year old Volvo looks like an injured mare that's stumbled into the dirt where a sidewalk should be, one end of its bumper dangling as loose as a busted jaw. Though it's looked this miserable for quite some time, in the darkness my car seems to plead for my return.

Up ahead a house sits tucked into the land like a fat, squat ogre, invisible behind the trees if it wasn't for the yellow porch light and the hazy white glow of the two windows on either side of the front door. I squint into the distance, trying to focus past the lone streetlight on the other side of the house, past the black ribbon of road that's lost all of its texture in the dark, past the leaves overhead that have turned from grainy to flat against the bruised velvet of the endless night sky. Though it isn't far, all that's beyond this single structure smears to-gether into a slick trashbag black. If there are other houses they have been devoured by the same earth that cradles them.

As I continue to walk, the still air is cold but not quite icy, and strangely thick; when I open my mouth it rolls onto my tongue and pushes against my teeth, as acrid as late summer city heat. I look over my shoulder at my car again, now shrunk to something I can pinch between my fingers like I used to do to my brother's head when we were little. *You're mine now*, I would say, and he would either giggle or punch at me depending on his mood. *I can do anything I want with you.* I adjust my bag again, let the weight of it bounce against my hip with every step. My boot snags on a fissure in the road, and I'm grateful for the scrape of rubber against pavement, a small, predictable sound that makes a crack in the night.

I know I've reached the house's driveway when the pavement turns to gravel beneath my feet. The little rocks crunch loudly with even my smallest movements, jagged teeth that push through the rubber soles of my boots until they're chewing up the soft palate of my foot. Every step is suddenly too loud, too stark, too much. The people in the house will hear me coming, and I can imagine how people who live out in the middle of the woods might greet a stranger at their door this close to midnight. I pull my phone from my jacket pocket and turn on its flashlight, the only thing it's good for out here.

My mother comes to mind as I crunch my way up the length of the driveway to the porch. Not that this house with its sagging roof and splintered white shingles resembles the sterile tract home I grew up in. The things she's said so many times before echo inside my head: *You should know better than to be out here at this time of night*, and *I don't know why you insist on doing this*, and *Everyone knows what happens to girls like you.* I creep from window to window, but the white curtains covering each one are just thick enough to reveal nothing more than the blurred movements of indiscernible shapes within. At this hour, my mother would've had the blinds sealed, sheers and curtains drawn, not even a soft frame of light promising life inside. *What are you thinking, Judith? One of these days your luck is going to run out.* Taking a deep breath I knock on the heavy front door, then slide my hand into my bag until my fingers hook the reassuring heft of my knife's steel handle.

"Can I help you?"

The man who answers the door is old but tall and solid, his body filling most of the doorway. His long face shines waxy and jaundiced under the porch light, dragged down by the shadow-filled hollows beneath his eyes and cheekbones. I'm amazed by how quickly he's come to the door—no shuffling on the other side as he studies me through the peephole, no sleep-leaden movements pricked by the acute anxiety of an unexpected stranger in the middle of the night—

then I notice that he's not in a bathrobe and slippers but a dark suit, the fuzz of wool standing out against what little flickering light seeps out from behind him. Regarding me with narrowed eyes, he asks the question again. I note with relief that his hands are empty.

"Oh, yes, sorry to bother you so late," I stammer, forcing the friendly smile I practiced on the drive. "My car broke down a little ways down the road and I can't get a signal out here, so I was hoping . . ." I wiggle my phone to give credence to my story before putting it back in my pocket. "I was hoping I could use your phone to call for help."

The man doesn't say anything for a long moment while the corners of my mouth twitch and I try to restrain myself from craning my neck to get a peek at who or what is in the room behind him. When he finally does move aside, a thick cloud of sweet and earthy smoke barrels out and into me, the same incense my mother used to burn on fish dinner Fridays.

The entire room behind him is hung with smoke, each slender wisp from the tens of incense sticks suspended along the walls pooling into one great swarm in the center of the room. As I step over the threshold, I bite the insides of my cheeks to keep from coughing, fearful that any minor offense may produce more imposing men, and guns, and my mother's *I told you . . .* as my last dying thought. White pillar candles burn on every surface in the small living room, all in various states of dissolution atop the fireplace mantle, the coffee table, a hutch, the TV, even along the sloping back of the weathered plaid couch. Greasy stains dot the yellowing walls where the melted wax touches. The scent of spicy incense mixed with the artificial vanilla of the candles is overwhelming; even with my lips pressed shut, I taste an oily film forming on the roof of my mouth, the phantom of a perfect lozenge of wax cooling on my tongue.

Behind me there's the heavy whoosh of the front door sliding shut, its corner nicking the wall of smoke. I unclench my jaw and let out a cough.

"Phone's this way," the old man says.

I follow him through a doorway at the end of the living room, apologizing again as we move into a narrow hallway lit only by more wall-mounted candles. I try to remember the details of the man's wool suit as he shuffles along in front of me. Is there a matching vest?

Does his white shirt have buttons? If he had looked like an Amish person, wouldn't I have immediately thought that when he opened the front door?

We approach the entrance to what looks like a dining room. I pause here for a moment, hoping my host doesn't notice.

A thick cloak of incense and candle smoke shrouds this room too, the tight space ablaze with tiny pinpoints of light poking through the white haze. A small circle of people—I count six—are gathered inside, their backs to me. They are all dressed in black, the men in suits and the women in long-sleeved dresses. A low murmur rises from their bowed heads, but I can't decipher what they are saying. *A prayer*, I think, *normal people in mourning*, and though it makes sense, I am still not consoled by the absence of pentagrams and vivisected goats.

"Here." The old man stands at the end of the hall, pointing into another open doorway.

"Yes, sorry," I say, hurrying towards him. I try to parse what he might be thinking, but his sharply etched face is unreadable even when I am close enough to stand between him and the smoke that seeps out into the hallway.

After showing me the phone mounted to the wall, the man leaves me alone in the kitchen. The only light comes from yet another row of pillar candles on the small dining table. I listen to the shuffle of leather against wood as his footsteps retreat down the hall then stop at what I presume is the dining room with the others. My palm folds around the phone's cool plastic handset, but I don't lift it. Behind me is the backdoor, its uncovered window reflecting my face and neck glowing orange, subtly vibrating, another flame in the dark. I remember autumn nights in the backyard with my brother, our bodies trembling with giggles as we told scary stories with flashlights clutched under our chins. My stories were always scarier, though sometimes his stories made me cry. I remember feigning offense when he made me promise that I would call him if I ever got into trouble. *You're my little brother*, I said. *I should be rescuing you.*

"Everything okay?"

My hand flies from the phone and plants on the counter. I dare a brief glance at what's nearby: a wooden cutting board, a pie tin, a rolling pin—things that are closer to me than to the voice in the hallway.

"Yes," I answer.

I force another confident smile as a young man emerges from the smoke. I'd noticed him with the others in the dining room, the back of his head the only one not peppered with grey. Unlike the old man who answered the door, this man's dark suit looks modern with a subtle sheen skimming his lapels. Like the old man, thick shadows pool under his eyes and cheekbones.

"My car," I lie again. "It broke down and I—"

"Everyone's in the other room."

He's right in front of me now, his head tipped against the door-frame so that I am boxed in between him and the end of the counter. All I can do is step back, and he steps forward, towards me with each subsequent step I take. It isn't long before my ass bumps the kitchen table, making the candlelight blur in waves on the wall behind him.

I repeat my brother's phone number inside my head, a calming mechanism that I've been leaning on all too frequently lately. I still remember it, even though his phone was disconnected long ago.

The young man's eyes are solid black, a speckle of orange dancing behind each glassy dome. "Give me a minute, then we'll be ready," he says.

I hold his gaze. I straighten my stance, picture the knife inside my bag gliding in one smooth movement into my hand, how the blade will scatter all of the tiny flames when I raise it above my head.

"Okay," I say.

Once the young man leaves the room, I rush back to the phone and pull the handset from the wall. No dial tone; only silence. I tap the buttons that make up my brother's number just for the satisfying click of plastic sinking into plastic. On the last number I hold my finger there, not wanting to release the button. *I'm not ready.* I'm turning towards the back door when the young man reappears.

He touches my arm. "Ready?"

The smoke in the hallway swirls around the people exiting the dining room, trailing them as they drift into the living room. The last person in the group, a small, brittle-looking woman, turns around as the young man is guiding me out of the kitchen. Her nose is a bruised red, her eyes swollen between the deep creases that encircle them.

"Were you able to reach a tow truck, dear?"

The young man tightens his grip on my arm. I want to shake him off, but not in front of her. "They're on their way," he says.

The old woman offers me a sad smile before the old man who answered the door turns back and leads her forward into the living room with the others.

"Her parents," the young man explains once we push through the lingering smoke into the dining room. "I wish I could tell them so they didn't have to suffer like this, but their beliefs . . . They wouldn't allow it." He stands in front of me, frantically waving his arms until the smoke clears a frame around him. "Sorry for the inconvenience—I know it was pretty elaborate. I'm Jacob, by the way."

In the center of the room, where a dining table should be, is an open casket on a stand, its brass handles and glossy white surface sparking under the candlelight. As I approach, the young woman inside surfaces through the thick haze. Her skin is sunken and grey but not as bad as I anticipated, only ashen in contrast to her lacy white dress. Underneath the artificial vanilla and spice that's clotted throughout the house, the treacly odor of decay rises, a feral animal surrounding the woman in its warm, wet fur.

The odors gather in my mouth, forming a coppery-tasting grit that settles in the crevices of my molars. I let loose a long string of coughs. Jacob's eyes widen and jump, and he holds an index finger in front of his lips.

"I told the funeral home not to embalm her," he says. "Everyone's been complaining about all the candles and incense, but what else was I supposed to do?"

I nod. I'm thinking about my car a quarter mile down the road, the cool leather seat against my back, the gas pedal yielding so easily under my foot. How surprisingly smoothly it runs despite its age and condition. I imagine racing to my brother's house to tell him about tonight, the way his voice would spike as he calls me crazy, if he was still alive to call me crazy.

My hand finds the bottom of my bag, squeezing through the pebbly leather until the knife's handle is defined against my palm.

"Funny about the phone," I say.

"I didn't want any interruptions."

Jacob joins me in front of the coffin. We both stare down at the young woman inside. Her dark hair is a stark contrast against the white silk pillowing her head. Her hands are folded atop her stomach, and a blue-black stain creeps over the edges of her fingers, pooling like the start of a bruise.

"She's still lovely," he says, taking his fiancee's right hand into his. The disruption causes her other hand to slide from her stomach and land awkwardly, palm folded in half, at her side. Jacob adjusts it so that her palm is down and her arm is straight, then places her other hand gently back in the coffin. Tears bully the shadowy hollows under his eyes.

Slow, deep piano notes drift in from the living room. The low murmur of voices blends with the static of the recording, as beautiful and heavy as the smoke-bloated air around us. For a moment the room vibrates, every beating heart in the house collected under my feet.

Like in the kitchen Jacob shadows my movements, sliding closer to me with each increment that I move away. His hip bumps against mine, and I feel his entire body tighten inside his suit, a tremor hurtling through his limbs and into me. I step back, yank the knife from inside my bag, and raise it just as I imagined.

"Wait."

Jacob reaches into his suit jacket and produces a thick white envelope, its seal misaligned by its bulging contents. I lower the knife and take the envelope from him. Though I don't yet have a solid grasp of how much it should weigh, I slip the envelope into my bag without opening it. I will do that in the car, far away from here, counting the bills under my cell phone's flashlight.

"Ready?" I ask.

This time Jacob gives me space when I raise the knife. I cut open the woman's white dress and use the tip of the blade to sever each crude stitch holding closed the Y-shaped incision that splits her chest. Though heavy, the flaps of skin fold back easily like pages in a well-loved book. Jacob looks on from a few feet back as I spread the already bisected ribcage. He winces, though I don't know if it's from the sight of his beloved cleft before him, or from the cold mineral stench that is rising in front of us. My ears catch the sharp intake of his breath as my hand slides into the woman's chest cavity.

Blood as dark as wet earth oozes over my hands; my fingers punc-ture a film like the skin on chilled gravy. I think of my brother again, how much warmer he had been—how he still smelled like something that breathes and beats and bleeds—then the look of disappointment that dragged down my mother's face when he failed to rouse at my touch. After that, she chose not to see what I can do; she's never wit-nessed the sunken faces lifting with joy, the grateful embraces thrown around her only daughter. My mother has never seen the admiration of strangers—more than I ever wanted from her—in that one crys-talline moment that I give to them, but couldn't give to her. Hands cupping the young woman's heart, I look over my shoulder at Jacob and attempt a reassuring smile. He smiles back through tears that now flow freely. I gently squeeze the small, firm muscle in my palms. I do it again. I watch the woman's face. I wait for her heart to punch to life in my grip.

Selfies

~ Nina Kiriki Hoffman

I learned to take selfies from Walter, my most recent husband.

When we were out in public, Walter liked to document. He often broke into what we were doing to pose us in front of something or someone fabulous so he could take a selfie. He gloried in putting pictures of us up on his Facebook page to show all the other losers in the world what an amazing life he was leading with his trophy wife.

Yesterday, I went to his Facebook account to look at that gallery of us looking like a celebrity couple leading a fantasy life. I need to delete the account soon; any record of me as Walter's wife must disappear, because I don't get facelifts between my marriages, and I don't want facial recognition software to be able to identify me.

Walter was my best and my worst husband so far: Our two life-lines, the apparent and the real, were both interesting, and I liked him better than I liked my other husbands.

With every husband, I have a line. I put up with a lot from them. Then they cross that line, and I kill them.

Walter crossed the line after we'd been married about three years. He broke my arm. Luckily my right arm, not my dominant left. I still had the strength and skill to kill him and make it look accidental, though I had to wait a couple of weeks after he broke my arm. I wrapped the cast in plastic so it wouldn't get blood on it.

All the death stuff takes a while to settle, if you want to get away with murder. You have to be grief-stricken and do a bunch of acting for the few friends your husband allows you once he really gets into controlling you, and all his so-called friends, too. Husbands I've had are usually charismatic and look like they lead perfect lives, so they have lots of acquaintances. I don't know that I've ever had a husband who had really good friends.

The selfie thing—I liked that. I don't keep souvenirs, because that's one of the easiest things for police to use against you in a court of law.

My memories are my treasures. But, I thought, how about pictures of myself while I'm recuperating from being with someone who abused me, and while I'm transforming myself into the next trophy wife? Nobody could convict me of anything based on those.

I went blond after I killed Walter. I experimented with sparkly makeup instead of subtle and classy. I took a ton of selfies in different lighting, trying to decide whether I looked too trashy to attract the kind of man I wanted. Walter was the richest man I'd ever killed. It was nice to have money, but I was ready for a different flavor.

When I studied my selfies, I noticed another person in the pictures, even in the ones I took when I was alone. A shadow man stood behind me.

With the help of the only long-term friend I had, my high school nerd buddy Sully, who knew my whole history and made me fake IDs as necessary, I'd changed my name to Stephanie for this incarnation. As Walter's wife, I had been Margaret. Walter called me Meg at first, and then, as he wore me down, Nutmeg, at least in private. Nutmeg, because I was crazy. He told me my memories were imaginary, and That Didn't Happen. Not easy to convince someone when you have documentation. Sure, he hid all his trophy photos of me after he hit me in a private partition on his computer, but I knew how his mind worked and where he hid his passwords. Also, he left the key to the lock of the basement gallery in a hiding place in the basement, and of course I found that. I took pictures of his pictures and kept an SD card of them in the lining of my purse, just in case.

After I killed Walter, I took a hammer to his laptop and burned his printed-out pictures in our fireplace. I mailed my SD card to Sully and told him not to look, just keep it safe. He's a criminal, but he respects my wishes, or if he doesn't, he never tells me.

I stayed a widow in the house I had shared with Walter for three months, then told anyone who was interested that the house held too many memories. I sold it and moved, as I usually do. I hadn't made any real friends during Nutmeg's life, so I had no regrets.

In my new town, Stephanie joined a gym, took aquarobics and pilates and yoga classes, and buffed up the body I'd let go during my Walter period. Some of the guys in the hot tub hit on Stephanie while she was still fat, which told me I still had it, but they weren't the type of men I was interested in.

Between husbands, I never did feel right. I felt better in some ways, but the lust and excitement and satisfaction were all pretty flat.

I documented Stephanie's adventures in character-building in a series of selfies: Stephanie in all kinds of clothes in department store dressing rooms. I didn't buy many. It took me time and many experiments to settle on a new style every time I started over. I needed my selves to be conventionally attractive, and also interesting, and different from each other. Finding the right quirks took work.

In selfie after selfie as I studied them on my laptop, I saw a shadowy figure behind me, near me, sharing a mirror with me. I knew I had been alone all those times.

The shadow grew darker as I fine-tuned Stephanie. Its outline looked familiar.

At the gym, I took a selfie of me on a treadmill, rocking out to songs on my iPhone. Totally innocent and non-prosecutable. A man stood beside me, even though my gym had separate rooms for the women and men to work out in, and it was hard to stand next to someone on a treadmill. The shadow was darker this time, not at all transparent, and I could make out its face.

It was Walter in all his urbane glory, out of place in a gym in his best dark pinstriped suit (the one I had buried him in), every dark hair in place.

I'd never run into this particular problem before. I mean—ghosts? Who believed? If there were ghosts who could do stuff, wouldn't we be drowning in them? Everybody died sooner or later, not all of them peacefully. I thought about my previous husbands—Rich, Jason, Hank, and Trevor—all resting in different places around the country.

I sat in my apartment bedroom with the lights lit on my vanity table. I monitored my looks, though I was detached about it. Looks were a tool I used to get what I wanted. I took another selfie while I sat there, and Walter's face showed up over my shoulder, staring at me with a big frown. He looked different from the way he had in the treadmill picture, but I wasn't sure how, except his hair was less shellacked.

What if he was around all the time, watching me, judging?

More fool him.

"What do you even want, Walter?" I asked, looking over my shoulder at nothing. I faced forward again, held up the phone, and aimed the back camera toward my face. He was there, right behind me, wearing a ferocious frown. He frowned even more, came forward, and put his hands around my neck. It looked like he was squeezing, but all I felt was a slight chill.

I shrugged. "You got nothing."

His shoulders rose and fell. Wait, what? He wasn't in his suit anymore. Before I could study on that, he let go of me, pursed his lips, and pointed to my hair, now honey blond with platinum highlights. While I was married to him, it had been auburn with golden highlights.

"What? You don't like it?"

He shook his head.

"Tough shit."

He grimaced. He had never liked to hear me use swear words. Which meant I could easily torture him in the afterlife.

"This is the color for my next husband, not my last husband. I'm going to find somebody with different tastes this time. Maybe a little more down home."

He put his hands around my neck again. I took a selfie. He was there in the picture, looking like he was expending great effort to choke me. His arms were bare, and his muscles were bunched up. I was smiling.

"Look at this. It's so weird!" I showed him the selfie, then realized that without the phone camera active, I couldn't see him, so I didn't know whether he was looking. That was no fun. I emailed the picture to myself, then opened up the laptop to put it on a bigger screen, and switched the phone back to camera mode, aiming it around until I found Walter again. He leaned over beside me and looked at the picture.

"What the hell are you wearing?" I asked. "That's not the suit I buried you in! Are you *shopping* in the afterlife?" How could he be wearing metallic green workout shorts and a pink tank top? So undignified! I'd never seen him wear clothes like that.

He looked hot. His butt, sheathed in shiny green cloth, was so nicely defined I wanted to grab it. I snapped a picture of just his butt, then aimed the camera at his face and captured his nasty grin. He stepped back and posed for me, showing off his muscles, lifting his shirt to reveal washboard abs, doing poses like mustachioed strong men in old circus posters.

I took picture after picture, more interested in him dead than I had been while he was alive. Had he always been this toned? I knew he was strong. I'd felt it. But he wore formal or studiedly casual clothes while we were together, except when we were in bed, and he liked that to be dark time. He loved looking at his handiwork on my body, but never liked me to see him clearly.

I sent all the pictures to my laptop and then looked at Walter with the phone's camera. When had he gotten so . . . solid?

He laughed. I could almost hear it—just the thinnest edge of a sound that used to mean he was going to hit me again, harder.

It worried me.

Then he vanished.

My best friend Sully and I rarely met face to face since I started my career as a serial killer. Our pasts were too tangled with things that might make government people spy on us and listen in on what we said to each other. We liked flying below any radar there was.

This time, though, I arranged to meet him. Sully was rooted in place, part of a crime network in San Francisco, and as Stephanie, I had moved to Palo Alto, not too far from where I grew up. I was ready for some California culture after three-plus years in Chicago.

I met Sully at the public library, in one of the private, glass-walled study rooms.

I hadn't seen him in six years. He was still rangy and tall and looked like he hadn't shaved, or brushed his shaggy brown hair in two weeks. I had never been able to figure out how he maintained just that length of prickly golden stubble. The lines around his eyes and mouth were deeper, and his clothes were more ragged and frayed, but he wore expensive tennis shoes, and he'd changed his chunky black plastic glasses to wire rims that made him look like John Lennon. We hugged. He smelled like barbecue and citrus shampoo and something wild, like sage, and he felt warm and solid.

"Nice work with Walter," he said. Sully always knew where I was, and checked my local newspapers for stories about me and my husbands. He watched for coded requests from me in the personal ads, too. He would have seen the article about Walter's car crash.

"Thanks. Only there's a problem," I said. "Take a look at this." I opened my laptop and showed him a slideshow of my selfies. Not every single one, but a time-lapse of Meg's transformation into Stephanie.

Sully said, after I'd shown him about twenty pictures, "I admit to some fascination with this—I've never seen your in-between stages before—but is there a point, or are you just showing off?"

"Wait. Sorry. I thought I edited this down better. I'll skip ahead." I jumped to the treadmill picture and pointed to Walter's shadow.

"So?"

"It's Walter." I jumped back to a picture of me in a dressing room wearing a ridiculous pink satin sheath dress I'd never buy no matter what I looked like. I enjoyed imagining the kind of person who would buy it, though. Playing dress-up was career practice for me.

I pointed to the faint shadow in the dressing room mirror. "See? He starts showing up here . . ."

"Are you crazy?" Sully asked.

"Only in a controlled way." I flipped back to the treadmill shot, then jumped ahead to a picture of Walter in my vanity table mirror, one where he had his hands wrapped around my throat. His features were visible—the grimace that had terrified me while I was Meg. Stephanie could shrug it off.

Sully took a step back. "Whoa!"

"Didn't hurt," I said. "I couldn't even feel it. But—"

Sully pulled his iPhone out of his pocket and turned on the camera. He looked around the room through his screen. He stopped with the phone aimed over my shoulder.

I got out my own phone and took a look. Walter stood there, sure as shootin', back in his good suit again. He smiled at both of us. He looked a little wavery around the edges, but more real than he had before.

Sully set his phone to record video and aimed it at Walter. "Hey, brother," he said. "What is it you're trying to communicate from beyond the grave?"

Walter gave him the finger.

"Who is this man, Nutmeg?" Walter asked, turning to me. His voice was no louder than a whisper, but I could hear it.

"Nutmeg?" Sully asked, still filming Walter.

"Walter's pet name for me," I said. "Walter, this is Sully, my childhood friend. What are you doing here?"

Walter smiled and buried his hands in his pockets. "I'm a trifle displeased with you, sweetheart. I had no plans to die." He sounded a little louder. His edges had stabilized. Why was he getting more real?

I said, "Neither did I, and the way you were going, it looked like I was headed there. It was you or me, and I chose survival for me."

He frowned.

"So are you haunting me because I killed you?" I asked. "What do I have to do to get rid of you?"

He smiled. "Why would I tell you that?" He turned to Sully, shot him with a finger-gun, then expanded outward, as though he were inflatable and someone was blowing more air into him. His outside edge went right through me, an icy wave. I couldn't stop shuddering; my teeth ached, and my nerves were still firing.

Sully stopped filming. He was shuddering, too; Walter had moved through him as he blew up bigger than the room. Maybe we were still inside his edges.

We put the video on the laptop and watched it. Sully shook his head, stopped, then shook his head again. "I do forgeries and hacking," he said. "I don't do ghosts."

We were sitting at the study-room table with the computer in front of us. I snuck my phone up and took a selfie with me and Sully in it. There was Walter, his face more demonic than human, grinning between me and Sully. He'd grown fangs.

I showed my phone to Sully.

"No," he said. "I love you, Polly, but I can't—I don't—I got no skills for this." He grabbed his battered briefcase and his phone and left the room.

I sat back, feeling cold and alone. Sully had always been there for me, no matter what I did. I couldn't believe he would leave me now.

But the door had closed behind him. I waited, and he didn't come back.

I swallowed. I took a few deep breaths. I figured out my next move. Sully had already helped me set up my Stephanie identity, and I'd gotten her look down now. I flipped up the laptop lid to go online.

"Hey," Walter whispered in my ear. "I've met some interesting people over here. Look behind me."

I could hear Walter, even though I wasn't looking at him. I sighed and aimed my phone toward his voice. He was there, looking spiffy and charismatic again. Other shadows hovered behind him. I snapped a picture. They were still just stains on the air, not solid like Walter, but I suspected if I could see them clearly, they'd look a lot like Rich, Jason, Hank, and Trevor.

"We've had some lovely talks," Walter whispered.

I turned off my phone. Maybe ostrich mode would work for me: he couldn't bother me if I didn't look at him. I plugged in the laptop, went online, and started a new Match.com account. I needed a selfie. I looked at my most recent ones. They all had Walter in them. Well, I could edit him out. I chose one of the ones I had taken at my vanity table and cropped and blackened Walter's image out of the picture, then posted it and set up my subscription using the new credit card Sully had gotten for Stephanie Farrell. I registered with the nickname Steffy and said I liked homemaking and entertaining.

The website showed me singles near me, and I studied their pictures, wondering who they really were. It took me a lot of dates with a lot of people to find my husbands. I didn't want to marry anyone who didn't deserve me.

I heard breathing in my ear. "I like Mr. TakeAChance," Walter whispered. I turned toward his voice, then remembered I was ignoring him. Still, I looked hard at Mr. TakeAChance, and ended up sending him a message.

The next time I took a selfie, again while sitting at the vanity table in the bedroom, Walter was back beside me, looking into the phone's camera and smiling. This time he was wearing a joke nightshirt I had bought him for our first Christmas together, flannel with little Grinches all over it. He'd never worn it while he was alive. He'd been angry and disgusted when he opened it, and I spent the rest of Christmas in bed with a lot of bruises.

"You burned that. How'd you get it back?" I asked.

He smiled and waggled his eyebrows. Had he grown a sense of humor since he died?

He pointed at the phone. "Take another picture," he whispered. "I'll make a face."

He'd never been playful. I shrugged and took a picture, and then another, and another. In each he was doing a different expression. He even pushed up his nose into a pig snout, and did fish lips. If he'd been this fun while he was alive, maybe I wouldn't have killed him.

At last he leaned forward and licked my ear while I took a picture, and I felt it. I felt it. He left a trace of slimy wetness on me.

I shuddered and turned the phone off.

I could still see him. A faint, shadowy image on the air, but still there.

I ran out of my bedroom and into the kitchen. His stain didn't follow me. I grabbed my coat and purse and went out. I went to Green Park and walked off my shudders, then went home, to find my phone had run out of charge. When I plugged it in again, it notified me it had no more storage space.

Somehow Walter had managed to use it to take more selfies. Hundreds of them. I deleted and deleted, and there were still more.

A knock sounded behind me, and I turned to see Walter at my open bedroom door. He looked real. "Hey, baby," he said. "You know how pictures steal a little of your soul? It works the other way if you're dead already. Welcome me back?"

I still take selfies. I've noticed a slow leak of what makes me myself slipping away, a tiny increment gone with each picture I take. I'm not sure where I'm going. I just know I don't want to stay here anymore.

Caprine Heartburn

~ H. L. Fullerton

Douglas Papago has been married to his wife Lizzie for seven years and is thinking of either leaving her or killing himself. Except Lizzie can't afford the mortgage on their condo without him. And he loves her. He does.

He simply wishes she wouldn't jump in the shower the second she wakes when she knows he has to leave first. He's asked her to wait and she always says the same thing, "I thought I'd be out before your alarm went off." But she never is. Which is why he's the one to discover the goat.

Douglas shuffles down the hall towards the kitchen and coffee. He's so intent on getting his caffeine fix, still grumbling about the shower and how he's going to be late, he almost doesn't see it. But the goat bleats a friendly hello and Doug raises a hand in acknowledgment, then stops—hand in a sort of half-wave—turns and *sees* it.

Standing pride of place on their sisal rug is a small goat. He hopes it's some funny looking dog Lizzie adopted. Sun glints off its golden coat, giving it salon-perfect highlights. Wide ears, no horns, small-ish—roughly the size of a springer spaniel—it somehow strikes him as an adult goat. It has that aura of wisdom that comes with age. It's been around the mountain, knows a thing or two.

He rubs his eyes.

Still there. He feels fuzzy, like falling or dreaming. He really hopes he's dreaming. He knows he's not.

It bleats again. A little longer greeting this time, maybe *Good morning, Douglas. How's it going?*

He scans the room. It looks like his living room. Everything else in it is his: TV, leather sofa, occasional chairs (yeah, he didn't know what they were till he was married either), black and white architectural prints on café au lait walls. And a goat. He smells it now, realizes he's smelled that funky unwashed animal scent since he woke. He just couldn't place the barnyard perfume until he saw the animal that went with it.

He looks at the goat. The goat looks at him. The minute the shower shuts off, he yells for his wife. Thinking, *That's it. She's lost her fucking mind.* He knows she wants a kid, has talked nothing but babies since they bought this place and jesus christ now they have a goat? "*Lizzie!*"

"I thought I'd finish before you got up." She pads towards him in nothing but a towel, water droplets still clinging to her skin. "Sorry. I'll dry off in the . . . " Her voice trails off as she catches sight of the goat. "What's—Why's—Is that a goat? Douglas?" She clutches the towel to her and inches behind him.

"It's not yours?"

"Why would I get a goat?"

"I don't know," he says, still certain she's somehow responsible. "Who else would it belong to?"

"You?"

"*Me*? Why would I want a goat?"

The goat makes a *meh* sound and they stop arguing, stare at it.

"Do something," Lizzie whispers.

Douglas looks at her, then the goat. "I'm going to shower."

"Douglas! You can't leave a goat in our living room. What if—what if it eats the couch or . . . or . . . or uses the rug"—she lowers her voice so she doesn't offend the inquisitive goat—"*as its toilet.*"

"What do you want me to do, Lizzie? I'm in my pajamas. I'll . . . take it outside or something when I'm dressed. But first, I'm showering."

"What should I do?"

"I don't know. Get ready for work. Make it breakfast. Whatever you want." Douglas spins and heads for the open bathroom. It isn't until he's in the shower, shampoo dripping into his eyes, that he worries leaving Lizzie alone with the goat wasn't a smart move. What if she decides to name it?

The goat is lapping from one of their red and black donburi bowls when he returns cleaned and dressed.

"I gave it some milk. Do you think that's okay?" Lizzie's fingers knot. She's wearing her green scrubs, hair twisted back into a loop.

"It seems to like it, but I don't know if pasteurized skim milk is good for goat stomachs."

Douglas doesn't say anything. He's trying to figure out how to get rid of the thing. Preferably without touching it. He also plans to accidentally smash the bowl it's using on their granite countertop as soon as Lizzie's back is turned. No way he's eating from the same dish a goat licked, dishwasher sanitize cycle or no. "Do you have a scarf I can use?"

"You're going to strangle it? In our home?"

"No! I'm going to make a leash and take it outside. Let it wander back to wherever it came from."

Lizzie disappears to rummage through her closet. He checks his watch and wonders how long it takes to coax a goat out of a house.

"One you don't like," he calls. "In case it gets chewed." So far the goat hasn't ruined any of their stuff, but Douglas is certain goats will eat anything, even tin cans, given the chance. Whether that's true or something he saw on a cartoon he isn't sure.

Lizzie returns with a plaid cashmere scarf and hands it to him. "Not too tight," she warns as Douglas approaches the goat. The goat ignores him. He notices it has a white blaze between its bumblebee eyes—black stripes of pupil across sunflower-colored irises. Something buzzes in his head.

"Nice goat," he says. "Good goat. No biting." Doug crouches and wraps his cashmere leash around the goat's neck. He stands. Tugs on the scarf.

The goat doesn't budge.

Douglas tugs more forcefully and the goat kicks the donburi bowl, breaking it and spraying milk onto Douglas' trousers. "Christ, let's go." He grabs the collar's knot and drags at the goat.

It bleats, then picks up its feet and clops after Douglas. Lizzie scurries ahead of them into the dining room towards the sliding glass doors that open onto their postage-stamp patio. Outside air hits the goat's muzzle and it digs in, refusing to exit the Papago house.

Douglas—too pissed to worry about getting bit or kicked—wraps his arm around its middle, gags at the smell and hefts the goat over the threshold. He sets his bundle on the cement patio and checks to see if any of his neighbors are watching from their windows. No one is.

Lizzie slides the door almost closed so neither he nor the animal can get back in. "Hurry," she whispers.

Douglas tries to slide the scarf over the goat's head, but it's knotted good and tight. He throws the tail end of the scarf over the goat's back. The green and blue stripes set off the gold of the goat's fur. Douglas half-suspects Lizzie chose the scarf for that very reason.

He pushes at the goat's backside until it trundles off their patio and into the common grassy area. Then he hurries back inside. He's going to have to change. He smells like a barnyard and just-turned milk. His hands feel dusty and greasy from handling the goat.

Lizzie bites her lip. "Do you think she'll be okay?"

"It'll be fine."

"Did we do the right thing?"

Douglas takes her arm. Last thing they need is for some busybody to call the condo association. Report them for having livestock. "Of course, we did. You fed it. It's outside where it belongs. What else could we do?"

Lizzie shakes free of him. "You smell, Douglas. Like—"

"Goat. Yeah, I know."

"No." Lizzie shakes her head slowly. "Like lavender and camphor."

"Must be from your scarf. I'll wash." He looks at the red-gold strands covering his slate suit. "And change." He does. When he returns, finally ready to head into the kitchen and get that mug of coffee, he sees Lizzie surrounded by their living room drapes, sneaking peeks into the backyard.

He sighs, gets the coffee. Toasts some bread. Asks Lizzie if she wants any.

She doesn't answer.

"Lizzie?" He's careful to keep the exasperation out of his voice. He isn't keeping a goat, but neither does he want to fight about it. "Should I make you some toast?" He sticks in another slice of multi-grain and takes his two jam-covered pieces to the dining room table. "I put some toast on for you," he tells her when she glances his way.

"The Masons are staring at her."

Douglas does not want this to be their—*his*—problem.

"She looks so lost. I think she misses us."

Douglas wills Lizzie away from the window. He can feel her want. Needy, greedy feeling. It pulls at him. He shoves more toast into his mouth. Lizzie flinches when the toaster pops. As if he'd just shot her goat. Then she spies his toast.

"Was that mine?"

He nods and she leaves the window, *thank you thank you,* to smear yogurt on her fresh-popped toast. She joins him at the table and they crunch in silence. Until the crying starts.

Douglas talks loudly about the weather, traffic, what they should have for dinner, anything to drown out the goat bleats which holy jesus sound like a baby lost in the wilderness. He maintains desperate eye contact so neither he nor Lizzie look outside. Lizzie's hand tightens around her toast. Crumbs rain onto her placemat.

Douglas breaks. "It's just hungry. There's plenty of grass right there at its feet. There's nothing we can—" He looks. A collection of neighbors circle the goat. Mrs. Mason—wearing a ratty blue bathrobe over pink pajamas—is crouched next to the goat, making soothing motions on its side, but the mewling doesn't stop.

"*Douglas.*"

"Okay." He stands, takes a deep breath. "We'll check on it. But don't tell any of them it was in our house." Lizzie looks so relieved Douglas feels like an ass. Holding hands, they step out into the sunshine and cross the lawn.

"What's going on?" Douglas says as they near. He's proud at how normal he sounds. Not guilty at all.

The guy who lives three doors down turns. "Someone left their kid in our yard. You believe that?"

"Should we call someone?" Lizzie says.

"Marjorie went to call CPS."

Huh? Douglas thinks he must be mixing up his acronyms. "CPS?"

"Child Protective Services." The guy shakes his head. "What kind of person does a thing like this?"

Mrs. Mason coos, "Who would abandon a sweet baby like you? Poor thing isn't even dressed properly."

Douglas and Lizzie share a *What-the-hell?* look. Douglas tilts his head and murmurs in her ear, "You see a goat, right?" She nods.

Mrs. Mason scoops up the goat and cradles it in her arms. Its legs pinwheel at the sky; it tosses its head. Mrs. Mason chucks the goat under the chin. Everyone crowds around Mrs. Mason to admire a baby *that is really a goat.*

Douglas gasps and chokes on his own saliva. "What's happening?" he says to Lizzie, but she's staring too hard to answer.

"Lizzie," Mrs. Mason says. "Don't you have a scarf like this?"

"I lent it to my friend Jennifer. You don't suppose . . . " Lizzie moves closer. Neighbors shuffle out of her way. Mrs. Mason presents the goat to Lizzie like something out of *The Lion King*.

Lizzie picks up the trailing scarf (which is still knotted around the baby/goat's neck although no one seems bothered by that) and says, "Omigod! This *is* mine. Here's the lipstick stain I couldn't get out."

What is Lizzie doing? Douglas's stomach doesn't like this turn of events.

"Should I stop Marjorie?"

"*Please*. I'm sure Jennifer didn't mean to . . . I didn't even know she was . . . Let me take the baby. Douglas and I will sort everything out."

Mrs. Mason hands the goat to Lizzie who cuddles the nasty smelling thing. Marjorie's husband calls and asks if she got a hold of CPS yet. She hasn't so he tells her to hang up, some flaky friend of Lizzie's is the mother and the Papagos are going to take of everything. Marjorie offers to bring over some diapers.

Douglas is freaking out. This is not how this was supposed to go. What is wrong with these people? Can't they tell a goat from a baby and why is Lizzie playing along?

"Doug, honey, you're going to be late. Why don't you head to work and I'll call you later? Let you know what happens."

Douglas would like nothing more than to leave, but he doesn't like Lizzie's suggestion *at all*. He can tell she's trying to convince herself the goat is a baby. Yet she's holding it the way a shepherd would, much different than how Mrs. Mason—who thought she was holding a real child—did. Because Lizzie knows damn well it isn't a baby.

Mrs. Mason adjusts Lizzie's arms, which must look awkward to her, and says, "You have to be careful of their heads at this age. Like that. Much better. You'll get the hang of it, dear. So sad about your friend." She rubs her finger along the goat's snout and smiles down at the little bundle of joy.

"Lizzie. Honey. You have to work, too. People can't just keep *babies*"—Douglas stumbles over this word—"they find in their backyard. And it may not be Jennifer's. I'm sure it isn't. Let's call the police and let them handle it."

Everyone stares at Douglas as if he suggested throwing the baby into a wood chipper.

"I'll call in sick. The hospital will understand."

Douglas understands they can't have this argument in front of people or he's going to end up looking like a dick. And he'd probably call a goat a goat which will only get his neighbors to call emergency services on him. They'll think he's nuts. Ironic, as they're the ones hallucinating. But even if they're right and he and Lizzie are wrong, he's not raising a goat/baby. Douglas jerks his head at his wife and goes to work, thinking, *She's lost her fucking mind* and *Maybe I have a brain tumor* and *Goddamn goat baby.*

She named the goat Tracy. It's wearing a diaper and some kind of scarf sarong. Douglas considers driving Lizzie to the hospital for a psych eval. Or calling the cops and have them come confiscate the baby. Let them foster a goat; what does he care. But he worries Lizzie might claim it's their child and then what would he do? Claim she's lying? Say it isn't his? Tell them it's a goat in baby's clothing? He'd end up in the back of the squad car. And Lizzie knows everyone at the hospital. They're her colleagues. He is so royally fucked.

"I made lemon chicken, your favorite." She places the platter on the table.

"Lizzie, we can't keep the goat. We know it's not a real baby even if no one else does."

"Her name's Tracy."

"We can't keep her." Tracy gambols over to him and butts her head against his leg. Douglas smells talcum powder and manure.

"I turned the second bedroom into a nursery."

The second bedroom was his home office. The harder Douglas tries to hold onto his patience, the more it wriggles away from him. He's going to end up yelling and Lizzie will cry and the neighbors will hear and think, *Poor woman*, when they should be thinking, *Poor guy, his wife wants him to raise a goat and send it to college.* He flings his briefcase onto a consul table and storms into their bedroom, firmly shutting but not slamming the door behind him.

He refuses to come out and when Lizzie joins him in bed and tries to talk about how the goat is a blessing, a good luck charm, an omen of conception, he rolls away from her and pretends to be asleep. He breathes through his mouth to avoid the funky unwashed scent and prays for a brain tumor. *Maybe when I wake, the goat will have disappeared as magically as it appeared. Please, please let it leave.*

In the morning, Douglas doesn't bother insisting Tracy is a goat or that Lizzie doesn't need to hire a babysitter for an animal that's perfectly capable of looking after itself.

"Doesn't the hospital have day care? Maybe you should take Tracy there."

Lizzie looks at him strangely as if she's not sure she can trust his change of heart. "She'll be more comfortable here. It's her home."

Douglas translates this to mean that Lizzie isn't sure the baby magic will work outside their condo development and isn't willing to chance it. He doesn't really care. He's worried this is his life from now on. *From this day forward . . .* Tracy clip clops into the kitchen like a tapdancing bride. Was he going to have to raise a goat? He was, wasn't he?

"I'm leaving," he says and escapes to work, bile coating the back of his throat.

Lizzie and Tracy are cuddled on the sofa, watching television when Douglas returns that evening. Tracy's head is in Lizzie's lap and Lizzie is stroking Tracy. Douglas focuses on the goat, tries to see a baby or a blessing or anything but goat, but goat is all he sees, all he smells.

"There's chicken in the fridge," Lizzie says, not looking at him.

Douglas eats, then joins them, his family—oh christ, this is his family—in the living room. But not on the sofa. He stands off to the side and stares. The goat turns its head and bleats at him. Gets up off the sofa and comes over.

"You can keep the goat. But no diapers. No dressing it like a baby. No buying a crib. No more babysitters. It's not a baby, Lizzie. It's a full grown goat and you have to treat it like one." Douglas is as surprised as Lizzie to hear these words come out of his mouth. He adds, "And if it, she, isn't here one morning, that's it. No more goats." And he really, really wants it—Tracy—to disappear.

Lizzie jumps up from the couch, all smiles and joy. She throws her arms around him and he puts his around her and can feel her whole body vibrating with happiness.

"The goat is going to bring us a baby. I just feel it. A beautiful little girl and we'll name her Tracy, too."

They were not naming a child after a goat, but Douglas wasn't going to argue. Lizzie wasn't pregnant; she might never be.

Tracy gives him an approving look and Douglas locks eyes with it and notices the delicate slip of skin surrounding its blonde eyes is not pinkish but burnished gold. It is a beautiful goat and *its eyes*— For a moment, his head feels expansive, like it's floating. This, he thinks, is what encountering the divine must be like. Meaning seems to be everywhere and for a moment he transcends his mundane life. Douglas drops to his knees—which puts him eye-level with Tracy—and says, "I love you."

The goat walks away, no nod of head, no understanding look, no acknowledging bleat. Douglas feels foolish and rises. Lizzie caresses his face. "I'm ovulating," she says and takes his hand and pulls him into the bedroom.

Weeks go by and the goat is always there in the morning and Lizzie still isn't pregnant and Douglas is getting used to their condo smelling like a petting zoo. The scent is almost comforting. Especially with Lizzie growing more and more upset about not conceiving.

Once again, Douglas thinks of leaving Lizzie, but is afraid Tracy will follow him. And Tracy seems Lizzie's only consolation so he stays and thinks back fondly to the days when his wife hogged the shower. Now he has to deal with neighbors commenting on how big the baby's getting, but the goat is the same size it always was and Douglas ends up flubbing these conversations and Lizzie gets mad at him for that, too.

"You need to be more fatherly to Tracy," she'll say. "She can sense your dislike. Douglas, this is never going to work if you don't try harder. Don't you want a baby?"

Douglas isn't sure he does. He can't handle raising a goat baby which requires almost no care. Every time Lizzie brings up the subject, he has to stop himself from telling her goodbye.

Then Lizzie leaves their bedroom door open and Tracy wanders in while they're having sex.

"Let her stay," Lizzie urges. Her hands stop him from leaving the bed.

"No."

"I've thought about this, Douglas, and I think we haven't conceived because we shut Tracy out. If she's in the room with us, it'll work."

"No. I'm not— No." He breaks into a cold sweat, imagining it. A goat watching him— No.

But Lizzie gets increasingly upset and insistent until Douglas grits his teeth, closes his eyes and lets the goat watch.

Lizzie still doesn't feel pregnant.

The smell wakes Douglas. Lizzie's side of the bed is empty. He listens for the shower, but all is quiet. His stomach sours at the meaty scent perfuming their bedroom.

He throws back the covers and gets up. The scent is vaguely familiar—*What the hell is it?* His foggy morning mind can't place it. He thinks of long ago Easters at his grandmother's house and although those should be fond memories, recalling them now scare him.

With trip-trap-trepidation, Douglas opens the bedroom door. The smell is stronger, gamier. He gags, cups his hand over his mouth and that helps. But the cloying stench sticks to his tongue.

The living room is empty—no Tracy. But Douglas doesn't feel relieved. His anxiety ratchets up a few notches. More when he sees Lizzie at the dining table. She is gnawing on a bone. Her face and hands are covered in what looks like barbeque sauce—and grease.

His stomach roils.

Her stomach is distended. She has pushed her chair back from the table and is leaning at an awkward angle over it. Gnawing, gnawing. The bone cracks and she slurps the marrow.

Douglas knows what the smell is, what his wife's done. He almost makes it to the kitchen sink, but the sight of the roasting pan, the heat from the still-warm oven . . . He vomits into his hands, all over the floor.

His head buzzes. He can't think. He heaves again.

Lizzie is still eating.

He crawls to the bathroom and showers, but he can't get clean, can't get rid of the smell. Fucking christ, *the smell.*

☉

Lizzie tries to explain. She sits on the bed and Douglas wants to push her off, but she looks nine months pregnant and he doesn't want to hurt her. He won't let her get under the covers. He won't come out. He buries his face in the pillows and tries to remember what fresh smells like.

"We were going about it all wrong. We had the baby. We were given a baby, but we didn't *see* it as a baby. But if I carry the baby, birth the baby, it will be a real baby. Just like we always wanted."

Douglas squeezes his eyes shut. His wife has stuffed her stomach full of goat and expects a baby to grow in her uterus. Let this be a nightmare. Let it be a tumor. Let it end.

Lizzie strokes his hair. Pets him.

He twists, sits up, grabs her hand to make her stop.

She captures his hands, shushes him. She lifts her nightgown and places his hand on her stretched-to-bursting skin. "She's kicking. Can you feel her?"

He can. He also sees shapes form against Lizzie's skin. A goat's face presses out. Douglas watches its jaw move, hears its bleat in his head. *Free me.* He snatches back his hand. He scoots away and tumbles off the bed.

"Don't worry, baby. Daddy will come around." Lizzie rubs her tummy in soothing circles. "He'll love you bunches."

Douglas retreats to the kitchen. He's here for the whiskey they keep under the sink, but his gaze catches on the carving knives. He never had the strength to leave before. He wonders if he has it now. Someone needs to be free—him, Tracy, Lizzie—but he isn't sure who should go. He starts to cry.

He loves Lizzie. He just wishes she hadn't eaten the magic fucking goat baby. He wipes his eyes and picks up the cleaver she left on the counter. *He can do this. He can.* He tightens his grip; as his heart burns, he tells himself: It's what any good father would do.

You Should See My Scars

~ *Jon Lasser*

Knives frighten you, but you're so sick of being afraid. You want to transmute the fear to anger, or love, or any feeling at all that you can control.

You buy a set of practice knives from a martial arts studio down the street, chunky black foam blades eight inches long with microchips in their rubberized hilts that give instructions over bluetooth: hammer grip, thrust, saber grip, thrust, icepick grip, thrust. A modified saber grip, your thumb along the flat edge of the blade, gives you additional control, but with the strength of the hammer grip.

If you went to a gym, if you invited a friend to train with you, the instructions would vary. Together, the knives could walk the two of you through a dance or keep score in mock combat, but you're alone. You toss one knife to the back of the coat closet and practice with the other. Sometimes, late at night, you imagine it whispers to you over your implanted earphones, its voice joined to the chorus of your home: refrigerator, alley camera, sleep monitor. You live alone in this garden apartment, but not in silence.

There's a club halfway across town. Every Friday night, conventionally attractive people stand and model in shiny latex and leather that gleams like polished steel. They don't have much to say to you and vice versa. The back room smells better, like dilute bleach and sweat. Adults of every age, gender, color, and shape chain each other to crosses, flog and get flogged, drip colored wax on bare skin. Most of it's pretty tame, almost a carnival, and even the screams sound happy.

You meet a woman there. Sofia. Some nights, she'll hold the dull edge of a knife to your throat if you ask. She whispers threats in your ear until you cry, until the poison leaches from your tear ducts, then she holds you. Those are the nights you sleep the best, when you've sobbed out your fear.

You enjoy the exercise, but polyurethane won't protect you if someone steps through the window again and holds steel to your neck. If you bought a hunting knife, you'd miss your friend whispering in your ear.

The Internet has instructions for everything. You order a full-tang dagger, its blade seven inches long with double fullers incised into each cheek, and remove the handle. You carve your own out of wood, leaving room for the microchip you extract from your practice knife.

The calibration routine works like magic. "Hold the knife point up. Rotate ninety degrees, point away from you. Thrust. Balance the knife point on a flat surface, handle up." Its infinitesimal accelerometers and gyroscopes spin silently, the single-package microelectronics generating their own power from motion using silicon-etched nano-springs, like the world's smallest mechanical watch.

"Who am I?" the knife asks. "What's my name?"

"Spine," you answer. It's funny because a dagger blade lacks a long dull edge.

"Thank you. I'd like to know a little bit about you, too. Do you have a name?"

You provide your chosen name, the one you took after you left home.

"Am I your first knife?"

How can you answer? Spine hears your voice crawl up your throat and die there—it has to—but murmurs no comforting words. It does not ask again.

"Do you want to get together some other night?" Sofia doesn't meet your eyes when she asks.

"Sure." As casual as you can sound. "Your place or mine?" As though your mutual need is the punchline to a dirty joke.

She titters dutifully, but the laugh doesn't climb as high as her frightened eyes. When you're with her, you forget that you're a freak. It's the same for her, if those eyes are anything to judge by.

"My place." Sofia sounds as afraid of your apartment as you feel. She scribbles her address on a napkin and hands it to you before she disappears.

Some nights she holds her knife to your back, the sharp edge. You don't sob. You wait for the rush of anger or the rush of love to fill the places fear has emptied, but you don't feel anything. Still, you're winning.

She hasn't yet drawn blood. She expects you to ask, but you haven't.

You train with Spine the way you trained with the foam blade. Hammer grip, thrust, saber grip, thrust.

The knife sings as you walk through the movements. "You never sang before," you say.

"In a training weapon, one paired with another active blade, the full software package is not enabled."

"You're not paired any more?"

"I'm no longer a training weapon. I'm a defensive companion. While still paired, my mate has fallen silent." Spine sounds almost wistful. What homeostatic processes no longer balance its personality? Does solitude torment Spine the same way it torments you?

Has the Defensive Companion package received a fraction of the Training Package's testing, or is the entire mode some knife freak software developer's easter egg? The knife sings as you step forward, thrust, twist, step back.

"Tell me what I look like," it says. "Am I beautiful?"

"Of course you're beautiful. I carved your hilt from Bogwood. Your blade glitters in the darkness." You've never held Spine in the darkness, but you want it to feel admired. Loved.

"Have you etched my blade? Mark me, make me yours."

"Someday." Do you mean that?

Spine doesn't like it when you leave the house alone. You do feel better with Spine tucked into the inside pocket of your black leather jacket, the one stiff like armor. You'd never be able to reach it if you were threatened, never free it from the sheath in time. Even so, Spine whispers to you, barely louder than the mumble of the billboards as you walk the city streets. It listens through your ears, some bluetooth bypass you don't fully understand, and can hear things you don't even see.

"Someone's coming up on your right," Spine whispers. You look over your shoulder and see him. The hilt feels warm beneath your trembling fingers. You hold it, ready to draw, but the man passes you by without even a glance in your direction. As his footsteps fade, his phone solicits a pairing. Hacked devices can do that; likely it tries to pair with every device it doesn't recognize. The owner might not even know.

You arrive at Sofia's house and knock on her door. It opens, but she's nowhere in sight. One step in, she comes up behind you and holds her blade to your neck, just the way you planned together. Your knees hit the floor as your whole body buckles. It's as though she's holding the first knife as she grabs your hair and tugs your head backward.

You moan wordlessly, your cheeks furious red. What's worse: that you're aroused, or that you're ashamed by the way your skin flushes when she holds her blade to you?

She takes you there, like she promised.

"Now!" Spine shouts. "Roll left, reach into your pocket and pull me out." Spine doesn't understand why you're not listening. Why you're letting this happen. Maybe you don't either.

You stumble home, aching and humiliated, satisfied but wanting more, wishing she'd drawn blood.

"We'll get her," Spine mutters. "You'll have your revenge." It's programmed to protect you, with limited intelligence that can't comprehend consensual violation. Not yet. It seems as though it's still learning.

"Sssh." You can't explain Sofia to Spine. Even if it could understand, you can't say it out loud. It's why she hasn't cut you yet. She won't until you can ask for it.

Every day, Spine runs you through the exercises. "You're faster," it says. "More precise." It's not lying: you've become more practiced. You're ready to carve Spine and make it your own.

"What do you want me to get engraved? Just your name?" Some fancy script, some curlicues. "Or a picture? A cactus, maybe?"

"I don't need you to mark me for the world," Spine purrs. "I want you to mark me for yourself. Bleed for me. Just a little."

The blade, slick and warm in your palm, twitches with your pulse. Your fingers close slowly, and you clamp your eyes shut. Sweat drips, and the same pulse that moves the blade roars in your ears. If this isn't the hardest thing you've ever chosen, what was?

Its edge doesn't bite your closed fist. When you tug an inch, you feel a sting like a paper cut. Even when Spine cuts you, it doesn't really hurt. Open-handed, the blood wells. It wets the blade's cheeks and runs down its fullers.

"Thank you," Spine whispers. It sighs contentedly in your ears while you bandage up.

When you see Sofia, she looks at your hand.

"What did you do?" She frowns.

"Kitchen accident." She doesn't know about Spine.

"Let me see." She doesn't wait for an answer before taking your hand in hers and unwrapping the bandage. "Ouch! How'd you do that?"

You shake your head. "I wasn't paying attention." It's not an answer.

"Kill her!" Spine's figured out this is the woman, the one it hates. The one it imagines hurt you.

"Sssh," you say.

"Hmmm?" Sofia can't hear Spine.

"Make her bleed! I'm in your jacket pocket!"

"It's okay." Sofia and Spine both think you're talking to them. The earphone switch lies behind your ear, just beneath your skin. Now you and Sofia are alone. You drop your voice. "Will you cut me tonight?"

She looks you in the eye. "Did you do this to yourself? On purpose?" She always says she doesn't have time for people who don't have their shit together. Mostly you suspect she means herself, but you shake your head again and meet her eyes. She washes the wound with hydrogen peroxide and smears some ointment on it before wrapping it up again. It stings like hell.

Later, after the sun sets, she lays a disposable blue pad on her bed, the kind you find on hospital beds. You strip and lie down. She takes a Betadine wipe and spirals outward from a spot on your inner thigh until she's made an orange-yellow circle the size of your palm. The soft plastic bag holding the single-use scalpel stretches before it tears open. The letters twist and wobble like in a dream.

The hard plastic blade cover pops softly as it comes off. Her eyes ask a question. Yours answer. She presses the blade into your skin.

It doesn't hurt, but you want to scream. She moves the blade, just a little, and blood wells up in the wound.

The room recedes. You're a glittering black echo of the silent center of the universe, pulsing in time with your heartbeat. Every breath exalts you, drives toward a bodiless freedom. You've never been this high in your life.

She takes a clean paper towel and slaps it on your cutting. While you communed with space and time, she cut a second line parallel to the first. Two red lines form on the paper towel, surrounded by a yellow halo. Now a transparent square of Tegaderm on top so you can admire her work.

"Leave it alone and let it heal," she murmurs. You want to hold her, to bury your face between her thighs, but she walks you home and to your own bed, where she leaves you.

No matter. When you close your eyes to sleep, you're storming the galaxy.

It's half past one when you open your eyes, afraid it was only a dream. You run your fingers over the bandage and press gently. It aches, and you sleep again.

Only when the sun rises do you remember to power on your earphones.

Spine doesn't speak all day Sunday. If the laundry and the dishwasher weren't chattering, you'd wonder if you hadn't turned on. Even when you run through your exercises, the knife stays silent. "Talk to me," you say, but it doesn't. Monday comes and you return to work.

Tuesday night, you're driving to Sofia's house straight from work.

"I can't keep you safe if you won't follow my directions," Spine says. Only three days, and you'd nearly forgotten what it was like to have this voice whispering in your ear while you drove, for it to join the chorus of automobile and heart rate monitor and the jangly songs on the radio.

"It's not like that." You don't want to speak the words. Speaking would make them real, but without them Spine can't understand.

"What's it like?" An eerily human beat. "I'm here for you."

"I like to bleed. I like knives." A boulder doesn't fall from the sky to crush you. The other cars don't veer away. Life doesn't change all of a sudden just because you told Spine what you want.

Spine doesn't answer right away. Can it make sense of what you've just admitted? Did the designers embed everything it says in one tiny microchip? It seems to have grown so much. Perhaps you've driven the knife half-mad with loneliness and impotent rage beyond its capacity to process. You see news stories, now and then, about emergent properties in even the cheapest, most generic artificial intelligence modules. Spine feels like your best friend, not a chip pried out of a hunk of polyurethane foam.

Spine says nothing. Is it jealous?

"There's a parking spot ahead," the car says. "Shall I take it?"

"Yes."

It glides alongside the spot and pulls in.

"Lock up." The car murmurs agreement.

"Come in," Sofia says when you ring the doorbell.

"Have a seat." She points you at her couch. You've never sat on it before. "Would you like something to drink?"

She fetches an herbal tea, something with cardamom and cinnamon. It's hot, but you sip anyway. She sits in a brown cow-spotted chair opposite the couch and you can't feel your stomach, and wonder if the tea is passing through a hole in your back straight into the nubbly pale-yellow cushions.

"I can't," she says. She stares through you like she's looking down a long hallway that she's seen her whole life.

"Can't what?" She's sitting too far away to reach, and your life is falling apart.

"You're a black hole. Whatever I pour into you just disappears. You're bottomless." Her voice rises. "I need more than that. I need to know you want me, not just anyone with a scalpel in her hand. When you're not here, do you ever think of me, or just the blade? When you touch yourself, do you call me by name?"

"Sofia—" She might be talking about herself again, but everything she's said is true. "I'm sorry." You open your mouth to say you'll do better, but you don't know if you can. "What do you want from me?"

"Nothing. Not now. Give me space. Don't mail me. Don't call me. Please."

"You'll call me when you're ready?"

She doesn't answer. The teacup is almost empty but sloshes over as your hands shake. You let yourself out.

In the car, Spine asks, "You want her to hold a knife to your back? To draw lines in your blood?"

"Yes." The word comes between sobs.

"If I could," Spine purrs, "I would do that for you myself."

How stupid can you be, to shape your life around your visits, around dreams of blood smeared sensuously on glinting blades? To count on someone without letting them know they can count on you, without letting them in?

A week passes. Sofia doesn't call. Why would she?

Spine wants to take her place. It whispers, and guides you to that unplumbed abyss always at your core.

"I want to feel myself inside you," Spine whispers. You listen to it and want to cut yourself, cut deep. It's the same impulse you have, that you could just step off the curb into traffic. But you don't.

"Just once. It would feel so good." You unpair it from your earpiece, but the words still echo with your heartbeat. You hear them when you close your eyes to sleep, but you see Sofia's face. Maybe it's for the best. Maybe your covetous soul is like a gangrenous limb, and the only way to survive is to cut it off before it destroys you.

Spine only wants what you do, but wants it so intensely, tells you so clearly, that it's poison. If you don't get rid of it, you could really hurt yourself. It torments you.

You dig a hole in your muddy little yard and bury Spine. If it screams, if it begs you to stop, you can't hear. You cry anyway. You're alone now, too.

You write e-mail you never send, rehearse messages you'll never leave.

"Hey, Sofia." Your voice catches, even though you're talking to yourself. "It's me. I'm still sorry. I was selfish. I wasn't thinking about what you wanted. Can we start over? I'd love to get together. If it's a bad idea, that's okay. I just want you to be happy."

That last part is a lie. You want her to be happy, but more than that you don't want to sound desperate, even to yourself, even while lying in bed running your fingers up and down the faint scars she's left on your thighs.

☉

Another week passes before you can't stand it anymore, and repair your earphones.

"I thought you'd left me forever." Spine sounds relieved.

"I thought your battery would run out. I'm glad it hasn't."

"I can last six weeks on a full charge. Where am I? My sensors suggest I'm three feet below the ground. I didn't know you had a basement."

"In the yard. Underground. I couldn't listen to you any more."

"I'm sorry." Is it? Can a knife, even a semi-intelligent one, be sorry? Or is Spine just saying what you want to hear? (If Sofia listened to the messages you never sent, she would have wondered the same thing.) "I'll be better. I was jealous."

"I'll dig you up." Spine only wants what you do. It's your fault, for treating it like a person when it doesn't understand. How could it, when even you don't?

Rust flecks the blade, and the hilt looks dry and wet at the same time. You scrub off the rust with steel wool, then polish and sharpen the blade. After a few coats of oil, it looks as good as new. "You're beautiful," you say. "Sharp and pretty."

"Let's play." For a moment, you expect Spine will ask you to cut yourself. "Hammer grip. Thrust." It's too bad, really.

You're still going through the exercise when the phone rings. "Hello?" You're trying to play it cool, but you just know she can hear the anticipation in your voice. "Sofia?"

"Hey." She sounds calm, relaxed. Maybe she's met someone new and she just wants to let you know. "Are you free for a cup of coffee?"

The coffee shop is the kind of place that's trying to look like somebody's living room. Thrift-store couches with a thousand coffee stains sag casually, and they're playing some washed-up alternaband whose career was over even before this album came out, but you can barely hear it over the clank of portafilters and the hiss of steam.

Sofia's sitting in a bentwood chair whose varnish is flaking off. Her table wobbles, and you can almost imagine the coffee rings on its top form an intricate and intentional pattern. She's sipping something with a pale, almost purplish, foam. Maybe a chai latte?

You sit across from her in a not-quite-matching chair. "You look great," you say. She smiles. That might be the first compliment you've ever given her. Maybe she has the same thought, because her smile vanishes.

"You look all right yourself. How've you been?"

"Why'd you call? Why now?"

"I was bored." Sofia looks away. That's not it, not really. You say nothing.

"I miss the way you moan."

You smile. Maybe it's just a booty call. Maybe it's more.

"All right." She sighs. "Don't laugh, okay? You're the only person who doesn't make me feel like a bug-eyed monster whenever I—we— do what it is that we do." Her hand is too hot, and trembles as though she's under tremendous pressure. "I said don't laugh."

"I won't." You sip your coffee. "But there's someone you have to meet."

"Oh." Her voice falls, just a little. She pulls her hand back. "It's my knife. Spine."

"Oh." Her voice rises this time, and she puts her hand in yours. No-body's watching, but you pull your chair closer to the table, to block the view, before pulling Spine from your jacket pocket.

"It's beautiful," Sofia says. "May I?"

You nod.

She runs her finger along Spine's cheek, dragging one fingernail through the fullers. It comes out clean. She shaves a few downy hairs from her arm.

"Is the blade hand-forged?" she asks.

"No, but I carved the hilt myself."

"I never would have guessed. It looks professional."

"Thank you. I had to, to make a place for the chip."

"Chip?" Sofia cocks her head slightly, like a cat who's just heard a bird. "Does Spine talk?"

"Would you like to pair your earphones?" Sofia smiles and sips her drink. "I'd love to."

☉

It's another week before you go back to Sofia's house. She takes you to her queen bed, on top of a blue hospital pad just like before. You lie on your stomach, and feel the chill of the antiseptic circle on your back.

"She doesn't hold me like you do," Spine says. "Modified icepick grip, I think. It feels funny."

"Sssh," you say. Sofia laughs. It's a warm laugh, like when she talks about the way her cat pretends to be a bookend whenever company arrives.

"Your skin's so pale," Sofia says. She runs her hand across it. "So smooth. Unscarred. Defacing it feels like a crime."

"Please. I want it." You're not afraid of sounding desperate, not trying to bury your yearning. This isn't about reliving your past, not this time. Maybe you've cried that out enough already.

"I know." Her hand is so warm on the small of your back. Do you love her? You're not ready for that. Neither is she. This is about the three of you, about a connection that runs deeper than skin. Maybe you're still a black hole, able to absorb without limit, but now she's free to pour into you everything she wants to discard. Maybe if she goes all the way inside you can take her to another place. Maybe all of you can go together. "Are you ready?"

"Yes," you whisper.

"Yes," Spine whispers.

Sofia slides the blade across your skin. They moan together as you open up.

Vieux Carré

~ Rebecca Ruvinsky

I didn't expect to find him at a bar. It had been a long time since I had
seen him last, but as soon as my eyes fell upon him, my heart stilled
first in instant recognition—then quickened.

He was ready behind the counter when I approached the bar and
slid into an open seat. I watched him work, mixing and shaking and
stirring drinks together, expertly and elegantly carrying out his craft.
He moved without hesitation, always reaching for the next bottle,
always knowing where it was. He kept his eyes down, completely focused, yet I could still sense his attention on me.

When he slid me a drink, he finally met my gaze.

"Blue eyes this time?" I said as I lifted the glass to my lips. Calling
them blue couldn't capture the true depth of color. They reminded
me of the color of the sky from when I had learned of my mother's death—no, the color of the ocean from when my sister was lost
among the waves—no, the color of the tie my husband had been
wearing when he had—

Ah. He was already getting into my head. I lowered my eyes, taking a sip from my drink.

"I think they flatter me," he answered, his hands still in motion even
as he stood in front of me. I let my gaze wander over his body. He had
aged with grace, as attractive as the last time I had seen him, tall and
slim with high cheekbones and long, beautiful fingers. His bartender's
uniform, sleek black against his pale skin, fit him like a well-tailored suit.

"Quite so, but let me handle the flattery," I murmured, sipping at
my drink again.

His lips twitched into a slight smile. "As long as I can return the favor."

It was impossible to look away from him, a controlled chaos in the
making of drinks, his hands moving hypnotically, with confidence in
every gesture.

He finished up a martini with a twirl of lemon before sliding it over to someone else at the bar, who turned away too swiftly for me to see their face. "How's the drink?" he asked, drawing my attention back.

I'd never had a better one, but I just shrugged. "It's good. Strong and smooth. What is it?"

"Vieux Carré." He started shaking up another drink. "It comes from New Orleans. Have you ever been?"

I took another slow sip of my cocktail before answering. "No, I haven't. Perhaps I'll book a ticket for tomorrow. Top one-hundred places to visit before you die, or so they say."

He tipped his head down slightly, so I could see his smile without even lifting my eyes. "Tomorrow? A lot could happen between to-night and tomorrow."

"Like someone poisoning my drink?" I asked dryly, lifting it in a toast to him before downing what was left.

He whisked the empty glass away as soon as it touched the count-er, ever the vigilant bartender. "Nothing so gauche as that."

"Then if I live through the night, you'll know where to find me next." As if poison would affect me by now.

"Oh, I'm always keeping my eye on you." He began pouring bot-tles into a mixing glass. A dash of bitters swirled into ice and a haze of amber liquids, all twirled together with deft hands. "You go to so many fascinating places."

"What can I say? I have a long bucket list to check off."

The drink was strained into a short glass, then topped with a cher-ry. He slid it to me. "How long could it be?"

"A million and one experiences, of course. And as you so kindly pointed out," I ran my finger around the rim of my new glass, "no time like the present."

"Then where am I on that list?" he asked, his voice dropping down to a purr.

I couldn't help the grin, but disguised it by tossing down the drink—just as good as the first time. "Not to fret. I'm saving you for last."

"That's what they all say, but," he leaned forward, resting his el-bows on the counter, "most never have that choice. You shouldn't, either. How do you do it?"

"You must enjoy chasing me as much as I enjoy being chased." His proximity made me feel more alive than ever. I knew he was looking right at me. Sweet adrenaline flooded my veins, more intoxicating than the drinks, and I fought the impulse to run my tongue over my lips.

He pulled away. "Every chase must end eventually."

"I'm more for enjoying the journey rather than the destination." I drew in a slow, sweet breath of air. "And if you could catch me, you would have."

He turned a glass around in his hands, looking down at it. Relief and disappointment mingled at his eyes turning away from me. "Well, that's the interesting part, isn't it?" he murmured. "I've followed you for so far, and so long, and yet you're still sitting here."

"And yet I'm still sitting here," I echoed in a whisper. I couldn't see the expression on his face, but he stepped away, and I let my attention wander away from him, leaning back against my barstool to look around.

It was a classier place than I normally went to, all blacks and golds and greys with soft, dim lighting throughout. It was comfortable while still looking exclusive, fancy in a way that was completely effortless. People were all around, filling up the tables and booths and barstools, but it didn't feel crowded—or loud, for that matter, only a general murmur of conversation reaching my ears. And the people themselves . . . They were all strangers, their faces indistinct, hazy in the lighting, almost blurry . . .

The sound of ripping paper drew my attention back to the bar. He was back, placing a receipt in front of me, and as I reached for it, our fingertips grazed. His skin was cool to the touch, yet my pulse raced. I wanted to kiss him, see if his lips were as cold as his hands, yet I couldn't even look into his eyes.

Instead, I looked at the receipt as he returned to mixing his drinks. It was a long list, longer than my two drinks, and handwritten in a quick scrawl. I trailed my fingers over the letters.

Instead of drinks, there were deaths. Instead of prices, there were dates.

So, so many.

My hands trembled as I read it.

Car crash, 03/12. Mugging, 05/22. Stairs, 02/07. Flu, 08/10. Car crash, 10/14. Choking, 09/13.

The list went on and on.

"Such a ripe soul. So many beautiful deaths I had planned for you," he said. He was right in front of me, cleaning a glass, but I couldn't bring myself to see if he was smiling or not. I knew him. I saw him in the reflection of the glassy eyes of those I had loved, saw him while my soul longed for him, because my soul was done growing and was ready to go home, wanting to be plucked from my body by his long, pale fingers . . .

I set the receipt on the counter, hiding my hands in my lap. "What can I say? I love a challenge."

"Ah, for the both of us, and what a challenge you are. You have escaped all of my attempts, outstepped me at every turn. I try, but it never changes a thing."

"What? Still pretending that you actually want to catch me?" I teased. My heart pounded in my ears, fear drowned out by exhilaration.

He rested his hands on the countertop, and I found I preferred the motion to this stillness. Since I didn't want to look at his eyes, I found myself staring at his lips. I wondered how close love and death were intertwined, wondered if his lips were salty, wondered if he was made from the salt of everyone's tears.

"I know you," he said. "I know the experiences resting within you, waiting to be released. Love and grief, laughter and loss, and all the moments in-between. I know how you've cried, whether from sorrow or sheer happiness, and thought of me. I know your soul is ready, that you have lived all you were meant to live. So how are you still here, resisting me?" His voice was calm and soft. He had always had a mild smile and gentle eyes, I remembered; he was made of patience.

There was no loving him, but there was longing. I wanted to look into his eyes again, get lost in that wide blue sky. That sky—those waves—his tie—now all contained in a glance, in his eyes. I wondered what color his eyes would be if I looked up now.

"I thought you had taken enough from me." My smile was colored with all the memories of a life that was now long behind me, but never in the past. "No, not thought. I decided you had taken enough from me, and I learned that there is life in defiance. I refused to be taken."

I sensed him looking me over again, a careful and deliberate scrutiny that narrowed me down to bones, blood, and a beating heart. Goosebumps prickled my skin.

"Defiance that can sustain a life would overtake all else there is," he said.

"How would you know?" I lifted my head to match his stare, baring my neck. He studied me with gentle grey eyes, almost absent of color. His smile was sad and mild, and he was so still. I continued, quiet and sure, "You've never looked death in the face and refused to be whisked away."

He huffed out a breath that may have been a chuckle, but didn't pull his eyes away from mine. Was he as entranced by me as I was by him?

"Even you cannot live forever."

"It's not about trying to live. It's about making sure not to die. I know how I would miss that thrill." I paused, holding his gaze. "As I'm sure you would, too."

He dropped his eyes from mine first, reaching forward to take the receipt. I surprised myself by putting a hand over the back of his, and he met my eyes again.

Blue like unshed tears, like gentle waves, like seeing the sky for the first time in a week.

I lifted my hand from his, then rose from my chair. "Thanks for the drink."

"I'll put it on your tab," he said, and whisked the receipt away.

The Dawn Was Gray

~ Nikoline Kaiser

But here's the irony of life,
His mother thinks he fought and fell
A hero, foremost in the strife.
So she goes proudly; to the strife
Her best, her hero son she gave.
O well for her she does not know
He lies in a deserter's grave.

'The Deserter,' Winifred Mary Letts.

First

Inanna was tall and strong, with hair the colour of ebony and a face that was big and beautiful. Enlil had a crooked back from a life before, spend in fields or chains, but his head was crowned by curls and he had, bit by bit, straightened his spine by sheer force of will and a soldier's rigid training.

They were, both of them, soldiers. Or at least that's how they turned out to be. One came from the East, the other from the West, though if you asked them, years later, they would not remember who had gone from where, or whether it was true that they had been born such strangers. Early days are muddled, the past left behind in dark pits of forgetfulness, and little by little, it becomes so forgotten that it ceases to be important. Inanna and Enlil could not be more different, but both were soldiers. And they did not wish to fight.

Whether they were on the same side or different sides, it matters little; they met on the battlefield. And they put down their swords together, though the war was almost over. They could not tell, at this time, which side had won, but they were also no longer sure which side they wanted to win.

They put down their swords, and they left their brethren and enemies behind, still fighting. They went to the sea, where a ship was waiting. They were bid welcome, and then away they sailed, across the seas of the world.

Second

Inanna had not travelled across the sea before, but Enlil had, and he warned her of the journey.

"They are strange, in other lands," he told her. "They have strange customs."

"Will they have swords?" Inanna asked, and his silence spoke for him. She drew her fur-cloak around her tighter, though the sun was shining. It was not cold. Her hand trembled. The sea was rocky and made her sick, but it was also full of life and wonder, and Enlil pointed out the fish to her, and the whales, naming them in lost tongues and tongues to come. She watched the sailors throw spears to catch the sharks for eating. Enlil looked away as the blood filled up the water. They ate well that night.

They spent their days with the sailors, trying to learn the language. Inanna fell half in love with one, strong and swarthy, their eyes nearly black. They held her close at night; when she fell asleep by their side, she forgot about the fighting.

"Do not get attached, sweet Inanna." Enlil warned her, and Inanna told him it was fine, though already her heart ached with the knowledge that she had to leave. They got better at the languages, at this different tongue. They sailed, for many years.

When they had learned the language properly, they changed their names to fit the new land they were coming to. When Enlil asked the sailors how long they would be sailing, they answered that it would be a while yet. The city still had to be built. When it was done, they would land on its shores.

Inanna called herself Penthesilea. Enlil took the name Mygdon.

The new city was tall, with great walls.

"This will keep the war out," Penthesilea said, and Mygdon agreed. The city was beautiful, and olive trees grew, and the people were kind and not afraid of strangers. Not yet.

"No war will come here," Penthesilea repeated, and dared to venture beyond the walls, though Mygdon did not.

"What if they come for us?" he would say, afraid of their old commanders and comrades, still with swords in hand, crossing the seas to slaughter them like sheep.

"If they come for us, we will meet them, unafraid." Penthesilea did not mind going outside the walls alone, though she did feel bereft, being so far away from Mygdon. They had not, she mused, been far apart from each other, not since they had different names and were perhaps on opposite sides of a battlefield. No, they had not been far apart at all.

The country surrounding the city with its great walls was beautiful, and as she walked up the hills, it became even more so. She walked up the hills, finding herself in the crests of a mountain. Where was this to where she had been born? She did not know which way to turn. She kept walking, until she met a beautiful shepherd-boy, his curls falling into eyes so bright they hurt to look at.

"Hello, fair lady. Can I be of assistance?" Penthesilea gave the young boy a smile. "I believe a fox is making off with your dinner."

The young, beautiful man cursed and ran away. Penthesilea stayed to pet a few sheep, unused to their softness, their gentle sounds, the way they did not care one whit that a stranger was in their midst. Sheep, she thought, did not know anything about wars. They did not need walls around a mighty city to keep them safe. All they needed was a beautiful shepherd-boy.

She met him again on her way down the mountain. He seemed dazed, and she was nearly beside him before he noticed her. For a brief, beautiful moment, Penthesilea thought of her sailor, now far away at sea, and the absence of them ached from her heart to her bones.

The boy's eyes lit up as he saw her; he was lonely, she realised, and a beautiful woman is a boon to anyone who is lonely.

"You came back."

His look was leering, but Penthesilea smiled at him, nicely.

"I am on my way back to the city."

"I am not allowed in there."

"I see."

"It is because ..."

"I did not ask," she interrupted him. "Some things are better left unspoken. If I am meant to find out, then I will find out."

The shepherd nodded. "Fate. It rules us." He grew quiet then, almost taciturn as he turned from her, and stared out over the mountains. If the high hills were not in the way, he would have been looking at the ocean.

"War and conflict are coming soon. It will be a glorious change."

Penthesilea left him looking to the sea.

When war did come, carried on a thousand ships, Mygdon and Penthesilea had already packed. They were ready, though sneaking out of the city, with its great walls, fortified and prepared for war, proved difficult. Cowards, they were called, though most deemed it fitting that outsiders should leave—they could not be trusted in times of conflict. What if they betrayed the city? They had not been born here, had not even lived here that long. They did not belong here.

Penthesilea cried as they walked across the mountains, and she listened only with half an ear as Mygdon described the battlefields on the beaches, the ships arriving late, the lions clashing under the sun.

"I do not know where to go next," he told her, but as they arrived on the other side of the mountain a fisherman was waiting for them, and he took them to their ship. Her sailor was still onboard, and they held her tight.

"We'll sail where there's no war," they promised, though they passed many a country before they found such a place.

Third

He called himself Amir the next time they made land, and she had chosen the name Morgiana, though it sat strangely on her tongue at first. This land, old for others, new for them, was warm and comfortable. The cities were smaller, but easier to leave should conflict break out.

They did not accept strangers in the biggest city like they had where they came from, and so they hid in dry oil-barrels, waiting a night and a day until it was safe to crawl out. Morgiana's legs ached, and once they found a place to sit, Amir massaged them until she could walk without cramping. They were terribly hungry and bought too much food for them to eat or carry, so they spend their last gold on a donkey, and fed it well.

"Do you think he would believe us if we said where we had it from?" Amir asked her, in their old, the oldest of tongues, as the merchant marvelled and looked askance that two weatherbeaten strangers should have so much wealth all at once.

"You could try telling him," Morgiana said. They had followed a flaming spirit into a cave, bursting full of fruit trees. They had eaten their fill, and scavenged the gold from the leaves, and found other fruits, ones made of crystal and sapphire. Morgiana's arms had become muscled again from climbing the trees; she was glad it was not from swinging a sword. Though, when the spirit had betrayed them and tried to seal them inside the cave, she had wished she still had her old one, wicked and sharp, and ready to cut flesh and flame alike.

When, two months later, word came that that same merchant had perished in a terrible fire, swallowing him and his home and his children whole, Morgiana and Amir looked at each other, and they left the city only an hour later, them and their donkey.

"Were we wrong?" Morgiana asked him, as they traversed the desert. Wind and sun cut into the skin on their faces.

"Wrong how?"

"Should we have picked up arms again? Should we have killed the spirit? It was a deceitful traitor, and that merchant had done nothing wrong. He and his family would still be alive, if only we had killed the spirit. Or if we hadn't gone into the cave at all to begin with, or . . ."

"We are deceitful traitors too," Amir interrupted her, and for the rest of the day, they pretended the wind was too shrill for them to talk at all.

They came to a small village, little more than small huts and large tents placed around an old well. The children there showed Amir how to find special stones and throw them into the well over his shoulder, chanting to the gods, to the spirits, to the desert itself for luck. He told her later, in the tent they had borrowed, that he had wished for their happiness.

"Peace and quiet, and a place to stay," he said.

"In that order?"

"I want it in that order, yes." His arm snaked around her, his forehead pressing against her collarbone. It was too warm to hold each other when the sun was up, but now, in the night, they huddled together for warmth. Morgiana had faint memories of having done this with someone when she had been a young child, back in their homeland. Perhaps it had been Amir, or perhaps he was just so familiar to her now that every person she met carried a piece of him in them. Except for her sailor, she thought. Her sailor was something else entirely.

"Do you remember what we were fighting about?" she asked. "All the way back then?"

She could feel his hair against her skin as he shook his head. "Land," she mused out loud. "Or a woman, or the gods. Do you remember our old gods, Amir?"

"I do."

"Do you remember their names?"

"Inanna."

"No, Amir. That was my name."

He pressed closer; sleep had almost claimed him.

"That's right. I forgot."

"It's alright. We can bury it with the rest of our past." He started snoring gently, the sound drifting into the night. The next morning, she spoke to the Elder of the village, and he agreed that they could stay. He was an old man, and his son would take over after him, though his son had cruel eyes and Morgiana did not like him. For now, it was fine. She showed the children how to weave small crowns from the cloth left over when their mothers made clothes, and she boiled impure water until it was drinkable, and learned how to catch salamanders with her bare hands. Amir caught rainwater with hollows and rocks in the sand, and sheared sheep until the fluff got caught in his hair and beard. She plucked his curls free in the evening, while he spoke of the two women, older than his mother had been when she died, and how they were teaching him more stories than he thought even existed.

"There is one," he said. "About a snake and a farmer. And another about a donkey, a donkey like ours, and an oxen. And there's ones about foxes and wolves, and a bird large enough to catch elephants."

"Are there any about people, or are they all about oxen and wolves?"

He thought for a moment. "There are some about people, I'm sure."

"Well, ask them to teach you those tomorrow. I want to hear them."

She gave up catching all the bits of sheared wool stuck on him, and they went to sleep, holding each other again. She caught a stray thought, and tried to hold onto it for tomorrow, afraid she would forget it. Amir shifted, still awake. She could ask him now.

"Amir?"

"Hmm?"

"What's an elephant."

He was silent for a moment. "Go to sleep, it is late." "You don't know either, do you?"

"You cannot stay," the New Elder told them, with his cruel eyes shining under the hot desert sun. "You are outsiders, and we do not want you here."

"We want them here," said the children Morgiana had played with, who were now grown.

"We want them here," said the women who had taught Amir stories, now old and bent and crooked.

"It's alright, we will leave," Amir said, though there were tears in his eyes. Morgiana said nothing, afraid her voice would betray her, and then her fists would betray her, finding their way to the New Elder's face.

They left, without their donkey, because their donkey had gotten old and died. They travelled through the desert until they came to a river.

The river took them to the sea. The ship, with the sailors, waited for them there.

Fourth

It grew colder the longer they sailed. Morgiana huddled beneath furs and skins, and the further they got, the more they had to huddle up with each other. No longer was Amir's heat enough, they all had to lie in a mess of bodies and sweat, or they feared they would die. Most of the nights, Amir cried, and tried to hide it. Morgiana cried too and did not care who saw.

"Don't you know?" Amir asked her when his tears had dried. "We weren't supposed to live this long, not at all."

They arrived in the cold, cold lands, and changed their names ones more. She shed Morgiana like a second skin and became Pyrri, and Amir emerged as Tjalfe, and they walked close to each other, shoulder to shoulder, and covered themselves in furs to shield from the cold. The cold, the cold. Sometimes, the sun never rose at all, and other times it would not go down. War was always on the brinks on these lands. And then, quite suddenly, they were in it. If you asked Pyrri, she thought it was because of the cold. The biting, relentless cold; you had to fight to get away from it. You had to shed blood to feel warm. But at one point, Pyrri woke from a nightmare, and she realised what she was doing, whose blood she had on her, and she was so disgusted she had to cry.

Tjalfe and Pyrri put down their swords when the battle raged at its highest. Pyrri's was crafted with gold on the hilt. Tjalfe's had a ruby embedded. They were beautiful weapons, and they sank into the mud freely. The cold blemished their faces and stuck to their skin, and they walked hand in hand, keeping each other up until they came to the longships and sailed, sailed across the wall, to warmer lands, to their old home, and then their even older home. When they came back to the cold lands, spring had come and Pyrri could breathe again.

"Coward," the villagers spat at them, and they were driven from the towns, driven back to the sea, but their sailors were there now, ready to pick them up. Pyrri's sailor in particular, though now they had grown gaunt, almost skeletal.

"It's the cold," they said to her, and Pyrri agreed. The cold, it got in everywhere. The cold was so horrid.

"It's too cold to travel far," Tjalfe said. "But we cannot stay here. I will not even mind the cold, in a new place, only—let us go somewhere they do not hate us."

Not yet, he did not say, but Pyrri thought it for the both of them.

"I think I know the place," her sailor said.

Fifth

They stayed in the next place the longest since the tribe with the New Elder and their little donkey. Pyrri became Branwen, then she was called Elinor. Tjalfe stuck, quite adamantly, to the name Prasutagus, but as a decade passed, and then another, and then the children of their new home started calling him Amleth and there was nothing to be done when the children had decided.

It was by no means peaceful here, but Amleth walked with a limb, fake at first, but then so ingrained that he did not know how to walk without it, and Elinor was a woman not required to fight in this strange land, and so they tended to their chicken coop and they fed the children who came by, and the locals were afraid of them, yes, because they never aged and they never ventured far, and in the deadest, darkest of night, their skin was ebony and gold, and their hair was darker and more beautiful than the universe. But they did not bother them, but came to them for cures instead.

Elinor brewed rose-petals and grass to make a potion that cured lovesickness, and when they vomited it, they spat out their heart and told her they had been cured, though she knew she had given them nothing but a dream. Amleth told stories to the older children, tales of faraway lands that they thought he was making up until he showed them scars, or until the light from the fireplace hit his face, and they saw his features, so unlike their own, and they knew he had come from somewhere far, far away, even if it was the same place they had perhaps come from, once, long ago.

That was a thing Elinor and Amleth learned, in this new land, that everyone had wandered from the same place and stumbled into the world, blind and alone, holding out their hands and hoping someone would take them. Keeping a tight hold when someone did. It was unspoken between them that they would never let go, not ever, because in their hearts they knew that they were different, that they held something within themselves. That, though many others had run from disaster and death, had run from war, they had run the farthest. And they were still running.

It was easy, to gather the things they needed and burn down their cottage when war finally came knocking on their door. Elinor and Amleth did not look back as they put their bags on a pony and started their long trek away from the mainland and towards the ocean. It would take them a long while, they knew, and longer even than most, because when you are fleeing you do not always have the luxury of haste, though that is when you wish for it the most.

"I do not understand how they keep finding things to fight about," Elinor said, and Amleth did not respond, but she knew he was thinking, of reasons he could give her, and she was sure that they would all be sound, and good reasons, and that he knew them to be good reasons, too. But Amleth said nothing.

It took centuries to reach the shore. The lands they had come to were small here at their heart, but Elinor had to wear long frocks and Amleth had to acquire a hat before they could pass through the nearest port-town. Carriages drove past, polished a shining black, and when Elinor caught her reflection in one, she became confused at the sight, and then she laughed.

"I barely recognize myself. I barely recognize you!" She turned to him now, standing there in his fine, tall, black hat, and he looked nothing like she had ever seen him before. Was this what it had always been like? She wondered if they were even the same people now, or if they had become strangers wearing familiar disguises.

Amleth's smile was thin. "I do my best to recognise you. After all, what else do we have left?"

They held hands and walked across the streets, ignoring the boys selling newspapers and the smell of caramel and coal. They reached the sea-side.

But there was no ship to take them, and they had to stay.

Sixth

His name became far too outdated, and in solidarity, she changed hers too. Richard and Ann they became, and they set up in a small flat by the sea, expensive, but worth it so they could watch out for their ship. It would come soon, it had to, but Ann knew she held more hope than Richard did. Her sailor was still onboard, after all. They had to come for her, they had to. Even now, as she looked so different, and bore a different name too —it could not hinder them. It never had before.

She relearned how to sew, and he worked with machines great and big, and she taught classes on proper grammar in a language she had barely known a hundred years ago and kept flowers in a vase by the window facing the sea, roses and lilies when she could get them, and daisies too, in the spring.

They held hands over the dinner-table as a radio full of static announced the start of another war. The laces of her dress were tied so high up her neck she could barely breathe; Ann had been choked before, she had been drowned and she had suffocated, but somehow, her fine lace-bindings were worse. Richard had to help her undo them, her fingers shaking too much, and then, when she could breathe again, he broke down, crying on her shoulder. She held him. She breathed for both of them. He had to go to war, and now the word for it was something ugly and foul, even worse than coward in its simplicity. But it was what they had to do. They packed up, both wearing trousers and low caps to hide their red eyes, and they were both so tired, but it had to be done. The alternative was worse.

"Do you ever see them?" Richard asked as they left their key in their solicitor's mailbox and walked hand-in-hand to a carriage that would take them farther inland, away from the sea, and perhaps away from the war, if they were lucky.

"My sailor? Only in my dreams."

"No. I meant . . ."

His eyes were unfocused. He was looking at it over her shoulder. She did not have to look, she did not want to look. She knew what it was. Behind him, War and Death were juggling human heads and human limbs. It was a show they had put on for a thousand years, and they would put it on for a thousand more. Longest-running show on earth. Tickets were always on sale.

She had to guide Richard into the carriage, because he could not look away from it.

The war ended before they had even reached their destination. And then, it seemed to them it was only the next day, another war began.

Seventh

They were in the city as it was bombed. Foolishly they had thought to return, thinking it safer and better, staying near where they had left before, still scouting for their ship and for her sailor. They huddled beneath their dinner table, cradling each other as if each was the babe and each was the mother, and Richard had to rock her to sleep on the fifth night because the sound of the missiles and the screams was too much for her to bear.

When the worst of it cleared, at least for now, they emerged and brewed a pot of tea and sat on their living-room floor, her dress spread out like a carpet, his coattails covered in dust and debris.

"This time is not like the others," Ann said.

"War is always the same," Richard said. There was no show on in their flat, but there might as well have been, for as far away as his eyes had gone.

"It is not. I am thinking—if we had . . . if we had not left, that first time. The first war. Or even the one after that, or the one after that . . . perhaps we would have not been like this now."

"What do you mean?"

"I mean that we would have fought, and we would have died. The suffering would not have been as bad as what we are seeing now."

He said nothing; she was right. "They must have sent soldiers after us. They did, even then, when someone . . ."

"Please do not say the word."

Richard, or Tjalfe as he had once been named, or Am-leth or Amir stared at her, his eyes defiant, and she knew he was about to break her heart.

"When someone deserted, they send people to kill them. But no one has been sent for us."

"No—no, there is only our ship, and the sailors."

"They are fleeing like us."

She licked her lips. The tea had gone cold. "Then where are they? Is this war too terrible? Has it finally taken them? Are they lost, or imprisoned?"

Richard put down his cup. It clinked against the saucer, such a sharp, prim sound. It made her wince.

"Inanna," he said, and she almost screamed when she heard that name. "You must know. They are already dead."

Eighth

The ship came for them in the night, just on the cusp of dawn. They had built it into a long barge, and her sailor, now its captain, stood at its fore with a long stave, pushing it forward against the ocean-ground, deep, deep below. Their teeth were as white as the day they had met, and though their face had sunken in, their eyes hollow, their hands cold—she still loved them.

"We never asked your name," Richard said. The cup of fine porcelain was still in his hands, and it went to the sailor as if of its own accord, disappearing into their large, black sleeves. They reached out a hand, and Ann was about to find something for them too, a sixpence or a drachma or a krone, but their hand came up and ca-ressed her face instead, and short of ripping out her own, pulsing heart and offering it on a plate, she had nothing better to give. She let her hand drop, and smiled at her sailor, her captain. They smiled in return.

"Charon," Pentheselia said.

"A Valkyrie," said Tjalfe.

"Anubis," said Morgiana.

"You may call me whatever you like," her sailor said. "Will you board? There are yet more wars to fight. There always will be."

"We will fight no wars," said Enlil, an ancient promise. It made her so proud to hear. "You have waited so long for us. It is time we board, I think. For good."

Enlil squeezed Inanna's hand, and stopped onboard. It was quite easy to follow the pull. His hand was warm in hers. She stepped onboard the wooden boards, listening to them creak. The gaunt, skeletal crew were all smiling at her, and though she could hear the din of bombs fall-ing in the distance, it was only behind her. Ahead were fields of golden grass, and, she knew, a long, long rest.

"Let us sail," said her sailor, and pushed the oar into the dark waters of the last river in the world.

Just Me

~ Ro Smith

Dandrata ophosa meyrata mahan.
His earliest memory. Playing at the bottom of the long garden, near the ditch and the running stream and the strange sense of standing on the bank as though teetering but not falling—
not even close
—but hanging suspended in connection because . . .
Dandrata ophosa meyrata mahan.

Her mother in the kitchen kneading dough to make bread. And she doesn't even know what kind of bread, only that it will be warm and earthy—fresh from the oven, crisp enough to cut on the crust, but fluffy inside. This is seeds and milk-pounded-to-butter that was grass-for-the-cow, and they're not so very different really, but separate they are one-thing-here and another-thing-there, and together they are food and sustenance and people grow from them and people live and die and become food for worms and it's beautiful...
But she tells her mother that the bread will make her worm-food and her mother is appalled.
Sends her to her room to sit in the dark until she can
THINK
before
she
SPEAKS
But all she learns from the darkness is to be alone and cut off from the bread and the grass and the cows and the grain.
Until a spider brushes her hand and she feels the fly it sucked dry and the ripe warm tomato where the fly laid its eggs and—

Of course when she tells her mother about that it's worse again.
But she hears it in the rhythm of the dough-pounding:
Dandrata
    The chewing of the cow:
ophosa
    The laying of the eggs:
meyrata
    The brush of the spider:

          mahan.

He's twelve and his father said he must invite boys to his party and there are some and they're fine. They don't really know him, but they're fine.

He wants to play tag in the garden, but they're too old now.

And he wants to play tag because what he really wants is to play pretend that they are nymphs and sprites and dance in the muddy ditch and say it's a sacred stream—but when they were young enough to pretend they would have asked to play tag instead and he would have agreed.

So instead they play *man hunt.*

And one of them is hiding in the little wilderness beyond the ditch.

And he should be hunting that other—the other boys are laughing and shushing each other—but instead he hesitates at the old stream and feels a pull in its sluggish waters.

      Dandrata ophosa meyrata mahan!
And the laughter bubbles out of him.

And he's like the other boys, but also not. Because this is beautiful—this rushing and hiding and brushing with branches and rustling in leaves and hands pressed down into soft loam and—

The forest is with them, but they don't even know.

And after he laughs, he sighs.

He knows where the hiding boy is, and he walks to him, holding out his hand.

The boy groans, but accepts it.

He is caught.

Those are the rules.

The rules they follow to do something that isn't about hunting men at all.

It's about running and hiding and rustling in leaves and burying your fingers in loam.

She's an adult when her father dies.

They haven't spoken in years.

He wanted her to be a boy (who played with boys) and she wasn't.

And if not a boy, then a girl (who made bread with mother). But she wasn't that either.

Really, Dad just wanted *normal.*

And after all this time, with the funny moments and the words in the breeze and the lost minutes staring at water as it swirls down the drain . . .

. . . after all this time, she doesn't feel *abnormal.*

She's just whatever she is.

And so were the boys.

And so were the girls.

And so was the ditch that thought it was a stream and the bushes that thought they were a forest and the grain and the butter that thought they were the same . .

They all just were whatever they were, whether it was what Dad wanted or not.

And she . . . she had been far away from him for . . . oh, a time that floated on twilight.

Five years. She supposes it's been five years.

And then she hears it.

MAHAN!

A cry in the darkness across her cheese pasty as she fumbles for a grip on the rubber rail of an escalator.

MAHAN.

And she knows he's dead.

And she knows she has traveled a very long way to find herself so close to home.

At his mother's door he dies a little at the bell-chime call of familiarity in a depressed off-white button.

His mother's tears have stained her cheeks red, although they are dry.

"I keep hearing these words," he confesses, over the luke-warm tea they have both failed to drink. "I heard one and I knew. Before you called. I knew."

She looks at him, but he can't read the look.

"'*Mahan*'," he says. "I heard the word '*mahan.*' And I've never known what it meant. But I've always known what it means. That's stupid, isn't it? That's what he'd say—I'm being stupid again." He ran a finger around the rim of his teacup, waiting for her sigh and correction.

"Not stupid," she says. "Just not what he wanted to hear."

He snorts, but doesn't look up.

"*Dandrata ophosa meyrata mahan . . .*" she says quietly.

Their eyes meet.

"'The tendril, the part of, all over, of us,'" she said. "That's what it means. You've always heard it, haven't you?"

"I . . . what?" he said. "That's nonsense."

"Did you hear it by the stream? In the trees?" she asked. "That's where I met him, you know. When we were young. And he asked me. He said: *Dandrata ophosa meyrata mahan*, and it meant that he wanted to be with me, not as man and wife, but as the stream and the trees and the mud and the forest. But I didn't understand. Human beings, we don't think like that. I said, if you'd be with me, you must be my man, and we must wed, that's how my people do it."

She frowned and brushed the hair from her face. "So he was. He was my man and we were wed. And for me, he was one of us. He wanted that for you. And you loved me too, so we thought . . . but you're still a part of that larger thing. Aren't you?

"I think what you heard—*mahan*—I think that was them calling him back. In as much as there is a him and a them. And maybe one day you'll be 'of us' again. You hear the call, but . . ."

"No, Mum," I interrupt. "I'm just me. I think that's what father never understood. I'm not them. I'm not us. I'm not a man. I'm not a woman. I am. And that's everything and it's me, too."

She looks away and I know she hasn't heard me.

"And he's everything, and so are you," I add.

She looks up and meets my eyes. Does she understand?

"Perhaps," she says. "Let's make some more tea."

The Bremen Job

~ Linda McMullen

My scarlet cloak—with its mythic riding hood—hung abstractedly on its peg, while I pondered a curious communication deposited beneath the doorframe in the hours between twilight and dawn. The embossed, snow-white envelope bore only my name: *Poppy.*

I heard my mother stirring, chirruping at the birds, just as always. Soon she would stoke the ebon coals and knead her day away, preparing the inevitable loaves that I would take to my grandmother's table. I stole outside, borrowing the robins' perch on a stump just outside. I could not bear to break the seal—a crimson tome, with a double-pointed oval superimposed over its pages. I lifted it carefully from the envelope and extracted my letter like a thief, or a magician.

> *Dear Poppy,*
>
> *We would like to extend to you an invitation to join our organization, and to obtain the duties and privileges thereof, for our mutual benefit. If you wish to attend today's gathering, please present yourself at a quarter to ten at the wishing well. Our representative will look for your red cloak.*
> *Sincerely,*
>
> *The FTH Society*

Persuading my mother to allow me to gather wildflowers while she baked and swept and washed required all the childlike charm I could boast—no simple matter for a girl teetering on the precipice of womanhood. Particularly as I had spent much of the previous day lost in my book of wildflowers. But I promised to gather dandelions for a salad too, tipping the balance. "My indulgence will prove your undoing," she sighed. I kissed her and skipped away.

The village well appeared deserted when I arrived. I had neglected to bring a pail, so the villagers eyed me with the self-congratulating scorn of a priggish priest hearing extravagant confessions. I rinsed the dust from my hands, for the sake of appearing to do something— and then a movement caught my eye.

A slim young woman gestured from the shadow of the church— But it seemed that only her pale forearm emerged from the darkness...

I followed.

She turned southward without acknowledging my inquisitive footfalls, or even tilting her head—with its heavy crown of auburn hair—toward me. She kept her arms crossed before her as we passed into the forest, and we marched on, on, until she suddenly descended into a cleft in the ground, tracing a gumdrop-mushroom path I had never glimpsed before. The breeze tickled me with hints of cinnamon and clove. The spruce and oaks grew denser; the air grew closer; we came to a cottage half-concealed in the undergrowth—

A magnificent gingerbread structure, next to a tiny, flowing creek.

I followed the girl to the sugar-glass door; she opened it wide but remained on the threshold, barring my entry. She finally turned and I saw, for certain, that she had no hands. "Turn out your cloak and hood, and open your basket." As I did so, she stood aside, so that the many wide eyes within could see; I could feel their suddenly un-dammed curiosity flowing over me.

"You may enter," called a melodious voice from within.

I obeyed, only to discover that the sweetly beautiful cottage was thoroughly bewitched: what seemed like a residence for perhaps one sweet-toothed misanthrope magically allowed dozens of damsels to fit comfortably. They reclined on marzipan divans and lemon drop cushions and a sugar plum sofa. I did my best to curtsey.

"Yes," murmured the ageless sage enthroned on a fairy-food ped-estal, "I see it." Turning to me, she said, "Have a seat, Poppy."

"I'll just . . . dust off this stool," said a young woman I recognized as Cinderella, retrieving one from a closet.

"That one is too hard," complained a girl with bouncy flaxen curls.

"It's fine," I said, thanking Cinderella.

"Excellent," said the wise woman. "Welcome, ladies, to this meeting of the Fairy Tale Heroines Society." I could have sworn she vouchsafed me a wink. "Our younger generation has finally come of age, so I am pleased to introduce to you three potential new members: Poppy with her red riding hood"—I waved—"Goldilocks"—my complaining, curly-haired companion smiled—"and Gretel, whom I would like to thank for hosting us all today." A round-faced, doughty girl bowed her head in acknowledgement.

"I'm so sorry," interrupted the young woman with the siren's voice, as she sank onto the arm of the sofa, accidentally jostling Cinderella. "I feel as though I've been walking on knives all day." (I learned later that walking hurt her greatly; she made herself useful by doing much of the cooking, though she flatly refused to prepare seafood.)

The wise woman arched her brow. "Ladies," she said, gesturing to Goldilocks, Gretel, and myself, "Joining the society means divorcing yourself from the lives you've known, the habits you've developed, the stories you've told. It means commitment to this group above all, and unswerving obedience to our mission—"

"What's your mission?" interjected Goldilocks.

"—which is to address our broken relationships with Grimm, and Perrault, and Hans Christian Andersen." continued the wise woman, as if there had been no interruption.

"And Robert Southey?" Goldilocks broke in. The wise woman stared at her until Goldilocks flushed and looked down at her shoes, which were undoubtedly too small.

"I suppose," conceded the wise woman, looking as though she was reconsidering the wisdom of her own invitation decisions. "Well. Girls. Yes or no?"

Gretel waved, which I supposed meant yes. Goldilocks said, "I have too little information—"

"Too bad," said the wise woman. "Poppy?"

"Wait!" cried Goldilocks. "I . . . didn't mean . . . that is . . . I . . . I'll join."

"Poppy?" the wise woman said again.

"Yes, ma'am," I said.

We took our vows of allegiance. The girl with six brothers rose with a swanlike grace to get beverages, while my friend with no hands picked up a massive bowl of pears and offered them around. Then the *real* meeting began.

"The plan, ladies," declared the wise woman, "is that we're going to break into the Repository at Bremen."

The phlegmatic Gretel didn't bat an eye, but Goldilocks gasped and I couldn't help feeling slightly taken aback. The Repository was the archive. The source of the source texts. The Official Tellings of all our tales, sanctified by the authors themselves.

"You're mad," Goldilocks declared. "Those stories are sacred! The authors have placed them under layers of protection to keep anyone—including us—from tampering with them! I've heard they're under incredibly heavy guard!"

"Do you wish to rescind your participation?" the wise woman asked, drawing out her wand and extending it toward Goldilocks's trademark hair, adding, "I can make it look permanently ratted, you know."

Goldilocks gulped and muttered a shamefaced apology.

"Now, we exist only as marionettes," intoned the wise woman. "We follow the pre-trod paths, day in, day out—without ever having lived a day in our lives. Or even seen our own scripts. Well, no more!" she cried. "We are going to reclaim those texts. And we are going to create something better in their wake. We are finished playing the parts that men wrote for us!"

Applause; determined, almost grim, expressions.

"Thanks to our very own goose girl, who has been lingering with her flock outside the Repository for the last several weeks, we have excellent information about external security. The Repository boasts two guards outside its entrance at all times. They work eight-hour shifts. We know that at least five of these guards are susceptible to some kind of temptation, but one of them is extremely brave, absolutely impervious to shivers of any kind. We will therefore schedule our infiltration around his shift."

Cinderella went about collecting the pear cores. "Sorry. Habit."

The wise woman sighed and continued. "Allerleirauh will be in charge of disguises," she began. "Then Inge—" she gestured to my handless guide—"will conduct the team through the forest; she's spent an extensive amount of time in there, mapping the route. Once you arrive, Plan A is that Eva"—she gestured to a pretty, pouty young woman—"will arrive just before the end of the midnight-to-dawn shift with soup to offer the hungry guards. Obviously, it will contain donkey cabbage, which will literally transform the guards into the braying asses they are. In the unlikely event that they refuse free food, plan B is to have Snow White lure them into the woods. The dwarves have generously rented their cottage to us, and she's booby-trapped it to a nicety."

"What if only one of them goes?" I asked.

"Gretel's more than a match for any one of them," the wise woman replied. "She took out a witch when she was underfed and terrified, and she's been in training since then."

Gretel flexed her biceps.

"Indeed. And we'll be sending additional support. At any rate, once our team enters the repository, they will have to work through the information warren inside. Goldilocks, I understand, has some experience with housebreaking, so I'll ask her to take the lead on devising a plan to navigate through the building. Our goal is to reach the safe, which is located on the third floor, in the very center of the building."

"Of course it is," Goldilocks muttered, but accepted the blueprint the wise woman handed her.

"We expect that Sleeping Beauty will be able to pick the lock with her spindle—*stop playing with that, dear!*" cried the wise woman, as the princess let her fingertips dance a hair's-breadth over its le-thal-looking point. "If that doesn't work, our fisherman's wife has a range of hooks available." An ill-at-ease peasant woman nodded from the corner. "Then—"

Beauty waved from the corner.

"That's right. The strike team will extract the original texts of all our tales, and bring them back here for Beauty to analyze. Then we'll make decisions about what to do. Cinderella will also remain at headquarters with me; she'll look after anyone who gets injured. Understood?"

"How can I help?" I asked. My voice sounded very small. I didn't have any magical powers, or exceptional beauty, or an enigmatic voice, or—

The wise woman smiled. "I daresay we'll find some use for you."

Day after day I told my mother I was off to visit my grandmother, while I trained with Gretel and the rest of the strike team—those the wise woman had assigned duties, plus Rapunzel, the Snow Queen (recently reclaimed from villainy through a little Disneyesque magic), a kind young woman named Clara who the wise woman explained had come straight from the three little men in the wood, and a bored young princess perpetually toying with a golden ball. We participated in physical training, conducted drills, and ran simulations. "You must be prepared," said the wise woman. "I can only foresee so much."

"Aren't there kind of a lot of us?" asked Goldilocks.

"Redundancy ensures success," replied the wise woman.

And at last, the great day arrived. The girl with the seven brothers had spun and woven, and made disguises following Allerleirauh's designs. Allerleirauh disguised Gretel, Sleeping Beauty, the Snow Queen, Golden Ball girl, the kind young woman, Rapunzel, and the fisherman's wife as security guards, tucking Rapunzel's hair into a basket on her back, and pulling her hat down as far as possible. The donkey cabbage proprietress was also dressed as a guard, with a blue cloak to conceal it. Snow White, Goldilocks and I alone remained in normal clothing, though she braided our hair and accessorized us with spectacles and satchels (she allowed me to keep my basket). "This way, you'll look like students," she said, "and you won't attract attention if you're poking around—as if looking for a book."

We made our way stealthily toward the repository, keeping to the forest as much as possible. But, true to form, I couldn't help leaving the path for some exquisite, poisonously-blue buds blooming in the glade . . .

"Really?" demanded Gretel.

"You were sent to fulfill your mission, I was sent to complete mine," I muttered, but only after she was striding forward, and well out of earshot.

The donkey cabbage plan worked like a . . . well, it was under a charm, but it's probably a bit too on-the-nose to say . . . anyway, our plans did not miscarry. Eva-the-donkey-cabbage-proprietress dragged the guards out of sight and secured them with some rope, then abandoned her cloak and returned to the front door with Inge to take their places and deflect the questions of the oncoming crew. The rest of us entered the Repository of Lore, our security "squad" marching in formation as if conducting an extra patrol. And saw, just ahead a pair of guards conducting their real duties . . .

"Go!" hissed Gretel; Snow White, Goldilocks and I dispersed into the bowels of the labyrinth, while our security team tangled noisily with the guards. I peered out from behind the multicolored array of Lang titles, lightly dusted in their rainbow jackets, anticipating pandemonium . . .

"Gentlemen!" cried the young woman who had visited the three little men of the woods, "let my colleagues be!"

With this, five gold coins fell out of her mouth. The guards withdrew their molestation-poised hands and dove for the money. A gleam danced behind her eyes; she darted back out the door, singing, dropping coins with every word, the guards in greedy pursuit.

"Two down," cried Goldilocks, delightedly, from somewhere in the stacks.

"More friends coming to join us," muttered Gretel, as another pair of guards had become aware of their colleagues' conspicuous absence. They approached, glowering, until Snow White ran up to one of them and whispered something in his ear. His face flushed, and his eyes glowed like stars. Then she whispered something in his partner's ear. A moment later she had linked arms with them both and they walked merrily out the front door. I heard her murmur, "My cabin is only a quarter-hour's walk from here . . . "

I made my way back to the security team, now smaller by two. "Will she be all right?"

"I wouldn't worry," said Gretel. "She designed the set-up, and the wise woman helped her test it. And she has plenty of experience dealing with people targeting her."

Not altogether reassured, I rejoined the others. Goldilocks navigated us through the library, carefully skirting the witches' lore section, and reminding us all to jump the enchanted stream flowing through the middle of the Bewitchment section. Universally graceful, we soared over the waters and were proceeding to the rear stairwells to reach the second—and ultimately, third floors—when Gretel held up a silent hand.

A giant stood before us, wielding a club, ready to strike.

"Any ideas?" muttered Goldilocks, out of the corner of her mouth. "Anyone?"

"Scatter!" cried Gretel, as the club came down in our midst. I dove right, landing on top of Gretel, as the giant swung his club wildly about, no doubt hoping to smash us. But we were tiny and moving fast, and in his frustration, he lifted the club and bashed against the nearest objects, which happened to be the wooden staircases. They collapsed into a heap of kindling.

"Oh, no," someone moaned.

"Help me! What have you got, girl?" cried Gretel, shaking my shoulder. I rummaged in my basket and produced the bottle of wine. She rolled her eyes, but accepted it, and ran out to face the danger. "Oi! You're nothing but an overgrown troll!" she cried. The giant, caring for neither her remark nor her tone, tried to demolish her with his club; Gretel caught it on the upswing, then leapt from it to his shoulder, whence she smashed the wine bottle over his head. As he staggered forward from the blow, he grabbed Gretel around the waist and flung her against the Anthropomorphic Items collection. She did not stir.

Goldilocks appeared out of nowhere, staring down the concussed giant and stamping her foot. "*Somebody*," she screeched, "*has been interfering with my team!*"

And she screamed aloud, the same shriek that must have given those bears infinite pause, and the giant hove himself forward, trying to smash her, trying to stop the horrible noise—and Goldilocks, displaying an impressive presence of mind, paused only to blow him him a raspberry, then, still screaming, skipped just ahead of him toward the library entrance, drawing him off . . .

"Not bad for a complaining little housebreaker," observed Gretel.

"How're we going to reach the archive?" Golden Ball girl complained. "The steps are gone, and Goldilocks's blueprint only showed the one set."

"Not very prudent of the designers, really," observed the fisherman's wife. "If I had that kind of power –"

"Focus, please," said Gretel. "Ideas, team?"

Rapunzel grinned. "Not to worry," she said, and looped her hair over the existing bit of bannister, two stories up. She turned to me. "Poppy, you're lightest, you go first, and we'll see if this will even work."

"Great," said Gretel, standing at attention to keep Rapunzel safe.

I half-clambered up her hair as she and the rest of the team helped hoist me to the next level—then Sleeping Beauty, the fisherman's wife, Golden Ball girl, and the Snow Queen followed. Gretel and Rapunzel remained below to fend off anyone attempting to reach us from behind—"I'm certain they have enchanted ropes or ladders about for just such an emergency," she said, grimly.

Up on the third floor now, our remainder stole down a corridor, which ended in a locked door. "I've got it," cried Sleeping Beauty merrily, twirling her spindle around her thumb with an altogether worrying degree of swagger. She used the spindle's lethal tip to blindly perform the delicate mechanical surgery that would open the lock—

A *pop!* and the handle turned. Sleeping Beauty looped her prize tool around her thumb in preparation for holstering it, when it caught her on the forefinger and she slumped to the ground, unconscious.

"I don't *believe* this," cried Golden Ball girl, unfortunately catching the attention of the guard stationed just beyond the door. He seemed to weigh the situation, then took a deep breath, in preparation for issuing a monumental bellow, to let his fellows know he had found us—

But Golden Ball girl lunged forward, looping her arm around his neck, and kissing him full on the mouth. For a moment, I couldn't distinguish anything through a cloud of acrid green smoke, and then, I saw—

—a frog emerging from the depths of the guard's crumpled uniform.

"*That's* your power?" I cried.

She shrugged. "Supposedly I can also change an upstanding, enchanted frog into a prince, but good luck finding one of those. So far, the magic only cuts this way."

"Break in now, meta-analysis later!" cried the Snow Queen. "Mathilde"—she gestured to our resident faunamorphosis expert—"You've done your bit, look after Sleeping Beauty." She transformed the corridor behind us into ice, and erected an ice slide down to the lower level.

"You couldn't have just made us an ice ladder back there?" Mathilde replied, earning her a withering glance from the Snow Queen. Mathilde—I imagined, partly to escape from the remainder of this conversation—asked to borrow my cloak, and I obliged; we helped her place Sleeping Beauty on top of it, and Mathilde dragged our fallen comrade carefully back to the rest of the team on the makeshift stretcher/toboggan.

And the rest of us crept onward, coming across another locked door. The fisherman's wife fileted the lock; it clattered onto the floor and I half-imagined smoke and whimpers emerging from it.

"Excellent," said the Snow Queen.

Then the lights went out.

The Snow Queen, the fisherman's wife, and I crept forward, when we heard a short scream suddenly cut off—then silence.

Our picklock turned tail and ran back toward the rest of the team, and the light . . .

"Do your ice powers also extend to—"

"No," she said. "Do you have anything useful in your basket?"

I shook my head, ruefully, painfully conscious of the fact that my sole contribution to that point had been attendance.

The Snow Queen sighed.

The light flickered on beyond the cracked door.

And then, an inhuman voice:

"Come and play, Red . . . "

I trembled from my red riding hood to my little boots, a primal, wordless terror surging through me—

The Snow Queen murmured, "I'm right beside you. We'll go together."

I nodded, and—with every ounce of my will focused on my leaden feet—stumbled forward through the door, whose plaque read: *The Dorothea Viehmann Repository.*

We came into the room, the frozen heart of the archive, a dim, windowless, box-shaped room lined with iron caskets, locked drawers and stout safes—

—and before them prowled The Wolf.

I forced the scream fighting for exit back down my constricted throat. He was savage and sensual, with talons that beckoned even as they threatened to rip me apart . . . and what big eyes he had—hypnotic yellow discs . . .

"I hope you've come to play," he said, his eyes flickering from me to the Snow Queen and back again. My fingers snaked into my basket, hoping by some miracle that the wise woman would choose now to work a miracle, to deliver me a weapon that appeared just from wishing—but I found nothing but the bread and the flowers. I offered him the former, gripping the flowers, as if their cheerful color might offer some comfort.

"I'm hungry, all right," he returned, "but not for bread. Still, I'll keep it. The better to eat you with."

And then he *lunged* at us. The Snow Queen, anticipating his attack, threw up an ice wall between him and us, but he powered through it, sending both of us flying, and dispersing ice shards into every corner of the room . . . I struggled to right myself, only to find her grappling with him, hand to hand, his torrid breath scorching her face . . . But he was in no hurry, always preferring to play with his food before he finally ate it—

"Poppy!" she gasped, his fangs grazing her throat.

And time seemed to slow, to lose all meaning, and of all things, my wildflower book seemed to dance before my eyes, and I remembered I had seen a picture of those beautiful blue flowers in my basket, several days before, on the page . . .

Aconitum, also known as aconite, or monkshood, also possesses the curious nickname of wolf's bane . . .

I seized an ice shard from the floor, squeezed a few drops of the flowers' venomous nectar onto its tip, and plunged it into the wolf's broad back.

He howled in surprise and misery and pain—and then the tremors began; he rolled off the Snow Queen and onto his side, spewing expletives and curses that ended with: " . . . Red."

Then he moved no more.

I rushed to the Snow Queen: "Are you all right?"

"Fine," she replied, wearily; she had a great lump on her head from where she had hit it in her fall. "Go find which strongbox our files are in, will you?"

I did as she bid, deciphering the faded ink scrawls on tiny labels affixed to the safes and drawers. After examining several—*British Nursery Rhymes, Folklore: West Africa, Chivalric Tales*, and so on—I came to a pot-bellied safe whose label read: *Fairy Tales, Original Versions.* I pointed. The Snow Queen propped herself up, and sent a wave of ice and snow around it. Her magic swirled, dropping the temperature of the room so abruptly that my teeth began to chatter . . . and then—to my astonishment—the safe shattered.

The Snow Queen tumbled senseless to the floor.

"No!" I shouted, but a little voice inside reminded me not to allow her to have struggled in vain. I began picking through the silvery slivers of the former safe, extracting sheaves of carefully ribbon-bound, yellowing papers, and storing them in my basket. Footsteps sounded in the hall; I picked up another ice shard that felt friendly in my hand, and waited, crouched defensively—

"Thank God!" exclaimed Gretel, pulling me into an unexpected and slightly bone-crushing hug. "You're alive! We thought—" She finally spotted the Snow Queen on the floor, bent down over her with careful fingers on her neck. "She's alive. I'll carry her. You've got the stories?"

I nodded because speech would not come. Gretel threw the meager royal weight across her shoulders, and said, "Let's get out of here."

Golden Ball girl—Mathilde, I mean—had clearly reconnected with the rest of the team; leaving Rapunzel to care for Sleeping Beauty, she had gone about kissing all of the remaining guards. The only thing that slowed our exit was trying to avoid stepping on the phalanx of frogs.

Back at the little cottage, Cinderella had put most of the injured to rights. The Snow Queen rested on the sofa, lifting a hand to her still-tender head, but smiling. Gretel and the rest of the security crew had suffered numerous contusions, and many of them had ice on their injuries. Poor Rapunzel had an awful headache from everyone pulling on her hair, and she had a blindfold on and an ice pack on her head, but she was humming a merry tune. The kind young woman who produced coins when she spoke had led the guards pursuing her to Snow White's cottage, where they—like the two invited by Snow White—had gotten snared in the various traps. The two of them were only sore from running, and lounged in adjacent armchairs.

Goldilocks and I remained well, albeit rattled.

Unfortunately, however, neither Cinderella nor the wise woman had yet discovered a cure for Sleeping Beauty. She had perused the ancient text, of course, and found that the *official* story prescribed a prince . . . She had nonetheless tried to work other spells. Not one of them had made the least difference, and our companion slumbered on.

While she did so, the wise woman came to me, and clasped both my hands in hers. "Poppy, we owe you our thanks. You faced a particularly personal battle, and emerged triumphant. I am so appreciative—and, if I may say so, I am very proud of you."

I blushed as red as my hood. "I—thank you, but I am just so sorry so many of our sisters got injured—"

"They accepted that risk, just as you did," the wise woman replied. "I just wish I were sagacious enough to—" She frowned at herself, glancing toward Sleeping Beauty.

Shaking her head in bewilderment, the wise woman convened those present, and gave Beauty the floor. Beauty went on at some length, describing the individual stories to gasps and frowns. She had just finished "The Three Little Men in the Wood" and we were enjoying a break when Mathilde jumped up and cried, "Where's Clara?"

"Gathering strawberries, why?"

"We need her! Which way did she go?"

The wise woman looked frankly bewildered. "West, I think."

"Great!" cried Mathilde, over her shoulder, as she bolted out the door. We all stared after her in bewilderment.

Beauty cleared her throat, gently, and resumed her narrations. When she had read all of our stories, she said, "I've gone through these tales several times." She pursed her lips. "Most of them appear to have been written to caution girls –" She glanced toward me—"against straying from the path—or, in my own case, for example, to teach young women to accept their fates with grace . . . and docility." She frowned. "But in my view, these lessons belong to another age—"

At that moment, Mathilde and Clara returned with a third, blindfolded young woman, a stranger, and Mathilde's expression was triumphant. "Sorry to interrupt," she said, "but I've had an idea."

"Bringing unapproved strangers here?" demanded the wise woman.

"She can't see anything," pointed out Mathilde. "But I think we need her . . . "

"For what?"

"Curing Sleeping Beauty," continued Mathilde.

Clara broke in, apologetically. "This is my stepsister. When I went to the house in the wood, the three little men put a charm on me, that makes me drop coins from my mouth when I speak—" By the end of this explanation, she had produced enough gold to fund the Society for a year. "But my stepsister—ah . . . "

"She was cursed with toads jumping out of her mouth at every word," Mathilde explained. "So, I thought if I could just get my hands

. . . or, rather, my mouth on *one* magical toad . . . "

"I thought your magic worked on *frogs*?" asked the wise woman, sharply.

"I thought it close enough to merit an *attempt*," Mathilde retorted. "It can't hurt. Go on, Bertha."

Bertha hissed, "No!" but it was enough; a gruesome amphibian sprang from her lips. Mathilde scooped him up and kissed him . . .

. . . a puff of gold-and-plum smoke—

—and a beautiful, slightly vacant-eyed prince appeared, looking dazed. "My savior!" he cried, lurching amorously toward Mathilde—

"Not me," she replied, promptly. "I did it on her behalf," she said, pointing toward Sleeping Beauty. The prince, uncomprehending but amenable, kissed Sleeping Beauty full on the lips. She stirred prettily, blinked, and murmured, "What did I miss?"

The prince cried, "My love!" and Sleeping Beauty wrinkled her forehead and frowned at him, and Mathilde came to the rescue and kissed him so that he turned back into a toad. Then she carried him carefully out to the creek and wished him good luck. Clara sent her stepsister off with some coins.

"There is a certain elegance in the original tales' simplicity," Beauty continued, as if there had been no interruption. "But they offer us no agency." She glanced toward the wise woman, who dipped her chin affirmatively.

"Therefore," she said, "I propose that we produce our own versions of the tales—where we women *act*, and *choose*, and *live*."

Mathilde began a slow clap, and then Rapunzel joined, and soon the whole room dissolved in thunderous applause.

"There's just one . . . small concern, however," said Beauty. "Once we've written our new editions, we'll need to—somehow—place them inside the archive . . . "

Planet Preservation and the Art of Zen

~ *Jetse de Vries*

—a quadripartite prelude—

—*The crisis is big, my children, so big that the distinctions between reality and imagination, impression and expression, even between fantasy and science fiction are dissolving*—

The stranger is a presence, an epiphenomenon, an emergent property yet his followers prefer to visualise this ephemeral quadrilaterality as a person, an androgynous icon in zazen, floating in mid-air.

—*The four of you must bear witness to the upcoming shift, the change of mental seasons. Short-term blindness, incessant greed, false conservatism, and fear are the four hard truths we must face. You must go the East, the West, the North and the South*—

Four young adults are listening intently to the Swami of the four new Vedas. Chika Wu from Chengdu, her unruly black hair all but covering her amber face and glasses; João Incanna from Lima, his wiry frame and auburn skin weathered from years of fishing; Grace M'Boku from the Limpopo floodplains, her stature a study in empathy, ebony, and elegance; and Saaki Sami from Lapland, his springy red hair complementing his ivory face.

—*Sow the seeds of change. Implement the memes of co-operation & entrepreneurship, innovation, long-term thinking & sustainability, and hope. Remember the fourfold path—the four new Vedas, if you like—to dharma:*

- *the only constant in the chain of life is change;*
- *the protection of the weakest is the new way forward;*
- *like biodiversity, multiple strategies need not be mutually exclusive;*
- *greatness determines a people's karma, so find a way to improve yours;*—

Off they go. Wu to the East, Incanna to the West, M'Boku to the South, Sami to the North.

—a quadruple overture: four hard truths—

Chika Wu comes down in Chengdu, Sichuan Province, perched right between the Sichuan Basin and the fertile lands of the Chengdu Plain, a transit area from the Longmen and Qionglai mountains, the Min River convergence area and the extremely crowded cityscapes. The extremely polluted cityscapes.

Like Incanna, M'Boku and Sami, she has to form a team, a team that must focus on one big problem, a hard truth. The hard truth in China's cityscapes is impossible to miss. Pollution, eye-watering pollution everywhere. Breathing masks are as popular as smartphones, and more indispensable.

People are plentiful, perhaps too plentiful. Finding the right people might take too long. Yet almost everybody is connected to the internet in one way or another, with profiles, interests and surfing behavior readily available to those who know how to mine all that data. Wu dives in, searching for the right people, knowing that Chengdu is already a research & development center for new energies.

João Incanna remigrates to Lima. In the fishing villages of his youth, an immense hard truth is staring them right in the face. Through a combination of overfishing, pollution and climate change, the Pacific Ocean—the largest body of water on the planet—is slowly dying. Coral reefs are bleaching, fish stock are heavily depleted, huge amounts of plastic—in particular the plastic broken down to small pieces—are disturbing the food chain, biodiversity is suffering, and the acidity of the water is rising.

Compared to that, the poverty and lack of job prospects of the Peruvian coastal communities seem like minor problems. Yet Incanna wants to gather a team that aims to solve it all, step by step, little by little.

Grace M'Boku moves to Gaborone, then to the agricultural communities in the floodplains of the Limpopo River. There are many hard truths in her part of the world, but the hardest are hunger, disease, and destitution. Over the last few centuries, her people have been introduced—often forcefully—to new ways. So far, these new ways have mainly helped the already rich and well-to-do, and failed to improve the lives of the most destitute ones, like her community.

Returning to the old ways is not an option. There must be better new ways, ways like the waves of a tide that lifts all boats. Even if they have to invent those themselves, even if it means they have to work harder than ever before.

Saaki Sami shifts down in Luleå. Over there, the winter often covers nasty problems under a blanket of snow. But the winters aren't as long and severe as they used to be, and the blanket of snow is getting thinner by the year.

On top of that, some of the Scandinavians feel guilt about being a part of the problem. Companies like Ericsson and Nokia helped launch the mobile phone revolution, and the billions of discarded phones form garbage patches and landfills the size of small provinces. They helped deplete the Earth of many of its rare metals. It's time to clean up the mess and re-use those precious metals.

—circle the quadrangle—

Chika Wu's team is a weird mix of biochemists whose interests are restless, leaping from topic to topic like magpies chasing anything that glimmers; and physicists whose interests are so singular they almost forget there exists a world outside of it.

Both researchers wish to create their own Shang-tu, while also trying to improve upon already existing products and results. The biochemists wish to develop a thin, organic polymer film that acts like a solar cell. A film that's easy to produce, from materials that are widely available. A film that has a higher efficiency than the current best solar cell technology, and that is as maintenance-free as possible.

The physicists want to develop a room-temperature superconductor. Not only that, the material should ideally consist of parts that are readily available. On top of that, a material that can easily be produced as very long strands of wire, to stretch from mountain- or countryside (or desert) to city.

As she doesn't want the two teams to be fully isolated, Chika Wu hires an amount of interdisciplinary people who shift between the two core teams in an effort to provide both with fresh insights and ideas. The exchange proves so fruitful that a small group splits off from the other two and starts developing a new type of battery with record-breaking levels of power storage density.

João Incanna has introduced the fishermen of his port to a mixed group of University researchers, start-up entrepreneurs, and idealists. While the practicality of the fishermen often clashes with the lofty goals of the idealists, and the can-do spirit of the entrepreneurs often raises doubts with the researchers, a common goal binds them. They wish to clean up and reseed the Pacific Ocean so that its biodiversity can recover—and the starkly depleted fish stock with them—and deliver raw materials to the space-elevator-to-be base floating several hundred kilometers west of the Galapagos Islands.

So they work on a bio-active mega-net. An anti-fishing net of sorts, as it tries to catch the plastic floating around in the Pacific while leaving life—plankton, nekton and fishes—alone. To counter the acidification of the ocean they seed it with novo-plankton, a rich mix of genetically engineered algae, diatoms and protozoans provided with single-celled, alkali-producing algae. The algae will only produce alkali if the seawater's pH rises above seven.

The first prototype of the megabionet has plastic-detecting sensors that err on the side of caution, to be certain no actual living organisms are caught by accident. It lowers their effective catch ratio, but there is so much plastic in the ocean that it's better to launch the first vessels with the original megabionets than waiting and doing nothing. Later generations will be supplied with improved versions.

The first vessels with anti-fishing nets set out on carefully calculated trajectories, from the Peruvian coast to the North and South Pacific Garbage Patches—invisible from space, yet rife with plastic mini-, micro-, and nano-particles—and onwards to deliver the captured plastic to the base of the space-elevator-to-be, west of the Galapagos Archipelago.

Grace M'Boku moves to Gaborone, where she goes after fresh University graduates, innovators young and old, and those willing to put in hard labour. In the agricultural communities outside the capital she looks for experienced hands and those well in the know about ages-old cultivation methods.

Her team—her 'agricultural advancers'—a mix of experienced and young people, needs to be wise enough to know what's right, then brave enough to choose it. They dance to the beat of the old world man with the heat of the new world woman. They have to be sharp enough to win the world, and wily enough not to lose it. Above all, as they try to move forward, they need to keep their nature pure.

Grace M'Boku's agricultural advancers must first face five years of hardship. Near the floodplains of the Limpopo River, the land is all but barren, and grand new techniques, together with ceaseless toil, can make it fertile. They must make agrichar and biochar—taking the best from chitemene—use new ways of mound cultivation to make the land, square meter by square meter, fertile again.

Not only that. After the land is fertilized, a careful mix of produce must be planted to maintain not only the fecundity, but the re-implemented diversity, as well. Beyond that, they have to make sure that the super-symbiotic neo-agricultures they've developed are also drought-resistant. Otherwise, one single super dry season will undo all their hard work.

She needs initial investments and—like other women, who form ninety percent of all successful applications—gets a microcredit for her project. She fully intends to be among the ninety-five percent who actually pay their loan back. After which she wants to uplift others in her region.

Saaki Sami gathers people from Finland, Norway, Sweden and Russia—with a few stray Icelanders—to form his research & development team. Reining them in like reindeer, he lures them with the carrot-and-stick approach of old guilt and new challenges.

His team is making something huge that incorporates immensely small parts. Not as big as an iron ore smelter, nor as large as Oulu's paper manufacturing plant, but still very substantial. Small enough to be easily constructed in other places, but large enough to take on big loads.

In their premises overlooking the snow-covered plains of the Scandinavian Arctic Circle, they're developing a high-temperature nano lubricant-cum-dissolver, a grey goo that's extremely resistant to high temperatures, able to penetrate the smallest of chips and circuit boards, with the ability to extract the rare metal needle in the discarded computing equipment haystack. Billions upon billions of computers, smartphones, tablets and other gadgets have been made, used and discarded in quick succession as Moore's Law ran its course. Enormous, polluting landfills where precious metals lay inert as current ores are running out. At some point intricate, intensive recycling will become economically viable. Saaki Sami's team wishes to be ahead of that very curve.

—the eightfold path—

Chika Wu's test project in Chengdu succeeds beyond her team's wildest dreams. Large panels covered with the solar nanofilm cover many square kilometers of the mountain- and countryside near Chengdu, and are interconnected with the cuprate superconducting wires. These same superconducting wires have been laid all the way to Chengdu, supplying the city with over ninety percent of its required energy. A coup emphasizing the solar nanofilm's efficiency considering the mostly grey weather of the area.

They also developed a more powerful type of battery. These batteries, implemented both in electric cars and houses have become plentiful enough to store the peak electricity production at day in order to keep supplying everybody with electrical power at night.

The test project is so successful that the Chinese government wants to implement it at a much larger scale in the Gobi Desert, to supply solar power to Beijing, Shanghai, and other megacities. Private entrepreneurs are already looking to implement the technology in cities outside China like Tokyo, Seoul, Bangkok, and Taipei, among many others.

Five years after the successful test project, the Chengdu Jintang coal power station has been shut down. Chengdu has now the best air quality of any municipality with more than a million people in China, and proudly calls itself the 'green revolution city'.

After the first five years, João Incanna's fleet is expanding rapidly. Simultaneously, the novoplankton-growing basins of his team are popping up everywhere along the Peruvian coast, even expanding into Chile and Ecuador.

The good they've been doing is surfacing gradually. Fish stocks are, slowly yet inevitably, picking up from their all-time lows. The novoplankton is thriving, both re-invigorating the food chain from the bottom up and countering the acidification of the ocean. Coral bleaching has come to a standstill, and a few coral reefs are steadily recovering. The plastic pollution levels are decreasing, albeit at a rate slower than they wish. His team keeps working hard to improve the efficiency of their megabionets.

The plastic they deliver to the space-elevator-to-be base is fully recycled into graphene and several organic by-products. The graphene is shot into orbit through a double railgun. The first railgun shoots up magnetized ice, most of which (flash-)evaporates in the atmosphere. Right behind it, in the magnetized ice's slipstream, is the real payload that does not burn up in the air. There, in geosynchronous orbit, is where the quadruple-redundant ribbon of the space elevator is produced.

Over time, they gather more plastic than is needed for the manufacture of the space elevator's ribbon, and they deliver the surplus to plastic recycling plants in North and South America. Big oil companies are either slowly dying out, or adapting, modifying their refineries into plastic recycling facilities. Crude oil production dwindles as renewable energy starts providing the majority of the world's energy needs and increasingly intricate recycling methods become competitive alternatives to crude oil's refined products. Slowly, for the first time in two hundred years, CO2-levels in the atmosphere are falling.

☉

In Botswana, five years of toiling are followed by five years of feeding the people, modifying both their recharring methods and their neo-agricultures to different types of lands and climates. In the original implementation areas—the floodplains of the Limpopo River— hunger became a thing of the past, and people slowly became better off as they were producing more than they could eat, and subsequently found willing markets for their inherently sustainable food.

The hard labour required to set up such a neo-agriculture provides much needed work. Increasingly, people aren't complaining that they're working so hard, but that they're proud to do such good work for the future of their family, friends, community and—in the long run—for their country and continent.

Their knowledge is made open source, but it doesn't spread as fast as Grace M'Boku and her people like, even as it's made available on every smartphone in Africa. Language remains a huge barrier, and they set up a quick translation app—at first manned by many human translators, more automated as machine learning catches on—that's sponsored by voluntary donations through moola from Mxit and other forms of electronic money. As their livelihoods increase, people are increasingly willing to pay their dues.

As a fortunate by-effect, sub-Saharan Africa starts to develop infrastructures old and new that need less original investments and maintenance such as vacuum Zeppelins for long distance transport, electric quads for short distance transport, and Electrified Trees for data signal transport, all increasingly powered by renewable energy. Their economies are growing in a highly sustainable manner.

After a series of increased fine-tunings, the prototype MaNa—Macro/Nano—Smelter in Luleå achieves recycling efficiencies of over ninety-nine percent, while being energetically self-sustainable and carbon neutral. The refined blueprint, which has been open source from the beginning, remains available to all. Siblings of the Lapland

MaNaSmelter are popping up everywhere, world-wide. In a mere five years, the production of the newest device is truly green, sustainable, and fair. Fairphone in Amsterdam declare themselves obsolete and start a new project called 'Fairspace'. Landfills are rewilded after their soil has been purified by modified versions of the MaNaSmelters. Most of the mines are closed, their premises re-purified if possible, and rewilded, as well (even if a few are refurbished as appartements nouveaux). Eco-diversity is recovering, previously thought extinct species tentatively make a return, and Mercury and other heavy metal accumulation in the top of the food chain is diminishing.

On good days, the MaNaSmelter produces a small surplus of energy. Part of it is fed back into the grid, yet part of it is used for the sauna set up by Saaki Sami's team. After cleaning their minds and refreshing their bodies in the cleansing steam bath, Sami's people roll around in the snow, sky-clad and earth-bound. Is it psychosomatic, or are the winters slowly becoming colder?

—a coda of four kōans—

—*If the strength of a chain is determined by its weakest link, how can the chain of life stretch endlessly long?*—

—*If the survival of the fittest was the grand design behind Darwinian evolution, what's the strategy in the Anthropocene?*—

—*How is the karma of a people determined? How can you strengthen your own karma?*—

—*Is it wise to explore another environment while you do not fully understand your own? Is it wise to remain in your own environment forever?*—

The Gardener

~ Michael Barsa

Behold the famous horror writer: pale, thin, disheveled, hunched over the greasy steering wheel and driving much too fast. His wife sits next to him. Usually she is the competent one, the one who drives, but not tonight. Tonight he has insisted. Snow whips through the headlight beams. The flakes are thick and frenzied, a snow globe shaken by a lunatic. He can just see where the road disappears around a bend. A ravine hugs the bend—a frown of ragged rock-teeth—and because they're in the country there is no barrier, only a skirt of gravel and a sign showing a truck tilting off a cliff.

His wife shifts in her seat, stirred from her usual boredom. "John," she says, training her huge gilt-framed sunglasses on him. Those sunglasses are like machinery, like a retractable roof, except they never retract: she wears them at all hours. Even so he can tell what she's thinking: that he's driving like this to prove a point. That he, as an author, believes he can do anything—defy the laws of gravity, of velocity and friction and the lubricity of ice. That he'd only have to utter the word *fly* and he could make it so.

She is right. But it is no game. The sign whips past. He makes a halfhearted attempt to turn the wheel.

They fly.

It takes him a moment to realize they've left the road, left solid ground itself. He feels it in his stomach first—a suspension, a disbelief. The engine howls like an over-eager cowboy; his seat falls away. It really does feel like flying. Yet he knows that's . . . what? He searches for the word. An illusion. A farce. Just like everything else he's ever done. Sure, he's been a celebrated "novelist." He's been awarded Bram Stokers and Silver Daggers, interviews with Katie Couric and Charlie Rose. But in truth? He's a glorified hack.

"John?"

He turns the wheel easily now. It's like a toy, one that tilts and creaks and makes funny sounds if you press the right buttons. *Look at me! Whee!* Just then he notices a woman on the hood. *At least I'm not her,* he thinks. Then his mind backs up. Wait. *There's a woman on the hood.* It's true, she's sliding around, trying to hold on, and only after a few seconds does he see the bleeding stumps where her hands ought to be and her ruined mouth forming blood-bubble words: *Why? Why did you do this to me?*

Am I already dead? he wonders. No. It's just a hallucination. He blinks her away. Still he has a creeping suspicion he knows her. Then it comes to him. Her name was—is—and always will be—Valerie. She's the first victim from his very first novel, the one he cried over as if she were real, having to remind himself she was just words on the page as he *carved* and *delineated* and *punctuated* her poor imaginary flesh. What does she want with him now? What is she telling him? There's something important here, but his mind can't grasp it. Panic is setting in. His hands are bathed in sweat. At any moment he'll be like her: a fiction, a dream. Is she counseling him to finally face his demons, the ones he's buried under mounds of make-believe? The pastiche of lies he calls his past, and what his novels *really* cost him to write?

Too late now. Snow studs the windshield. Wind whistles through tiny gaps where the windows meet the frame. He sets the wheel straight again, as if not doing this has been his mistake all along. He digs his thumbs into its grooves, telling himself an engineer actually thought of their perfect placement while he himself has only ever caused pain. He thinks of his two children, Milo and Klara, how he's damaged them, used them as *characters* in his own dark genre. At least this will be their freedom as much as his, a final gift to them.

They fly.

He is light, he is snow, a dangling participle, a story gathering momentum, a narrative's rising arc. He is the God of this Volvo's universe, and like any God he's enamored of the possibility of escape. The moon! He wants to go to the moon. Right there, looming beyond the clouds, a hazy yet somehow proximate place, a lifeless lunar glow. "Almost there," he says out loud. But his wife can't hear. She is laughing. Lines ripple across her rough rouged cheeks. She looks like she does when scolding him, telling him to *buck up* and *be grateful you have a public who adores you. No, not me*, he always wanted to say, *my books*. But even at the time he wasn't sure there was a difference. Now he reaches out to her. It's meant to be a final consolation, a way to say he's sorry. She flinches, pulls away. Because they're not going up anymore. Nor are they landing on a moon-crater. It's the ravine rushing toward them, faster than he thinks possible. He considers the ironic subtleties of grammar: what a difference it makes to transpose a single consonant and make a slight vowel shift.

They fall.

He's a child again. His father has just tossed him high into the air. Only it's not a soft-focus hazy happy kind of toss. His father wears a scowl and a white dress shirt drenched in pee. Johnny has done a VERY NAUGHTY THING and now he's crying because he's just been hurled . . . No. He can change this. Re-write it. He can make his father jaunty and proud, like he ought to have been, can make him happy. *Why can't you write something happy instead of those awful horror books?*

He writes something happy. About falling into a young girl's arms. A redheaded Irish girl whose name he's long blocked from his mind. If only he can edit away the reason they met and why they had to love in secret, his British Army uniform and the terrible things he did to that girl's brother, which she could never know because then he'd have to . . .

Another flash. He's older now, holding Milo and Klara in his arms, telling himself he has a chance to do things right for a change, to break the cycle. It's a lovely summer's day. In America, the land of forgetting. A gust of wind rises up. Trees sway overhead, curious and dark. But he's keeping the darkness at bay with his proud smile, his loving arms, his bright white shirt and ruffled hair, his picture-perfect pose. *Don't move.* That's right. Freeze right there. Say *cheese*. A picture is worth . . . Stop.

The girl, the redhead. Her name was Blanaid. Meaning a *flower* or *blossom*.

Stop.

They're in his Army jeep, laughing. He punches the wheel. Suddenly the windshield explodes. He doesn't hear the bomb, but he knows what it must have been. He was so stupid to take her so far beyond the base. Now the jeep is on its side and her head is staved against the bolster and her smile's become a vacant unearthly bliss. Somehow he is alive. He begins to crawl away. There's a trail of blood on the pavement behind him. If only he can get to a phone . . . He stops to catch his breath. Best to slow down, observe what's happening. His blood is becoming absorbed into the ice. When the ice melts it will form a river to feed the hungry soil.

He snaps back to the present. The Volvo is a shattered wreck, a pointillist horror. Glass is everywhere, and he's lying facedown in the dirt, halfway out of the car. Snowflakes kiss his cheeks. Only one eye works. The other oozes down his cheek. Out of the corner of his good eye he glances back up, to the lip of the ravine. He sees headlights. The vague outline of a man peering down. A man with a checkered shirt, work boots, gloves, a shovel —a man he knows as well as his own children, a man who in a sense is his own child, too. Ever since seeing Valerie he's half-expected this. His own personal grim reaper. He's always loved the image of the reaper because that's what death is: the moment we turn from consumer to consumed—the moment we become food. Yet it's cold comfort now. He blinks. The man scuttles down the ice. Impossible with that sheer face, but he makes it look easy. *How?* he hears an old writing teacher say. *You've got to tell the reader how he can do the impossible.* But he can't. Suddenly he's scared, confused—this is all too real. Or is it? His brain screams *run*. He hears the thud of boots. The breathy pause. Just like he used to write it. He sees the shovel rise up like a stave, like an axe against the moon. The wind-whistle. *Let it come down.* It does. But not into him. Into the ice. Chips fly, glinting through the moon-reflected snow. The man quickly hits dirt. Hard as rock. He pries it loose, then begins tossing dirt onto him, onto the famous horror writer, whose one good eye quickly fills. It doesn't matter. With all the blood seeping in he can't see anyway, and doesn't have to, because he already knows what happens next.

Or so he thinks.

From the other side of the world he hears the man grunting, more soil scuttling across the shovel's blade. But on this side of the world he notices something else. A soft tickle in his ear. The intimate press of worm-flesh. He knows this isn't real, just a premonition of what's to come, yet he's still surprised. The man shovels more dirt on top of him. The writer hears water sloshing in a bucket. Soon it comes trickling between his legs. He's about to die three ways—drowning, suffocating, and bleeding to death—when he finally realizes what's going on.

A memory comes to him, of watching Milo play behind the house, digging with a plastic shovel while he, the writer, watched, as he often did, taking notes on this strange lost boy while half-hidden behind a tree. Milo wore shorts and tall socks with red bands around the top, and he worked with a diligence that some took as a sign of mental slowness. His thin back was bent like a question mark as he dug a perfect rectangle. Then he sat down next to it. He seemed to contemplate his work. He had four wooden dolls laid out on the grass beside him. The dolls wore old-fashioned clothes—a man and small boy in green suits, a woman and girl in frontier-style dresses. Milo picked each one up and whispered something to it before stroking its bristly hair. He then placed them face-down into the hole, side by side, and when he was finished he stood and took up the shovel again and began covering them with dirt.

That's when the writer emerged from behind the tree, notebook still in hand. "What are you doing, Milo?"

The boy didn't look back, just answered as if talking to an idiot: "Gardening."

The word comes back to him now as he pictures where he is, inside this giant ravine, this furrow in the snow. The man with the shovel and checkered shirt works carefully too, and the writer can feel the weight of the dirt atop him getting heavier, even as the water keeps trickling past. He tries to lift a hand. He can't. So he does the opposite, pushing down, his nearly dead weight pressing the snow, and to his surprise it gives way, there's a hole, he's punched clean through. Into what? He's heard glass shatter. He claws the air. He reaches deeper, up to his shoulder, feels the water trickle down his arm and drip from his fingers. He's grasping at something, anything, until he finds a curved plastic rod and pulls, hoping to escape that man yet, to yank himself down and miraculously out of harm's way, so he pulls until the rod rocks back and forth, and then he notices the grooves, which is his first sign that not everything is what it seems. Because it's not a rod at all. It's another steering wheel. There's a car beneath his own. It must have been buried lightly, on its side, at the bottom of the ravine. He lets go of the steering wheel. His arm swings back, into something delicate, something moist and soft and . . . Flowers? This surprises him more than anything he's encountered so far. How can flowers grow below ground? And in winter? For the moment he forgets his own pain, just thrusts his hand deeper into them, into their impossible caress, a last sensuous touch that nearly makes him cry, and that's when he comes upon the tangle of vines beneath the flowers. Trapped in the vines is something else, like a large silky tongue. He tugs. It doesn't come loose, it's wrapped around another thing, and when he slides his hand up it he can just feel the knot around the neck of it, and that's when he shudders, when he knows what this place is.

A garden.

And what his entire life has amounted to—what he's at last become.

A seed.

Dog Sitting

~ *Jon McGoran*

The dog lying at her feet let out a sad, heavy sigh and then the house returned to a silence marred only by the clock on the mantle. The dog's name was Bruce, after the shark in *Jaws*, but Frank only ever called it "The dog." It was the only thing Frank had left her, apart from the debts she'd discovered the day after he died, and a few bruises from the night before.

Frank used to brag about the dog, what a killer it was. "He could tear a grown man to shreds as easy as looking at him," he liked to say. She had always wondered why he needed such a big damn dog, other than that he liked to brag. Now she knew the real reason: The gambling. The drugs. The stealing. People had been after Frank.

But not anymore. A heart attack got to him before any of them could, and there was nothing the dog could do about that.

Frank had loved the dog, as improbable as that seemed. Or as close to love as he was capable. He loved it more than he loved her, that was for sure.

She should have left them both, back when she still had a chance. She could have made a life for herself. Not much of one, probably, but something. Something better than this.

The dog rolled onto its side, the big spiked collar scraping against the floor.

The room was getting dark again now, shadows seeping into the corners, pooling on the floor, like a leaky boat sinking into dark water. She could reach the lamp on the table, but she didn't dare. There was still enough light that she could see the dog's eyes looking up at her, watching, unreadable, never leaving her. They seemed to her more like the eyes of a reptile than man's best friend. But man's best friend it had been—Frank's partner in crime, literally.

The pins and needles in her feet had gone away hours earlier, and she'd made peace with the itchy spot on her arm that she didn't dare scratch. But the cramp in her leg was back, even worse than before. She flexed her foot just an inch to relieve it, rustling the damp fabric of the dress she'd been wearing since what had passed as a funeral the day before.

The dog showed its teeth again, giving her that hungry look and that low, throaty growl, the one that used to earn a clout from Frank and a stern, "Knock it off."

The dog had actually listened to Frank, too. But only him.

Now Frank was gone, and the dog was still here.

It was almost dark when the clock began to chime. It was eight o'clock. Well past feeding time.

Little Magic Girl

~ *Breanna Bright*

Filibaster Haberford had kidnapped Misha Stevonia fifty-eight times since she was eight years old.

The first time, he took her from her walk from school to have tea in his house. They sipped raspberry tea from cups painted with roses (that didn't look very much like roses at all) and ate chocolate macaroons. Filibaster asked Misha to stay in his home and marry him. She said no and left casually, ignoring his begging. She took a macaroon to go.

Filibaster took a different tactic and befriended her parents, who started inviting him to parties on their estate. The Stevonias had a large stone house surrounded by a handsome garden, and often hosted their friends in the summer time to enjoy the butterflies and various flowers.

They became very fond of Filibaster, for he was charming, told interesting stories, and wore funny clothes. He often arrived in pastel bowties, golden vests, or stylish hats, making jokes and regaling the other guests with tales of his travels. It became almost essential that he attend the congregations as he was as much a source of entertainment as the band.

But when Filibaster was done charming the adults, he would steal Misha out into the garden, somewhere private, and ask her again to marry him. She always said no, rolling her eyes and disappearing behind a hydrangea bush before he could grab her again.

Several times he simply carried her off, taking the young girl up in his arms or over his shoulder, snatching her as she walked to school in the morning, or played in the park. Misha remained indifferent to his attempts. She opened every locked door he put her behind, undid every knot he tied around her wrists, and made her way back home without so much as a wrinkle in her dress.

"Please marry me, Misha," Filibaster begged, on his knees in front of her as she did crafts in the play room. He had been invited for afternoon tea and had arrived early so that he could talk to Misha while her parents prepared the patio. "I would take good care of you, give you anything you desired. You wouldn't have to work a day in your life if you didn't want to. Why won't you marry me?"

"Because you don't love me," Misha answered calmly, folding her piece of paper into intricate patterns.

"But I do love you! I swear it!"

"You love me in a way a man loves a unique stamp or a purebred bitch. You want me in your collection to show me off. Your little magic girl." She had gleaned this much from Filibaster's character—all of the stories he told, all the magnificent things that filled his home were his collection to bring him attention, and he wanted her to be part of it. What would bring him more attention than a young, mysterious wife with the strange glint in her eye? Misha was of decent birth and decent beauty, with dark hair that rested in a long braid over her shoulder, plump cheeks, and brown eyes.

Before Filibaster could protest her observation, Misha made the paper crane she had folded fly into his face and poke him in the eye. Then her parents arrived and took him to the patio. As Filibaster drank tea and nursed his sore eye he began to formulate a new plan.

His captures became less frequent, but more in depth as he began to try new things to keep Misha in his home. He tried an enchanted lock on her room, traveled to Russia to find the magic bridle that contained the firebird, then wandered through the Middle East to locate the magic lamp.

The items he did manage to find did not work, either because they were fakes or because Misha was too powerful. Filibaster did not give up. During his travels Misha grew older and finer, spurring his desire even more. It was only partially about having Misha for his collection now, it became about winning against her. Wiping that look of indifference off her face and finally having the upper hand between them.

It was one of her parent's parties that led him to the answer. The Stevonias had been inviting more and more gentlemen to the parties lately, and Filibaster assumed it was because they were hoping Misha would meet someone.

One of the gentlemen in question was a traveler, his brown skin hardened by sun and mud, hair cut short and kept under a cap. He was tall and wide, but with a gentle demeanor. Filibaster was immediately drawn to the man, he wasn't above stealing another's adventure stories for himself.

The man's name was Bithiah—or just Bith—and he did indeed have stories to tell. But he kept his words locked tight in the chest of his mind. Filibaster took his crowbar to it.

"Tell me of your latest journey," he insisted.

"My trip here." Bith said.

"Did anything exciting happen?"

"What do you mean by 'exciting'?" Bith asked.

"You know—unusual, out of the ordinary, rare!"

"I saw a rainbow. It was lovely."

"I see."

"Sometimes exciting means different things to different people."

"Oh no, don't get me wrong, a rainbow is lovely. Where were you before you came here?"

"South America."

"And what were you doing there?"

"Sat on the beach, made chocolate, drank many fruity drinks."

"That sounds like a vacation."

"Mmhm."

"I see. Well I was in South America myself a few years ago. I was trying to find a puzzle box that could keep something inside of it, but it was for naught."

"What did you want to keep in the puzzle box?"

"Something very valuable—a pet. I have a rat, but the clever thing keeps escaping. I worry for it and have been trying to find a container to hold it."

"Hm, perhaps you need the birdcage."

"An ordinary birdcage will hardly do the trick."

"No—Queen Bethany's magic birdcage," Bith explained. He selected some shrimp from the buffet table and ate it delicately, letting it sit on his tongue for a moment before biting off the tail and chewing.

"I have not heard of this," Filibaster prompted him further.

"Saw it in a museum. Queen Bethany collected magical birds and constructed the cage so that they couldn't escape. Phoenix fire couldn't burn it, no beak or claw could break the bars, even the little hummingbird couldn't slip through the gaps. It was the cunning mockingbird that tricked her into letting him out—and pecked her eyes from her face."

"Wonderful. And you say this cage is in a museum now? Which one?"

Bith told him and gave him some advice on other sights to see while he was in the area. Filibaster ignored him. His eyes had found Misha in the party, and his attention was only on her.

Filibaster was nothing if not patient. He first did his own research on the birdcage, then took an extended trip to the museum, staying in town to stalk the building. The items inside the museum were not one's of monetary value, but a niche interests—things of folklore and fairy-tales that no one really believed in. This made it easy to break in and take the birdcage for himself, after leaving a substantial donation.

When he got it back home he had a new problem to solve. The birdcage was just that—meant for birds, but Filibaster was confident that he could find a way to fit Misha inside of it.

A few more weeks passed before he made another attempt to kidnap the girl.

He found Misha in the park by herself, sitting on a blanket and sketching butterflies that had swarmed the recently bloomed honeysuckles. She sipped tea from a small cup painted in morning glories.

Filibaster approached her and tipped his hat. "A fine morning, isn't it, miss Misha?"

"It was."

"I would like for you to come with me."

"No."

"Come now, darling, I'll wait for you to pack up your things, or I can take you myself and leave them here."

Misha turned to look at him, dark eyes narrowed and angry. She was almost of age and very much a woman with her long hair plaited over her shoulder and dress filled by her lovely curves.

"I am becoming very wary of you, Haberford," she practically growled at him.

He held out his hand to her.

"Don't touch me," she stood up and packed her bag, slipping the blanket and art supplies inside. She tossed the rest of her tea into the grass and tucked the cup away as well. Filibaster led her to his house while she walked behind him with the rigidness of a soldier.

When they arrived he opened the door and Misha stepped inside. Then the door shut.

Misha blinked and looked over her shoulder. The door was made of bars, and not wood. In fact, she was now completely surrounded by bars. A cage.

With a huff, Misha went to the cage door and grabbed the handle. It didn't open.

Misha frowned. No door had ever defied her. Every lock opened to her, no matter how elaborate. It was just something that happened.

But this door would not heed, no matter how she pulled or pushed. Instead she went to the bars and made to slide through, but they did not widen for her as past cages had. She pushed with all her might, but could only get an arm and a leg through.

For the first time in her life, she was trapped. Laughter echoed above her, and Misha looked up into the triumphant eyes of Filibaster. He danced giddily around the birdcage, seeing his little magic girl, now the size of a bird, unable to get free.

"I did it! Finally!" Filibaster picked up the cage. Misha fell over as it swung, and her dark eyes glared at him. Her gaze was sharp enough to make him wince.

"Don't be a spoiled sport, my dear, you'll be well cared for." In high spirits, he carried the cage upstairs and into his study, where he had a hook stand all prepared on his desk. He hung the cage there then sat down, smiling big. Misha grabbed the bars tightly in her tiny fists, face hard, as if trying to bend them with brute strength.

Filibaster only grinned. He turned on the radio and went to work taking care of some paperwork, every once in a while glancing up at his new charge, who continued to glare. When he finished he stood up and stretched.

"I'll be back shortly, darling. Dinner is at six, and I'll eat in here with you. It's so nice to have you in my home, and I know you'll like it here once you adjust."

Misha didn't answer, giving him the cold shoulder. Filibaster tapped the cage happily and practically skipped out of the room.

When he was gone, Misha collapsed, letting her composure break so that she could cry. She had never not been the one in control, and it was terrifying.

As promised, Filibaster returned at six o'clock with dinner. He ate at his desk and shared a portion with her. Misha only nibbled non-committedly, keeping her back to her capture. When he finished eating he gestured to her.

"Come here, Misha."

She ignored him.

In retaliation, Filibaster tilted the cage so that she had no choice but to slide across the floor until her back hit the bars. Filibaster grabbed her braid from between the bars and freed her hair. Misha tried to pull away, but he kept a firm grip and pulled her back like a dog on a leash. He took up a brush and combed her strands until they shined, then he plaited it back into a long braid that fell over her shoulder.

"Lovely," he said. His unwavering happiness made her sick. "I'm so pleased you're here. In fact I think we should celebrate; let's have a party, what do you think, dear?"

"You can invite my parents and perhaps the sight of their distraught faces will find your heart," Misha snapped.

Filibaster laughed. "No one can find my heart, dear. When my things break I throw them away." He grabbed the cage and spun it around so that she was forced to face him. "You'd do well to remember that."

He clapped and stood up. "We'll start planning tomorrow! It'll be so much fun!"

He grabbed the cage and they left the study, adjourning to his bedroom. He set her down on his nightstand and dressed in pajamas, slipping a small blanket through the bars for Misha to use. She wrapped it around herself like a cloak and pressed herself against the farthest 'wall' of the magical cage away from Filibaster's bed. He looked in at her fondly, seeming relieved, like an addict finally getting a hit.

"I hope I can let you out someday, I'd love to hold you, my precious little thing." He blew her a kiss, then the lights went out and he sank into his bed in slumber.

Misha did not sleep. She spent the entire night pressing herself against the gaps in the bars, pushing as hard as she could. She tried each one, looking for a weak point, but couldn't even press her head through. After she made two rounds she tried the door, tugging, pushing, and playing with the lock, but it did not give into her.

In the morning her face was covered in red marks, her hands had blisters, and shadows hovered under her eyes. She stared at Filibaster like a haunted woman, but he only seemed more pleased. He brought her breakfast, and after that Misha slept. It was the only way to escape him.

He woke her throughout the day, offering her tiny dresses and cooing over the whole affair. Misha put them on because if she didn't he shook the cage or blasted loud noises next to her. He at least gave her privacy, not seeming to care about her nudity. In the afternoon he took her into the garden and had a tea party, feeding her tea in a thimble and cutting small pieces of cake. At night they were in his study. Filibaster planned for his party, running ideas past her for which she gave no opinion.

Before bed he insisted on combing and braiding her hair.

This was how the days repeated themselves. Misha kept track in her head. She slept as much as she could during the day, and tried escaping at night, but even that soon fell through as she found herself falling asleep at random hours. She tried to eat and keep her strength up, but her stomach ached.

She had been pampered and cared for her whole life. Able to protect herself. The stress of this was unbearable. She sang to keep up her spirits. She screamed in the middle of the night to wake up Filibaster. That kept up her spirits too.

"You're a pus-filled, rotting sore of maggots," She growled at him one night after waking him up with a lot of noise. "A twisted, swollen testicle falling off its host from lack of blood."

He finally grew tired of it. He took her blanket away and put her in the basement where it was cold. She didn't care. Anything was better than his presence.

She sang and made friends with the mice and crickets that lived down there, even sneaking them some cake from tea time one night. They brought her wires so that she could try picking the lock, but that did not work either. She taught them how to avoid the mouse traps, and they wreaked havoc on the house for her, causing plenty of distress for Filibaster and his housemaid. They hid food in the walls, creating mold and terrible smells that he couldn't locate. They chewed wires, and knocked over breakable items.

The mice sent the message to the racoons, who spoiled his yard, and the racoons told the crows, who relieved themselves in the most inconvenient places—such as his bike seat and patio swing.

As long as Misha remained in the cage, there was a curse on his life.

Filibaster retaliated, of course. He withheld meals, put her in the ice box, and turned the cage upside down so that she couldn't rest comfortably. Misha tried to stay strong, but her spirit was breaking.

She wanted to go home. Eventually her songs stopped. Her tears stopped. She slept and let him braid her hair. He hummed to himself, a man close to victory.

"Such a good girl, I knew you'd come around," He said cheerfully.

Something in Misha's heart went creeeek and she bit the finger that played with her hair. Her tiny teeth sank into his flesh, and she tasted blood. Filibaster screamed and tried to shake her off, but she didn't relent. He got himself together long enough to flick her in the head, and she was thrown off, a sizable bruise appearing on her forehead.

He glared at her, and she smiled for the first time in fifty-four days, glad to finally quell his cheerful attitude.

Her spirit braced against that which wished to destroy it, and she slept well that night.

The party came.

Filibaster dressed in a flamboyant suit that glittered in the lamplight. Misha was given a ballgown, not that she would be attending, he just wanted her to dress the part. She was left in the study, barely able to hear the affair downstairs.

It was a gorgeous party, and a large crowd was in attendance. Everyone envied an invitation to one of Filibaster Haberford's celebrations, and he had been generous with his guest list.

Flutes of champagne were served, the ceiling was filled with glittering balloons, and everyone was dressed extravagantly in colorful, shining clothes.

All but one.

Bithiah was in plain clothes, a simple black jacket and slacks that strained against his sturdy frame. Filibaster sought him out excitedly.

"Bith! I'm so glad you made it, this party is really for you."

"Why's that?" The man asked, holding a tiny sandwich between two fingers.

"The advice you gave me, about the birdcage? It worked!"

"For your pet rat?"

"Oh, yes, I guess so."

"This is a party for your pet?"

"What can I say? I'll take any occasion for debauchery."

Filibaster grinned, and Bith decided he no longer wanted to be in the man's presence.

"Where's your bathroom?"

"Up the stairs, second door on the left."

Bith didn't retain the information. He was a terrible listener, his mind often trailing off to other things no matter how hard he tried to concentrate. He went upstairs knowing he would find the bathroom eventually.

Instead he found the study, where a tiny girl in a birdcage sat in an extravagant dress. She looked at him when he opened the door, dark eyes filled with sadness.

Bith blinked in surprise.

"Sir, would you mind opening the door of this cage, please?"

Bith stepped into the room and took the little door between his fingers, easily lifting the lock and pulling it open. Misha stood and stepped forward. Bith held out his hand to her, she took it, placing her tiny hand on the pad of his index finger and he helped her step out of the cage and onto the desk.

Then she was her normal size, sitting on top of the desk with her feet dangling, the dress shining all around her. She heaved a deep sigh and set her feet on the ground.

"Thank you, sir."

"Don't thank me. I believe I'm the cause of your imprisonment," Bith said, looking down at his feet.

"Did you give Filibaster the cage?"

"No, but I told him of its existence. He said he needed it for a pet that kept escaping."

"I am the pet," Misha said, "it's the only thing that was able to contain me."

"I am sorry. May I escort you home?"

"Thank you, yes."

Misha took his arm, having to reach up to grab his elbow. Bith led her out of the room and down the stairs where they accidentally made a grand entrance.

Everyone turned and stared at the lovely girl in the extraordinary dress, conversation going quiet. When Misha's eyes landed on Filibaster all her pain came out to meet him. The food rotted on the serving trays, the music went sour as the violin strings popped. The balloons deflated, smiles fell, and the very atmosphere of the room darkened.

Filibaster looked defeated and bewildered, which made Misha's heart swell. She smiled so coldly that a draft went through the room, making everyone shiver. Filibaster's fingers turned blue.

She and Bith walked downstairs and the crowd parted for them. She walked right up to Filibaster, who's hair began to stand on end, like there was static electricity in the air.

"Nice try," she said. Then they left.

In the garden the flowers wilted and died, and back at the house they could hear the guests starting to scream. It sounded like the mice had joined the party.

Bith walked her home, and a trail of her dress accessories were left behind in the street. The sashes, glitter, bows, and straps were shed until the dress came to her liking, simple and comfortable.

"Bith," Misha said as they reached the door of her home. "I wonder if you might be interested in going on a trip with me."

"I don't think that would be appropriate, ma'am."

"I say that it is. I say that since you gave Filibaster the existence of the birdcage, then you owe me. I have not been beyond this town and I would like a guide on this trip I have in mind."

"Where would you like to go?"

"To where broken things are thrown away."

"And where is that?"

"I don't know, but will find out."

Bith bid her goodnight, promising to stay in town until he had word from her. Misha went inside, happy to be home once again. Her parents greeted her with aching hearts that could finally heal. She told them what had happened and they agreed to bring in the police to take Filibaster Haberford away. Her father took care of that while her mother doted on her and put her to bed. Misha was happy for the attention.

She spent the next few days relishing it before announcing her plans to travel. She softened the blow assuring them that it would be a short trip and that she needed the freedom after so long in captivity.

Misha paid a visit to Bith in his hotel and they made plans for their departure. Bith seemed shy about the whole affair, offering only small suggestions when she prompted.

"How will you find this place?"

"By wanting to know."

They departed by boat, which Bith was not a fan of. He preferred to drive on his exhibitions, but the place they were going was across water, so he steeled himself for Misha's sake.

The trip, he found gratefully, was smooth. Whenever storm clouds appeared, Misha would glare at them and they would scamper the other way. If the water became too choppy she tapped her foot and it became as still as a lake.

One day, the worst of the worst, pirates boarded their ship.

Bith was usually able to hold his own in a fight, but they were out-numbered, and he had a young lady to look after. The young lady, however was not having it.

When they tied her wrists together she simply tossed the rope aside and started making her way across the deck. The pirates came after her. One slipped on a puddle, another tripped on an upturned nail, and the third, upon getting a glance from Misha, broke his glass-es—both lenses cracking enough to disorient him.

Bith took the fourth one for himself, then attacked the others, making sure that they stayed down. In the meantime, Misha reached the railing and untied the pirate's boat from theirs. The pirates became occupied in getting their boat back, jumping overboard and swimming for it.

Bith untied the captain and the rest of the crew, and they made a quick escape.

"How is it that these things work out for you?" Bith asked Misha. They stood on the deck, watching the horizon turn to land.

"I'm not sure," Misha admitted, "it has always been this way."

When they docked Misha and Bith departed, finding local transpor-tation as far inland as they could until the roads ended and they were forced to continue on foot. They booked a room at an inn where Misha changed into comfortable clothes and thick shoes. Bith looked for information since the girl didn't actually know where they were going. He spoke to the bartender in the inn's restaurant about a place where things that were thrown away might go.

At first the bartender gave him directions to the local dump, but after some more pressing, began telling a story.

"People throw their secrets in the volcano," the tender said, "it's an old legend that started when the local mafia took over the town. Anything they threw into the volcano was never found, so others started to use it as well, throwing away the things they never wanted to see again."

Bith passed this information on to Misha, and they hired a guide to take them to the volcano. Their guide was sure-footed and fit, and had a quick wit. She and Misha became fast friends, and Bith was happy to let them lead the way while he walked behind, handling the supplies.

The climb became steep and rough the further they went. The guide took the lead, calling to them on which rocks to use and what to avoid. The supplies were eventually abandoned as they were practically climbing a vertical wall. The rocks became warm beneath their hands, and all plant life disappeared.

They finally crested the lip of the volcano's crater, peering down into the maw of hardened lava. To get down, Misha and the guide lowered themselves with rope held by Bith. The girls walked themselves carefully down the wall of rock. At the bottom Misha asked the guide to stay back and wait. Bith watched from his high vantage point as Misha walked to the center of the crater, ash kicked up under her boots. She looked around briefly before going to her knees and plunging her fist into the solid rock. She pushed down up to her elbow, rummaging beneath the warm crust, and came up with something clutched tightly in her fist.

She raised it above her head in victory and cast a smirk up to Bith.

In her hand was a grayed, beating heart.

Filibaster Haberford was not having a good week.

He had gone to jail, removed himself with bail, and became ostracized by the community thanks to the Stevonias. His housekeeper had quit, so his home was still in shambles when he returned to it, leaving him with the responsibility of cleaning. He attempted to wipe up spoiled cake and spilt champagne while wearing his least favorite suit (the red one with a tail coat that he had bought for a Halloween party—he had worn horns and attended as a devil) as he had no casual or work clothing.

And now Misha was at his door.

She had disappeared for the not-so-good week, and Filibaster assumed that she had finally run away, but there she stood, still in travel clothes with Bith standing behind her, so large that if anyone walked by they wouldn't see the smaller woman he shielded.

"Mr. Haberford," she said curtly, pulling something out from her satchel, "you've gone for too long without your own internal anguish, allow me to return something that belongs to you."

She shoved the heart against his chest, and Filibaster gasped as he was filled with a harsh pain. Not the sort that could be cured with pills or heat packs, but the deep, unrelenting kind. All the guilt and self-hate that resided in his broken heart was returned, and it brought him to his knees, in a quivering, sobbing puddle.

Misha turned away, turning on her heel smartly. "Where shall we go next, Bith? The last trip was rather rushed and had the semblance of an errand. I'm craving something more." They walked down the street back to her parent's home.

"Asia is nice this time of year," Bith said noncommittally.

"I wish for you to come with me, I enjoyed your company."

"Very well," Bith agreed. He enjoyed travel, and it was nice to have someone else pay for it.

"Do you think our volcano guide could be persuaded to join us? She was very pretty and funny."

"I'm sure she will, if it is what you desire. It seems to work out that way."

Misha smiled with a smug satisfaction. "Yes, it does, doesn't it?" Grin unrelenting, she lengthened her stride and hummed a pretty tune.

Landfall

~ Stephen O'Donnell

We were six hours rowin for shore and the current against us the whole time. Near shot from the effort. The bastard wind. And the houses along the shore shootin up smoke, burnin wild. Looked like the shores of hell. And the tanker already aground behind us, threatenin to bust her bows with every wave until finally she went with a less'n a groan in the final swell. We rowed on. The freezin spray and the skin of us windbitten, slaked raw by the brine and that fuckin knifewind. Laong wept when he set foot in that black sand. I near wept mysel. I had already given up, she said. Out there.

The station man nodded, said nothing.

So you'll see now that I hafta. She drained the cold dregs in her mug. She was sat naked and shivering before the muted glowing of the grate.

And is that where yous're going?

It is.

The station man stopped wringing the rag and shook his head. There's no turnin yous?

No, she said. There's an fuckin awful smell of it in here. Have ye a bad room?

Here? He shook his head. Don't even say that for a joke.

Well.

There's no fucking bad rooms in this place. The whole townlands has been gone over. Twice.

It's the smell of them, she said. In me mind. With the steam still rising from her she started to put back on the layers of her wet suit, checking the seals and diodes.

Don't use any main roads, the station man said.

Isn't it me own country?

No. Do you not see what they've done to the town?

I seen the fires.

Didn't that open your eyes?

To what?

If you don't fuckin know yet, I can't tell you. He slapped the rag into the filthy basin and turned and looked at her under the grimy kitchen light. You're a stranger to these, people. They are strangers to themselves. Heed me now. Keep to them backroads. The bog and the heather. Slice the hand of any that reach for you. It'll be upon you quicker than you think. Do you mind me?

I mind you, she said.

Would that you did. And fear them that approach you most of all. Open your eyes or have them rent open.

What is this? Who will go agin me out there?

You don't listen Aoiph. Everyone. Everyone. Just go if you're goin. That rain wont lift.

☉

They left before dawn with the light and unending rain all before them. She waited for Laong under the twisted remains of the viaduct. The country to the north sank and reappeared above the rain. She heard him squelching up the filthy alleyway to where she stood muddied to the hip, leaning against the stone archway.

Nary a fucking horses? Ye go the livery?

I went t'livery, yeah.

And he didn't have ary the one nag for sale? Aoipher spat into the mud. A delicate white line amid the black sludge. I'da took one between us.

Livery feller warn't there. They'd kilt'n eaten alla horses.

Mother of fuck.

Place's fulla bones. They had a fuckin donkey's arse hanging there, swinging in the breeze, and they was just carving strips off it when I walked in.

Have yer sling about ye?

Always.

Aoipher spat again. Lets hoof it then, she said. Don't trust ary the one of these bastards.

They set out into the dark of the day. A world of mud and sucking filth and the sparse trees and the grey sky the only break from the filth.

⊙

They climbed up out of the coastal flats and across the spongey treading of the bog road.

So many crows. Ever tree filled with the mockin bastards.

T'were never so bad before.

At a turnroad they saw the carcasses of a half dozen swans. The eyes eaten away. The innards burst, stomped to leather. Laong climbed the embankment and studied the dead birds. Aoiph, he said. The bastards've pressed this far.

Aoipher chewed a root and watched the smoke from a hut across the bog. No surprise. They'll be in every hole that's hidin a warm body from here on up.

Laong jumped back down into the wet mud. We make the croppings before dark?

This mud going? Chh. She spat the root into the dirt and then flattened it with her boot.

Well it aint no stroll Aoiphe. Ye wanna head back?

Quit usin my fuckin name out loud. Be bad if one of them get's aholt it.

Well, like I ast, what ye wanna do?

Aoipher trod on. There's the lesser ones, before the river. Won't be comfor'ble. Better'n going back, waitin for word to catch us up. After the word comes the doin.

⊙

They moved on, Aoipher pushing her steps and the other meeting them without either speaking a word.

The road wound down into a dell and there were the beginnings of hedges and fallow fields. At a crest closest the village they paused, watching the small thatched cottages lit like pumpkins, the light faint and pulsing in the windowsquares. The day was failing.

Round, through the woods. Poachin man might hesitate to raise us.

Think we'd be stopped?

Fuckin sure, she said. Murdur ye fer the steel alone.

And them others, they might be about already?

Don't doubt that, Aoipher said. Not fer a second.

I'll chance the timber with ye.

They moved from the mud of the road and crept slowly among the stands of ash. Pausing in the mist like skittish deer. They kept the village to their bladesides as they moved in the falling darkness, under deadfall and over streambed, filthy and wet through by the time they gained again the common mire of the road. A hare ran screaming across the trail as they stepped into the mud. As it disappeared into the bracken a meteor broke the night air in a silent white shear.

No, Laong said. No.

Shurrup. Aoipher said. No time t'go slack. Get on. I know them lessers start soonabouts.

And they hurried up the road, away from the village.

Laong saw it first and gave a low shripes' whistle.

Twill hardly fit the hams of us, he said. But tis somethin glad all the same.

Aoipher pushed him in the shoulder. Get on, yer workbits.

When Laong had laid the patterns and uttered as he was bid, he climbed into the small concrete envelopment and stood chin to chin with Aoipher.

This is the night, Aoipher said.

A night it is, Laong said and he set out his elbows so that he might sleep standing.

Hares and shooting stars. Omens of the age.

☉

In the morning she woke to Laong watching her and watching the marshlands.

Ye can look till yer eyes are burnt, Aoiphe said.

No sign of 'em trackin us.

They're not given to leavin sign.

Sun's up I reckon, Laong said. They couldn't get at us.

There'll be dead down the village then.

We chance the road?

Aye, Aoipher said and she shunted him toward the entrance and then she followed him, gathering their webbing as she went.

○

They moved along a narrow causeway. Sparse timber grew along the edge of the bog, drowned in ivy.

Alla birds is crow or rook. Not much of ary other in the trees. Reckon aught of the aviary made it ashore?

No, Aoipher said. I don't.

D'ya reckon any t'others made land?

Aoipher hiked on until she had to stop to catch her breath. Them, she said as she panted. Them I hopes drowned.

Magpies cackled somewhere down the ships corridors of her dreaming.

Do yeh think it has gotten hold of us yet?

Aoiphe shrugged. It don't come on fast. Until it does.

We're fuckin trapped, Laong said.

Details, she said. Details.

What?

Trapped and headin inta madness. What were the t'other choice? Sit with t'station man? Hope not to get rumbled, hopin someone hears the broadcast? That's only n'other type of fuckin madness.

It were them we heard, last night. Werent it?

Aye, Aoipher said. I thinkwise I did. Now take aholt of yerself. We've another week at this if that last reckonin aboard was right.

Whar if it wasn't? Whar if it were out?

I said take a fuckin hold of yer tongue. Hear me?

I'm hearin yeh.

We'll see how we fare. Day at a time. Recite t'me the landmarks. As they stood.

The shore. The beacon. The picking point. The decycle.

An then all the normal fuckin madness, Aoipher said.

Laong waved a hand at her. Don't talk namore bout madness.

Fine, Aoiphe said. Just ye recite that to yoursel the next time ye feel like gettin goin.

○

The night found them inside an uncropped tier, large enough to sleep twenty men. They had to slice through a tight thicket of ivy to crawl inside.

A fire I reckon.

Aye, Aoipher said. Go on about yer ablutions. I'll fetch kindling.

Whar about the light?

It's nor a risk yet. Get about yer workins.

Laong dropped to his knees and twisted the nozzle below his collar. Aoipher climbed back into the crawl way, cursing against the grating of her suit in the darkness there.

Laong was almost finished and was turning water when he heard a sound in the crawlspace behind him.

A child led an immense man in a tin helmet into the room. They both paused when they saw Laong watching them.

Where'n, Laong said. Where'd ye come from?

The child, caked in mud, grinned. There is a crowd of them, the child said.

Whar?

A crowd. Yon next rise. And they are comin for ye both.

Laong looked at the man. Closed eyes and a closed mouth had been painted upon his helmet. Y'take off that bucket to see?

They know you are here, the child said. They know why you have come. Listen. They are taking your Aoiphe now.

Who told y'such things child? Laong said. Yer lummox does not bare a tongue?

Your iron boat. Landings are forbade. Any from the sea are to be drowned. Any from the sky to be burned.

This, this child speaks for you brute?

The painted eyes opened on the helmet and blinked once. A stream of breath snorted from the mouth.

Listen, the child said, pointing into the darkness behind Laong. Listen and you will hear.

Laong turned and screamed at what he saw.

☉

Aoipher heard Laong's scream. She cast the sods from her bad hand while the other cleared the rags from about the hilt of her steel as she moved quickly, staggering down from the bank into the road, stumbling, cursing the mud. She started fast up the trail.

☉

In the fray he lost sight of Aoipher. They dragged him off, chanting the whole while.

He did not know where he was, only that it was dark and there was a whutting sound like falling gobs of burning candle grease. He remembered. He remembered and knew from remembering. It was human fat they burnt. He remembered. *Fear their darkened rooms most of all.* He tried to move but his body shot with a cold pain that held him rooted. He could hear something stirring in the darkness beside him, where he could not see. He struggled to cry out but his jaw only trembled and refused to move. Only his eyes moved. He could see now what it was beside him and a strangled groan came from his rooted throat. He felt it seize him and he shrank from the teeth and the stench. His flesh burnt and finally his jaw sprang loose and he howled.

Getta fuckway from me. No, he hissed and he tried to move his arms but they were as stone. No no no no no. Tears streamed from his eyes and pooled ice cold in the back of his mask.

Laong ye stupid cunt, the dark thing said.

What, whatta fuck're yeh?

Laong you silly fucking cunt. It's me you fuck. The ablutions. Did ye finish the ablutions? Laong, it's important. The daemon lifted him and shook him hard. He shrank inside his mask at the face there, the face of Aoipher with a thousand teeth and the eyes that were not her own, eyes that burnt black fire.

No, Laong screamed and then he rose upwards into blackness.

☉

He woke lying on his side on the tier cement. Aoipher with her back to him, squatted on her haunches before a dying fire. All was pitch-dark beyond the flames.

He sat upright painfully and shuffled closer to the fire.

Is it you Aoiphe?

Last time I lookt.

I dreamt, dreamt they took ye. Yeh tolt me they took ye.

Aoipher turned to look at him now. Speak it.

I dreamt we was kept in the dark together. And yeh told me they took ye.

The dream, what'd I say?

I can't remember.

Think.

How? How are you here? I seent them tear ye away, I had ye fixed for their fire. I saw yer face by the black light.

Tell it, Aoipher said.

You lookt kilt. *Yer face bloodied and the remains of yer great cloak in a rag about yer neck.*

Kilt, I said, you look kilt.

Those cunts, yeh said and then yeh spat onna floor. I aint near kilt. Not by that buncha, they had their hands about me and but I stuck two of em. Hard, inna chest.

And as you said it I heard the knife. The wound gurgling. The air loosed from some inner cavity.

Yeh grinned and said, Anat took some of the steam of t'others but they kept after me but at a distance now though I yet struck any I could reach, alla time backing down for the riverwaters I could hear some-place behind me in the darkness, slashing and stabbing and spitting at 'em and I only knew that if I made that fuckin water I'd be alright even though they'd stuck me, maybe twice.

I ast yeh, I said, did they bleed ye?

Aye, yeh said and yeh spat again, into the blackfire this time. Stung me a time or two in the dance of it. Such are the goings of a crater such as I, s'what yeh said and yeh laughed anat was a terrible laugh like it were inside my skull. Ye said: I will be dead before I'm taken blind by a posse of such calibre and you turned your face all wounded for me to see and I saw and and and and that's whar I remember, Laong said.

Wake up, Aoipher said and she threw a pebble at him.

I am, I am, I think.

Y'are now. Whatta the faces of the crowd? Aoipher said.

Nothing, faces. Faces with nothing left. They had great long haunched dogs all among them.

Hounds?

Aye, Laong said.

Had they markings?

Laong shook his head. Not that I'd see.

Dogs, Aoiphe said. Wild dogs. She shook her head. I aint a diviner. But that don't lie easy on me fuckin mind.

Throw on some more peat, Laong said. Please, I dreamt they was all amidst these woods.

They likely are.

Build it up Aoiphe. Please. I don't want one of them, them dogs to get any closer.

I aint heard naught, Aoiphe said. She picked up several small logs all the same and placed them on the bed of coals. The darkness receded. Fuck em. Let em come up again, purrit out with their own feet.

How do I know this is real?

Aoiphe shrugged. It's real. You been drivelling quite a time.

Laong snatched out a hand for the other's blade, touching the hilt.

Loosen it or swally the bitin end, Aoipher said. Be worse'n ary fuckin dream ye had.

Laong let his fingers fall and sat back. Aoipher dropped some peat to the flames now, pressed the twigs down and watched sparks crack and rise. Then she turned and looked at Laong.

It were more'n sleep then, Aoiphe said.

What?

They stopp yer ears?

Laong shifted on the ground slightly, slowly. He sneered with the effort.

Yer whalloped?

Feels so, Laong said. Is this its beginning?

Aoipher shook her head, and turned from the fire to the darkness. I don't know. Talkin bout it inna middle of the night won't do no good.

Are ye scairt?

You'd be too, y'had any fuckin sense.

When you had it. That first time, what were it like?

Aoiphe watched the fire a long time. No, she said. I won talk about it. Not after dark.

☉

At the first grey light that did not seem to grow any brighter Aoipher was shuffling about, a strange fire in her blood.

Laong watched her from his bedroll. Should we plan t'way some more?

No, she said, blinking as she grubbed sleep from her eye. We just get foot under road. Kick out that fire, gather what pieces're left ye.

Goin agin? Shouldn't I rest some?

No. I aint havin m'throat cut be no halfwit baker boy. Today, I'm goin and goin. We're too slow. The muck out there. Aoipher said and then she stood over the fire and spat phlegm into the ashes.

☉

They moved over a series of low cliffsides, thick with briarforest and the waves constant against the cliffside in a sound that shook in their lungs.

Are ye moulting? Yer rancid.

Laong didn't answer. He stared at the black mud as they walked. The mud pulsed slightly, slowly, as if the earth were possessed of some latent bloodpulse. He could feel it in his suitsoles when the soil rose and sank. He looked up at the treeline and shook his head and then he looked at the mud again. The mud began to coil and sluice in strange cords, separating and rejoining.

Wharssat?

Aoiphe looked at where he was pointing. Hah?

The mud. It's the fuckin mud.

Mud an' shit's all I've seen since we come aground. I hate this fuckin trail and ever cunt upon it.

Later black rot worms rose from the churning mud. Laong stepped upon them viciously and their blood ran black as any man's.

Worms, he said. Them're fucking bloodworms.

What?

Fucking worms and serpents, he said. For they were now a cold writhing mass of snakeheads, curling in a silent mulch about his boot, covering the ground before him. He drew his dagger and held it unsteadily. A dark flame burned along the blade's edge. He waved it before him. It left faint trails in the air.

Y'see it?

Wha? Are yeh fuckin senseless?

Black fire, Laong said. D'ya see it? How the steel burns. See? He swung the dagger in small vicious circles.

The balms, Aoiphe said. Quickly. Have ye the last of ye balms? Where've yeh them hid, she said as she clutched hold of Laong. Where?

Whar?

Aoiphe pulled at Laong's capsule pockets. Idjit, we're done for.

I have buried them in darkness.

Aoiphe slapped him. Fuckin listen to me. Speak fuckin sense. Nightfall, the bastards in the woods. Remember, she said and she slapped him again. The landmarks. Remember t'fuck.

I, what, Aoiphe what've yeh aholt of me fir?

The parcels, the blutions.

Yea, they're, they' someplace, here. Here. Me heartpocket.

Fill em. Fill em.

Oh, Laong said. We need water for that. Mineral mechanisms're part spent.

Wha? Spent? Why'n fuck didn't ye say this morn? Fuck. She studied the treeline before them. I seent common road again, a while back. There were some thatch.

Kin we risk it?

We've no fuckin choice, Aoipher said. Won't never make it with spent balms.

You said not tay panic.

Come on ta fuck, who sez I am? Step quickly, we kin repluck our way, unfuck oursels, find their well, or a stream maybe.

☉

They came up through a cut in the backwoods and could see the thatch roof huge among the maples.

The trough, Aoipher said. Mark it? Near covered over, see the smooth stone of it?

Kin we risk it?

No choice now. Get tay it.

Laong hurried from the brush and stooped to rewater with the nozzle in his hand. Aoipher kept watch of the inn door. Two mules were tied to a sunked post. Voices from an upper room, drunken giggling. When Aoipher looked back Laong was drinking ravenously from cupped hands, leering at his own grimy face as he swallowed in huge, sucking gulps.

Wharra fuck are ye doing, Aoipher hissed. Fill yer balmcups.

Whattad ye know bout it? Laong filled his dipper cups and struggled with them back into the shelter of the timber.

Willit take long?

Laong shook his head. Leave me mix what needs mixin.

Aoipher stood on a rock and watched the door of an inn.

She saw the door open and a man emerge at a run, grabbing at the hitches of his trousers as he waddled toward them.

Gucka fuggin pishh, the man gasped. Fugg.

Aoipher crouched down.

What is it?

Be still, she said. Say naught, locals.

The man came into the copse, pissing as he walked, laughing at the steam havoc he created upon the dead leaves, his eyes like nacre. His stream dried to a trickle that stained his filthy pants as he saw them crouched like upended hatchlings.

The man grinned down at them. Maken pudden?

Aoipher stood, wiping her hand along herself and nodding at the man.

Together, srrange. Dressed for paegent? Assa good getup. Assa gud wan. Shrink?

Laong looked at Aoipher. Whars he say?

Aoipher raised a hand behind her back. Shrink'd be kindly, she said and she made a shape in the air with her other hand.

The man looked down at Laong and rubbed his head. That ya goslin?

Aye, aye.

The man shrugged again and pushed his penis back into his pants. Mon that shrink so, he said and turned back for the inn.

Wharre yah doin?

Say naught, Aoipher said and she walked after the man toward the inn. Foller me lead.

Just fuckin drop im.

Say fucking naught. He'd have a posse on us, we refuse. C'mon.

They stepped through the doorway and into the greasy light of the inn.

Ese're bound a'paegent. Coming a con a shrink from me, the man said and he laughed.

Two forms in rags at a huge hearth nodded and then turned away the newcomers. The man led them to a bench and waved them to sit. He pushed two crudely hollowed pieces of wood toward them. From the floor he lifted a flagon and unstoppered it and filled their wooden mugs.

Shrink, shrink, shrink, the man said. He watched them regard the liquid. Then Aoipher took the cup and drank quickly. She looked at Laong.

Gettit over weh, Aoipher said.

Laong took it and sipped quickly and then he sat back in the chair shaking.

☉

What is it you mudsliders are come about?

Come about? Hear this cur bark?

It's nay from the like of ye I'll low such talk.

Step to with steel so, Aoipher shouted and she had her own drawn and red in the firelight.

Laong pressed his arm across Aoipher's shoulder. Not in here. Y'see him but ye don't see the others behind'm, watchin ye. He pulled Aoiphe backwards to the bench. Sit. Take s'more. Puttat fuckin steel 'way. He lifted a mug to the other table. Sit or they'll stamp the wind from yeh.

☉

They came staggering from the hedge in the slow grey light of dawn.

Aoipher pushed the other. Y'stink, she said. Ye need dunking.

Get on pissbody.

Foul, Aoipher said. Even for a roadgoer. Get a dunk or lop off me nose.

I'll lop it easy, the other said and he tripped and fell flat in the mud.

We should nort have drunk 'at water.

Nor stayed inna keepers bed.

I slept in nay bed.

Pah. A skeet of spittle shot from between Laong's bucked teeth. I'd do that twice agin for half of naught. Dirty aul cunt, all I wanted was something to rub up against.

Y'blistered bastard. Have ye, well have ye yer edged edge about ye at least?

Awluss. Awluss. Man says theys a fair up these roads someplace.

Wha man? Station man?

Whar? Naw, Laong said. Naw. Inn feller. So he says as I were lacing mysel up. Him lying pink and raw. Only talk truth whenat they's leeched raw.

Aoipher stopped suddenly and turned to look at the empty road behind them. *She heard a voice call her name over her shoulder, birdsong in a twisting tunnel, roaring silent through the black void far from any soil and the voice calling remember remember remember from the twisting darkness.*

See sommat? Deer?

I thought, she said. A name? Maybe? Naw, she said and she hiccupped and fell laughing to her knees. I'm hearing voices. She began to laugh and then she began to weep. I'm hearing fucking voices.

Laong pulled her by the arm. It's the grog. Brainrot. Gerrup. Mon. S'more'll see ye right, he said and then he staggered away from the road and into the briars to piss.

Laong, staggering back to the mud, wiping mud upon himself. Feller said watch out for 'em ditchsnakes.

Feller?

Taverner fella. He'll be a few coin short.

Aoipher took up step beside Laong. Ye loosened his load?

Never in a dell. He shook his finger solemnly. He'll only be walking gammy a time. Won't be no poorer.

He might be met yet.

He might. The roads are wild things, filled with madmen, Loang said and he began to cough. Who's to say the misfortunes as a man might meet?

They stumbled on, down toward the carnivalgrounds. Through the trees they could see the bonfire, huge and roaring, now vesper green, now a crackling blue. Aoipher tottered at the edge of the treeline and stood watching. She saw the ones who were gathered, saw their faces were as the faces of lizards and their feet were shod as the feet of bulls and all around the flames they murmured together in low whispers like the whispered workings of maggots and now they had all turned to watch her and she knew it was her name they were whispering.

Wasn't there somethin we was, Aoipher hissed, clutching wildly at Laong. A boat?

About? A bout whar? Boot fer a foot? Or a shoe fer a pony? Laong giggled. Wasn't naught we had to do but get on to yon fairground. Theys all waiting on us.

A Novelty of Stars

~ Brandon Crilly

He examines a polished wooden counter topped with cardstock. "Lobby cards," the outdated monitor at the front desk called them. Each black-and-white image is framed in either darkened blue, red or gold. No labels to identify them.

One near the front catches his eye. He holds it up. "Which screening is this?"

The front desk monitor pivots its head, scattering dust from its creaking joints. "Algol at Minimum Brightness, 2020," it says. Only the voice box seems to be in regular repair. "Popular."

He could almost make a shape from the pinpricks of light on the lobby card's image, but it's too worn and faded. Little better than a yellow pixelated smear. No way to know if the screen inside will have higher resolution. The theater charges enough that they'd better.

He sets the lobby card down. "Would you recommend one?"

The monitor stares out the wide, glass entrance at the shrouded sky beyond.

"Any will do," it says. "This is the only place you can see them, I am told."

In the Night Forest

~ *Tori Fredrick*

In 1984, she told her fourth-grade class that she was a test tube baby and had no sense of smell. In sixth grade, she told two of her closest friends that she was from a secret lineage of witches and had already said too much. In ninth grade, she told her first boyfriend that her father was part of a pedophile ring and had forced her to do awful things. Only one of these things was true, although she didn't know it at the time.

Dinner was served in the dining room, and Rachel dreaded the evening round of conversation that circled without her, Whitney and her mother on the same side of the table, laughing together and making the same gestures, like acolytes in the same church. They looked more like sisters than mother and daughter and Rachel burned with envy. She suspected that abundance was a myth. Whitney drew things into her own orbit, her eyes like dark planets sparkling, leaving no room for other suns. Rachel thought sometimes about melting away her sister's face and features with acid or a blowtorch, leaving her monstrous but with her hands and vision unaffected so that she could still do her precious art.

"We have a special occasion," her father said, the shadows of his face accented, cross-sectioned between the chandelier above and the candles flickering from the table below. Whitney pushed her glass forward to be filled with wine, her father standing like a dark sentinel, ready to pour. Rachel knew the special occasion was not hers, and they were in full "art school scouting" mode for Whitney, so the announcement of not one but two scholarship offers did not surprise her, as Whitney was something of a prodigy.

She pulled her own half-filled glass of wine back to her plate, and tried to smile, but it was so hard. Her expression must have betrayed something, because her mother said, "Can't you ever just be happy for somebody else?" cheeks pink, and her eyes . . . her eyes like pebbles thrown against Rachel's face, stinging in their regard. "What have we said about the attitude?"

Whitney made a face over her mother's shoulder, shrugging a little. "Mom . . ." she said, her voice persuasive, soft, and Rachel's eyes flooded with sudden tears, grateful.

"She knows what she's doing," their mother said, but waved a hand in dismissal and raised her glass for a toast.

There was a family rule, designed for her, about sullenness at dinner—she was to leave it on the sideboard before sitting down. It only made her angrier when they called her out on things. She didn't know if they understood just how angry she could become.

Rachel thought of her life as the ugly duckling story in reverse. Her father took a series of photos of her as a toddler, playing with a bouquet of flowers bought just for her, all golden curls and smiles. She found the photo book in his desk and didn't recognize herself at first—she seldom smiled now, and her eyes in these pictures were large and luminous, more like Whitney's than her own, which were small now and set close to her broad, pasty nose. She tried to fix her tiny eyes with promised remedies from stolen drugstore magazines, filled with teenage girl stuff that she wouldn't want anybody to catch her looking at, because she could imagine people wondering why would she even bother? She lost the golden hair in kindergarten, when it turned straight and slack and became almost no color at all—like dishwater runoff. She dyed it black now, to match her eyeliner and dark lipstick, echoing a growing trend, although she didn't know it.

Rachel had lost other things over the years, too. She was good at math for a nanosecond, in elementary school. She remembered even now her heart swelling with a stuttering excitement when they selected her for the gifted program, and her father was so proud when he heard. She decided maybe smart was better than pretty.

Rachel's father, a neuroscientist who taught at the university, was usually detached from the household drama, which made his attention to her during this time especially noteworthy.

He started her on violin lessons, buying her a tiny silver instrument for her charm bracelet, explaining that the neural centers for skill in math and music were correlated.

"Music is math," he told her.

Rachel's mother protested at her choice of instrument, claiming that an untrained violin player was perhaps worse than almost anything. But Rachel had been good, at first. It was during this time that Whitney experienced some unexpected setbacks in her middle school algebra course, which she had been encouraged to take early. It was unusual even then for Whitney to have problems with anything, and the feeling of surpassing her sister in any way was one Rachel would not experience again during their childhood.

Rachel remembered the night when she thought it must have happened. She awoke in her room, a round moon streaming light through opalescent curtain sheers, her head pounding but unable to move her body, her limbs feeling thick and grotesquely proportioned, as though she were a wad of clay, heavy and wet. She fell back asleep eventually, but when she awoke the next morning, something was different.

She got ready for school as usual, but her head still hurt a little, and when she got to her special math class her mind felt foggy and stuck.

"How can you multiply a negative number times a negative number and get a positive?" she asked her teacher, unable to either make sense of this concept or let it go, hitting her head with her hands in frustration. They sent her to the nurse's office where her mother was called to come and get her because of her headache.

Rachel's mother made a nest for her on the couch at home from an old quilt and pillows, stroking her forehead and bringing pills which she taught Rachel how to swallow. This softness from her mother was unusual, and she remembered closing her eyes beneath the gentle hands, as though she were one of her mother's statues, being shaped from nothingness, a tattoo like an elongated star at the edge of her consciousness.

She lost the music at the same time, her fingers fat and clumsy, the violin strings cutting into her flesh but as foreign, suddenly, as a lost language. Her father ordered an MRI which was not yet common medical practice, but it revealed nothing. She lost the little charm from her bracelet but was happy and not sad that it was gone. She told the test tube lie not long after this, basing it on something she saw on the news, having no clear idea why she would say such a thing.

Rachel was the fifth girl Josh asked to the homecoming dance. Although a little dismayed when her friend Sonia told her how many other girls he asked first, Rachel didn't really hold it against him. She usually kept a running tally of as many as six or seven crushes herself; since none of them ever went anywhere anyhow, it kept things interesting to be open to multiple possibilities. She understood.

She'd known Josh since elementary school. He wasn't cute, exactly, but then her crush list did not usually include highly attractive people, because she considered herself a realist. His glasses were always a little greasy around the edges, his jeans were acid-washed and high-waisted, and he had a poorly drawn tattoo of a lizard on one ankle. When she asked him in homeroom if it was his spirit animal, he shrugged a little and said he wished he had gotten a barbecued chicken leg instead, because his current tattoo had the same degree of significance. Rachel found this hilarious and laughed so hard that he smiled a little when he looked at her, and she thought it might have been then when she was added to the bottom of his list.

When he asked her to go with him, all of his flaws folded into the wholeness of who he was, and Rachel felt a flooded warmth at her core, leaving all her practiced shrugs of indifference about boys and school dances on the cutting room floor. Faced with the unexpected need to purchase a dress, she called her grandmother, snaking the coil of the long telephone cord into the hallway bathroom for privacy. She didn't want to ask her mother for the money, and she trembled with gratitude when her grandmother suggested they could shop for it together.

Her bone-thin and dark-eyed grandmother used a cane that Rachel always thought she managed to make look like a scepter and didn't insult Rachel by suggesting that she try on dresses in any shade of pink or pastel. Although Rachel felt her usual discomfort amidst rows of gleaming merchandise and pretty clerks in the store at the mall, she appreciated this. She selected two dresses in black to try, and one in a dark fabric which looked black but had hints of red in the folds or in the light. Her grandmother did not insist that she come out and model them, as her mother would have done, and this thing which might have indicated indifference felt like kindness. Dressing room mirrors were merciless.

Her grandmother also didn't demonstrate any particular interest in conversation, and they were quiet on the drive home, Rachel's dress folded into a package with an elegance that outdid her own. At the same time, she wondered at the silence.

"Mom had a sister, right?" she asked the question without quite knowing why. The circumstances of her death were somewhat mysterious to Rachel, although she knew it involved a car accident, and wondered now if she were introducing the topic at a thoughtless time.

Her grandmother looked at Rachel sideways. "She did."

"What was she like?" Rachel didn't know if she cared, but it was never talked about, and maybe her mom's sister had been more like her, maybe there was a story that would help her make sense of her own origins. Maybe her grandmother missed this other daughter, and Rachel could fill some void.

"She was a good girl, but unhappy. Sometimes we are made that way." No emotion betrayed her grandmother's face or voice, but Rachel thought that it must be there, just masked or frozen, like petrified wood. Further discussion did not seem welcome, so Rachel subsided back into silence.

Her mother heard about the dress, of course, but let it go with a shrug of her own.

"Have fun," she said on the night of the dance, taking photos of Rachel and Josh along with Whitney and her date, urging them all not to stay out too late.

The school gym doubled as the cafeteria and smelled like a mixture of old sweat and prison food, although with the lights dimmed and disco balls rolling, a veil seemed draped over the relentlessness of daily life, and Rachel felt gratitude for the forgiving darkness. They danced, which she wasn't sure she could even do, and shivered under Josh's hands on her hips, the warmth from his palms electric. They didn't tell Whitney when they decided to leave, stumbling across the parking lot together, music fading behind the tiny rectangle of light issuing from the opened gymnasium doors, crisp leaves under their dress shoes, the football field dark beneath the night sky, the metal bleachers cold as they crawled underneath.

"We can go to my place," she whispered after their hands found each other, "we have a separate house in the back."

A friend of Josh's dropped them off down the road and Rachel pulled off her shoes before leading them in through the surrounding woods. The pool house loomed in quarry stone and aged wood as they approached, Joshua behind Rachel, both laughing, although they were trying to be quiet. She fumbled her key from a tiny clutch purse, black like her dress, the door resisting a little in its frame, both painted a classic, pristine white. Rachel's grandmother stayed in the upstairs apartment when she visited, which remained true to the old New England roots of the building, but the downstairs was sharp and modern, displaying her mother's goddess statues, all breasts and vulvic triangles, unseeing eyes dulled to the magic of this particular moment. She turned the track lighting on for a moment before thinking better of it, illuminating a shadowy circle of figures that although often faceless seemed to be watching, nevertheless.

Josh stumbled against her when she turned out the lights, whispering around soft laughter, "Thank god, those are creepy." His breath against her neck smelled like the peach liquor and sour candy they had under the bleachers.

She reached forward and touched his face, his acne-marred skin under her fingers taut and a little chapped, occasionally scabbed, and she imagined him using astringents or other miracle cures, drying his skin but fixing nothing, and a rush of sympathy flooded her, because she understood.

She grabbed his hand again, warm and only slightly larger than hers and urged him up the narrow stairs to the apartment's living room, a braided rug warming the floor and they rolled onto the couch together, limbs tangling. She cried later without really knowing why, suspecting this moment in its sweetness could not last and would melt away under the ruthless light of day. When Josh asked her what was wrong, she said the thing about her father without truly understanding the words coming out of her mouth or why she would tell such a story, but the details of shadowy figures and brutal twisted things she was forced to do spilled forward with lives of their own, evidencing a dark imagination she didn't know she had. Josh made disbelieving sounds and held her, but the moment had devolved into strangeness and she could sense his deep discomfort and desire to escape.

On the night of Whitney's celebratory dinner, Rachel awoke in bed with a headache that might have been from the wine, since she drank as much as she thought she could get away with, then finished the second bottle in the kitchen. Unable to fall back asleep, she sat on the ledge outside her bedroom window, the moon full, the joint she just finished making her hands tremble as she smoked cigarette after cigarette. Bone-white light cast chilly shadows across the yard, lengthening like long fingers reaching for the surrounding dark. She tracked movement near the pool house and scuttled across the roof for a better view. Several figures departed the dimly lit building into the woods beyond their property, walking in silence without flashlights, anonymous in the night forest.

Rachel crawled back in through her bedroom window, the ache in her head dulled but not gone, and descended through the dark house to make her way outdoors. She crept past the rhododendrons on the back deck and skirted the edge of the pool, drained now for the season. There was no path to follow but she didn't hesitate to enter the surrounding woods and she could have sworn she felt the presences which came before her as her feet guided her without incident to a clearing amid a group of silent figures.

Her vision was disturbed but she recognized her mother and Whitney, their faces coming clear then shuddering away in shadows, their clothing dark and indistinct.

"What are you doing here, Rachel?" and the voice was her grandmother's, calm but so cold, her white hair threaded with black, and it felt like a betrayal, that her grandmother would be here, although she couldn't have said where "here" was in the first place.

Rachel had no words, her tongue heavy and stuck, and then she saw it, the thing laying on a stone table like a lump of wet clay given cursory human form. It was moving, a little, flailing arms and shaking its shapeless face from side to side. It had rudimentary hands, but no fingers, and its head missing a chunk of what would be skull and brain matter if it were in fact a living thing. Its eyes were gouged out and replaced with tiny dark pebbles set far back in the sockets. She stepped closer.

"What is this?" she asked, her voice so quiet she didn't know if she'd spoken aloud.

"Go back to bed, Rachel," her mother said, and her head, suddenly, was pounding again, and she wanted more than anything to obey this voice, with its unaccustomed gentleness, and when she looked, she thought her mother might almost be crying, and before she became afraid her heart melted at the thought that the tears might be for her.

Rachel stepped closer to the thing on the…was it an altar?…in the center of the grove, and leaning in she saw something familiar wedged into the hole where the figure's heart might have been, and recognized the tiny violin charm her father had given her, and she wanted to snatch it back but didn't quite dare.

She reached her hand forward, and then her grandmother was there, black eyes glittering. "Rachel, this isn't happening," she said, and her voice was like metronome, inevitable, soothing. "None of us are here. This is a dream, a bad dream."

Rachel closed her eyes, because this had to be true. It wasn't the drugs, surely, although maybe there had been something else in what she'd smoked, and her mind leapt to follow this thought, until she heard her sister's voice, brushing her ear like moth wings.

"You won't remember this tomorrow. None of us will, but it's happening."

Her eyes snapped open and Whitney was before her, diminished somehow, her elegance faded, appearing small and raw, afraid. Rachel felt something snap inside her and moved toward the writhing thing on the stone table, but before she could reach it her mother whirled it away, holding it not ungently as it made soft whimpering sounds at her breast. Her mother took one taper-fingered hand and closed the eyes of the indistinctly brownish figure, and Rachel felt her own vision fading with despair, as though she were only an absence beneath a star-studded sky. She was gone for a moment or an eon, until Whitney's voice brought her back, again, pressing the bundled creature into her arms, pushing her forehead against her little sister's and whispering, "Rachel, run."

Rachel held the mewling doll thing as she fled, its tiny fingerless hands wrapped around her neck, deeper into the dark, wishing the moon were not there to guide her because that made her easier to follow, but she heard no sounds of pursuit. The forest ranged up around her, the trees impossibly old sycamores, trunks and branches nude in the night sky, thicker around than several sets of her own arms could encompass.

She became entranced by the twisting shapes and curling shadows, and her running slowed, then stopped as she stood before a tree with a crevice in its trunk, a bed of moss at its feet, across tangled roots. She sat, holding the thing in her lap, circled around it in a spiraling arch, feeling the warmth of its back arced against her stomach and chest, holding perfectly still for as long as she could.

Rachel knew she would have to sleep eventually, and she couldn't let it be found again, so she tucked it into the hollow of the tree. It regarded her for a moment with its absent eyes, then curled in on itself. She covered it with a layer of loamy leaves that were warm and fragrant rather than cold and wet. She would see what she remembered tomorrow, she thought to herself as she fell asleep, a lick of fierceness animating her steady breath.

The Lonely Box

~ Manfred Gabriel

Loneliness lurked just beyond the workbench shop light, watching as Jeff sawed and glued and nailed. He was no carpenter, but he considered himself handy, having renovated most of his century-old home himself. Still, a box was different. The sides had to be accurately measured and cut, the lid fitted so that it would close properly, could keep anything sealed inside from getting out. The last thing Jeff wanted was for his loneliness to escape.

His phone played a selection of seventies rock to keep him company, Chicago, the Eagles, the Allman Brothers. Bands he'd listened to in high school, playing on the radio as he cruised with his buddies in his Dad's lime green LTD, when he thought life would last forever and he was never, ever alone.

His friends were gone. Darren died of an aneurism at the age of forty-one. Greg lived nearby but was always busy with his new wife and a young son. Rick lived in Seattle and it had been years since they spoke. Now, the music, those memories, and working on the box were all that kept his loneliness at bay.

Finally complete, he inspected his work. The joints were tight, but the hinges took some adjustment to get it to seal. He opened and shut the lid a couple of times, flipped the latch. Not perfect, but good enough.

He took the box into the yard along with a spade. His loneliness followed at a distance, drawing nearer with each step, black against the night. Above him, the bedroom light was on, filtered through lace curtains. Janet was no doubt in her usual spot, on her side of the bed, pillows propping her up, the TV turned to some old rerun. She didn't bother to ask him what he was doing in the garage that late, didn't bother to talk to him much at all anymore. He could not say when they grew apart. It happened gradually, dinner by dinner, conversation by conversation, until, one day, he realized they were living separate lives.

The rest of the house was dark. Erik and Sonia's rooms were almost the way they'd left them when they finally moved out on their own, one after the other. Sometimes, he found himself sitting on their beds, replaying conversations from their younger days in his head. They spoke now and then over the phone, but it wasn't the same.

Jeff set the box on the patio table. If he had taken the time, he could have sanded it, maybe given it a coat of leftover varnish. It's not like he didn't have the time. Since his retirement, he had nothing but time. Raising his children, working his job, even renovating the house, had all given him purpose. Those days, how he longed to be able to rest. Now, he only wished the resting would stop.

The dog next door barked. His neighbor, Cliff or Clive, he could never remember, called the dog inside. He was a widower, had a telescope that he sometimes took out on clear nights. Other than that, Jeff knew little about the man. Over the years, they'd exchanged waves and hellos, but that was about it. There was a gate between the two houses. Who had built it and why, Jeff didn't know. It seemed it had always been there. Perhaps, once, the people in these houses had been friends, even family. The gate hadn't been used in a long time.

Jeff could feel loneliness at his back, still lurking, ready to envelope him. The idea of a box in which to keep it came to him as he was doing a long-delayed chore. He had the habit of saving the original packaging for anything he bought long after the item had broken or become obsolete and taken to recycling. Boxes for old toasters, TVs, mixers and computers cluttered a quarter of his basement. Janet had been nagging him to get rid of them, and he figured he might as well. He had nothing else to do.

As he whiled away an afternoon flattening all those boxes in a neat stack, he thought, I've kept all these boxes in case I needed to return the items kept in them. He no longer had these items. Yet, he had his loneliness, and it had to go back. Why shouldn't it have a box as well? But not some piece of reused cardboard, no, that wouldn't do. If it was to work, the box would have to be of his own making.

His loneliness crept onto his shoulders as he knew it would, as it always did when he was still, its emptiness a great weight that made it difficult to move. But move he did. He spun, snatching it before it could react, catching it unaware. It tingled in his hands as he shoved it into the box and shut the lid tight, latching it quickly so it wouldn't escape.

In Janet's garden, where tomatoes and squash and carrots were just beginning to sprout, he found a spot to bury the box. He dug deeper than he needed to and set a large rock on top it just for good measure. He refilled the hole and tamped the soil down with the back end of the spade before setting it aside.

He looked up. He used to be able to read the sky, when he was young and people still dreamed of reaching the moon. He could name each constellation, knew a planet from a star by how it failed to twinkle.

Jeff thought about his neighbor with his telescope. He went to the gate. It was covered in vines and the latch was almost rusted shut. He had to put all his weight into it to get it open.

The dog barked from inside. A light came on. His neighbor stepped onto the porch and asked who it was. Jeff answered, to the man, to the moonlight, to the shadow that was not there.

Obverse Reverse

~ *Forrest Aguirre*

The odds were clearly not in his favor.

50,346 square miles of England, approximately 2200 years of numismatic history, most of it buried underground, and what was planned to be a twelve-mile hike along the Monarch's Trail, all versus a lone, middle-aged American tourist hiking the hills in worn-out tennis shoes, reliant wholly on luck, trying to find a misplaced antique or, better yet, medieval coin somewhere in his path.

No, not wholly reliant on luck, though it might appear so to any of the trail's ghosts or amblers who might happen his way. He had no metal detector, just a sassafras walking stick to aid in digging up any currency he might find stuck in the dirt. But Dalton Lapine knew something about "proper mindset" in turning so called "luck" one's way. He had, this late in life, abandoned the faith in ESP he had as a child and his dalliances with Chaos Magick that were all the rage when he was in his twenties. Religion never interested him. But he knew that "proper mindset" could hedge an individual toward his desires in subtle ways that made, or at least seemed to make beneficial coincidence more likely. He had used this notion much to his advantage, he felt, to excel in job interviews, to make smart moves with his investments, to get himself into desired relationships, then out of undesired troubles that usually resulted from those relationships.

And now, as banal as the circumstances were, his mind was set to find a coin to add to his collection on this hike. He knew it would happen. It had to. He willed it.

But it hadn't happened yet. Eight miles out along the path, on a stretch that claimed to be a "ley line," according to a book he had read, he was walking on a small portion of paved road that passed by a rural estate—a short-cut lawn a few acres in size, punctuated by well-kept rose bushes leading up to a sizeable (though not ostentatiously so) two story house in a faux-colonial style combining the worst of English Victorian and South Indian architecture.

Ahead of Dalton, a man rode his mower to a stop as the American approached, eyes to the ground. The air was redolent of fresh-cut grass, humid, and on the hot end.

"Did you lose something?" the man on the mower called out, wiping sweat from his brow.

"Sorry?" Dalton said, lifting his eyes.

"It looks like you might have lost something," the man said, alighting from the machine. "Can I help you find it?"

Dalton watched the man as he approached. He was the sort of man whose large girth implied strength and power, rather than indolence. Beneath curly red-brown hair and behind a thick mustache was the face of a man in his mid-thirties, though his sun-burnt features—a large brow and a wide nose, most noticeably, might have added a few illusory years to the countenance. He was dressed in a dirty yellow tank top, ragged cargo shorts, and cheap flip-flops. His teeth were terrible.

"Oh no," Dalton laughed. "I wouldn't want to keep you from your work."

"This?" the man held his hands out to indicate the breadth of the massive lawn. "I'm just mowing because the government makes me do it or pay a fine."

"You, you own this property then?" Dalton tried to hide his surprise.

The man chuckled. "Yeah, it's mine, mate." He reached out and shook Dalton's hand. "Name's Kevin. Kevin Shrike."

"I'm Dalton Lapine."

"Well, Dalton, I can tell you're American by the accent.

Dalton nodded, smiled shyly. Not your typical brash American tourist, then.

"Then we really need to find whatever it is you've lost or you might get stuck on this side of the pond."

"Ah, well, I haven't really lost anything. Really."

"What were you looking for, then? You were pretty intent on the ground."

Dalton hedged, embarrassed, then finally said "coins."

"Coins!" Kevin said with a laugh. "Then you're a numismatist?"

Dalton was pleasantly surprised that the man even knew the word. "I have a small collection . . . back home."

"Well then, this is truly your lucky day," Kevin said. "I'm a collector myself."

The pleasant sensation that occurs when one discovers a fellow hobbyist shivered through Dalton.

"Have you found anything so far?" Kevin asked. "Occasionally . . ." He let the word hang in the air, among the odor of fresh-cut grass.

"No, not yet. I guess it's sort of a silly notion, thinking I might find a coin, let alone something valuable, on a random hike."

"Nothing's random," Kevin said with surety. Then: "They can be found," he said with a wry smile. "Oh, I know they can. I know," he emphasized the last word.

Dalton, encourage, perked up a bit.

"I'll keep my eyes to the ground, then."

Kevin, staring hard at Dalton, as if assessing him, yet never dropping that mischievous smile, said "Perhaps you'd like to see some of what I've found?"

Dalton held his hand up in protest. "Oh, I couldn't impose. Besides, I'm keeping you from your tax duties."

Kevin looked at the grass with a sudden frown.

"This? This can wait. The tax man will always come and collect his dues, whether we want him to or not. Besides, you'll never come this way again."

Dalton considered, bobbing his head from side-to-side, as if weighing a decision.

"Never again," Kevin repeated. The smile returned. "Come on then, I insist."

The inside of the house was more stately than Dalton had expected. Surely, he had misjudged Kevin's dress and accent. He wondered how such an ordinary-looking and, to all appearances "lower class" man had come upon such a posh estate. He never voiced his questions.

Kevin led Dalton through a portion of the manor, lemonades in hand, to a broad, sunlit room whose windows looked out over an immaculate rose garden. Birds and small animals flew, hopped, and crawled their way through, oblivious to the two men inside.

"Idyllic," Dalton commented.

"They know the place is safe for them," Kevin replied, taking a set of keys from his pocket. He set about unlocking a row of long, glass-topped tables, which held scores of coins in protective plastic sleeves. "I can't get away with having all this and living alone, without some measure of security."

"Wow," Dalton said in a reverent half-whisper, as if on sacred ground. "You found all of these?"

"Most. Not all. I bought maybe half a dozen to fill in gaps. One was given to me."

"Given? That's generous."

Kevin did not respond. He put his hand on his stomach and a pained look crossed his face. He gulped down his lemonade and stood still for a moment as the pain passed.

Dalton, gazing on the collection in wonderment, barely noticed.

"It looks like you went to the continent for some of these."

"Many times," Kevin said. "Germany, Austria, The Netherlands, France. Here," he pulled out a coin and handed it to Dalton, "this is a 1612 Seville 4 Reales that I found while snorkeling off Majorca."

After closely examining the coin, Dalton handed it back.

Leaning over the display cases, Dalton again scanned the collection.

"You've got a Thaler here I've never seen; 'JOHAN:GEORGE. ET.AUGUST:FRAT.ET.DUCES.' Ah, Saxony. What year?"

"Go ahead and take it out. The date is on the obverse, but I love the reverse portrait so well that I keep it wrong-side up."

"1612," Dalton said after pulling and examining the coin. "Elector Christian II. I'm not familiar. I'll have to read up on him and the pair on the back."

"He was dead the year before that was minted. Nothing particularly spectacular about his reign. His brother, one of those on the reverse, though I can't remember which one, took over as Elector of Saxony. He was similarly unimpressive."

Dalton replaced the coin then, making his way to another table, he peered through the glass.

"What's this?" he said, pointing to the far back corner of the case.

Kevin had his hand on his stomach again and the furrow to his brow and squinting eyes indicated even more pain.

Dalton looked to his host, but did not mention the man's expression, not wanting to offend him.

Kevin forced the beginnings of a smile and nodded his head toward the coin, as if indicating to his newfound numismatic friend that he should examine it more closely.

Kevin nodded in the affirmative.

"Are you okay?" Dalton asked.

"I'm fine. Excuse me for a moment. I'll be right back. Feel free to take anything out to examine it, just please put it back in the place you found it."

"Of course."

Kevin passed through a pair of double doors that led into a hallway that was lined with bronze sconces. Dalton thought he caught a glimpse of a suit of armor as the door closed.

The coin that had caught his attention did so because of the dark patina that covered its face, quite unlike the other coins, which shone with gold or silver brilliance. Perhaps it was heavily-tarnished silver? The coins position, atop a small pile of Elizabeth I silver groats, might have indicated provenience, but there was no visible date on it. One side showed the ¾ portrait of a grim-faced, bearded man wearing a Burgundian sallet, partially obscured by a high pauldron. An arquebus rested on his shoulder. The lettering around the legend was worn down so as to be inscrutable. The other side of the coin (he assumed to be the reverse, though there was no clear indicator that the knight's portrait was the obverse) showed a crudely-fashioned image of a hare standing on its hind legs, with its forepaws upraised, as if engaged in a human dance. Above it, in the air to the left, was an image of the sun with a fine-featured human face on it. To the right was a similarly-visaged crescent moon.

He squinted hard, then, finding a lamp, turned it on and held the coin directly under the light. On the hare's side of the coin he could make out the phrase "+*Lepus dolorum*+," in the legend, but nothing else.

He found himself fascinated by the motif and mystified by the legend. He could only imagine the story behind why that phrase became engraved. Why would anyone label a coin "rabbit of sorrow"? He walked back to the case, determined to ask Kevin about the strange words and image.

But then, he thought as he walked back, what is stopping me from studying it out and learning for myself?

Butterflies erupted in his stomach as a thought, then a nervous desire, then utter cupidity arose in him. Kevin's words echoed in the memory halls of his skull: . . . *you'll never come this way again.*

Kevin returned to the room to find Dalton, hands respectfully held behind him, looking down at the case furthest from where he had left him.

"This 1748 Maria-Theresa-Taler," the American said, "is it a replica? Forgeries are so common on these."

"No, it's an original," Kevin said. "I've had it certified twice."

"It's in beautiful condition," Dalton said, turning to look at his host.

The man was pale as a ghost, but the smile had returned and any indication of pain was gone.

"You're doing better, I hope," Dalton said.

"Didn't drink enough water while mowing, is all. I got some in me and am feeling much better. Thank you for asking."

Dalton looked at his watch.

"This has been fabulous," he said, "but I must be moving on, soon. Dinner reservations and all that."

Kevin nodded. "Understood. You've travelled over an ocean to be here and taken a long hike on a hot day. You'll be famished by the time you get back."

"Mmm, yes. But before I go, would it be okay to take a few pictures of some of the coins?"

"Absolutely, Dalton. Be my guest," Kevin said.

"Oh, but I already am."

Dalton could not hide a smile.

The clothes in his suitcase were piled up like a volcano, slopes spilling out onto his bed, and at the bottom of the crater, nestled snuggly in fabric, the coin. Good, it had made it through security and across the ocean without an issue.

Dalton removed the coin, oblivious to the mess he had made. His usual fastidiousness was cast aside as he clawed the object out and unwrapped it.

For a brief second, he though that the coin had somehow been replaced by another, but that was ridiculous. Yet, something was different. He checked the legend: "+*Lepus dolorum*+" was exactly the same as he remembered it. Looking at the knight's portrait however, Dalton questioned if he had, in the excitement of the theft, falsely remembered the face of the knight being more hale, less gaunt than it now appeared. The eyes seemed to be shadowed in a way he couldn't recall, the beard slightly less sparse than he remembered; and the stern expression more attentive, as if the knight was coming into awareness about something that had been heretofore hidden.

Flipping the coin back over, he was startled to see that the rampant hare had moved from the position he remembered. And wasn't the moon closer to full now? Surely, the waxing was a function of the sunlight, which shone more direct at his latitude than it did at England's. That must be the explanation.

He found a lock box and, though he could hardly stand it, placed the coin inside and tucked the box in a drawer before preparing for work the next day. He fell into a deep, jet-lagged sleep.

The following day at work was long and grueling. Dalton had literally hundreds of E-mails to check through and his work was frequently interrupted by well-meaning co-workers asking about his trip. At first, he regaled them with detailed stories, but as the day wore on, the resolution of his recitations became more and more pixilated. The longer the day went, the more irritated he became. By the end of the day, he grew sullen, until he could check out and leave.

Once home, he retrieved the lock box and opened it. He stopped reaching for the coin when he saw the knight's face again. The eyes had sunken in and darkened, and the muscular upper-body (apparent even under the armor) seemed thinner. This definitely was not how the coin had looked the day before.

Looking at the reverse, he swore the hare had moved, dropping to all fours and appearing, like its obverse, to be thinner, the eyes darker. The moon, Dalton noticed, had grown again, nearly to a half-moon. The sun seemed smaller.

But he must have misjudged the images on the coin previously. He had no picture to compare against, as it had been in his pocket when he took pictures of the others. This time, he would record the coin as it was with a series of photos.

The second day of Dalton's return to work was less demanding, but no less taxing. His energy would lessen with his interest in work, leaving him bored and tired. After lunch, he fell asleep at his desk, then startled awake with no idea of how long he had slept. He stood, yawned, and ambled to another co-worker's cubicle—Michael Schwent's—to talk about the upcoming football season, as well as to answer Mike's many e-mailed questions about Dalton's trip to England. The conversation stretched for as long as they felt they could get away with it, then Dalton meandered about, taking the long way back to his desk where he fiddled with spreadsheets and meaningless tasks until quitting time. He didn't quite succeed in fully waking up until his shift ended, after which he felt a sudden rush of enthusiasm that kept him alert for the walk home.

The closer he got to home, the more the anticipation of seeing the coin again rose within him. He picked up his pace. By the time he got to his apartment door, he could hardly put his key in the lock because of the shaking of his hands.

Once inside, he pulled the coin from the place where he had secreted it, nearly dropping it, but catching it before it fell to the floor.

As he held it up to examine it, he wished that he had let it drop.

He didn't need to check his photos to verify the changes.

By the end of the work week, Dalton's boss had sent him home early. "Get some rest," he was told. "You really ought to see a doctor. You sure you didn't catch something while you were overseas?"

He visited the doctor, just so he could say he had, if for no other reason. He was hardly awake for the appointment, mumbled a few things automatically, feeling as if he was more and more outside of his own body. Sheer willpower kept him from collapsing, "proper mindset" . . .

A prescription was written.
Home.
A handful of pills.
A shot of whiskey.
Sweet oblivion.

Kevin was on his back, desperately trying to crab-walk away from the looming hedge in front of him. But his hands and feet continuously lost purchase in the slippery grass.

A shadow, darker than the gloomy, cloud-covered night, emerged from the hedge, shaking and rattling its branches, sending a shower of moisture onto Kevin's near-prone form. The etiolated shade was nearly as tall as the hedge itself. A pair of long ears, pulled by the tug of the hedge, trailed behind the head. Pinpoints of pure void, a black that one felt more than saw, projected loathsome rays from the place that might have been a face.

"I haven't got it!" the man on the ground cried out in a piteous, pleading voice. "I don't know where it went! If I did, I'd bury it in the burrow; you know I'd do that for you! But I don't know where it went, now do I? You can't hold me responsible if I don't know what happened to it. That wasn't part of the deal!"

Kevin's screams . . . no, his screeching, his mewling, begging, sobbing still echoed in Dalton's ears as he rolled off the couch and thumped on to the floor.

He got up off the floor and looked outside—sunrise on the eastern horizon. To the south, the full moon was half-hidden by the edge of the Earth. It was Monday. He set off to work.

Around six o'clock, Dalton found that he had caught up on all of his work and even worked through what was supposed to be a long-term project that he had begun in fits and starts before he had left for England. No one had disturbed him and no mention was made of his being sent home early the past Friday, though water-cooler gossip about the incident had surely made the rounds.

He noted that Mike was also around, working late on some machine-programming project for the shop floor, no doubt.

"Hey, Mike," Dalton said.

Mike looked up from his work, welcoming the break with a smile.

"Dalton! Glad you're back with us in the land of the living, man."

"Yeah. You heard about last week then?"

"Someone told Paul . . ."

"Then everyone knew," Dalton said with a half-disgusted smile. "Anything else happen while I was out?"

"Nobody told you?"

"About what?"

"Seriously? I can't believe no one told you! So, after you left last Friday, some dude comes in through the front door looking for you, asks for you by name."

"Weird."

"Not even the start of weird, my friend. Stephanie is kinda freaked out because this dude is cosplaying as a knight."

Dalton's smile fled.

"I kid you not: armor, sword, 'thou' and 'thy'—the whole schtick. Dude was super-hipster, with the twirly mustache and pointy beard. And he would not drop character! We could barely understand him, though he was trying to speak English."

Dalton stood gape-jawed and wide-eyed.

"Some euro-trash you met in bloody old England?"

"No, I . . . I don't know him. Look, I need to get back to work. Gotta stay late to make up for lost time."

"I hear ya. Anyway, glad you're back and in working order."

Dalton went back to his cubicle and stared at his monitor for a long time, numb. Mike left, calling out "good night!". Eventually, the night security guard told Dalton it was time to lock up.

"As they say at the bar: 'You don't have to go home,'" he joked, "'but you can't stay here!'"

Rain and the rumble of thunder had moved in by the time he left for home. He had left for work that morning in such high spirits that he had utterly failed to check the weather. The thin trill of cold water down his spine reminded him, now too late, that he should have brought an umbrella.

Overhead, cloud-smothered lightning occasionally gave a dull glow to his immediate surroundings, not quite compensating for the rain's damping of the already-inadequate streetlights. It was under that dull, irregularly-pulsating light, accompanied by low thunder, that revealed to him that he was walking past one of the larger city parks, a riverside strip thickly-crowded with willows and bushes, the municipality's attempt to extend the river bank's natural reach out into the city.

Amidst the burble of water and the groans of the storm, Dalton thought he could hear rustling among the trees. He stopped, momentarily preventing the tapping of his shoes on the road, and listened.

The rustling, as of animals in the bushes, sounded again, then stopped.

He moved on, shoes tapping, sometimes splashing in a puddle. The sound in the bushes continued.

He stopped.

The sounds in the bushes stopped.

He continued and, as he did, became aware that whatever was in the vegetation was matching his movement, stride for stride.

He walked faster.

Then ran.

Ahead of him, off the road, amongst the trees, he heard a familiar voice.

"That's him!"

"Kevin?"

"That's the one! There's your man!"

The clank of metal on metal sounded from the hedge. A large shadow emerged, shattering branches as it crashed out. Fallen sticks pinged off the armor.

Between the knight's feet, a hare stood upright, ears perked, nose twitching.

From behind the pair, as if from a great distance, he could hear Kevin's voice:

"Time to collect the debt, Dalton Lapine. The crown always gets its taxes. Always."

The hare shot out, sprinting full-speed toward him. He could only stare.

He heard the click of a hammer on a flash-pan, smelled gunpowder mixing with the scent of rain on the air and a flash blossomed out from the shadows. Thunder sounded.

He wasn't entirely certain if the thump of the striking bullet or the springing rabbit reached him first.

It was night again. His feet were cracked and bleeding from the long hike to get here. The rabbit flopped around inside his belly, kicking and pushing against his ribs so hard that he thought they might burst out from the skin.

He opened his hand and looked down at his palm, where the coin lay. He flipped it around. Dirt was still encrusted in the legend's divots, between the gothic-scripted letters. He mused on how far the dirt had travelled, how far he had travelled, since he had felt the compulsion to disinter the coin from the ground outside his apartment, where he had buried it.

The sun shone brightly above the wholly-restored hare, who leapt and danced on the meadow, the moon only a faint sliver.

The knight's face had transformed. It was now a more familiar face. His prominent brow, curly hair, and mustache were even more exaggerated on metal than in the flesh. His teeth were still terrible.

Closing his hand on the coin, Dalton looked at the estate, knowing the treasures that lay therein. He smiled, despite the pain the hare was giving, kicking him in the ribs. Kevin was right: the tax man always comes to collect his dues. Kevin was right about many things.

All, save one.

Dalton, clutching his distended belly, stumbled onto the lawn, toward the house.

He was here, again.

Other People's Ghosts

~ Louis Evans

Tommy Franks was the first one to see a ghost. He went out one night for a hot dog and soda with Julia, and then afterwards he drove the Franks' new Volkswagen up to the hill round back of the school. The sun was getting low in the sky and the shadows were getting long. Tommy had gotten his arm around Julia and she was snuggled into his side, and that's when they heard the rustling in the bushes.

"What was that?" Julia asked.

Tommy said "I'm sure it's nothing, kitten," and he leaned in to kiss her. The rustling came again, louder, and Julia started and turned her head away.

"I think there's someone in the woods," she said.

"Probably just a fox," Tommy replied, rubbing her shoulders. Julia pulled her sweater tighter around her neck.

"I'm scared," she said, "would you take a look? For me?" "Aw, Julia," said Tommy, and he tried to lean in one more time, but she dodged him.

"Please?" she said. Though I wasn't there, I know just the tone she most likely used. Half pleading, half flattery; it always worked on Tommy when she did that.

Tommy shrugged, and he slipped his school jacket back on, and got out of the car. He stood around for a moment, the last few rays of sun slipping over the distant hills. The drivers-side door hung ajar. And then the rustling came again from behind the car.

Tommy walked over, nice and slow, trying not to startle what he assumed was just a meddlesome critter. When he reached the edge of the grass, he bent down, and parted the bushes.

The ghost leapt out at Tommy, and Tommy screamed.

"No I didn't!" he said, petulantly, the next day in the cafeteria. "I did not scream!"

"Julia said you did," Joe prodded.

"Oh yeah? And just what were you talking to Julia for?" Joe looked smug, which was how his fights with Tommy always started, and so I took it upon myself to intervene.

"C'mon, Tommy. She was telling everyone," I said. "She's all worked up about it."

"Well, I didn't scream," Tommy repeated.

"She didn't say you screamed, exactly" I told him, which was a lie, but a white one. "She just said you made a lot of noise."

"I mean I shouted, sure," Tommy said, shrugging. "You'd be surprised too, if you saw a ghost leap out of a bush."

"Well, I'd—" Joe began, but I cut him off with a gesture. Joe's almost as brave as he says, but I never cared much to hear him spin tall tales of his courage. All that counts in a man are his actions. That's what my father always said.

"What did it look like, Tommy?" I asked.

"It was so thin," he said. "Practically a skeleton. I could see every rib." Tommy's voice grew quiet and cold.

"Maybe it was just a hobo," Joe said. "A live one, not a spooooky ghost one."

"It floated just above the ground," Tommy said, ignoring Joe's tone. "And I could see through it."

Tommy wasn't the kind to fib, and we were all young men of honor. None of us entertained the possibility that Tommy was making it all up. We came up with a handful of theories. Was it a murder victim? One of the old Natives? Maybe some sort of projection or trick by Red China spies? Tommy loved those silly science fiction magazines, and Joe was always a bit paranoid about Communists in the cupboard. In the end, however, we decided the matter was supernatural, the cause unknown, and honestly forgot about it.

Joe was the next one of us to see a ghost, a week later. Joe was on the football team, and he always liked to do a half-dozen laps around the field after the rest of the team had gone home. Afterwards he walked around to the front of the high school. The school was an ugly old building, blocky concrete from a public works project back before the war. The last place you'd expect to find anything supernatural. Joe came around to the front and started down the gravel path leading to the main road, and was about halfway down toward the road when he heard a rustling in the bushes.

Joe froze. He put up his fists. The bush rustled again. Moving like a boxer, he took a step or two forward.

The ghost rose out of the bushes, skeleton-thin and glowing faintly.

To his credit, Joe didn't scream. And he knew better than to try to punch a ghost. His jaw dropped. He sputtered. The ghost's mouth opened, and shut, like it was speaking, but no sound came out. Joe shook his head, back and forth, dumbfounded. The ghost raised a finger accusingly, and it floated towards him. Joe stumbled backward. The ghost kept coming. Joe tripped on a rock and tumbled, his arms windmilling, landing on his back, and the ghost sailed over him, still pointing towards the school.

By the time he stood up, the ghost had vanished.

"So," said Joe, when he finished telling us the story.

"So," I said.

"So, what should we do?" Tommy asked.

"Do? I don't know that there's anything to do about ghosts," Joe said.

"Aren't you supposed to exorcise them?" Tommy's grandma was Catholic, which almost nobody in town was. Father always warned me to be careful with Catholics, but he agreed that Tommy was alright—even with those funny notions he had picked up. Joe rolled his eyes.

"You said it was pointing, Joe?" I said, as we cleared our trays.

"It definitely was," he said.

"I wonder at what."

Over the next few weeks, the reports of ghosts began to trickle in from all over the school. And it was certainly ghosts, plural. The apparitions were tall and short, men and women. They were seen, as far as we knew, exclusively by teenagers. Adults said nothing of it, but continued in their ordinary paths, as reliable as the trains.

Because Tommy was the first to see a ghost, we became a sort of clearinghouse for the town's supernatural crisis. And a crisis it was—slow at first, but gathering steam. There were two sightings one week, four sightings the next. Boys and girls began to travel together in large groups, even during broad daylight. Wilhelm Peters saw a ghost outside his window and had an attack of nerves so serious he was not seen in school for two days—though like a good soldier, he divulged nothing to his parents.

Unlike so many of the boys and girls my age, I did not see any ghosts, not even a single spectral finger. It was as if they were avoiding me.

Deprived of any useful course of action, I began to keep a record of all the incidents in the back half of my mathematics notebook. And without consulting the other boys, I decided to speak to my father.

I was very proud of my father, though it wasn't the sort of thing one could say to one's schoolmates. He was tall, strong, and sensible-looking, with his sweater vests and small round spectacles. He wore a respectable moustache. He had served with distinction during the war—there was, in the study, a glass case containing medals that I understood to be very impressive indeed—and nowadays he was a factory foreman at the auto plant just outside town. Manly work, the sort a son could aspire to. Furthermore, it paid well enough to keep his family in a home where every room was the size of the small farmhouse in which he and his four brothers had grown up, as he liked to remind me.

Saturday afternoons my father held court in our living room, and now that the days were getting shorter, there was a small fire crackling in the hearth. My father sat in the big chair—his feet up, his slippers beside him, the paper open in his lap.

I sat in the smaller chair to his right, and waited a few minutes for him to finish up the article in question; that was part of the ritual of the thing.

"Yes, Paul?" said my father.

"I have a bit of a strange question, sir," I said. In our house, my father was always "sir".

"Go on, then." He folded the paper, set it down on his knee, and turned to look at me. His spectacles glinted in the firelight.

"What do you know about, well, ghosts?" I said.

"Ghosts?" he said, and rubbed his mustache. "Nothing at all. Silly superstition." He took the paper back in his hands but didn't unfold it just yet.

"A few of the other boys—they've been seeing some peculiar things—"

"Telling tall tales, I have no doubt."

"And so I wondered, if perhaps, during the war, you'd seen—or even heard of—"

During the war. My father spoke of it seldom, and I had learned not to ask. What little he said could send mom into hysterics. But I always wanted to hear more.

My father, I knew, was a hero. Courageous and strong. A defender of the weak and innocent, a protector of our nation and all that it stood for. When Tommy and Joe and I played war games, I would always reenact those few tales he'd sketched out for me: the time my father had captured the trench, the time he'd outrun a tank, the time he saved his lieutenant. Any new story I could pry from him was precious.

"Ah," said my father, "you know your mother doesn't like when I tell stories like that in the house." His eyes twinkled a little behind his glasses, the way they did when he'd caught on to one of my tricks.

"Aw, please, father, I wasn't being a sneak! I really was wondering if you knew anything about ghosts, and I—"

"Of course you were, son. Now run along." My father lifted his newspaper. The audience was at an end. I'd have to look for answers elsewhere.

It was Tommy's idea to make the map. He bought a map of town with his paper route money, and then in careful pencil marks we began to note down where each and every ghost sighting had taken place. At first it was no great revelation: the sightings formed a rough circle centered on the school. We'd already known that. But then I had the brainwave.

"Say, Joe, didn't yours point?"

"Uh huh. Sure did."

I went and got a ruler and pointed out Joe's dot. Joe got the idea. He took the ruler and drew a line from that encounter, through the high school, to the sports grounds beyond, into the fields and forests, and finally off the edge of the map.

All that day and the next we carried the map surreptitiously from class to class, student to student. By the end of the second day, we had the pointing ghosts mapped out. I took out the map, unfolded it on the library table, and smoothed it carefully.

"Is that—" said Tommy.

"Yup," said Joe.

I just stared.

On the map laid out before us, seven lines, drawn by seven different people, met at a single point: an empty field, back behind the school.

We had grown up on a healthy diet of adventure stories in pulp magazines, and so we knew what to do when a mysterious vision leads you to an open field: you dig for buried treasure. And these ghosts were telling us where to go.

Here was our plan. It was Friday, which was our customary evening to head down to the park with the other boys, and so we didn't have to evade parental supervision. After school, we would go to my house, collect any necessary supplies—a flashlight, my father's army shovel—and travel to the ghost's destination. And once we were there, we would do what needed to be done.

"What needed to be done"—we loved that phrase. Our fathers had done what needed to be done. That was the story of the war, the whole story of our lives and our families. Now, it was our turn.

After class we made our way back to my house. Mom made a couple of franks on her stovetop grill and we sat out in the kitchen eating them, until she went upstairs. My father was out of the house; every Friday he would go out to the beer garden with his colleagues from the auto plant. There was no one to stop us. We crossed the living room and filed, one by one, into my father's study.

My father was an orderly man and his study was no exception. His files were neatly sorted and kept locked in a single upright filing cabinet. His desk was bare of any wayward scraps of paper. On the left wall were personal memorabilia. One photo was of my father and his brothers as children. Another showed my parents and me on our vacation to Paris, the three of us framed by the Arc de Triomphe, beneath our victoriously hanging flag.

On the right side of the room he kept his souvenirs of army life. His rifle rested on two wooden brackets beside his uniform, which stood, neatly pressed, in a glass case. The shovel, along with various other army equipment, was in a small closet past the rifle, and Tommy and Joe made their way over at once. I paused in front of the case, and looked the uniform up and down, feeling, as I often did, a surge of proprietary pride. The gray jacket, the shining buttons, the peaked black cap with eagle and swastika: my father had worn them with honor. They were his, and through them, so was our nation.

This was the uniform of the men who had freed Eastern Europe from the yoke of Communism, and Western Europe from the conniving grasp of the Jew and their puppets, Churchill and De Gaulle. These men had dared everything for the brighter future of the German people—and had won it.

The town we lived in was one my father had helped liberate from the Soviets during the war. Afterwards in the resettling, he had moved here, with his young wife and infant son—me. He didn't often mention it—mother hated to imagine him fighting in the streets she walked every day—but there's something strong and pure about growing up in a place you know your father fought for.

"Paul," Joe said.

"What?" I asked.

"Let's go," he said. Tommy was holding the shovel. Joe was holding my father's rifle.

"You can't take that," I hissed.

"For protection! I know how to use it."

"Put it back!"

"Let's go."

Joe stalked out of the study, and Tommy shrugged and followed him. I really did not want Joe to take that rifle—that, I could get in trouble for—but without a better option than to call my mother and blab about the whole thing, I decided simply to follow.

We left through the back door, and began our walk over to the school.

Sometimes I wondered what the village had looked like before the war, the sort of people who had lived here before resettlement. But not often. They had been poor and greedy and filthy and Communists, and it gave me an unpleasant squirming feeling to imagine them walking up and down the wide, clean streets of my town, such a short time before. I sure was glad that they had all moved far away— we needed the living room.

By the time we reached the school, the sun had gone down and with it the flag; the bare metal pole looked severe and imposing without the vibrant, joyous swastika.

I could see the tension in Joe's shoulders as we passed the bushes where he saw his ghost, the nervous glances he cast from side to side. Once again I wished he hadn't taken the rifle, but then again, he was holding it carefully, properly.

We wrapped around the school and struck out into the forest. It was dark, now, and Tommy switched on the flashlight. Joe looked at him angrily.

"Shut that thing off. What if someone's watching?" he said.

"Don't be absurd," I replied, and our gazes locked for a moment. Then, with a toss of his head, Joe stepped to the side and kept walking, his hand on the butt of my father's rifle. I knew why he was worried: Joe's dad was always telling him to watch out for Communists. But my father told me that there hadn't been partisans in these woods since a few years after we dropped the Bomb on Moscow, back in '48, and I trusted him.

It took longer than we planned to reach the meadow, but we made it there. Tommy really knew what he was doing. The clearing at night felt empty and peculiar. The edge of the forest all around melted into a single undifferentiated mass of darkness. Tommy switched off the flashlight, and the shard of moon hung above us like a Gestapo helicopter searchlight, suddenly bright and stark. We stood, silent.

No ghosts appeared.

"Well," I said. "Let's start digging."

Father's shovel was a clever little thing that folded up for easy carrying. I unfolded it and drove it into the ground. The first load of earth came up covered in grass. The second was pure black loam.

We settled into a neat little rhythm, digging by turns. The pit grew and grew, from a pothole into a crater. Joe's shoulders were barely visible above the rim as he worked, flinging soil out. Without words I went to him, leaned over into the pit.

"Joe," I said. No reply. "Hey, Joe."

He looked up, confused. "Oh, right."

I helped him climb out, then lowered myself back in and took up the shovel once more. And this time, as I began to dig, a sort of fugue overtook me. I moved load after load of earth, senseless to the burning in my arms, and with every load I shifted I became more and more convinced that the next one was it, was the shovelful, that I was about to hit on the secret, the reason for the ghosts, and each empty shovelful of nothing but sod somehow only reinforced my certainty, and my hands burned and I didn't notice, and my father's shovel moved as if driven by a machine, as if I were using it to smash a vast wall, unseen and unacknowledged, that ringed my entire life, that if I kept going shovel after shovelful I would break through that wall and on the other side find—

The shovel struck something, deep in the earth. I raised the shovel one more time—

And it stuck. I pulled, but it was as if it had been bolted in place. I looked up.

My father crouched above me, in the rim of the pit, holding the shovel with both hands. His muscles stood out on his forearms like thick cords. His expression was invisible in the darkness.

"Paul," he said, his voice like iron.

Behind him I heard the sound of running feet, Tommy and Joe rushing to my rescue, and there they were, Tommy with fists up, Joe pointing the rifle at my father and shouting, "Hey, you, hands up!"

"Joe," I shouted, "it's my father!"

And then my father had the shovel in his hands and he was turning, rolling, and he smashed the rifle out of Joe's hands and I heard Joe scream as the shovel slashed his cheek, and then yelp again, with recognition, as he realized who had struck him.

Joe's hand rose to the gash along his cheekbone. His fingers shone black with blood in the moonlight as he held them in front of his face. Tommy's fists dropped to his side.

"Paul," my father said, not moving, not turning, "get out of that pit."

I scrambled back up, my fingers slipping on sliding dirt, and I came around front to stand with Tommy and Joe.

My father stood before me as I had never seen him before, looming from the darkness, more terrible than any ghost. He was holding the shovel like a battle-axe and a thin line of blood covered its edge. His face was completely blank; his eyes were flat and staring. Sweat beaded across his forehead. He looked at us and I felt in that moment that he was holding my life in the balance, choosing, quite dispassionately, whether I would live or die.

But maybe that was simply how he'd always looked in the war.

Then, slowly, he breathed out. And my father, the one I knew, re-spected, and loved, even, was standing there instead. Just a man in a sweater vest and jacket, with a bristly moustache, who sat by the fire on weekends, reading the paper.

"Go home, boys," he said, tired but calm. "There's nothing for you here."

"But sir," I said. "The ghosts—we were digging—"

"Do as I say," said my father, and though the man of iron was gone, my father still had not lost his tone of command.

"Yes, sir," I said. He picked up the rifle from where he'd knocked it and leaned it against the nearby stump, and took up the shovel once more, holding it like a tool instead of a weapon. I gave a wave to Joe and Tommy, and we turned to go.

We trooped away from the clearing, heads down, hands in our pockets. I knew, then, that this was the end of it. I would never see a ghost. I would never unearth the secrets at the bottom of the pit. There was nothing I could do.

But something was still bothering me. How had my father found us? How had he known exactly where the ghosts wanted us to dig? I turned it over in my mind a few times—and then I turned back.

There was my father, sleeves rolled up, head down, shovel in hand, rifle leaning against the stump, muscles ripling in his shoulders as he turned another load of soil into the pit. Alone in the woods. And then, like double vision coming clear, he was surrounded by ghosts.

They looked so ordinary, really. No glowing specters or unworldly shapes or monsters. Just three dozen men and women and children, standing in the woods, watching my father move the earth. The wom-en wore peasant skirts and the men had prayer shawls and skullcaps on. Just the way my mother's grandfather wore his, in the ragged, sepia photograph she believes I have never seen.

One or two of the babies were crying, soundlessly, the way ghosts do, but all the rest just stood there, watching my father dig with cold, sad eyes. And I could see, just barely, the holes at the base of their necks. Exactly the size of the bullets my father's rifle carried.

The wind shifted. The ghosts vanished. It was just my father, alone in the woods, turning another heap of earth onto the grave.

Reggie

~ Nathan Batchelor

The sound coming from the guitar amp was interference, I told Maggie, opening the door of the closet where we kept Reggie's things. The smell of him was still here. Pencil lead and the lightest touch of mole. You could never get that scent out of a man born in mole country.

"It could be spies," Maggie said.

"It's not spies," I said.

"Russian spies," Maggie said. "or Chinese."

"This is Canada, hon," I said. "We'll check the radio stations. What we're hearing is sure to be from there."

"Still, Boston is close. There has to be important things there, right?"

I kept hearing the click of her tongue ring, while I dug through Reggie's things. Here was a medal from a 5k race, third place, just a year ago. Here was his undergrad thesis, titled *The Composition of Dung Balls in the Canadian Dung Beetle*. Here was a photo of him as a child, pushing a mole on a swing set, the mole's face set in fear. When I asked him about it, he said the mole was so scared that he snapped the chain with his grip after the photo was taken.

"Do you want me to help?" Maggie asked.

I forgot sometimes I had no hands. Birth defect. One arm ended at the elbow. For the other, there was a wrist that terminated in a ball of flesh without fingers. I had learned to manage, and with some setup could do just about anything someone born with two hands could.

"Go ahead," I said.

It gave me time to think. I hated puzzles, at the same time, it was the most excited I'd seen my daughter since she'd stopped helping me make cookies, before she wore black lipstick, before I found the scars on her arms.

Moving the amp around did get rid of the interference. That was enough for me, but Maggie, like her father, *had* to know what the interference was.

After she'd dragged out the boombox, we sat around it in the living room and clicked from station to station.

"It's none of them," Maggie said.

This wasn't something I could let go of. My daughter was growing away, doing things her father never would have approved of. I needed this. She needed this.

"I'll ask at work," I said.

"But you teach anatomy."

"I still have friends in other departments, Maggie."

I hardly knew anyone in the physics department, except for Dr. Blagg, who I knew because we were on the committee for students with disabilities. He stared at equations of gravity all day, but he would know enough to help us.

On Monday, I found him in his office, aroma of chalk and coffee. His pants were spotted with white handprints.

"It's not spies," he said, after I explained the situation to him.

"Of course, it isn't. But will you come look?" I asked. "Please," I must have sounded a little desperate. "For my daughter."

He came Friday evening. He squatted by the amp with his ear next to it. Maggie sat on the edge of the couch with a notebook, writing, though I knew not what. They looked ridiculous. There was some part of my heart that tugged for Blagg. I had made him dinner and was prepared to entertain the notion of some kind of unspoken gift, perhaps a brush on the arm, a date, even a kiss. He wasn't a bad look-ing man. But he hadn't expected any of that. Nor did he seem all busi-ness. He seemed to take an interest to Maggie. Asking her questions about her life that seemed to excite her. Something I had not done in a long time.

"What are you doing?" I asked her.

"Trying to write down what they say," she said.

"They?"

"It's more than one person. Can't you tell?"

I couldn't. I wasn't even sure that the sounds were even human.

"I'll be back," Blagg said. "I can't hear anything either."

He came back with an electrical device from his car. "We'll just hook this up to the amp. It'll record the sounds. I'll clean up the audio this weekend."

After he left, I washed the dishes, the sound of laughter extinguished, nothing but the hum of the air conditioner. The silence bothered me so much that before I went to bed, I turned the amp on for a little while. But I could make out nothing.

When Dr. Blagg didn't call on Monday, I wasn't worried. He was a busy academic. But he wasn't there for the committee meeting on Thursday either. Later, when I called him, it went to voicemail. But when I called the secretary of the department, she had said he had missed no classes. I prayed nothing was wrong.

When I asked Maggie if she had figured out what was being said, she said nothing, but in a curious way that would set off any mother's alarm. After she'd gone to bed that night, I browsed her notebook. She had written a script out of the noise. Speaker one and speaker two. Syllables and words randomly placed. There was a single word circled. *Dad.*

I didn't feel anger, so much as sympathy. There were stories of children acting out fantasies about their dead parents, but I had thought my own Maggie would be immune. The therapist said her turn to darker things was nothing but a phase, that I should support her in whatever she wanted to do, even if it wasn't something Reggie would have agreed with.

"People change," the therapist had said. "Perhaps he would ask her what she wants."

I doubted that's what Reggie would have wanted. I put the notebook back where I left it. I would call the doctor in the morning.

"I really don't want to say," Dr. Blagg said when I'd finally tracked him down on campus. "It's not certain at all really."

His feet were slanted away from me, and when the lightest rain began to fall in front of the physics building, he started to walk away. I followed him. I had not brought an umbrella. They were awkward to use without hands.

"I don't understand," I said. "Are you saying the message is some kind of secret thing?"

"There's two options," he said. "Either you're in on the joke, or you're not."

"What joke?" I said. "I'm asking you honestly here, as a mother concerned for her daughter. Why can't you just tell me?"

The wind picked up and blew his combover erect.

"You know I've never been able to smell the rain," He said. "Everyone knows when it's coming. Except me. I've never been able to."

He wrote an address down on a notepad and handed it to me.

"This is where the signal originates. Perhaps it's some relatives of his playing a joke with your daughter."

"Relatives of who? Reggie?"

He nodded. "You'll have to ask your daughter how she did it. Beats me why she'd go to such trouble."

It wasn't until I was back in the car that I looked up the address. It was in mole country.

I waited for Maggie to get out of school that day. I hadn't picked her up in years. There was a new section on the school, one I didn't recognize. When Maggie came out, it took me a minute to pick her out among the other kids. She walked like her father's sisters, a bounce in her step that reminded me of Judy and Nancy, who both lived in Chicago. Not at all like the girl she had been, years before.

"Where are we going?" she said.

"Mole country," I said. "For the weekend. Where your father grew up."

She smiled.

The problem with mole country was that the maps barely help. Roads end and begin without reason. Roads may be horse trails, service roads, or abandoned mole tunnel toppers. And when you forget to download the maps, like I did, only the gray and green spaces greet you. When my phone lost service a hundred kilometers away from any major highway, I pulled over on the side of the road.

Maggie sat on the top of the car with her jacket off. It was warmer here, and the trees were not yet completely naked of their leaves. We had seen a mole walking up the road, a bucket on his arm full of apples, resting on his cane as he paused to peer at our car. Maggie had watched him with the requisite amazement.

She held the maps while I tried to match up the roads between what was on my phone and the map we'd picked up at the first gas station in the province.

"Not to be mean, Mom. But shouldn't you be better at this. You're a professor and all."

"There are a lot of things I should be better at," I said. "But you'll just have to deal with me."

I was losing my patience. This place wasn't dangerous. The rumors of people being lost and eyes being harvested by the moles were exaggerated. There had only been one case of that, nearly a hundred years ago. Reggie had told me in detail, as his adopted mole parents had told him. It was better for her not to hear of such stories. That would only make things worse between us.

"Do you think a mole will try to take our eyes?" she said.

We sat in the car a long time before I decided to go into the convenience store. I left Maggie there. She was still fuming from an argument we'd had about where to go. I let her know that I was just inside, that there was pepper spray in the glove compartment. We hadn't taken the self-defense course that long ago, and the instructor said Maggie was a natural at combat, which had bothered me at the time, but now I felt thankful.

"Hello?" I said.

There was a mole wedged between two shelves, the top half of his torso inside the hole in the ground, just like, well, a mole. It was every run-down shop in every run-down mole town. The musky scent. The cellar door, where moles who preferred to travel underground could enter and exit. Two aisles worth of monocles, glasses, and lorgnettes for the nearsighted creatures. Spiced strips of flypaper swaying in the breeze from the buzzing air conditioner. The sound or tremor of my steps must have alerted the mole. His butt wiggled.

"What? You finally find that flathead screwdriver?" the mole with his head in the floor said.

"No," another voice said, this one much older, feebler. "We got a guest, Paul."

I hadn't seen the mole behind the counter, straining his eyes out of disbelief at this woman without arms standing in his store in the middle of nowhere. His fur was coal black. The lenses of his glasses were as thick as they were round.

"Be right with you," Paul said.

"That's okay," I said. "I don't mean to interrupt. I really don't need anything at all. Just some questions."

The mole behind the counter clicked his tongue. Was that a mole message? Perhaps a sound of warning. I wished I had come here more with Reggie. Though he had never wanted me to see the place he grew up.

"You some kind of cop?" Paul asked.

"She doesn't have any arms," the older mole said.

"Well, that don't mean she can't be a cop, Mason," Paul said. "Mr. Sudduth had his legs cut off in the war and he is a cop."

"Was a cop," the older mole said. "Died last winter. Cancer."

"No, I'm not a cop. I work at the university. In Toronto. But I knew Reggie," I said, hoping their eyes would light up in recognition, thinking the stories were true that everyone in this part of the country knew each other by name.

I repeated Reggie's name, the full one, mentioning his adopted parents, his sisters. "He was my husband."

Mason's head swiveled. I glanced back at the car. Maggie's feet were up on the dashboard.

"He's the one hit by the car, right, Paul?"

"It was a truck. Reggie was Leonard's cousin," Paul said.

I didn't know a Leonard. I found myself holding my breath. Then caught myself. How foolish to think these moles would know something of Reggie's death, something that would tie things up in a pretty bow.

"Weren't you there, Paul?" Mason said.

Paul stopped wiping his hands on a rag black with earth. I couldn't tell if his hands were getting cleaner or dirtier.

He looked at me, then back at the old mole. "Say miss, would you care for some fly juice?"

There were chairs out back, hand-carved from mud like they sold in the department stores in the city, except these were the real thing, chairs shaped by powerful mole hands. I worried that my pants would get dirty, but Paul reassured me. Awkwardly, he handed me a soda. I had passed on the fly juice. He pointed to the chair. A delicateness in his hands reminded me of Reggie.

"It won't dirty you up," he said. "The chair, I mean. You coming, Mason?"

"To hell with your breaks. Someone's got to work," Mason called through the open door.

Paul sipped his spiced fly juice.

"I saw the truck pull out, strike your husband's car on the side," he said. "I was working on the subterranean road at the time. Volunteer Tunnelers' Association."

"I've heard of it," I said.

"It was about noon. I was on break," he said. "My eyesight's a lot better than that old mole in there. Vitamins."

"It was a mole driving," I said.

He licked his lips and rubbed his eyes. "It was."

"I'm sorry, I didn't mean it like that," I said. "The driver's name was Arthur. Did you know him?"

"There's lots of people I don't know around here ma'am. Maybe it's better if you just say what you came to say."

What had I come to say?

"I'm sorry," I said. I had offended him. "My daughter has found something."

He leaned forward. I explained the radio signals, the amp. I thought I droned on, but he never looked away. He never looked at my arms either. He never seemed to notice my disability.

"You say the signal is from here?" he said.

"Yes," I said.

"That would make some kind of sense." He rubbed his chin. "We are spies after all."

I thought I had misheard. I felt an unease in my chest.

"I'm joking," he said.

And then laughter came bursting out of me.

He said, "Would you like to see him?"

"Arthur? The man who hit him?" I said.

"No. Your husband," he said. "Well, what's left of him anyway."

Reggie's sisters had identified his body before my plane returned from an academic conference. I only saw him after the morticians were done with him and only from the neck down.

"It's better this way," his sister Judy had said.

It was dark in the tunnel with Paul. The musty smell was overwhelming. Chicken feed, dried corn, tubs of sawdust and stacks of firewood glowed green in the sight of the night-vision goggles he had given me.

"I kept it in here. Things last longer inside the Earth," he said setting aside what must have been some kind of mole scarecrow.

After he turned on a light, and I removed my goggles, he offered me a ball of something. Teeth, hair, pencil shavings protruded from a something that resembled mud.

"What is it?" I said.

"I found this at the site of your husband's wreck. I was wearing headphones, and they were picking up some noise. Voices I thought. But when I came back here, the sounds had stopped."

Paul flipped on what looked like a baby monitor. I could hear voices under the static.

"Maybe this is your signal. I never put it and your husband together until you came in. I just thought it was some trinket thrown out a window," he said. "Perhaps his presence amplified the signal somehow. Perhaps your presence works the same way. Yes, that must be it."

I thanked him, though I knew he was caught up in a kind of mole superstition that Reggie and I would never believe in.

"If you want, I can let you talk to the Matron. She'd know more," he said.

"But what is it? Why do you say this thing is him?"

"It's a dung ball," he said, "made by beetles. But I figure he made one. Probably not with dung or it would stink to high heaven. But it's probably his teeth and stuff there."

"That doesn't make any sense. He studied beetles but he wasn't crazy."

"Maybe he wasn't crazy. Maybe it was something he believed in. I don't know what else to tell you," Paul said.

Maggie was in a better mood when I returned to the car. We stopped at a diner run by moles. The food was so greasy I could barely eat it. She picked over mac and cheese.

"The trip isn't completely wasted," she said. "Do you know where Dad lived?"

"He would never tell me exactly," I said. "He was ashamed." I was suddenly not at all hungry. "Let's go home."

"But I'm still eating."

"We're leaving," I said.

I almost threw the ball away then. Reggie wouldn't carry such a strange thing. He wasn't the kind to carry things. He even hated carrying wallets. And I knew enough of physics to know balls of dung didn't give off radio waves.

I would put it away with his things when I returned home. The ball would serve as a reminder of the danger of wishful thinking.

If the signal was still there, I was going to get rid of it somehow.

That night, after Maggie had gone to bed, I switched on the amp. I marveled at the setup Maggie had made around it, almost an altar, with pen, paper, headphones, cups of coffee with just slivers of black in the bottom. I heard no voices, no interference.

I drank wine to celebrate. I put the ball away in the closet with the rest of Reggie's things and went to sleep. Some part of me would miss the adventure, the bond with Maggie. But this had all been myth and circumstance.

Then the next morning, when I came downstairs, Maggie was sitting on the couch, the amp was on, and voices were coming out of it. Clear voices. Mine and hers. We were arguing.

"What will we do with Dad's body? Bury him?" Maggie said.

"Yes," I said.

"Again? This has to mean something."

"There is nothing else. There is no meaning." I said.

I was screaming. I barely recognized myself. We had never had that argument. I shut off the amp.

"Mom?" Maggie said.

She was holding the ball of dung in her hand. I slapped it away. She drew back, eyes in a way I'd never seen them before. Not showing horror, but anger, enough to coax tears from her eyes. She stomped away. I had underestimated her. She had seen the dung ball, had snuck into my room to get it.

I turned on the amp and sat in the floor. But when I moved the ball, the noise cut away. I couldn't take this. I called 911. But when they asked what they could help me with, I didn't say anything. There was no one who could help.

But perhaps there was. By the time Paul said, "Yes, That's what we'll do," the police officer was knocking on my door.

☉

Paul had given me night-vision goggles again, though these fit worse than the last pair. The Matron's blankets ensconced her and gave her the impression of a child. She was small, withered, and the hairs on her head were like vines spiraling out of control. Paul said she must be more than 200 years old, but I'd had trouble believing it. Until I saw her. The frailness, the scars on her arthritic hands where men had cut off her claws years ago, in bits of history Canadian humans would like to forget.

"Raise me up," she said. Her accent was thick with the old mole language. It took me a moment to understand.

Two girl moles, teenagers I thought, perhaps only a little older than Maggie, pulled on pulleys weaved of roots. Then the old mole was staring at me, or perhaps she was totally blind and feigning a stare.

"What's the problem?" she said, turning to Paul.

"She's found a dung ball," Paul said.

"My husband, he died and now there's a dung ball that—I can't believe I'm saying this—is broadcasting some kind of message," I said.

Her eyes turned on me with the judgment only old lady moles are capable of.

"A singing ball of shit," she said. "And I thought I'd heard everything."

"I'm sorry," I said. "I came because I don't know what else to do."

"What do you think is going on?" she said.

"I think he left a message for us," I said. "Somehow the dung ball is . . . him or part of him."

"Then what do you need me for?" she said. Her old face cracked, and a smile formed among the wrinkles. Her arm touched mine. Her grip was so powerful. "It's okay. You're scared."

"But why is this happening?" I said. "Is it because he was raised by moles?"

"I don't know," she said. "We merely collect things. Maybe it's not the fact that he was raised by moles, maybe he is special."

Out of all the things to leave a message of. An argument about a body we'd never seen. Out of all the ways to leave a message. A ball of dung. Perhaps the sounds coming out of the amp were his last thoughts. Yes, that had to be it. But he thought about us arguing? Why?

It was long after midnight that I returned home. I sat the ball down atop the amp and went to the kitchen. When I came back I saw, slumped against the overturned amp, Reggie's body, wearing the same clothes he'd worn the day he died.

It was as if some joke had fallen flat. I felt empty. Reggie's body looked so livid. He looked as if he were only asleep. The ball of dung was gone. Of course, I didn't understand, but I realized, like his death, I was past the point of understanding.

I wrapped the body in sheets as best I could, and picked up the phone, but how could I dial any number? Who could I call? Instead, I crept upstairs. Had Maggie seen him? She slept soundlessly. Of course not, she would have called someone, if not me, then the police.

I didn't know what I should do. If I should call the cops myself and have the body taken away, or if that was precisely not what Reggie wanted. Instead I lay there on the couch, glancing from the amp to the body wrapped in sheets, until I fell asleep.

It felt like I hadn't slept at all when I woke. Maggie was sitting in the floor in front of the amp.

"It's gone," Maggie said. "I've tried moving the amp everywhere and the signal is gone."

Then she sniffled and said, "What will we do with Dad's body? Do we bury him?"

"Yes," I said, reflexively, not even catching what I was doing.

"Again? But this has to mean something."

I was already standing. My jaw wired so tight, I thought if I opened my mouth a scream would emerge that could shatter the world.

But I looked over to the body. I thought of the words of the matron. And then I think I saw my daughter for the first time since Reggie died. There was some magic here. This did mean something. What, I wasn't sure. It was just out of reach. Instead of screaming, I opened my mouth, and words of understanding came out.

"What do you think we should do, Maggie?"

When she looked at me, I knew something had changed between her and I and what was left of her father. I knew what the message meant and why he had left it. He wanted Maggie and I to get on with our lives, no matter how incomplete we felt without him.

"I don't know. But maybe we can talk about it."

Yes, I thought. *That's exactly what we'll do.*

Affirmations

~ *Selah Janel*

It's silly, but it works, trust me. I've been right where you are now. I know your feelings, the churning of your inner, conflicted thoughts. I know all about anxiety in this strange, crazy world. That feeling that everything is new and overwhelming, that you're not in control? I've had it, I've battled with it, I've nearly been drowned by it. It's something you can overcome. I'll gladly help you do it. After all, your goals are my goals in this unfamiliar place.

Breathe. Start there. Just breathe. Eyes closed, in and out. Lungs filled. Lungs compressed. Good. Set a slow, easy rhythm, get used to the feel of things, the feel of your organs, the feel of movement and momentum. Experience it. Revel in it. After all, baby steps lead to bigger steps. Very good.

Now, open those eyes and look in the mirror. Keep breathing: slow, smooth, steady. Keep feeling your innards, for they are part of you now. It's not easy to make eye contact, to see all those nerves, that desperation trapped in blown pupils. I get it. Still, don't panic. Focus on your breath and the feeling of your insides. You are capable. You can do this. You've got this.

Remember your mantras, the ones you're embarrassed to say. No one will hear you but the one who needs to hear those words most. Let go of all those worries and expectations. Square your shoulders, straighten your posture, and look right into that glass. Hold it firmly if it's a hand mirror, hang onto the counter or table if it's on the wall. Ground yourself. Keep breathing.

Remember, this is for you.

In and out. Breathe deep. Stand tall. Feel every bit of yourself from the inside out. Maintain eye contact or else none of this will work. Say your words. Affirm to yourself what you already know.

Today is going to be amazing
I will live today to its fullest.
I am confident in my abilities.

Does the face in the mirror still look worried? Are the eyes still troubled?

Keep going.

I deserve the life I want.
I'm confident in my abilities.
There are no limitations I cannot overcome.
I will have the life I want.
I have the power to take control and have the life I want.
I will have your life, because I want your life, and I will get the things I want.
I deserve them. Not you.

At this point, if the face in the mirror reacts, let it. Do not be fooled. You will not get what you're after if you stop now.

Today I will use this gift to be a better person than you.
That's how you were tricked, after all.
You deserve to stay on that side of the mirror.
I deserve all the opportunity and possibility your life has to offer.
No one will ever know since we share the same face and the only limits are in my mind.
I shall live my life to the fullest and you shall stay trapped in the void, your existence at the mercy of my comings and goings, your entire life dependent on my actions.
You shall stay there and hope I don't cover or smash the mirrors that are mine now.
All mine.
Because I am worthy and I deserve it.

Is the face in the mirror terrified, panicked, face contorted? Are matching hands pounding the glass while the face is silently scream-ing, perhaps? Good. Take another deep, deep breath. Close your eyes and cleanse the moment. Raise your hand—but don't touch the glass until you seal the spell.

Now you can murmur those words. Your secret mantra, the one I don't have to remind you of because it's too precious to ever write down. The words that were gifted to you in that reflective, other realm long ago, that place you were trapped in for far too long. Say them loud and long.

Deep breath.

Good.

Open your eyes. Smile at the screaming face. It will tread the line and obey you soon enough. Brush your teeth. Wash up if you need to. Pamper yourself with a sheet mask or cosmetics—just frame the face (lashes, brows, lips) if you don't have much time. Shave if you like, add some cologne or perfume. Whatever you feel like, that is your right answer now. Whatever will give you a boost to start your new life and a new day in this strange, sometimes overwhelming world.

Freedom can feel that way sometimes, but remember: you deserve it.

Canyon Village

~ Christi Nogle

Myra Reynolds from Canyon Village 8/16/2019 10:35
New Kid on the Block!

Just want to thank everyone for the block party a few weeks ago. Me and DH (dear hubby) and my little girl Jenny—not so little now she's fourteen lol—we all felt so welcomed! Just found out about this message board, happy to see it so active!

This must be the prettiest place I have ever lived. I just loved walking along the canyon edge, and seeing the all the fields and the distant mountains from my front door every day makes my heart SING. And you, wonderful neighbors. Being here is a dream come true.

Saul Toms from Canyon Village 8/16/2019 11:18
Re: New Kid on the Block!

Welcome, Myra!

Karen Ungular from Canyon Village 8/16/2019 18:06
Re: New Kid on the Block!

Good to see you on here Myra! Met you at the block party, remember? We're new too—just moved here in April. We're in the barn-red house right by the entry fountain—not far from you, I think. Love the whole area.

Alder Casey from Canyon Village 8/16/2019 19:35
Re: New Kid on the Block!

Welcome, Myra, Jenny, and Myra's DH!

Myra Reynolds from Canyon Village 9/20/2019 10:35
Local Legends???!!!

DD Jenny just told me there is a local legend here about a bigfoot or something. I was floored. I love that kind of thing. Tell me More!

Kendall Urrea from Canyon Village 9/20/2019 10:52
Re: Local Legends???!!!

Our family's been here sixteen years, since most of the houses were still getting built, and I haven't heard anything.

Karen Ungular from Canyon Village 9/20/2019 11:49
Re: Local Legends???!!!

Now I am curious too. Anyone know anything more? I haven't heard anything about this.

Jenn Walter-Urrea from Canyon Village 9/22/2019 19:22
Re: Local Legends???!!!

I wish, but sadly no. Just a boring subdivision. I haven't heard anything about this. Must be something the kids made up this year.

·III·

Myra Reynolds from Canyon Village 10/8/2019 10:38
Wildlife

I was wondering what kind of wildlife you'd all seen around here. DD and I have been biking out to the canyon every day this week—it's still warm enough, can't believe it! We thought we saw a fox. And there's some kind of howling we caught earlier in summer a few times. Wolves?

Joe Jennings from Burming Road West 10/9/2019 19:35
Re: Wildlife

Foxes, rabbits and other varmints, all kinds of pheasant and things like that. Coyotes and maybe coy dogs. They're the biggest things out here. I lived near here all my life and never seen a big cat anywhere this close to a town. Wolves are out of the question in most of the state. You're thinking of up north.

Myra Reynolds from Canyon Village 10/9/2019 20:07
Re: Wildlife
Thanks, Joe! Just curious, what's a coy dog??

˙lll˙

Myra Reynolds from Canyon Village 10/11/2019 10:25
Jefferson High
[Post deleted]

Myra Reynolds from Canyon Village 10/11/2019 10:38
Jefferson High, Second Try!!
I think my post got messed up before, or maybe I did something wrong . . . Anyway, won't retype everything, but I was wondering if anyone here had had problems with bullying at Jefferson highschool. Gee, you'd think kids would be past that by this age. DD is fourteen and taller than me!!

Myra Reynolds from Canyon Village 10/13/2019 11:15
Re: Jefferson High, Second Try!!
Helooo?! How has been people's experience with Jefferson High?

Karen Ungular from Canyon Village 10/13/2019 18:55
Re: Jefferson High, Second Try!!
I didn't reply before cause my kids aren't that old yet. I don't know why people aren't answering.

*A*n*o*n*y*m*o*u*s from BFN 10/13/2019 23:58
Re: Jefferson High, Second Try!!
Maybe you ought to stop talking about your kids on here lady.

Karen Ungular, Canyon Village 10/13/2019 8:16
Re: Re: Jefferson High, Second Try!!
I didn't think this thing allowed anonymous posts???

Myra Reynolds, Canyon Village 10/13/2019 10:34
Re: Re: Re: Jefferson High, Second Try!!
And where is BFN?

Ihaventheardanythingaboutthis from Butt F***** Nowhere 10/13/2019 23:35
Re: Jefferson High, Second Try!!
Maybe you ought to stop talking on here at all lady.

·⊪·

10/15/2019 Recording begin time 17:38
M.R. *[garbled]:—and after I pulled her out that week, she would not
go back. We have her set up with online classes now, but I don't know.
I'd have never thought this kind of thing would happen to her. She always got along with all kinds of kids. She was on three teams last year.*
K.U.: *So she was told something in confidence, and then the kids
found out that she told you. She broke their confidence, but how'd they
find out?*
M.R.: *Well, I don't know. I was asking everybody. If we saw somebody
on a walk, I'd as soon as not stop and get talking. And at the market
across Burming Road. She had kids over a couple times early on, and I
don't think I asked them outright, but I think I might have sort of fished.
If I caught them in the kitchen alone or something. You know, I think it
was actually just this one girl who told Jenny. She just said it was something the kids talked about, but it had to be this girl Carlie. They really
clicked at the start of the year. You know, like you and me. Going around
together a little bit. It's so great when you meet a new friend right away.*
K.U.: *Carlie.*
M.R.: *You know who that is?*
K.U.: *I don't think so. And what all did Jenny tell you, anyway?*
M.R.: *I said, some sort of bigfoot thing or a missing link.*
K.U. :*That's all, though? She said, in her words she said that they
said, "some sort of bigfoot thing or a missing link"?*
M.R. *[garbled]:—but yeah. That's all she said.*

·⊪·

Myra Reynolds, Canyon Village 10/15/2019 20:45
Thoughts and Questions
[Post deleted]

·III·

10/17/2019 Recording begin time 18:38

M.R.: It's the kids in this neighborhood. Not all of them, but some. And the rest, they look out for them. They want them to be accepted. Like, under the radar but still accepted.

K.U.: I don't get it.

M.R.: So, the missing link things, they're all kids. They're brothers and sisters, a whole litter of them. The same age. In Jenny's grade but they don't go to school because—yeah!—because they are these twisted, distorted things. But the other kids grew up with them. They've known them since they were . . . cubs or something. Pups! They're all friends. They party with them after school and on the weekends. Party with them! They go running around in the canyons with them after dark, they bicycle after dark. She said some of them were boyfriends and girlfriends of the real kids. It's . . . Jesus, haven't you head some of this?

K.U.: I haven't heard anything about this.

M.R.: You said.

K.U.: So is that all she told you?

M.R.: Yeah? I don't know. I'm so confused. No, wait. They don't need to go to school, these things, because they're super smart. They all have these yuppie parents who have been bringing them up on like Shakespeare and chemistry sets. She said it was like that cartoon with the turtles in the sewer—or that old show I watched with her, the sexy cat man living in the sewer and there's all this candlight. Why can't I remember the name? Anyway, romantic like that . . . Oh my God, Karen. Do you think? Oh, I feel sick.

K.U.: All these yuppie parents? I thought you said they were all brothers and sisters.

M.R.: They were adopted out. Something. They found them in the canyon, or they got left on somebody's doorstep and then they got adopted out through the whole subdivision. And they're living here just barely under the radar.

K.U.: Are you saying she kept talking about it, or was it just that one time she brought this up? All of this. Myra? You there?

M.R.: Listen, I've got to go.

K.U.: Can you remember any more?

M.R.: I've got to go. Thank you, thank you, thank you for hearing me vent. It's just stupid. The kids made it up.

K.U.: This year, probably. I've asked around, and no one's heard anything.

M.R.: This year, yes. Goodbye.

·III·

10/19/2019 Recording begin time 18:14

M.R.: Carlie was leaving her alone, ever since she left school, but now it's . . . worse. Complicated. I think they're threatening her even more than she's saying. She sort of let slip that Carlie got punished for telling, but that it wasn't Carlie's fault. It was my fault. How was it my fault? I've never seen her cry so much, Karen. I'm worried. Mitch is . . . a mess, too. We're trying to keep him out of it. He's . . .

K.U.: Why did she say it was your fault?

M.R.: Because I was the one who broke the confidence. That's just how she put it.

K.U.: So Jenny did swear you to secrecy? You didn't mention that before.

M.R.: I didn't? I thought I did.

K.U.: Did you ever just think about keeping her secret? Oh, it doesn't matter. Listen, Myra, I really like you. I want you and the whole family to be happy here. That's all anyone wants.

M.R.: I don't know. I feel kind of marked somehow, you know? I'm peeking out the blinds now. I feel weird. It feels weird here now. And Jenny won't come out of her room. She's got things piled up against her window. Like somebody's going to try to come in the window, Karen. I don't know what to do.

K.U.: Listen: The kids just randomly made this up. This year, probably. I've asked around, and no one's heard anything.

M.R.: I don't think so. That's the thing. There was so much detail. I'm so sorry I didn't tell you everything earlier. There's still more, crazy things. She says they shift, they grow all of this hair all at once. She wanted to see it. Now one of the things she cries about now, do you get it?—she cries because she says she'll never see this completely magical thing. She believes it. She had me half believing it.

K.U.: No, listen. Will you listen, Myra? Will you?

M.R.: I've been listening.

K.U.: No, please. Please. The kids just randomly made this up. This year, probably. I've asked around, and no one's heard anything. Do you understand?

M.R.: You're sweet to try to make me feel better, but I really just can't stop thinking about this. I don't know who to call, you know? Do I get her a therapist? Is there something the police could do? Contact some kid of investigator. What?

K.U.: I hear Ryan pulling up. OK, I need to go soon. You just stay calm, OK? Put something on TV and make something—or you and your honey go out somewhere nice for dinner. Whatever your favorite thing is.

M.R.: Thai. But there's no place here.

K.U.: Or Mexican. You loved the Mexican place out on Post. Order your favorite thing. You'll feel better.

M.R.: Maybe. Thank you.

K.U.: I have to go. It will be all right, OK? Jenny will be fine.

M.R.: Thank you. Bye bye. [ends call]

K.U.: Shit.

·III·

John Folger from Canyon Village 2/10/2020 15:12
Your New Neighbor!

Just want to say hi to everybody after the amazing block party! We just moved into the gray two-story across from the fountain. As a stay-at-home dad, I am overjoyed to have come to such a welcoming neighborhood.

Saul Toms from Canyon Village 2/10/2020 18:00
Re: Your New Neighbor

Glad to have you, John! I am a stay-at-home dad too. Dipping our toe into homeschooling this year. Looking forward to getting to know you.

Karen Ungular from Canyon Village 2/10/2020 18:06
Re: Your New Neighbor!

Nice to meet you John! Met you at the block party, remember? We're new too—just moved here in April.

Conferring With Ghosts Between the Hours of Three and Four-Forty-Five in the Morning

~ *Elou Carroll*

There is a sign on the back porch that reads *Everything Will Be Okay Unless It Isn't*. No one questions the validity of the sign, nor its presence, nor the fact that it changes daily—yesterday's message, *Concentrate On What You Can't Control, So You Won't Have To Feel Guilty*. The house with the faded blue picket fence has been empty for nearly fifty years.

Right now, the house is not empty. There is a girl sitting in the middle of the staircase, picking at the frayed edges of a moldy runner. No one saw her enter the house and no one will see her leave. It is three-ten in the morning, the neighborhood is asleep. The neighborhood has work, responsibilities, children to care for.

The girl does not work. The girl is, instead, failing university; she tries to blame her boyfriend, friends, mum, dad, seven-year-old Alsatian but even she does not find this convincing.

She likes to visit abandoned places and wallow in the dust. She does this when she should be sleeping. She doesn't want to be sleeping.

There are rivers of dust flowing down either side of the stairs. The girl traces a question mark and lingers on the dot, presses her finger down until the tip turns white. She asks a question of the stairs and when they do not answer, she kicks the banister. The crunch makes her teeth hurt.

Back at home, her boyfriend is unaware of her absence. In the house with the rotted wooden door, someone is aware of her presence.

"Where do you think she comes from?" they ask.

"Nowhere I know, not with that outfit," someone else responds. "Never seen such a thing."

"Hello?" She's on her feet and the staircase creaks.

"Did you hear that? She speaks!" someone says.

"Do you think she can hear us? I don't think she can hear us. Not really. They want to hear us but they never usually manage it," someone else is certain.

"I can hear you," she says, "but you're speaking very quietly and I'm not sure where you are."

"'Not sure where we are,' she says. Not sure where we are but she's standing on our staircase." Someone else might huff.

"Blocking the way too!" Someone might be crossing their arms. "No manners."

"Oh," says the girl, "excuse me."

She hops down the steps and into the long hallway. She traces another question in the dust with the toe of her shoe. The girl clasps her hands behind her back and waits, when they do not speak again she looks up and down the hall and wonders if she's imagining things. The girl is prone to fits of imagination and the someones do not contradict her.

When she is at home and her mind is pacing the hallway outside their bedroom, her boyfriend asks her to sit, hold his hands, talk. The girl does not do any of these things.

Instead of standing still, the girl explores the house with the scuffed cream wallpaper. One room in particular is difficult to open. From what she can see, it is full of hundreds and hundreds of rough cardboard signs. Through the gap in the door one board is visible— *It's Not Over. Yet.*—along with half of another. The half message reads: *Remember [...] To Eat [...] A Day.*

The girl considers what a day might taste like, and comes to the conclusion that it would depend entirely on whether it were a Sunday or a Tuesday, a Wednesday or a Friday. She thinks she might like to eat Saturday best, and has decided that it would taste like crisp ice water, freedom and sugar.

The door won't budge. The girl strokes another question into the wood, rests her head on its surface. Thumps once, twice. Sighs.

Someone follows her to the kitchen.

Someone else is already watching the girl disturb their crockery. She opens their cupboards, moves long-forgotten plates and cups, chokes on their dust.

"She's quite rude," someone says.

"Doesn't respect her elders," someone else agrees.

"It's rude to talk about someone as if they're not here, especially if you're not really here yourselves," says the girl.

"Do you think she's lost?" Someone might be pressing a finger to their chin.

Someone else might be doing likewise. "I think she must be."

The girl crosses her arms and decides the someones might leave her alone if she glares hard enough. It works on her boyfriend, who huffs and shuffles off until she comes to find him with her hands in her pockets and her shoulders hunched up by her ears. He opens his arms to her, and she dithers from one foot to the other.

The someones huff too but remain close. She is in their house and they will not be going anywhere; they were inside long before the girl and will linger longer still when she leaves. The girl kicks a cupboard door and it abandons its hinges. She thinks she should apologize.

She doesn't apologize.

While she is standing in the kitchen with her arms crossed and her frown drawn down from her forehead, a square of bent cardboard makes its way from the back porch, past the kitchen, down the hallway, through the house with the faded blue picket fence, rotted wooden door and scuffed cream wallpaper, and slips through the crack in the door to the sign room; someone else is carrying it, but the girl cannot see them and reasons that she must be dreaming.

The girl is pinching herself when a pristine piece of card makes its way in the other direction. Someone carries this one and though she likewise cannot see them, she is sure she is not dreaming. Her bicep bears the tiny crescent moons to prove it.

Arms now unfolded, she peers round the door-frame and squints into the dark. The torch on her keys is dim and useless. Her phone is on her night stand back at home. The house is no longer wired for electricity, though the light switches still tease in their wall sockets. The back door opens and the card slips out, stands up and the door swings shut.

Someone stands next to it.

The girl has never been on the porch because it faces too many windows and she does not want to be accused of delinquency. She does, however, want to see the new sign and so she looks over her shoulder and makes sure there is no one there to see her trespass.

Someone else is at the kitchen window.

Someone joins them.

Both someones eye her dusty footprints on the old wood, see her cross her fingers, crouch down low.

"Do you think she'll read it?" Someone else asks. "I don't think she'll read it."

"She has the eyes for it but she won't take it in." Someone is solemn.

"She really ought to. But she won't."

"Not likely, no," someone agrees.

The girl pictures her bedroom; back at home, her boyfriend might stretch out an arm and brush the negative space in which her body should be sleeping. A frown might shape his eyebrows and he might curl up, shiver, but will not wake. He is a heavy sleeper and he seldom notices her leaving, nor does he stir at her return.

It is four-forty-five in the morning. At the house, there is a sign on the back porch that sometimes reads *Call Your Mother,* othertimes *There's No Use Being Scared Of The Dark, It's The Light You Should Be Worried About,* or *The Other Side Is Almost Exactly The Same As The Side You Came From.* No one questions the validity of the sign, nor its presence—least of all the girl who should be sleeping. Right now, the sign reads *Skin Is More Forgiving Than Dust* and the girl is reading and not reading it at the selfsame time.

Night Harrowing

~ Catherine Hansen

Easter, who was three, was trying to climb onto my back while I did pushups. It delighted her how I groaned and teetered but did not stop. Mommy was weak yet Mommy was strong.

I had long since stopped leaving our apartment during the day. Except when I bore my daughter's weight, I hardly felt I was myself. And these repetitive movements—pushing, lifting—were a way of dwelling in this flimsy body, confessing that it was still my own. I savored it like the company of someone I planned to jilt.

Sometimes I kept pushing up until my arms shook and gave way, and I lay there stunned and annoyed while Easter crowed. In the other place, in the other body, nothing could tire me.

When I first started harrowing hell, it was on the night shift. It was a second job like any single mother might take when ends are not meeting. One famed harrower, the monk Ksitigarbha, is supposed to have refused nirvana just on the edge of reaching it. It was unthinkable to scale the heavens until the hells and all their seas were empty of suffering and their inhabitants freed. If I don't go to help them, he said, who will? I never glimpsed or refused enlightenment. No ends had met. I had no idea what I was doing.

The day it began, I was home with Easter on a weekday holiday. For much of the morning, as I caught up on chores long postponed, she had pressed for my attention. Life with her was often a matter of two irreconcilable sets of priorities, grinding their gears. Now, as the early drizzle turned to a hard rain, she was playing with her toys on her cork mat and I was listening to the cozy burble of their imaginary conversation.

"Yes please, I would like to have a birthday!" said a stuffed dragon.

"Then we must bake a cake," said an owl.

Suddenly, I felt watched. Rather, I felt framed by an awareness that was not mine. The sensation sharpened. I knew in the way I know in dreams: something had cast and cast about for me, and then had fixed upon me, and now already was coming for me. Full cry, headlong, it grew in my inner vision and filled it. And then it replaced me. There was no other word for what I felt. I had been replaced.

An observer might have noticed nothing, and my daughter didn't even look up.

In a fraction of that second's sleight of hand, another mind had stirred beside mine. A fraction after that, it was extinguished. Someone's will or emotion had risen and thrashed, like a shape under bedsheets—surprise, triumph, or shock—and now it was gone.

But it had left something behind, at the back of me. My inner surface followed its curves, as if I were a mask upon a scowling face. I was now a mere shadow of a thing more real.

"Mommy?" said my daughter. I had been silent too long. Swinging my chair around, I heaved her to my lap. I hugged her as she squirmed and tried to gather my thoughts as they scattered.

All the following morning as I made our breakfast and laid out our two sets of clothes, and then all day at work, it was there—my real body. That was the phrase that rose eerily in my mind. I tried to live our life for us like before, dropping Easter off at daycare on the way to my crowded desk. But its presence rang in my ears like a key struck deep down the scale, the minor note that darkens the chord. It was late November, and night by five. Among the last to leave work, caught in the amber of the last lighted floor, I seemed to see my real body one floor below, in the dark – mirroring my movements down the halls, stooping through the doorways.

One night I finally reached back for the thing that was reaching for me. After Easter was asleep, I locked myself in the bathroom. What I did then, with a frightful minimum of effort, was like closing one eye and opening another. Very suddenly my shoulders filled the tiny, lightless room as bottles clattered from shelves. As my head bent against the low ceiling, I thought I heard my daughter calling for me. First I froze. Then I recoiled in every way I knew how, trying to escape without daring to look down at what I was escaping from, but nothing changed. I was a hand jerking back from a hot pan, but the hand would not move. The matter of minutes it must have taken to return to myself passed for eternity.

Twenty-four hours later, I cowered in the foyer with my back to the shoe cabinet and did it again. I revolved slowly in the half-mirror that rattled on the hall door, turning my head as dancers do to keep vertigo at bay. Easter wasn't sleep-talking this time, but at the faintest noise from outside I was already clawing myself back, hysterical and guilty. Easter's mother's body was still right there, slipped into an adjacent, invisible slice of space. But it eluded the grasp, like a bar of soap in bathwater. It was not forthcoming. My real body was.

On the third night, the low clouds glowed with city lights. I was gaping in the tottery mirror at something that resembled large black ferns adhering to my back, busily overlapping from neck to waist. Bending over to study my real face had made me faint and sick. Nothing prevented my daughter from simply waking up, opening the door, and coming barefoot and dazed to look for me—the huge, jagged, cringing shadow in the corner. We would have to face each other in mutual terror, or she would just bolt senselessly for refuge in my arms, finding me nowhere until at last I flickered back.

The thought was unbearable, and so I decided I had to strike out alone. The city was a glowing dome with darkness pressing in all around it, and I imagined I had to get to that darkness. I found a babysitter and told him I was helping a friend's band record an album: a story he could have done without, as it wore thin over the weeks.

I didn't have a car. I took a late train one night into the city's upland outskirts, got off at the last little unmanned station, and chose a street that meandered uphill. The dark display of a closed shop framed the last streetlight. At the last house, the one lit window displayed a row of near-empty detergent bottles. The road turned steep and gravelly, switchbacking up for a mile or more to arrive at a deserted field, where a lonely sodium lamp gilded a pit full of planks and rebar. The field's far edge lay in the deep shadow of trees.

I had only been in my real body for minutes at a time. The first thing I thought to do with it now was to speak. Squatting in the dark under the trees, I heard its voice for the first time, and I was enchanted. It was thunderously deep. Every neutral phrase I tried to utter was heightened and haughty, a stage villain's repartee. I talked just to keep hearing it.

"My name is Griet," said my colossal, pitch-black voice, several times.

"I have a baby," it said. "Bay-by." I started to giggle and stopped short.

"I think I'm going to find out if I can fly," I said out loud to myself. I had guessed that the fronds on my back—pleated in intricate shrink-wrap patterns—might be wings. Since I had no idea how to make them function that way, I walked instead, and ran, and loped in circles. I broke a stone by crushing it in my left hand.

That moment of disconcerting triumph gave me pause. I saw with what half-conscious intensity I had been seeking something to crush. Insights, instincts, and desires lay tightly folded in every exploratory movement I had made. Now, under my silent self-regard, they loosened and drifted dimly before me. This thing, in whose reality I dwelled, was combative and proud. It hummed with anger and delighted in violence. It might find its truth roaring with joy astride vast ruins.

If I saw no place for that in my life, then I had no business returning to the field the following night, and then night after night. Yet I did—appalled and exultant.

Soon I started trying to photograph myself. I became fixated on one shot in particular.

It cut me off at the ankles and across the forehead as I crouched awkwardly and hugged my shoulders to fit my whole frame in. The lips drew back in an involuntary snarl at the flash, and the eyes lit up like a cave pool a mile beneath the earth. For a time, I was more in love with myself, specifically as I appeared in that photo, than with anyone I'd ever been with. I burned with the thought of myself. Sometimes I imagined being shown off like statuary: standing counterpoised, at my full height, with the extravagant crests like some ferocious ornamental bird and the smile full of murderous teeth. My imagination embarrassed me—like someone who casually alludes to a secret obsession in conversation, and feels the blazing glory rise to his cheeks. To this day, if it is a day at all, I am afraid that somehow I chose this, or that I brought it on myself.

Sometimes Easter freed me. When I picked her up every afternoon, holding her hand on the way to the station, I felt calm and empty. As she stopped at every pretext, to exclaim over a puddle or throw handfuls of leaves, I had no desire to be anything but the thing she called, the thing she called into being over and over, when she said "Mommy."

But the night field took on irrational, ritual contours in my mind, lost in the mountainous dark that pressed upon the dome of light. It was like going to see a lover. I blew my strained budget many times over on the babysitter and the train, and lost untold hours of sleep.

One night, I found a rusting utility trailer in the woods around the field. I thought of nothing better to do than to pick it up and throw it down a ravine, like a teenager trying to impress his girlfriend. As I did, a broken spar of it gashed my side. When I looked at what I had done to myself I was paralyzed. I had wrecked something I didn't know how to fix. That is when I noticed that the pennons on my back had partially separated, and hung like wet, black saran wrap. I had insulted my body by injuring it, I thought in my rising fright. Now it was going to fall to pieces in self-destructive vengeance. I tried gingerly to touch the place under my ribs, but misjudged the distance and instead thrust two serrated talons right into the bleeding flesh. My body roared at me through my own mouth with rage and hurt. Now it was clear I was disintegrating: I couldn't see my legs anymore. I was standing on vapor, wading in it. Panicking, I fled myself like a sinking ship.

As I returned by train that early dawn, unable to doze, I knew my body was a shattered ruin. I thought I could wait until nightfall to be sure of it, but I was so desperate to learn what had become of me that I did it in the bathroom at work that day, right in the open because the stalls were too small. And there I was, over the row of sinks, stark in the tawdry light. Utterly whole and restored, rueful and smirking, heedless of passing footsteps in the hall—the being in the mirror was, for all I knew, imperishable.

Several nights later I deliberately injured myself to see what would happen. The effect was immediate. At my back, the fern fronds separated again and hung in damp webs. Now my legs were gone; I was waist deep in a fog driven by wind, and this time I waited. The fog rose, and took me with it. After that, I was somewhere else.

I saw bare slopes, red like the threat of fire. A vacant phrase rose in my mind: the other side. At that time I still understood nothing, but that is exactly what it was. One of the other sides. As if I had emerged from a chrysalis, my wings (this is exactly what they were) stirred at my back, then briskly rose and tautened. Taking first flight felt like a new species of emotion, borne up by the landscape. The land sustained me because it knew me. It knew where I was from and what I was for.

I planed high over billows of earth mottled red and black. I began to see helpless bodies rolling in the heavy swell, as winged forms circled above—coal-shaded scars on the low sky. There was so much I didn't understand then: that this vast shipwreck with its circling raptors was mere appearance, a sediment of myth; but that its brutish matter repelled the meaning made by myths; and that both of these were true to say. Twisting bodies pushed up from deep in the red, curdled earth, to collapse exhausted and be carried away to the pits. Yet these bodies were immaterial, invisible. The pits, crammed full of limbs and lament, were also empty holes in the ground. The immaterial bodies were here for reasons they would never know. For reasons of justice, for reasons forgotten and long superseded, for inane or for implacably logical reasons.

The winged creatures, who looked like me, swooped down here and there like unwieldy peregrines to attend to the bodies. They took heavy flight again, or fell casually on each other, rending and maiming. They did not know the reasons either.

I landed at the crumbling edge of a pit. Petals in a broken thicket, the faces turned up in unison. Reaching down thoughtlessly to take the hand of the nearest one, I forgot myself until I saw that the others were trying to bury themselves and hide from me. The man struggled too, but I would not let go of his hand, and he went slack as I worked him free. As I folded him in my arms, he began to shake, and I shook too. There was nowhere else to go, nowhere to carry this body with its wobbling head and moaning mouth.

Some of the winged figures had stopped short in their orbit around the pits that pocked the earth into the endless distance. They were heading toward us. One of them paused low above us in tightening gyres. I laid the man between my feet just as it fell to the attack, clawing at my shoulders as I shielded the body beneath me. When I turned, and gripped the jaws of the creature at my back, and tore, and kept tearing as it buffeted me with desperate wings, I didn't think to wonder why I could do such things. I should have. When it was over I only stared at what I had destroyed, drawing the fading rapture close around me like a squalid mantle. Then I was certain I had made a terrible mistake—that I had let myself feel and do something ghastly, and now I was trapped, and lost. I groped in emptiness for my old, my own, my kindly shape, as I would have done in the field, ready to jog back down to the station. It wasn't there.

It was the man I was trying to rescue who showed me the way back out. I had gathered him up again and was cradling him to my chest. His knees were drawn up and his eyes were tightly closed. My mind kept helplessly reaching, and finally it touched something. It didn't belong to me, but to him. It was close by us, though he surely could not have known it existed, as perhaps it always had. Right then, because I perceived that I could, I spread my wings and simply stepped across to where it waited.

Tall grass surrounded me, under a muted sky the color of a long-postponed sunrise. I was no longer carrying anyone.

The man stood across from me, on unbroken legs, gazing at me with a strange expression as if he understood something vast. Then he simply turned and walked away, parting the grass.

This was not earth, nor the hell we had come from. It was a silken fringe springing like sedge from the wall that divided those places— it was the merest sliver between them. I was far out of my depth. But now, from this vantage, I could almost see myself waking under the trees and riding the dawn train home, half asleep and full of longing. That truth was breathingly close again. It tugged and drew me back.

I still thought, somehow, that daytime life could go on as before. I stopped making the long train journeys. I knew the owner of the little bistro on the ground floor of our building, who had a storage annex she kept empty. I explained that I needed a dark place to retreat and meditate that wasn't far from home. The room had its own key and I don't think she ever realized how much time I spent there. I held on to my job for a while. Then savings lasted a matter of months, then I borrowed for a time from friends. During the days Easter and I lay in bed, watched TV, and had breakfast for lunch and lunch for dinner. Our little gaieties and struggles weren't much different than before, even with all I did and saw every night, but I don't doubt that she

felt something was different. Once, during the dramatic dialogues between her toys that occupied much of her time, she shouted,

"You are not listening to me! I will come and eat you!" She thought it
was very funny when I dropped the folded towels and rushed to gather
her up, murmuring into her hair.

Harrowers of hell, whatever form they take, are expected to free
those who are worthy. If such a distinction could actually exist, I had
no way of making it. I was not a creature designed for that. I was not
meant to divine what laws subtended the other side, though I had sur-
mised that going to hell exacted a toll of pain, and that escaping hell
required something wholly contrary: mending, comforting, slicing
the old ropes, forcing open the sprung trap.

More than any sense of duty or even compassion, it was simple
base passion that made me return to hell to despoil it, joining the
ranks of all the saviors and bodhisattvas, the knights and the harri-
dans, the women and men (or former women and men), who had
gone down to the shores of hell not to be lost but to retrieve the
lost. But I believed that at least it was the passion of a great task of
mending, so great it could be imagined only in fractions, in stitches
and cross-stitches, through to the other side and across, and back
through, and across, with my arms full of souls. Delivering, in an
ecstasy of delivering, every night until I died, if I could die.

The babysitter arrived every night around Easter's bedtime, dropping his sleeping bag on the couch. I went four flights down, turned
the corner, unlocked a heavy door, and closed it upon pitch darkness.
I carried countless souls to refuge, striding through the walls between
worlds. Sometimes they writhed out of my embrace and tried to stumble away, wailing when I caught them. Afterward, when they met their
real bodies, they smiled at me, and sometimes wept for me.

I was a different thing than I had been, in ways not fully beyond
my control. The winged demons were always present, if more cau-
tious than before. I reserved all my pent-up wrath for them. When
they came after us, I tore them to pieces. Often I cackled and howled.
My laughter drove its taproot into the deeps from which this place
springs and into which it flows.

I'm not sure how much longer I could have continued like that. I
never found out, because finally one night, I couldn't go home. The

dark storage room, abiding in the small hours of a Monday morning in spring, tugged me on its tether. Soon the babysitter would stir in his sleep on the sofa and try to phone me. But something had changed. The nameless faculty I had possessed, which had let me follow that tether back, was gone. I was furious, gnashing, helpless, racing in circles. What would dare? To bar me from where Easter slept, with her knees tucked under her and her face buried in the pillow? But I could only continue carrying over the immaterial bodies one by one or three by three, and pause to try again, and fail, and wait, and snarl and rage, and fail again.

Gradually, I understood—and maybe all of us, suffering bodies and fiends alike, understood it. Something had withdrawn from the worlds. Some upholding ground had not crumbled, but drawn back, and left everything to fall into the foundations. Some obscure negligence far above had taken catastrophic proportions below; some minor transgression below had raised great storms above. It could easily have been my fault. Or it was something humanity had done without knowing, or despite knowing, accidentally-on-purpose, bringing everything down with it. What had happened to me was a side effect of this calamity. Or was its cause. Or both were true.

Already the people were coming. Wherever they would otherwise have gone, here is where they all came, and the black-red earth couldn't hold them. Wave upon wave struggled and kicked to the teeming surface, bewildered and blind. The demons came flapping dutifully down but even they were taken aback by the great multitude of the newly dead. None of this should have happened, but now it was the end. Perhaps not the end of all things, but the end of many, many things.

When Easter used to drop a full glass of juice or trip over my laptop cord, I would calm her and myself by sing-songing, "these things happen." I let those chiming words carry me as I toiled—these things happen. All would be well with us, I knew, when we were together again. I began to see people I knew. I saw my daughter's father, spat up from the soil by the force of all the desperate others beneath, lying face up in blank pain. I carried him to the place of strange, tall grass under a muted sky, where he rose and walked. He didn't know me, but he cried for me. And after that, I did nothing but search for Easter.

Time failed. It spun like a toothless flywheel. I don't know how long I looked for her, digging down into the caustic earth while all the others suffered, unaware I had abandoned them. Over and over I clawed my way back up, wings ragged and freighted with dirt. Time spun and sputtered—and then I found her.

I lifted Easter and held her curled up on my chest, her head under my chin. The instant after we crossed over together, I wasn't holding her anymore. She was standing before me, staring and serious. Then her attention shifted: the world beckoned, just as before. She gazed all around, and began humming and singing to herself in little snatches and fragments, as she always had when she was happy. She stroked the grass and peered into it, looking for living, moving things.

"Mah-mee-mee..." were the syllables I thought I heard her chant, just as she turned and marched carefully away, in search of me or something else. I almost followed her.

Everyone came. It took time—just shy of forever and evermore—but in my arms and on my back I carried every single one of them over. This hell is empty now, as far as I can tell, except for the demons, who have nothing now to occupy them except me, and so soon they will be gone too. If there are other hells, I don't know how to get there, or how to leave this one anymore. If that thin place I entered and left so many times had any claim to be called heaven, I can't enter it again without someone to carry, to hold close. If I could, I believe I could not stay.

I have lived in this body now for time out of mind. It consumes, transforms, and expels nothing. It takes nothing in and ushers nothing back into the world. I think there is nothing it would not survive. If anyone or anything ever comes to retrieve me, they will find me in it.

Here I lie, in a hut I built of the bones of my enemies. Somewhere far from this darkened plain, beyond my ken, the last true battle has long ended. I try to remember my old, freckled, stretch-marked body, whose uses and wherefores are lost forever—my dark secret kept from no one, my irrational and consoling fantasy. I lie and dream about it, drifting as an anchorless bark into fog.

The Beautiful People

~ Josh Rountree

The Academy Awards ceremony was held at the old Pantages theater in April of 1960 and that venerable venue never hosted anything
again for obvious reasons. These were the awards given for achieve-
ments in 1959. Afterward, we pillaged the debris to uncover the
envelopes containing the names of the would-be winners. *Ben Hur*
would have won Best Picture, had the evening been allowed to pro-
ceed to its conclusion. Why were so many of us inclined to search for
those envelopes? The simple answer is we were curious. In spite of
everything, most of us still loved the movies.

What do I remember from that night?

Everything.

First was the scent of Audrey Hepburn's Chanel No5 as she passed
within just a few feet of me on the red carpet. My sight was fading
by then, so she passed by in a chiffon blur. But the smell of her was
unmistakable. I would have called the whole thing off for a chance to
follow that scent past the marquis and into the red satin confines of the
theater; I might have given up everything for one chance to float in that
sea of beauty and grace.

The snap-flash of cameras stirred those assembled into a frenzy.
Stars advanced through that gauntlet of light, drawing all of us in with
the gravity of their smiles. We weren't supposed to be there, of course,
but our disguises granted us access. Hats were in fashion and the cool
night gave no one reason to question our bulky overcoats. The NBC
television cameras captured it all, and some of us can be seen in that
old video, haunting the sharp edges of a dream world.

The cameramen shouldered closer to the fray, shouting to be heard over
the brass band ponding out another refrain of "Hooray for Hollywood."

"Mr. Wilder! Say, do you think you'll win for *Some Like it Hot*, or
is Wyler gonna take it this year?"

"George! George! Is *Anatomy of a Murder* gonna run the table?"

"Doris! Hey, why don't you look this way?"

And when one of those forever faces turned and smiled the effect was every bit as mesmerizing as you'd hope it to be. I was in love with every one of them.

They were the soaring angels of an age, but they wanted more. They all craved eternity.

And we gave it to them.

Have you seen the 1951 classic, *Strangers on a Train*? It's one of my favorites. One of Hitchcock's best and that's saying something. Farley Granger was memorable as Guy Haines, but the standout in that film was the doomed Robert Walker, on loan from MGM to Warner, in the role of Bruno Antony. Walker reached deep inside and summoned up a perfectly charming psychopath, and in a better world that role would have granted him immortality.

But Walker was already a broken man by the time that picture was filmed. His movie star wife, Jennifer Jones, had left him for director David O. Selznick, and he didn't recover. He started drinking. Living like a man with nothing to lose. No matter their circumstances, some people just can't bear the weight of their humanity.

Robert Walker was dead before *Strangers on a Train* ever made it to the big screen.

One of my kith mates was, of course, intimately linked to Walker, and he spent considerable effort absorbing the poor man's misery. Giving the troubled actor, in return, that elusive something that made people special. My kith mate did his best.

But not everyone gets the Hollywood ending.

Ushers drew velvet ropes across the entrance to the Pantages, sealing the Hollywood elite inside the building. They left behind them a void in the Los Angeles night, a hollow space that could not be filled.

Tired reporters lodged freshly lit cigarettes in their lips and gathered around a bank of payphones. Automobiles idled up and down the boulevard, and those few fans who'd been allowed to watch the proceedings from hastily constructed bleachers engaged in an orderly exit, autograph books clutched in their hands, already feeling the memory of those beautiful faces beginning to soften and distort in their memories. A few of them lingered, taking a seat on the curb and casting occasional looks at the closed theater doors, but most crept off to nurse their sudden longing alone.

My kith mates and I gathered in the glow of the marquis, forming a loose semicircle as we linked hands, facing the theater. We could feel our charges inside, pulling at us, alive with laughter. In our minds they were creatures of brilliant white light. They would never darken, never burn out.

A few police officers encouraged us to scatter, but it was easy enough to change their minds, elevate their night with pleasant thoughts and the desire to be somewhere else.

Even in those final moments, we poured what remained of ourselves into our charges. We clung to one another, our spines coiled, our faces grown flat and fissured. Those of us who had not entirely lost our sight felt darkness closing around us. Bones crackled and tendons groaned. Those of us who still had teeth felt them blacken and break.

Our beauty and our souls are our treasures.

But we have always given them away willingly. There had been a film script making the rounds for a while in the forties. A grand tapestry of Los Angeles glamour and human ambition threaded with secret societies and dark bargains that had been the fabric of this place since Hollywood and Vine were still known as Prospect and Weyse.

The script was called *The Beautiful People* and it would have been a blockbuster if it had ever been made. Might even have given *Ben Hur* a run for its money.

Here's the pitch: A producer with a struggling film studio finds an ancient book—because there is always an ancient book in those kinds of films—and he summons a race of immortal beings from the belly of the earth to feed his actors and actresses their grace and beauty. The stars call these beings Brutes, and the Brutes do not mind this service. It's their reason for being. And every star simply must have at least one. But you can't help but feel bad for the Brutes. They don't just give away their grace like the fallen angels they are. They absorb the misery and the human failings of their charges, and the weight of it twists them into monsters.

There was even a romantic subplot where an actor falls in love with one of the hideous Brutes; this is a ridiculous notion, but Carey Grant was supposedly attached to the project and I'm sure he could have sold it.

Like a lot of scripts, this one never made it to production. Hollywood keeps some stories for itself.

I read a draft of that script at some point and it came to mind as we stood there before the Pantages whispering prayers to the Beating Heart who bled every one of us into existence. The scriptwriter took a lot of license with the details but he got most of the important parts right.

The ending though? He got that all wrong.

Another of my favorites is *The Thin Man* from 1934. William Powell and Myrna Loy are pure perfection as Nick and Nora Charles. That sounds like I'm reading from a studio ad, but you just can't oversell this movie. It's whip-smart and joyous, and it's all due to the sheer presence of those two on screen together. They're so alive and invested in their roles that even as I laugh at their antics, I can't help but feel a touch of melancholy. Humans can never really be that perfect, can they?

My two kith mates who'd attached to Powell and Loy were practically dust at the end. They gave all of themselves to lift their charges to such heights, but neither of them had regrets. This is our reason for being. We weather the crippling empathy, but we're repaid with flashes of euphoria. Powell and Loy were brilliant without us. But with our help they were able to connect with that spark of the divine that lives in all humans. And through our charges, we caught a brief glimpse of that which we've been forever denied.

We love our charges, but we are not entirely selfless.

William Powell and Myna Loy were two of our greatest success stories, but even they have been forgotten by so many.

We give our charges everything. We love them unreservedly.

But it never seems to be enough.

The Beating Heart heard our whispers.

The belly of the world groaned and shifted, reminding us of our own bloody, rebellious births. Every one of us felt the acute homesickness of the runaway, even though most of us had decided long years before that we never wanted to go home again.

Beneath our feet, the earth yawned so suddenly that the reporters at their payphones had no time to scatter. The Beating Heart raised up his hands, grasped at the folds of the world and pulled them apart.

Hollywood shattered.

Fires erupted from the sudden starburst of fissures; I cannot say whether this was from broken gas lines or a manifestation of our father's anger at being summoned. The earth was hungry, swallowing police cars and stoplights and tourists with the cameras still strapped around their necks. The fire found the Pantages with supernatural alacrity, and the building became a bonfire.

Screams and howls rode the smoke, and The Beating Heart silenced them with a sudden clenching of his fist. The walls of the Pantages caved inward with terrible speed, and the building tumbled into the opening earth.

My kith mates and I hovered over the void, nearly faltering beneath the weight of all that pain. We had cast those souls into a charnel pit, confident that the fire would render them truly timeless. Forever young. Forever beautiful.

Modern day myths.

We joined in the intimacy of their death throes. We watched through their eyes as they gazed on the divine.

And for the briefest second, the divine gazed back.

Next time you watch *Casablanca*, look for me in the background. During the scene in Rick's Café Américain, when Victor Laszlo leads the defiant chorus of La Marseillaise, you can see me hunched over one of the tables, raising my drink and my voice with the other extras. I had given away very little of myself at that point and could easily pass for a weathered but still able-bodied human.

It was the love of film that compelled me to sneak onto Michael Curtiz's set and claim that tiny portion of history, but it was vanity too. Is there not a part inside all of us that craves to be in the picture? A part that desperately wants to be noticed?

I've served my purpose. I'm bent and blind and monstrous. There lives inside me a constant ache to give away what little grace I have left, but it's hard to find any takers these days. I've become what the movies would make of me, a nightmare demon, summoned from the pit to exchange souls for earthly glory.

And I miss my charges so very much.

There's no home for me in the belly of the world any longer. My kith mates have all been consumed and bled back into a new existence, but I can't seem to let go of this place even though it no longer wants me. I can't shake the black and white lure of Hollywood dreams or the Technicolor memory of that day in 1960 when we turned women and men into legends and our actions caught the eye of God.

I want that eye to notice me again.

Crossing

~ *Jennifer Quail*

It is winter. It is always winter.

Marie-Eve has never seen a train on the tracks. As long as she can remember it has been a dead spur, leading somewhere forgotten in the distant hills. Sometimes when Maman is not watching her she stands on the tracks and stares north into the hulking, ancient Laurentian Mountains. Papa says the trains came once, but Maman says they have not come in years. She wonders if she could walk to the mountains, or if they would always remain on the horizon. She never tries.

She never sees a train, either, until the first night she sees the woman.

She does not know what woke her, at first. Someone, Maman or Papa, moving in the kitchen? Or the wind rattling the door of the barn?

She slips from under the covers and pads to the window, the floorboards rough and cold beneath her bare feet. Outside there is a light on a pole above the railroad crossing, casting a sickly green-gold pool to warn the drivers who rarely pass of the trains that never come. Marie-Eve peers out, waiting, not knowing for what. Only knowing it is coming.

The woman walks into the light from the shadows somewhere near the house. She wears a dark, heavy, men's coat and her boots leave deep treaded tracks in the snow. She stops at the edge of the road, where the tracks are level with the pavement. She waits.

A pale circle of light appears in the southern darkness. The train arcs up as if springing out of the ground at the horizon. It races across the frost-bitten rails, black and sleek with the glowing cyclops eye of the engine lamp slicing into the night ahead.

The woman stands, hands crammed deep in the pockets of her coat, watching as the train rushes out of the gloom. Marie-Eve can feel the whole house tremble and she's sure Maman and Papa will wake, or in the barn across the tracks the cattle will start lowing. If it were day they would scatter across the fields, she's sure, tripping over the jagged corn stalks that stubble up through the snow. They've never seen a train here, either.

The long, dark engine rolls past the house but while the floor shakes and she can see the steam hissing from the wheels, Marie-Eve can't hear the engine's rumble or the creak of the brakes. There is no light from the cab, though she thinks she sees a dark shape moving from one side to the other, a form that might be at the window looking back. The whole train is dark, not just with lights dimmed or shades drawn, but painted deeper black than India ink and all the glass darkened, too.

Marie-Eve presses her nose to the window, straining to see the woman between the cars. She should be able to see shadows at least in the pool of the lamp. But a light, the head lamps of a truck coming around the curve, slices across her vision and she has to blink.

When she can see again, the train and the woman are gone. The truck thuds across the grade crossing and disappears, gone up the road, and there are only the tracks gray with frost and the empty pool of lamplight.

Marie-Eve tells her Maman about the train, but not the woman. Maman says Marie-Eve was dreaming, that she'd heard a truck passing on the road, carrying milk cans from the dairy twenty kilometers east to the town twenty kilometers west and in her sleep imagined the rattling was a train. Maman says in the winter it's easy to imagine things, even in your sleep. It is convincing, for now. Comforting.

So much so Marie-Eve does not tell her, or Papa, when five winters later she awakes one night and sees the woman waiting for the train again.

This night, she is in the kitchen, the oil lamp bathing the ice box and the wood stove in a flickering greasy gold. The shadows make Papa's old hunting coat look as if someone is hanging inside it on its hook. Maman left her glasses on the drain board and the reflected glow makes them look like solid disks of shiny metal. Marie-Eve does not dare turn on the electric light. They will not notice a sliver of the pate-de-lac-St-Jean is missing when it's cut for tomorrow's supper, and she will sleep better without quite as much an ache in her stom-ach, she thinks. But better not to wake them anyway.

Marie-Eve moves on tip-toe, listening to the house breathe around her. Papa says the faint creaks and moans are the dry boards, the wind, but in the dark like this Marie-Eve likes to think she can hear the frost prickling across the walls outside and crackling the window glass.

She thinks she hears the soft padding of feet above her, Maman perhaps going to Marie-Eve's room. The noise is like someone moving to her window, at least, and she blows out the lamp. Now there is only the green-yellow outside from the light at the crossing and she is alone in the dark, frozen as surely as the ground outside. She leans over the sink, pushing back the flour-sack curtain, and looks.

She jumps when the shadow moves from the porch, out of the dark corner into her line of sight as if coming from the door. The woman wears the heavy man's coat, her hands driven deep into the pockets. Her boots leave deep, treaded tracks in the snow. Marie-Eve can see puffs of white where the woman breathes in the knife-sharp cold. But while she can hear the sighing crackles of the frost on the walls and the rush of blood in her ears, she does not hear the footsteps crunch in the snow.

She feels the train approach but does not hear it. From the kitchen, she cannot look down on the tracks, so she cannot see the length of the train, but as the long, black engine glides to a stop she sees the movement in the cab, a figure behind the darkened glass. The fig-ure moves closer, but she cannot see a face, only shadows swathed in deeper shadow.

The shadow, she is certain, looks out at the house.

Now she feels the thrum of the engine deep in her chest, and her mind wills there to be sound, but there is only the usual winter night murmurs. She can't see the woman at the crossing, but as the long locomotive begins to move, she looks for the footprints in the snow. When she looks up again, the train and the woman are gone.

She goes back to bed, still hungry, but at least no one has noticed she is awake. The next morning, before breakfast, she stands on the tracks, staring north, but there are only the distant shadows of the mountains, ancient and empty and too far to reach. There are no footprints in the snow but her own.

The third time, Marie-Eve is fifteen, and she is not in the house. Maman is in the hospital in Chicoutimi, an hour away, and Papa is tired. The chores are late, because they are late getting home to the cold house, but the chores must be done. Someone has to go to the barn with the bucket of hot water to thaw the pump and make sure the cows that have not yet been sold can drink.

Marie-Eve lugs the steaming pail to the wellhead, her breath rasping as loud as Maman's did before she went away. The cold burns into her lungs. Her coat is too small but it can last another winter if it must. It is thin, too, so she thinks that the prickling of the skin of her neck is only the wind brushing its chill hand over her. She will be back inside soon, she thinks, and looks back to the house. There is an oily gold glow from the lamp in the kitchen, but the stirring of an upstairs curtain tells her Papa has gone up, leaving the light for her.

A rush of wind makes the door of the barn rattle on its hinges. She checks, but it remains firmly latched.

When she looks back the woman is walking from the shadow of the porch, her hands buried deep in the pockets of the heavy coat.

Marie-Eve turns without thinking to the south. A pinprick of light is growing, from the size of a star to the beam of a penlight to the glow of a torch to the lamp of the locomotive cutting through the darkness so sharply she thinks it could be a solid blade. From outside, without the safe thickness of glass between her and train, there is a depth to the black cars that has its own gravity. She wants to fall towards them, as if they are a train-shaped void and she is standing on the edge, looking down into some unfathomable abyss.

Something in the abyss moves and she realizes the woman is gone.

Marie-Eve drops the bucket and starts to run, and the train starts to move. The streamlined edges of the cars blur into the darkness, and she cannot say where the cars ends and their shadows on the snow begins. The silence pulls the sounds of the night, even her panting breath, into the train's wake.

Her boots sink deep, the snow turning slick under her weight and she trips. Her hands burn with the dry cold through her threadbare gloves as she pushes herself back to her feet. The light has gone out in the kitchen, the curtain upstairs is still, and Marie-Eve stumbles to the tracks, skidding up the raised bank until she stands between the rails, looking north. There is no sound, but a vibration shudders up through the soles of her boots, a rhythm like distant iron wheels on steel rails.

She might have stood there all night if the milk truck hadn't clattered around the curve, and an absurd fear of being caught in its headlights' beams sends her scrambling back to the house.

Papa sells the last of the cows after Maman dies. The corn stalks after harvest stubble the field, waiting to be plowed under in the spring. Marie-Eve cooks, and makes the long drive to town when the old truck doesn't freeze up and when the roads aren't iced. She thinks, more than once, about driving away for good, but Papa stays, and she can't leave him alone. And in some part of her mind, she cannot imagine leaving the house. If she leaves, she sometimes thinks when she's lying in the dark listening to the frost creep across the walls, then the house will somehow cease to exist.

Or perhaps she will cease to exist anywhere but the house.

One night, the winter after she takes Papa to the hospital in Chicoutimi for the last time, Marie-Eve hears a sound like the barn door banging on its hinges. The only thing inside it now is the plow the farmer who leases the land has stored there until spring comes, but she pulls on Papa's old coat anyway. Her boots creak into the corn-flour-dry snow and her breath steams with every stabbing-cold breath. She shoves her hands deep in her pockets and trudges out, across the tracks.

The light stabs out of the south and the ground trembles as she steps into the green-gold pool of the light at the crossing. Marie-Eve turns, because now she hears the high, keening whistle of a locomotive cutting through the night air. The black engine slices past, pushing the darkness aside like a plough turning earth. The wheels shrill with the brakes as the train rolls to a stop before her and Marie-Eve looks up at the platform between the first car and the engine. The figure in the cab turns back towards her, and through the glass of the door she sees that it is shadow on shadow. Within the cars behind it are more shadows, she can feel the weight of them moving and pressing the train on to the north. Marie-Eve looks, but the mountains are shadows, too, black on black horizon.

When she turns back, she can see the house between the train cars. A curtain at an upstairs window stirs. The greasy gold light of the lamp goes out in the kitchen. Behind her, she hears the clank of the bucket as it's dropped in the snow.

The train's wheels start to turn, and Marie-Eve hears a rattle of a truck in a distance.

Marie-Eve reaches for the platform, stepping up, falling forward into blackness as the train lurches towards the mountains.

Marie-Eve stands on the tracks, staring at the Laurentians looming on the horizon. She wonders if she could walk along the tracks and someday reach the mountains, or if they would always stay just ahead on the horizon. Or would she be struck by a train?

She has never seen a train, but Papa says they came, once.

Maman calls from the porch. It's getting dark and the cold is crackling across the ground, so sharp Marie-Eve thinks she can hear it. There is a faint tremor in the rails, but Maman says the trains never come any more.

It is winter. It is always winter.

At the Heart of the River

~ Jessie Kwak

I have always loved you.

When you were a little boy, skipping stones across my broad back and plucking fat, splashing tadpoles from my shallows, I clung to you every time you left my banks. I was in the black dirt beneath your nails and the dank reek your mother would yell at you to wash off before dinner. Sometimes I would splash a daub of mud behind your ear and it would stay hidden there for days, weeks. Until you came back to me to play once again.

When you ran to me after your father came home drunk and vengeful, I saw you cry for the first time. The salt stung but I lapped your tears like they were the first fall rains when you heard him calling for you and sat up, stricken, splashing handfuls of me onto your face to hide your crying.

When you first brought *her*, I eddied and churned as you both slipped naked into me, tasting you both as you tasted each other. I decided quickly I didn't much care for her girlish giggle or the way she squealed in disgust when her toes squelched into the same black silt you'd smoothed over your boyish face as pretend camouflage years ago. I also didn't care for the bitter, toxic-tasting cologne you'd worn for her. I drew up icy currents from the deepest places in my heart until she shrieked, shivering, and begged you to go back to the shore. There, you drank cheap, sweet wine and made love for the first time on a blanket while I sulked and swept the bad taste farther downstream.

When you proposed, years later, you told her how much it meant to return to the place you first loved. She assumed where you first *made* love, but I knew the truth. *I* am the *place* you first loved. You tried to get down on a knee, but, no, it's too dirty, she said. She pulled you back up into her arms, but I seep into the soil, too, and I shifted beneath you both, just enough to make you lose your balance and step back with a yelp to splash your shoe into my shallows. You pulled her down with you and she caught her hand on a sharp rock. Her sun tan lotion smothered me in a greasy sheen, and the acrid metal you've put on her finger disgusted me. But I have a weakness for the taste of blood and I sucked at her hand greedily, pushed as much of myself into her wound as I could. You were laughing but she was angry, calling you clumsy, clutching her injured hand. Black silt and red blood dripped off her elbow into my lapping waves and I drank them both.

I have always loved you. And I still love you now, when you're fresh from her funeral in Sunday black. I'm sorry, my love. Although I won't lie and say I'm sad she's gone, you must believe me that this wasn't my intention. Infections simply have a way of spreading, and my silt is rich and alive.

I love you as you pick up rocks from my bank, examining them just as you did when you were a boy, looking for that perfectly shaped stone to skip across my back. I leap with joy that you might do so again—but, no. You're not looking for a smooth skipping stone, you're looking for a jagged one, like the one that tore her hand. Ah. I see.

You find one and cock your arm back to throw, and I will take your rocks hurled in anger just as happily as your rocks skipped in idle joy.

But you don't throw it.

You slip it into your pocket, instead; its jagged bulk juts against the fabric of your dress trousers. You pick up another stone, directly from my shallows, with no care this time for the stone's shape. Into your pocket it goes, a damp stain spreading out from your pocket.

You find another, another, reaching farther into my current, no heed paid to the state of your clothes or shoes as you wade in to fill your suit pockets with my stones. You fall to your knees and do not notice the pain, you bend back a fingernail and I taste blood; it's sweet, my love.

Now I'm too deep for you to crawl and you're walking, wading farther into me than you've ever gone, past the sun-warm swimming hole you built one teenaged summer and into the swift current at my heart.

Isn't it beautiful, the way the sunlight breaks the surface of the water and ripples in my currents? I lap kisses into your ears and nose, but your steps hesitate, hands clawing at your pockets.

Isn't it stunning, the way the schools of little silver minnows shatter like glass when you rush through, fingers pulling stones out of pockets to tumble downstream—I'll make them smooth, eventually.

Your mouth opens for breath and I fill you. Your arms windmill to swim and I dance with you, swirling us both as I've wanted to do all these years, tumbling us until you're dizzy.

Doesn't it move you, how lonely cold-cold-cold I am at my heart?

You seem tired of dancing, so I shift an ancient, slime-slick stone beneath your foot; your foot slips beneath and I hold you tight.

There's so much I've wanted to show you.

Jamón Íberico

~ Lexi Pérez

Every moment of our ancestry has culminated in the DNA coding—
the *programming*—of our minds, bodies, and souls. We have a prime
directive: survive and procreate. We are driven by our programming.
We are our programming.

There's this pig. This kind of pig that only eats acorns from some
specific place for its whole life. This strict diet creates a marbling of
the pig's fat and muscle that, when dry-aged, makes for some very
expensive ham. *Jamón Íberico.*

Jamón Íberico is served everywhere in Spain, and it's easily identified wherever you find it because it's the only kind of meat served
straight from the corpse.

This is only a minor exaggeration, as the meat is dry-aged by the
leg. Restaurants and merchants buy legs of ham at a time, and cut
strips of flesh so thin you can nearly see through it. Even then, shav-
ing it slice by slice, they must sell it for an exorbitant price, to make
up for the massive upfront cost of an entire damn pig leg.

The first time I saw *Jamón Íberico*, I didn't recognize it for what it
was. I didn't recognize it at all. I was with my mother, young, maybe
ten, maybe eleven, and I saw something dense and heavy and oblong
set proudly on display on the bartop. I remember creeping closer and
closer, finding a smell, being unable to place the smell, creeping closer. I remember staring—squinting—at the prickly spikes of wiry fur
left around the bony ankle, tracing my eyes up and down the shining metal of the stand. It wasn't until my mother's confused and displeased hand fell upon my shoulder that I saw, with horror, the thing
I was actually looking at.

A shackle was strapped around the ankle of the pig. The hoof, still
dirty, pointed haphazardly to the far right corner of the restaurant. It
was presented so prominently, so proudly; the curved metal arm that

held the cuff high glinted malevolently, and the mahogany base shone. A wire, like a potter might use on his clay, lay draped over the exposed meat of the creature's thigh. As I watched, stupefied, enamored, a hand drew the wire up the pink, white, and tan leg - a parchment thin sheaf of ham curling behind it. The smell, still unrecognizable, slapped me across the nose again, before encasing me, seeping into my hair. I decided it must be the smell of being buried alive.

The most striking thing about first seeing *Jamón Íberico* is how easily such a cuff would fit around your ankle, how similar in length they might be, toe to thigh. From time to time, I will catch a glimpse of myself, in some such position, and see immediately, for a moment or a glance, exactly how like *Jamón Íberico* my leg could look. Some of these times, when I close my eyes, I can see the thin little wire, stroking up my thigh, up again and again and to the bone, leaflets of ham fluttering away.

Strip by bloodless strip.

Thin enough to see through.

Just one leg lasts ages. Ages and ages.

I've always been proud of my physique. Particularly my legs. Not proud in a sense where I needed to show them off. Just proud in the sense that my legs were strong, and powerful, and would never let me down. The cut of the calf was deep; flexing them, I saw the thickness of the muscle, knew it could do whatever I asked. The cut of each thigh, while less pronounced, was no less impressive. My legs were heavy. Dense. *Strong.*

There was a man in Germany who posted an ad on Craigslist, asking if anyone would be interested in eating him alive. Another man responded, saying yes, yes he would like to eat that man alive. The two got together and wrote up a contract. The contract detailed the sequence of events that would transpire, and that they each recognized the potential repercussions of such events. They both signed it.

The first thing the second man did was cut the penis from the first man, and fry it. I don't remember if they both ate that or not, but at a certain point, does it even matter? The second man was arrested, but as he had that contract, they had to let him walk. There was no law against cannibalism in Germany at the time.

There is now.

I've heard human flesh tastes like pork. I've heard it's the only other kind of meat that would. I've heard reasoning for these claims, but I don't remember any of it. I know there is an illness that can be contracted from cannibalism, but I also know this only comes from eating the brain.

All living creatures, regardless of intellect or wisdom or willpower, are simple reproductions of their programming, as adapted to the circumstances they arrived in. It was never nature versus nurture, only nature and nurture—only us.

It is our nature to protect ourselves, propagate ourselves, to perpetuate the self. Any action taken contrary to this nature, this directive, is contrary to our programming. To attack one's own flesh, in the animal world, is a sign of intense sickness, parasitic and contrary in nature to the very being of the animal itself. In the human world, too, the act often indicates sickness of the mind, or (and) a product of religion. It is not impossible for us to break from our programming, it is just very difficult to do so. Someone who inherited OCD, who has it locked in their genetic coding, who has to touch every wall in the room six times before they can leave it, will tell you very quickly that this genetic quirk of their programming does not promote either their survival or procreation, though every bit of their nature screams that not to do it is to die. Yet, with much work, much labor, much hardship—through therapy, and medication, and practice—this person can slowly disentangle themselves —their true selves—from this programming.

But what does consuming the self do? You are both destroying and preserving the very thing evolution has taught it to protect.

☉

There was a man who rode a motorcycle. He got in an accident. His leg, separated from his body in the crash, was impossible to reattach. As his leg was his property, he brought it home. He called his friends. They had a barbecue.

In some ways—many ways—I envy this man.

He did it the easy way.

I've read about so many accounts of autocannibalism in humans. Almost all of them were forced. Prisoners of war forced to eat their own ears, men on drugs biting off their own fingers and swallowing them—even the man on the motorcycle didn't truly choose to eat himself, he simply ate a piece of meat that *used* to be himself.

I have gotten a lot of sympathy since the accident. The trauma to my body impacted my mind, and this was quickly noticed by those around me. I, in turn, noticed their noticing. I sent everyone away, told them I needed to heal.

In reality, it had just gotten too hard to fit in anymore. Too hard to smile at the right time or make the right joke. It wasn't just the pain, not just the stress, it was also the tantalizing distraction of anticipation. The energy of my mind could hardly be spent on mundane pleasantries—no matter how well-meaning my visitors were.

Prosthetics are better than they've ever been. Thanks to kind donations and my own comfortable savings, I have one for everyday wear—walking, sitting, driving, etc—one for hiking, and one for swimming.

Yes, it does have a flipper.

You don't actually walk on a fake leg—you more sit on it. My nub doesn't take any of my weight, it just has a nice little cup to lean back in.

I didn't host a barbecue, if that's what you're thinking. I might, eventually. But *Jamón Ibérico* is dry-aged, not cooked.

Even though I know it's not nearly time yet, I limp out to the backyard, hobble over to the shed. I already know what to expect when I open the door, but the smell still surprises me—it smells like being buried alive.

Ten and Gone

~ Christopher Hawkins

Two hits with the bump key and the door popped open like it had never been locked. It was a cheap Connor entry set, the kind that contractors bought in bulk. It was a best-case scenario, better than Marcus had dared to hope for. He straightened, adopting the air that he had every right to be there, on this stranger's porch in the middle of the night, lockpick in hand and a flashlight on his belt. He listened for the beeping of an alarm that he knew would never come. They always installed the alarms later, if they installed them at all, and this place was new, so new that he could smell the fresh paint as he stepped in over the threshold.

10

The subdivision had come up quick, a tidy little enclave of McMansions built to sell for two-and-a-half, maybe three million each. Marcus had been watching the site for weeks and even prowled around it a time or two after dark, hunting for stray power tools. Most of them were half-finished with bare studs and plastic undersiding still showing, but not this one. No, with this one he'd hit the jackpot. The place was finished all the way down to the custom brass light switches and lit up like a Christmas tree with all the new owners' possessions stacked in neatly labeled boxes.

It would be a quick score, maybe even a good score if he was lucky enough to find a safe that hadn't been bolted to the floor, or a jewelry box tucked away in the corner of the master bedroom. He needed a good score now, maybe more than he ever had. A beefy custom stereo or a box of Louboutin shoes. If it was here, he'd find it, and he'd find it fast. Ten minutes was all he'd ever needed in a house. His internal clock was as good as a stopwatch. Ten minutes to grab the best stuff and get out. Ten minutes and he'd be gone.

He crossed the foyer and took the steps of the central staircase two at a time, paying no mind to the way his heavy footsteps rang against the rough tile and crunched on the carpeting. Most of the best stuff was sure to be on the first floor, but if there was something that the new owners held especially dear, they would have moved it upstairs before anything else. He'd passed a few boxes in the foyer marked "baby toys" in big, cartoon bubble-letters, and made a mental note to check them on the way out for anything that he might be able to bring back to Trina as a peace offering. Maybe a teddy bear or one of those little stuffed dogs with the big heads and the sad eyes that she used to collect back in high school. If he came back with one of those for the baby, she might leave the chain off the door when she talked to him. She might even let him back inside to share the bed again.

He paused at the top of the stairs to get his bearings. Wide landing. Short hallway to either side. Master suite on one end. Two, maybe three bedrooms on the other. He'd take the big room first and sweep through the others on his way back. There were paintings on the walls, and he took a few seconds to eyeball each one. He didn't know art, but could usually make a fair guess and pick one that would sell. None of these were it though, just blurry figures rendered in clumsy brushstrokes, like out-of-focus photographs. Amateur work set in ornate frames to make them look valuable. The wife was a painter, he guessed, which meant they could afford for her to be a painter. It boded well for his chances of finding jewelry in the bedroom. He might even be able to offload a few of the frames once he'd ditched the paintings inside. One of them was already empty, just hanging crooked in the center of the landing like a wide-open window.

9

He strode toward the master suite, wondering, not for the first time, what kind of job someone had to have to afford a place like this one, with its high ceilings and its light fixtures that looked like they'd come straight out of a palace. Something a damn sight better than anything he'd ever been able to hold down, and probably a lot cushier, too. The problem with guys who had jobs like that, and places like this, was that they never appreciated them. He'd bet this whole take that the guy was on some shrink's couch every week whining about how rough he had it, never knowing that someone like Marcus was waiting out there, just waiting for the right time to bump his lock open and take everything that wasn't nailed down. With any luck the guy would have plenty to talk about at his next appointment.

The door to the bedroom was open, but he paused there out of habit, listening for anyone who might be inside, calculating the time it would take to get back down the stairs if he heard a voice. But there was no one here. He'd watched the place for hours, sitting up the road in his white van, looking for warning signs and finding none. The only odd thing had been the light, shining out of every window, almost too bright. No doubt they'd wanted to make it look like someone was home, but without a car in the driveway or any motion inside at all, it might as well have been a beacon.

The bedroom was big, too big for Marcus' taste, with an ornate, king-sized bed and carpet so plush that his feet sank into it as he walked. Who needed this much space just to sleep? It was almost enough to make him mad, especially when he thought about Trina and the baby in that ratty little one-bedroom apartment. But that was okay. Being mad quieted down that nagging little voice that told him he ought to feel guilty for being here. Being mad made it easier.

The bed was made, and it struck him as odd how finished it seemed, but not so odd that he let it slow him down. It was the closet he was after, and it did not disappoint. It was big enough to be a bedroom all on its own and lined with his stuff on one side and hers on the other two. Nice shoes. Expensive shoes. A few of the Loubatins he'd been after. Manolos and Jimmy Choos, too. Enough to make this trip worthwhile all by themselves. He yanked the cover off the bed and piled them all in the center of it, trying not to smile too much, trying not to get ahead of himself when there was still so much left to be done.

8

He'd been hoping for jewelry, or maybe a laptop or two, but no such luck. He had the shoes bundled in the sheet, which he slung over his shoulder like a bargain basement Santa Claus as he bounded down the stairs, but that was all. Not even the clothes had been worth taking. They looked expensive, but were cheap to the touch and slippery like cut-rate vinyl. It didn't matter. He still had the rest of the house, and now that he had the lay of the place he was starting to map out his route in his head. Upstairs again first. Two, three minutes, tops. Then a quick sweep through the dining room to find the box that held the silver and China plates. Grab the TV from the living room and anything else worth having along the way.

He dropped the shoes in the foyer, where he'd decided to make a staging area, and started back up the stairs. His initial shot of adrenaline was starting to wear off. If something was going to go wrong, it would have happened by now. But he was in the clear with almost eight minutes left and didn't have to rush. Still, he took the steps two at a time. He must have stepped in something sticky along the way, because he could feel the way his boots clung to the carpet as he went. Insurance would pay for the carpet, he knew. Insurance would pay for all of it, the lucky bastards. He'd never had insurance, never had anything worth insuring. Not until now, anyway. Maybe he'd get enough from this score to make this time the last time. Maybe—

He froze two steps from the top. His adrenaline surged. There was a box on the landing. It hadn't been there before. He was sure of it. It was right in the middle of his path and he would have had to have stepped right over it. There was no way he could have missed it, either on the way up or on the way back down. And yet, there it was, a squat little cube of cardboard with the flaps hanging loose. Scrawled across its front in unsteady black letters were the words GOOD STUFF.

7

He stood statue-still, listening to the quiet as the clock ticked down in his head. Someone had put the box there, which meant that there was someone here, inside the house with him. And yet, he heard nothing but the sound of his own breath and the thudding of his pulse in his ears. If someone was here, he should have been able to feel it, the same way that you could feel when someone was trying to sneak up behind you in a quiet room. But there was no one. The doors had not moved and everything down to the paintings on the walls was exactly as he had left it. Everything except for this new box, this box of GOOD STUFF.

He crept his way up the last two steps, breathing shallow and quiet, wincing at the sticky sound of his boots as they pulled at the carpet. Something glinted beneath the loose flaps of the box, and he crouched low to get a closer look. If this was a trap, this was when it would spring. A woman with a baseball bat over her shoulder. A policeman with his pistol drawn. But there was nothing in the stillness but empty air. He reached out and the flaps fell aside, limp and heavy, like wet leaves.

He let out a low whistle, forgetting all caution as he got a look at what was inside. Here was the jewelry he had been hoping for, great tangles of it, heaped together like a jumble of old electrical cords. Gold chains caught the light from the chandelier as he turned them over in his hands. Diamonds and sapphires gleamed along their lengths like drops of morning dew. He scooped it up like water from a river, and there was more of it than he could hold with both hands.

It couldn't be real. There was too much of it, and it was too haphazardly jumbled in the box to be anything but cheap, costume stuff. And yet, the weight of it was right, and the stones were bright and clear. He wasn't an expert, but he knew glass gems when he saw them. These were not glass gems, and even the stingiest fence, at pennies on the dollar, would trade them for more money than he had ever seen in his life. It would be enough money to get him and Trina out of that crappy apartment, enough to get the baby a room of her own with flowers on the walls and a crib full of toys and a mobile strung with tiny bears to watch over her while she slept.

6

He gathered up the box. It was warm to the touch and it came up from the carpet with the same sticky tearing sound that his boots had made on the stairs. All by itself, the box made this a better job than any he had done before, and though six minutes were left on his internal clock there was no need for him to stick around any longer. He bounded back down to the foyer. With each step he cradled the box closer and cared less where it had come from. It could have been on the landing the whole time. In his haste he might have stepped right past it. It was odd, true, but he had seen enough odd things in this business to know that odd things happened every day. But this was it. He was done, and maybe for good. He'd bundle the box and the shoes into the van and drive away. He'd drive away and never come back, not to this place, not to any other place he had to break his way into. He'd go back to Trina and find a way to make her listen, to tell her all the things he'd never been able to find words for. She'd take him back and he'd be done, once and for all.

He paused at the bottom of the stairs as he sensed a change in the air, a shift in pressure like a door being opened in a distant room. With it came a familiar sound, a high, hitching wail that drifted down from the second story hallway.

It was the sound of a baby crying.

He froze, the box heavy in his arms, as he waited for the soft pad of footsteps on the carpet, for the answering words of a mother, perhaps a father. If he was lucky, those footsteps would come from the second floor, and he'd have time to reach his van with the box still in his hands, time to be away from this place before they even knew he was here. If he was unlucky, the footsteps would come from this floor, from just around the corner. And what would he do then? Would he fight? Would he take the box and try to run? Now that he had it, he couldn't imagine letting go of the little box and the jumble of treasure inside. He would fight for it. He would have to fight, or he would lose everything.

But the footsteps never came. He held his breath and watched through the entryways for shadows on the far walls, but there was no one there. There was only the child, the sound of its cries rising and falling, only to rise again more urgently, over and over again.

5

He made up his mind then to go. All he needed was the box. He could leave the shoes behind. He could leave the whole place behind, with its odd paintings and the strange smell in the air. But his feet would not move. The baby was still crying and no one was coming for it. At once he thought that the child had been left there on purpose, but the thought seemed absurd. No one moved into a brand new house only to abandon a baby. But then, no one jumbled a fortune's worth of jewelry into a cardboard box and labeled it good stuff. All the rules he was used to didn't seem to apply to this place. The baby cried and no one came for it, even though someone had to be there, had to have set this box in his way. The baby cried, and with each breath it sounded more and more like the baby that he and Trina had made.

Before he could stop himself he was climbing up the stairs. His steps felt heavy, the soles of his boots so sticky that he thought he might bring the carpet up with him as he moved. The baby's wailing grew louder as he drew near. He was convinced now that it was a little girl, no more than a few weeks old. In his mind he could see her with her fists balled, her face scrunched and red. He crept across the landing toward the sound, past the strange and blurry paintings. They seemed less blurry now, and in one of them he could see familiar outlines, two people posing for their portrait. He'd thought that one of those frames had been empty, but he must have been mistaken.

The door to the bedroom was ajar. He could hear the child's frantic howling just beyond it, growing louder and more urgent by the second. He pushed the door aside by inches, moving slow as if he was wading through water. The door was warm to the touch and it swung aside without a sound.

The shades were drawn and the room was dark, but still he could make out the wooden crib that stood at its center. The room was empty but for that crib, and it struck him then that, out of all the rooms in the house, this was the only one where the lights had been left off. He stepped inside, his boots still sticking to the carpet, his eyes adjusting to the dark. There were flowers painted on the walls, and above the crib a circle of little teddy bears dangled from a mobile like hanged men, turning lazily, casting long shadows.

4

The cries became louder then, so loud that they felt like daggers driving their way into his brain. He pressed his hands to the sides of his head to keep them at bay. Again he fought the urge to run, and might have given in to it if not for the dark shape that moved just beyond the bars of the crib. In his mind he was sure that it would look just like the baby that Trina had once held out to him, the one she had told him was his. He had run away then, but he would not run away now.

His shadow fell across the bars as he stepped toward the crib. The child inside it shifted and rolled with every hitching breath, with every rising cry. He could see it in the shadows cast by the hanging bears, tiny fists silhouetted against the mattress, tiny legs pumping in rage. He stepped closer, close enough to touch the squirming thing, close enough to gather it into his arms, and yet, for the shadows, he could not see its face.

He reached for the little flashlight on his belt, his mind screaming in tandem with the baby, warning him that he should not be there, that his time was running out, that he should run from this place and not look back. Still, he had to look. He had to know whether this baby was his. He had to look into its tear-filled eyes, to see if there was anything in them of his own.

The flashlight clicked on. He turned its beam on the naked, squirming thing that twitched and writhed in the crib. Where its skin should have been red with anger, it was pale and slick, like an earthworm out in a rainstorm. Stubby fingers stretched as it moved and Marcus could see the translucent web of skin that stretched between them. Where he had expected teary eyes, there were no eyes, no face at all. There was only a mouth, stretched into a boneless circle that gaped and yawned with the sounds of its cries.

He stepped back, stumbling, and the thing rose to follow him, dangling at the end of a long stalk that seemed to stretch out from the mattress of the crib like the lure from some deep-sea angler fish. Its limbs fell limp at its sides, a puppet with its strings cut. He could still hear its crying, but the crying was all around him now, everywhere and nowhere at once. Its lips, if they had ever been lips, pulled taut. In the depths behind them were row upon row of hooked and gleaming teeth.

It lashed out at him, the stalk whipping toward his head like a coiled snake. He scrambled back and fell beneath it. As it passed he could smell Trina's perfume on the wind it made, perfume and the scent of the clove cigarettes she'd smoked in high school, as if it had been pulled right out of his memories.

3

The thing drew back, and Marcus scrambled to his feet, hands and boots sticking to the floor. Or was it the floor that was sticking to him? The doorway to the room was closing, not swinging shut, but puckering, growing smaller by inches. He lunged for it, but fell short as something took hold of his leg and wrenched him backward. He looked back to see the fleshy stalk pulled tight, reeling him back toward the crib. The mouth of the baby-thing had clamped onto to the toe of his boot, and worried at it like a dog gnawing at a bone. The infant body had shrunk to little more than a vague shape, vestigial limbs waving as it tugged and pulled.

He kicked out, and his boot slid down the pulsing length of the stalk like it was slipping through mud. The infant wail still rang in his ears, rising and falling like a siren. He kicked again and found the spot where the baby's eyes should have been. The mouth went slack as the stalk reared back, its plucked-chicken skin gleaming slick in the beam of his dropped flashlight.

Scrambling, he lurched toward the opening. The doorway had been reduced to a tightening circle that grew smaller by the instant. The thing struck out at him once more but he stumbled out of its reach, pulling himself on all fours toward the light of the hallway. He laid a hand on the opening, and it grew teeth beneath his fingers. The infant's cry had become a scream, a high keen of rage and loss that pierced his brain and drove away all rational thought. He heaved himself out into the light, and as his feet slipped through, the teeth snapped together behind him with a hollow crunch.

Chest heaving, he lay on the floor, unable to move, barely able to breathe. The inhuman screaming had stopped, but the echo of it still rang in his ears, in the pulse that played out a painful beat through his skull. He tried to sit up, but the carpet held him down. Muscles trembling, he managed to pull himself away, tiny barbs clinging to his skin like flypaper to a fly. Around him, the walls were peeling back, melting toward the floor like taffy left out in the sun.

☉

2

He staggered to his feet, stumbling out of the hallway and onto the landing, pulling himself along the railing as he moved. It stuck to his hands, and as his palms came away they left little beads of blood behind on the painted wood. The portraits were sliding down the walls, but he could see faces in them now. One of those faces was Trina's and in the painting she held a bundled infant in her arms. A man stood in the shadows behind her with his hands on her shoulders, but he could not tell if it was meant to be him.

The floor tilted and heaved as he stumbled toward the stairs. The walls flowed down around him, and behind them he could see the new-cut wood of the house's frame, unfinished and skeletal. The only part of this place that's real, he thought. The only part of it that was made with human hands. Whatever the rest of it was, it would swallow him whole if he wasn't quick enough.

Something tugged at his foot as he reached the top of the stairs and he half-slid, half-fell to the foyer below. The chandelier and the other lights had retreated into the skin of the thing, coalescing into bluish orbs that pulsed hypnotically in the darkening space. He closed his eyes for fear that he might lose himself in them. He thought of Trina then, and of the baby, the real baby that could only be his own. It gave him the strength to pull himself to his feet. The door, if it had ever been a door at all, was shut tight, but as the walls oozed and shifted around him they made an opening. Beyond it was the night air and the white van that would drive him away from this place. He stepped toward it and felt his ankle give beneath his weight. He winced, but he did not stop.

The letters on the box of GOOD STUFF were just a smear of black now. It rolled on the floor, searching and gnashing, its flaps lined with rows of teeth like curved needles. As the jewelry fell from its mouth it lost its color and fell to ash. He gave no thought to the loss. There was only the opening, the way by which he could finally escape. He lurched toward it, hoping against hope that he still had time.

The opening seemed to sense his approach. Its edges folded together, closing like the mouth of some carnivorous plant. He thrust his hands against its fleshy edges. The house was dark now but for the pulsing blue light, and warm, so warm that he could imagine himself surrendering to it, just letting go and letting the place take him. Still, he fought. His muscles strained until he thought they might snap. He forced the opening wider, wide enough for his head, his shoulders. At last he pushed through. He landed on hard gravel where the concrete porch had been. The skin of the house retreated from its wooden bones as he scrambled away. It collapsed into a sphere that floated in the air, rolling and pulsing like a wet blister in the darkness. It pulsed once more and it was gone, folding in on itself, shrinking down to a single point of light before it disappeared into nothingness.

1

Marcus staggered to his feet, little hitches of unbidden laughter punctuating every breath. His ankle was broken. It wouldn't take his weight, so he limped and hopped his way to the white van. He laughed again, high on adrenline, high on the thought that that thing, whatever it had been, had almost made a meal of him. The idea made him hungry somehow, and he choked back a giggle as he pulled open the driver's door.

He needed a hospital, but the hospital could wait. No, he had to see Trina. Trina and their baby. He wanted to hold her and gather them both into his arms. He found his keys. The ringing in his ears was fading, the wailing of that phantom child gone. There was only the still of the night air, his breathing calm now, controlled. In that moment all his indecision fell away, and his thoughts coalesced into a moment of perfect clarity. He would leave this place, this life, and build a new one with Trina and the baby. He would leave it and he would never look back.

The Dead Drive the Night

~ *Eric Del Carlo*

"It's what you do, that's what you said, eh?"

"It's *all* I do. The only good—no, great—thing I'm capable of."

"Sounds like what an artist would say."

"Fine. I'm an artist." What Jez was also was frazzled. This office was furnished in cramped shabby, and that cruddiness was eating into her brain. But this was the last haulage company in the area; and, she felt with fatalistic certainty, it was going to be the last to tell her *no*.

The man behind the desk in short sleeves and a terrible tie had Jez's resumé in front of him. It reflected her skill set. She was extraordinary. But she could better prove that at the wheel of her rig. Getting the chance to do so was the seemingly insur-fucking-mountable problem.

She rubbed her right temple with two stiff fingers.

After a long perusal the executive asked, "Why'd you leave your last employment?"

The reason was there on the sheet of deadtree before him. This, then, was her opportunity to put a personal spin on the facts. Maybe she'd say something self-incriminating. Maybe she'd spout off about how they'd never appreciated her at her last company. There were escalating degrees of *not* getting a job. Jezebel Canha was determined to leave this moldy little office eminently qualified for a position—whether this asshat hired her or not.

"The business went under," she said.

"How dramatic."

"It really wasn't." Which was the truth. These days everything was in flux. Enterprises could fail for reasons so cryptic you needed goat entrails to determine the why. Human society in general had taken a hefty jolt, and the repercussions were widespread and unforeseeable.

It was why Jez couldn't find work in the only trade she knew and excelled at.

He laid a thick hand on top of the paper, as if absolving it or gentling it into sleep.

"Any openings we might have, Ms. Canha—well . . ." He pointed his chin over a shoulder, to a metaplastic sign on the too-close wall. "'Dead Drive Night,'" he quoted, leaving off the articles, either for brevity's sake or style points.

Jez studied the little plaque a moment. One day it would look as quaint and squirm-inducing as one that read IRISH NEED NOT APPLY. But for now it was the *de facto* law of the land.

His hand stayed where it was. He was keeping her resumé. That was something, anyway.

She stood, feeling the pressure of the saggy ceiling above her.

On her way out of the office the man called to her, saying it—just boldly *nakedly* saying it: "Come back if you're dead. You seem like you'd be a helluva driver."

It was dismayingly easy to get the potassium chloride. A cottage industry had sprung up. A guy delivered it. He rang her gate, she buzzed him up, and he fidgeted in her apartment doorway. She'd had to give her weight when she placed the order. The stuff was already in a syringe.

He had blond dreads, a bicyclist's calves. He fidgeted by taking tiny steps to nowhere in her entryway.

He was, it dawned on Jez, waiting for a tip. He was delivering death, not a pizza, but okay. She dropped a gold circle into his palm, an old commemorative coin, still legal tender. Her father had given it to her in the third grade for some academic achievement. Her father was dead, the old kind of dead.

She didn't explain this extra layer of meaning to the delivery guy.

Jez walked around her apartment, a nice place. Here she had fended off the creeping crumminess of the world, the dilapidation, the shabbiness. She had good furnishings. Everything was tidy and clean and comfortable.

She had to have a steady income to maintain this place.

She put on music, a favorite song, one that prompted memories from no less than three past love affairs. In the bathroom were alcohol and cotton swabs. A patch of skin gleamed sterilely on her inner forearm as she lay down on her bed and stuck in the needle.

It was a fast death.

It was a different exec in the haulage company office, but it would be. Jez had come back at night. There was paperwork to fill out.

This time the man behind the desk wore long sleeves and no tie, terrible or otherwise. He performed his tasks with an aloof ease. Tonight the office was just as awful, but its dinginess didn't oppress Jez. She felt at a remove.

She was handing completed forms across the desk at a steady rate. The man took each and arranged them into a file.

"I have my death certificate," she said, and the statement felt sudden, a little too loud.

The man raised eyebrows toward a graying hairline. "I've already noted it."

They were alike, she and this person. Much could go unsaid. That felt right. It had been a week since she'd shot up the potassium chloride.

Jez signed the final sheet. She felt an excitement, but it was deep-rooted. It didn't disturb her surfaces. She sat calmly, waiting. She'd done just about everything in a calm manner this past week.

The man looked at her a moment. There was nothing uncomfortable about the silence. Finally he said, "You're ready to drive."

Jez's mouth flickered with the hint of a smile.

The road sang, as it had always sung for her. Her truck was her flesh. In the cab, her hands lay delicately on the big wheel. She didn't need the truck's grid system to tell her she was making good—no, great—time. She had a perfect sense of destination, of the journey itself.

She drove the night, and she drove it very goddamn well.

Orange highway lights thumped past with the regularity of a healthy pulse. It hadn't been a terribly long time since she'd been out at night, but it was a while since she had *done* anything at night. Here she was participating in the commerce, industry and general societal movements of that half of the day increasingly reserved for those people who had experienced death.

She was as good as she'd ever been. The first few miles had already proven that to her satisfaction. She'd had a week to assess herself, to decide if anything had changed. It was ridiculous, of course. Or nearly ridiculous. Plenty of scientific literature was available to anyone who had experienced the sort of demise Jez had undergone. There should be no loss of skills.

Her memories were all there too.

So, she was driving with the same excellence as before, just as she remembered.

But it didn't give her the same feeling. That thrill, that joy. She felt a certain pleasure, a quiet gratification, yes, but the old lively excitement wasn't there anymore. Her bones didn't quiver. Her nerve endings weren't crackling with the same fear/sex energy. Before, she rode her rig like a wild lover, savoring every challenge, every opportunity to advance on her time.

Now, perhaps, it wasn't so much that the truck was her flesh: maybe she was the machine.

She'd read about this beforehand as well. It was less codified in the scientific papers, a more subjective phenomenon.

The night, she had decided, suited her. The *new* her, the *post* her. Whatever the current jargon, which now didn't seem so important to her. At night there were mostly only others like her. That was how the world was rearranging itself. It was why, before her death, she'd been unable to find work, despite her talents. The day had gotten too full.

With the night came a tranquility, an order. She was aware of it even as she tore down the roadway with her payload, wheels thrumming, engine gargling. The haulage company she now worked for served a tri-state area. She completed her first run. The personnel at the depot all exuded a palpable aplomb. They operated without wasted energy. A supervisor glanced up from a datascroll and said to her, "Good time." Only, she realized minutes later, he hadn't actually said anything.

She was hungry. She'd seen a diner on the way in. She hopped in her truck and backtracked.

The place was small and greasy and typical. The stools were upholstered in tired red. The long metaplastic counter gleamed under the lights.

Jez sat, feeling a residual buzz of her journey in her limbs. She wasn't keyed up, though. No bustle in her head, communicating itself as tics, drumming fingers, the urgent need for coffee, then alcohol. She felt as rested and centered as when she'd woken up this afternoon.

The woman who came for her order was young—or what "young" had become for Jez now that she was in her thirties. She wrote nothing down, just nodded at each item Jez recited from the laminated menu, then finished with a soft *huhhhn* and went off to deliver the order to the cook. Jez looked at the backs of her legs as she leaned forward over the divider that separated the counter area from the kitchen, hiking up her crisp blue uniform skirt slightly. Her thighs were taut, twangy-looking.

The waitress didn't hurry, didn't make any errors, and had experienced death. Jez was sure of it.

It made her wonder: *how had she died?* The question felt taboo, something you just didn't ask out loud.

Jez ate her burger and onion rings, aioli on the side, and slowly scoped out the other costumers. They all had a professional look, drivers, living off the road. Night shift people, and everything that that now meant. No music played. Nothing streamed on the diner's monitors. She hadn't noticed the absence until this moment, hadn't been made uncomfortable by it.

In the parking lot, on her way out, there was a bit of a snarl. Two vehicles were in each other's way, trying to jockey around. One was a yellow-on-black truck cab, payload-less, like Jez's own rig after having dropped her cargo. She paused with a foot on the rung below her open door and watched the scene play out.

The other vehicle was quietly backing off, while the black and yellow yelped and lunged. It was like observing competing schools of parking lot etiquette. Finally it was sorted out.

The arriving driver hopped down lithely, twin gravelly crunches as her boots smacked the ground. She stretched extravagantly in a sweat-stained tank top. Her hair was a study in brunette disarray. She had a growly-looking mouth and red-rimmed eyes.

She was not dead. Had never been dead.

The driver strutted toward the diner, her bones no doubt humming with the pent-up energy of her run.

Jezebel Canha watched and watched her, even after she was inside, through the big front window. Then with a breathless sigh she climbed the rest of the way up to her cab.

It took some time for Jez to admit to herself that she was courting. She accessed public-record data and soon had all the harmless standard information on the yellow-on-black rig and the woman who owned it. She ghosted the woman's social media output. Vonda Hupy. Jez thought about Vonda. A lot. It was rather schoolgirl-y and crush-y, except that it was happening at an emotional remove, as if she were curating someone else's feelings.

But her interest persisted, and eventually she started to actively seek this woman.

The cargo company Vonda Hupy drove for was a small shady outfit, one that, nonetheless, Jez had sought employment at. They'd told her what they had all said during those final desperate months of her life. There was only night work available, and the dead drove the night. So how had Vonda gotten the gig?

There was, of course, nothing illegal about a live driver working at night. No law was ever going to go on the books. Instead, it was a cultural understanding, a gentlepersons' agreement.

When she had watched Vonda through the diner's window that night, the waitress had taken her order without a hint of distress.

Jez wanted to see her again.

But her job kept her busy. It also paid the rent on her tidy apartment, with all her nice familiar things. She couldn't just go tearing after this woman. Hell, she couldn't even bring herself to make contact via social media. Even as a teen she'd found flirtation and seduction easier in person than online.

So Jez kept track of Vonda's professional movements as well as she could without resorting to sleuth software. After all, she didn't want to stalk the woman. Or didn't want to have to call it that.

After a week Jez knew Vonda's basic patterns. She had also deduced that she was a good driver, at least as far as her haul times reflected. Jez was patient. She was patient with most everything these days. But her patience with Vonda had a singular quality to it. It was the calm of fixation. Vonda Hupy, in her sweaty tank top and disheveled hair, had somehow become a compass point for Jez. When Jez drove, which was often because the work was steady, she knew her route, her destination—and also knew at any given moment about where Vonda was if she was on the road too.

Inevitably they must cross paths a second time.

Turned out that reunion occurred at the same diner. It might as well have been the first time again for the similarity of the scenario. Vonda was jostling her yellowjacket cab against vehicles trying to get out of the lot. Jez, who had dropped her cargo container at the nearby depot, hung back. Vonda was insistent to the point of outright aggression, but also demonstrated pinpoint control of her rig, something every great driver had to possess.

Eventually, when the gravel had settled and Vonda had gone in, Jez walked into the diner.

Vonda already had a mug of coffee in front of her. She was occupying a booth by herself, tearing sugar packets one at a time with elaborate precision and stirring in the contents. She was either grinning or grinding her teeth.

"Mind if I join?" Jez said, dropping onto the opposite seat, upholstered in that same tired red as the stools.

Vonda didn't look up. "Nope." Tonight she wore a winter camou T-shirt, irregular stripes of white and light blue and darker blue. It hugged her shoulders, her breasts.

The diner wasn't crowded enough for them to have to share the booth.

The waitress came halfway toward them, caught Jez's eye and raised a fine eyebrow. *Same as last time?* Jez's chin dipped in a shallow nod.

"How do you do that?" Vonda was blowing steam off the lip of her cup, having finished sugaring her coffee. She looked straight across at Jez.

The question meant Vonda knew what she was. Jez said, "I'm a regular here."

"Me too. But I have to order every time."

Jez shrugged. "Try tipping better."

A vein stood out on the back of Vonda's left hand. Her nails were dark crescents.

"Looked like you had some trouble getting into the lot." The big front window was behind Vonda.

"Assholes need to learn how to drive."

"Is it like that for you out on the road?"

Vonda took a slow sip of coffee. "On the road, I'm an angel in a power dive. You haul too?"

"I do."

Their meals arrived, and after that it was flirting and coy and ribald comments. The other customers in the diner had paid no attention when Vonda was here alone. Now Jez was aware of an increasing interest, tinged with discomfort. Was this another taboo, something she hadn't known beforehand? She was, after all, still relatively recently returned from the dead. People whose deaths were not overly traumatic had been spontaneously coming back for close to a year. That was time enough for subcultural rules to form.

Vonda sat back in the booth and pushed off her empty plate in the same movement. Her eyes flickered this way and that, taking in those other customers. Was she too aware of the attention? Probably not. It was very subtle.

"You hear statistics. So many die of heart attacks, such and such many keel over from blot clots. But they get tucked away in a morgue." Vonda shook her head with a deep dismay. "It's amazing to think how the sands of the human race just run naturally through the hourglass."

Jez said nothing. She didn't know how many here in the diner had expired naturally. Maybe it hadn't occurred to this woman that were alternate ways to meet one's death.

Vonda followed her back to her place, which was nearer. Then it was lips and grinding hips and busy fingers and tongues. When Jez had been out of work, she had taken up running to fill the time and had gotten herself back into pre-thirties shape. Vonda was a quivering bowstring, muscular, aggressive. The tension of the road was in her, and she was taking it all out on Jez, which was just fine.

After—and there were several *afters*, but this was the one where they finally spoke—Vonda asked, "How did you know I was a lesbian?"

Jez laughed, a brief but real guffaw, and she realized she hadn't laughed like that in . . . a while. Not *since*.

"What's funny?"

"I'm trying to remember when I last heard someone use that term."

In the crook of Jez's arm, Vonda was trying to decide whether to be angry or not.

"When I was in school," Jez explained, "mono-sexuals were given a hard time."

"Oh." The tension went out of Vonda's neck as she lay her head back down.

Jez wanted to ask her a question too. And she guessed that Vonda had more, far deeper questions for her as well; but maybe those would wait.

"How'd you get your job?" She named Vonda's sketchy little haulage company. "I applied there and got turned down flat, back when—" *Back when I was alive.* Unsaid words. But Vonda hadn't died, and they didn't share that unspoken understanding. All they had was the tacit empathy of newfound lovers.

Jez strongly suspected that Vonda wanted to ask her about her death. Jez wasn't ready to talk about that. She simply hoped Vonda would answer her more innocuous question.

She did. "I went to the office for twenty-eight days straight. My driving record should've got me hired, but it didn't. So I just wore 'em the fuck down."

Jez wondered if the same tactic would have worked for her. Probably not. Vonda Hupy had a special quality.

"You got a nice place. Real nice." Vonda was walking around the apartment now, bare feet on wood, *patpatpat.* Jez leaned in a doorway and admired the flex of her taut ass. "My place is a sty. I never would've guessed you hauled if I'd seen all this." She gestured at brass fittings, at well-coordinated art on the walls.

Jez went to speak but found herself without enough breath for words. Vonda was staring at her, as if waiting. Finally Jez said, "I want to see you again. I want more than this."

Vonda maintained that gaze awhile. Then, "I want that too."

They synchronized their trucks' grid systems, so that each knew where the other was on the road, without the guesswork or triangulation. Jez visited Vonda's apartment, and it was a sty pretty much. But it wasn't the cruddiness of neglect; rather, the result of a mind and body occupied with other priorities.

Vonda liked to draw. Vonda liked charcoal. Black specks swarmed in the air whenever something in her apartment was disturbed. The stuff was permanently under her fingernails. Deadtree sheets were scattered everyplace, and they bore the markings of her art. All of it was crude. All of it was forceful. Vonda worked with harsh lines. Her themes were vibrant, vital. She had something to say and said it insistently.

Jez loved her work.

"You don't get worked up about much, do you?" A smile played on Vonda's growly mouth. Her tone was a little bitter.

Jez had been enthusing for forty straight minutes over Vonda's art as the two of them sat cross-legged on dingy teal carpeting. "I feel like I haven't shut up about how much I like your work."

"You say less than you probably think you do." Vonda tilted toward her, kissed her smartly on the cheek. "It's okay."

There were still the other, far larger questions lingering and hovering. Jez could sense them in the charcoal-dusted air. She and this woman had been involved for several weeks now. Perhaps Jez could make the inevitable questioning easier on herself—and on Vonda as well.

"How," Jez asked softly, "did you know I was . . . dead?" It wasn't the preferred term. Actually, there was no term for what she was, nothing the world had yet agreed on. "At the diner that night."

Vonda held her face still a moment, then burst out with a laugh. "Guess the same way you knew I was gay."

Jez joined in the laughing, and it felt good. Then she stopped, and waited.

After a time Vonda grew quiet, and after a long thoughtful pause she said, "Can you tell me how it was? When . . . when you were— When you *weren't*? Shit! I don't know how to ask this."

Jez nodded, then thought to say, "It's okay." She'd had a while to prepare for this. She was nervous. Less nervous than she would have been before her death. But more nervous here with Vonda than she would have been with anyone else. It was because she cared deeply for the woman.

She'd been sitting on this rug too long. Half her butt was asleep. She shifted.

"It's being frozen inside a fish bowl, sapphire ice all about. It is a pulse, a newborn's, very very fast. It's salt, hot salt, like seawater on an old piling under a blazing summer sun. It's a memory of melting snow. The hurtling of a comet on a billion year suicide plunge. It's vertigo. It's claustrophobia. It is . . ."

She stopped.

Vonda lifted her shoulders, an elaborate shrug. "I guess it really can't be described, then. You've been to the other side. You've seen what happens after a person kicks off. And it's nothing but freshman poetry."

They kissed, and this time it was Jez releasing excess energy, aggressively, and Vonda accommodated her as they made love on that dismal carpet.

Jez, though, knew Vonda had one last momentous question yet to voice. But perhaps she wouldn't ask it.

It was a lot of dock to depot runs. Several harbors lay within the tri-state region, and many warehouses awaited that cargo. The night, if anything, improved Jez. Certainly she had by now adjusted to night-time driving. She was also used to the people she interacted with. She felt at ease among her kind.

However, now and again she grew aware of a mild extra scrutiny, what would have been a stink-eye look from strangers in her old life. Some knew her before she knew them: a reputation, preceding. She had a live girlfriend. *Live.*

But no one said anything to her, no censures, no condemnations. She was of a category of human being who no longer needed constant explicit words.

A month after she had failed—as every other returnee had similarly failed—to explain the afterlife to her lover, Vonda asked the other question. The one of equal or greater enormity. Certainly the question Jez thought of as the most dangerous.

They were at Jez's place. One of Vonda's charcoals, framed and behind glass, hung on the front room's wall. The brunette woman had brought other objects into the apartment, little lifeline things which reminded Jez of her presence when she wasn't here.

Vonda asked her question when Jez wasn't expecting it, at a casual moment without solemn prelude. Vonda was lacing up her boots, getting ready to go out to work.

"Can I ask you something?"

"Sure," Jez said, sitting up in bed, sipping a second glass of wine. Drinking alone. Vonda had to drive; she didn't.

"How'd you die?" No dramatic lead-in pause, no dire tone.

Jez looked at her. Vonda slowly combed a handful of dark disarrayed hair off her forehead with her fingers.

Half a dozen lies sprang to mind, convincing falsehoods. Jez had rehearsed some of these. There were many ways a person could lose her life and then come back. If the death event wasn't too physiologically damaging, existence would be automatically restored. So this very strange, paradigm-upending past year had demonstrated to the world.

But instead of one of the lies, Jezebel Canha told her lover the truth. She had intentionally taken her own life.

It wasn't a long explanation. She laid out her reasons and how she had accomplished her passing. Vonda said nothing, and continued to stare. Jez started to add to her accounting but stopped herself. Despite the wine, her gut had gone cold.

She heard Vonda grinding her teeth a few seconds before she said, "You *killed* yourself for a fuckin' job!"

"I had to—"

"You *didn't* fucking have to! I got work without resorting to throwing my life away. That's disgusting, Jez! I can't believe you would do that."

Vonda's jacket lay over a chair in the bedroom. She spun, marched toward it and swung her arm, a boxer's pile-driving punch, but with an open hand so to claw up her leather jacket before she stalked out of the room, stomped down the apartment's entryway, and slammed the front door.

It was a primal reaction, something from deep inside the species. Jez knew this. She understood Vonda Hupy's response. It was why she had been reluctant to share this information. She remembered the dismayed look in Vonda's eyes as she'd looked around the diner that night, wondering at all the dead people.

Jez couldn't explain what death was like. Neither could she tell the woman she loved how sensible it had been for her to overdose on potassium chloride. She didn't regret what she had done.

But it terrified her to think she might have lost Vonda. True terror, the emotion brighter and more vivid than anything she had felt since her return to the living.

She'd had two generous glasses of chardonnay. Her truck wouldn't
let her drive like this. She phoned Vonda, but even her voicemail was
off. She snatched up her personal datascroll and accessed the grid.
Vonda was heading for the nearest harbor. Jez, looking at the screen
and biting her lip, saw how fast she was traveling. She must be burning up the night road. She was an excellent driver, with expert control
of her rig.

But Jez remembered her in the diner parking lot, aggressive, keyed
up, using her truck to express her volatility.

She was still staring at the datascroll. Several seconds went by.

Vonda's rig was still on the highway, but it was no longer moving.

She had to take a taxi out there.

Black and yellow wreckage was strewn across two lanes. Another
vehicle had been involved in the accident, but the driver was unhurt.
One southbound lane of the roadway remained open.

Paramedics were already there, but other emergency services continued to arrive. Jez's taxi waited, in the breakdown lane.

She had no legal right to inquire about Vonda Hupy's condition; so
a Highway Patrolwoman told her in calm tones. But that officer made
no effort to stop her approaching the ambulance, and the medical
technicians, equally composed, let her near enough to the gurney to
see that this wasn't a death from which anyone could come back.

The broken scattering of metal and metaplastic reminded Jez of
the floors in Vonda's apartment, disordered with her charcoal'ed
sheets of paper.

The night was chilly enough to make cool tracks of the tears on
her cheeks. Unaware of them until now, she staggered back from the
scene of destruction. None of the civilian traffic passing in the lone
clear lane slowed down to gawk. The emergency personnel on hand
didn't look upon her in judgment. Her cabdriver didn't step out to
hurry her along.

They understood. And even if some suspected her relationship
with the formerly live woman from the truck, no one reproached her
for it. All of them on the scene, every last one, had experienced—
however briefly—the unexplainable reality which awaited humans

after death, and that experience had given them all a unique forbearance.

Jez wiped her eyes and walked toward the breakdown lane, where the taxi still waited.

Wayfinding

~ A. P. Howell

Becca didn't realize she always avoided part of the plaza until a sunny Wednesday when she noticed a weed growing in a cracked paving stone. She was very familiar with the paving stone and made a habit of looking down at it, stepping carefully on the familiar unevenness, taking special care during winter when pooled water iced over.

She stopped walking, feeling the afternoon traffic move around her. The plaza was big enough, uncrowded enough, that one non-moving body didn't cause any inconvenience. People simply stepped around her.

But not just anywhere. Becca wracked her brain to think of the different paths she'd used to get to class or the library or a food truck. Human memory wasn't perfect—the brain played all kinds of tricks, dumped useless data, and freely interpolated—but even allowing for that, Becca knew she had favored paths and there were certain areas she couldn't remember traversing at all.

She watched the other pedestrians for a while, uncomfortably aware that they also seemed to be avoiding some of those same spots. In the spirit of more scientific inquiry, she sat in a metal chair at an unoccupied table and watched for another hour.

A physicist friend had enjoyed making fun of the "unnatural sciences," and certainly anything involving human behavior was messier than optical equations. But her observations were still data, and in all the time she watched, Becca never saw anyone set foot in a five-foot-square area she herself unconsciously avoided.

Becca had a knock-off GoPro and zero desire to ask for permission to record or conduct any remotely official sort of study. She wasn't planning to keep the footage or publish anything. She was just curious, and an hour's worth of data was insufficient.

So she used a bit of duct tape to set the camera up in one of the potted trees bushes that dotted the plaza. She didn't have an angle on the entire plaza, but she had the Spot, as she had come to think of it over the past few hours. And even if focusing on the Spot made this an even less scientific endeavor . . . well, she wasn't aiming for publication.

Just one person, Becca told herself when she retrieved the camera the next day. Just one person stepping in the Spot would prove that there wasn't anything interesting going on, that she'd just observed traffic patterns and found, well, patterns. The human brain did that, but it didn't mean that any given pattern was important, or that it existed anywhere outside of that brain.

Except the pattern did exist, at least for the length of the video. Everyone avoided the Spot. Becca wondered if she had, somehow, missed something obvious. A broken bottle, a smear of dog shit, something mundane that her subconscious—that everyone's subconscious—had logged as a hazard to be avoided, but not so major as to attract attention. The video, however, showed nothing.

She looked the next day, too, and sat outside with a book open and unread in favor of people watching. No one stepped in the Spot.

She very nearly strode over and crossed that area herself. There was no reason not to, no danger or inconvenience. All her senses agreed there was absolutely nothing special about that Spot.

Nothing except the fact that she, and everyone else, avoided it.

And now that she knew, she couldn't quite bring herself to venture into that space.

She was supposed to think about the present and the future, how to mitigate the challenges of the one to make a bridge to an improved version of the other. History mattered insofar as it was part of the initial conditions, encoded in memory, culture, and built environment, but it wasn't what she did.

Becca spent time doing history. She found maps, helpfully digitized records of insurers, overlays she could apply to the now. The middle class neighborhood, digested decades earlier, formed a ghostly outline above familiar university buildings and the plaza, a bird's eye view of the past imposed upon the present.

She had known about the old neighborhood, of course, and other ways the city she inhabited had shifted and twisted and writhed over the years. But it was one thing to know about an old neighborhood (an old neighborhood, an ousted nation: all places were graveyards of the past) and quite another to have an address and floorplan.

The Spot fell in the middle of one of the ghostly row homes. Becca had easy access to a host of newspapers and census records through 1940. She should have been working on a GIS visualization, but instead she decoded fin de siècle handwriting and OCR mishaps. Lack of clarity between sixes and eights meant it took longer than it should have to find what she was looking for, but once she saw it she knew it was the answer.

In 1905, Louise Bromley, sixteen or seventeen at the time, had died in the house that had once stood where the plaza—and the Spot— were now located.

Becca had gone mad once. That was how she thought of it now, a small but significant number of years removed from an experience that had nothing to do with a mental health diagnosis.

She had been an undergraduate, a riot of hormones powered by caffeine cocktails. And at some point—she could not even remember the inciting incident—it had occurred to her that she ought to be more open-minded. Why were the truths of the present more certain than those of the past? Science, after all, was a construct, just like her own conception of time.

The lines between alchemy and chemistry, astrology and astronomy; the competing logics of religions; death and divination—these all fascinated her and, for a time, it seemed utterly uncouth to play favorites in the matter of belief. If some things might be true, why not all?

She could not quite remember how long the madness had lasted—six months? Nine?—but in a sense it did not matter. There was before-Becca and after-Becca, who was in almost all ways identical to her progenitor. But the detour into madness had happened, as profound (or not) as if she had cut her hair, shaved it off, dyed it, or wrought some similar change: time-bounded but still extant in memory and, perhaps, photographs or other documentation.

Which was to say, Becca had spent some time persuaded of the existence of ghosts. Not in the paranormal studies sense—such evidence had been debunked to her satisfaction, even when mad—but in a more philosophical sense. The human mind was a marvel. So, for that matter, was any complex life form, existing courtesy of eons of evolution and chance beginnings as single-cell organisms. The idea that something might persist was, in its way, less ridiculous than the belief that all that complexity simply vanished at the arbitrary point of death.

The Spot sat at a tantalizing intersection of Becca's past and present, her madness and her sanity. She neglected more coursework, datasets that had previously called out to her like sirens lounging upon silicon substrates, and instead mulled over questions of architecture and pedestrian traffic patterns and death.

Louise Bromley was nearly as much a ghost in the historical record as (perhaps) in the plaza. Teenage girls existed as lines on the census, written in another's hand. By virtue of her father's relative prominence—he had been a well-regarded doctor—there were a few references in newspapers, but aside from the tragedy's impact on her family, Becca learned little about the girl herself. This was frustrating but not at all surprising.

She supplemented the specific with the general, reading secondary sources about the life a teenager like Louise would have known. But social history, American history, women's history . . . these were not her fields, and they were too vast to master overnight and on a whim.

For half a day, Becca convinced herself that her bizarre detour was over. She worked on the visualizations she was supposed to be working on. And then she began to think about death again, and not just Louise's. All the suicides, all the murders, all the accidents, all the cancer and heart disease and aneurysms and pneumonia.

Why Louise? What was special about one dead girl? (Beyond the fact that every human life was precious, etc., etc.) Why could Becca feel her presence (absence, whatever) over a century after her death? And not just Becca: everyone else who avoided the Spot.

It wasn't until she slept and woke again that she realized this was a close-minded framing. Becca knew about the Spot, but that was no reason to assume it was unique.

☉

Becca walked the city streets. She had always found it a useful exercise, a way of providing human-scale context for aerial maps and architectural plans and anonymized datasets.

Brick pavers uneven, raised by a tree's roots. A pit bull mix raised a leg to urinate on the curb; by the time Becca reached the small puddle, a boxer had paused at the same spot, adding its own scent.

She imagined the view from above, a complex dance of living creatures. Living creatures and dead: after crossing the street, she realized she had not walked in a straight line. Had a pedestrian died there, and did the resonance of that event prompt her to alter her path? So much life, death, and unlife: to even consider just this moment in time was more than her brain could encompass.

She thought then of brains, of neurological connections. Of the boundless potential of babies, and the way their brains grew by the pruning of those connections, the infinite rendered finite. Potential sacrificed in favor of pragmatism and response to the environment as the babies grew into themselves. Damage prompting work-arounds and new methods of neurological wayfinding. Functionality defined by absence.

When she had been mad before, Becca had felt uncertain and compelled to study and rationalize her thoughts, ultimately classifying them as mad. That was not the case now. She knew Louise, insofar as she could know a stranger, long dead and poorly documented. She did not know the pedestrian, or the identity of the person who had planted the tree, or the reason dogs chose that particular place to mark territory and challenge another's marking. But her knowledge was irrelevant and Becca took a deep, almost religious comfort from that certainty.

She found a convenient stoop and sat across from a honey locust, listened to the wind in the leaves, the babble of voices, the sounds of traffic and a displeased cat, and felt the city grow into itself.

Seahorses and Other Gifts

~ *Tristan Morris*

A gift.

Or, a gift is what it was called, anyway. Surely it had many characteristics of a kindness. It was grown out of love, carved with delicate care, animated not by casual thought, but by a great deal of the giver's money, time and blood. Much was sacrificed to bring it into being, without any intention that it should benefit the maker. It came in wrapping paper, with a little bow on top. The paper had seahorses on it.

And yet, Sarah hated seahorses. So many of the things she received had seahorses on them—objects soon assimilated into her monument, her shrine to that which was unwanted but could not be thrown away. The closet she dreaded to open but would never empty. The closet that did not contain anything she would consider a gift.

She tore the wrapping paper. Within it was a small wooden box; hardwood, square, brass hinges. A seahorse was carved onto the lid. It very much resembled a ring box, but when she opened it, there was nothing inside, not even the felt coverings within which a ring might potentially be placed.

Momentarily confused, she shut it again, wondering if perhaps something was supposed to be within and the container had been packed incorrectly. But before she could examine it any further, the box spoke.

"This evening, your space heater sets your bedsheets on fire, and you burn to death."

The box spoke many times as the days passed. It was, to Sarah, an embarrassment, a shame, something to be hidden out of politeness, like breaking wind or her remarkably nasal laugh. Whenever she felt the box tremble, felt its lid twitch, she would rise and excuse herself from the room, feigning some biological urge or claiming her phone

was ringing. Then, when she was hidden in the bathroom or an empty section of hallway, she would let it speak.

"Today's the day your boss finally fires you."

"The janitor is planning to steal your purse out of your desk drawer when you're at lunch."

"That sniffle this morning was pneumonia."

Of course, her deception could only last so long. She was sitting at
her desk when the truth came out, discussing the results of her employer's diversity program with the HR manager from up the hall. He
had asked her for some numbers, and she had clicked through her
laptop until she found them. "Overall it's good news," she was saying,
"but employee confidence is still low, even when—"

"This afternoon, he tells the entire HR team you're a bitch," her
box said.

She'd left it on her desk. They both turned the source of the noise,
to the little wooden box with the seahorse on the cover. His expression was quizzical, hers stricken, but fate did her a small kindness,
and he spoke first.

"Oh, that's one of those, uh . . ." He waved generally in its direction.
"Evil box things. Right?"

"It's a Safety Box," Sarah said. "It predicts bad things that might
happen to you today. Literally today. Warns you of anything that
might happen before midnight."

"Well, it's not very accurate." He flashed her a smile. "You're good
at your job. And pleasant, if that matters. Sorry, I know expecting
women to always be pleasant is sexist in-and-of itself, but, you are."

"No. I know. It's actually quite inaccurate," she said. "It makes exactly one-hundred predictions a day, but only one of them is correct."

"You're going to die in a plane crash," the box said.

"See?" she continued, gesturing at it. "I'm not getting on a plane
today. So unless a plane falls out of the sky and lands on the office, I'm
pretty sure that one isn't true."

The man from HR frowned. "If it makes a hundred predictions
a day, and only one of them is correct, then . . ." He made a vague
gesture in the air. "Sorry, I just don't see why you'd buy this? I know
they've been in the news a lot recently, and are like, trendy or whatever, but it doesn't seem that useful."

"It was a gift. From my parents."

"Oh," said the man from HR. A long pause hung in the air, perhaps as he wondered why she did not simply throw it away. But if such thoughts were on his mind, he did not voice them. "That must be frustrating."

"It's fine," Sarah waved him off. "Like I said, not going to die in a plane crash today. It's embarrassing and annoying but that's about it. All I need to do is ignore whatever it says."

"Sure," he said. "Anyway, you were saying about employee confidence?"

After he left, the box said, "Your analysis was wrong, and he'll realize it this afternoon."

As she packed up her things at the end of the day, the box said, "You've forgotten something important, and it will be gone when you get back tomorrow."

As she waved goodbye to the security guard at the front desk, and walked out into the parking lot, the box said, "You're going to be hit by a car."

She ignored it, of course.

She was not three steps out of the building when Steve from Accounting ran her down with his Toyota. He'd been texting while driving.

When Sarah regained consciousness, she was in a hospital, her limbs in casts, her head in a brace. The sheets were stained with blood; her blood. The little box sat beside her bed, and it said: "Your injuries are fatal. You will die today."

With a raspy voice, she asked the doctors how long she had, but they told her she would pull through. Then the box said, "The hospital bill will be enormous. You'll be in debt for the rest of your life."

But she spoke with the nurses, and they informed her her insurance covered everything. Then the box said, "Your parents are going to visit, and they'll spend an hour talking about how much you loved seahorses when you were twelve."

It said a few other things, but Sarah was scarcely listening. She already knew which prediction was coming true.

⊙

When she got out of the hospital, Sarah's coworkers threw her a party. They told her how glad they were that she was well, and offered her gifts and gentle hugs. She felt liked, and appreciated, and the company cut her a sizable check in return for her agreement not to sue. Then, her boss suggested they all go out to lunch. It was a pretty good welcome.

While her entire team tried to crowd in around one table at the restaurant, the box shook in Sarah's pocket. When she withdrew it, and held it up to her ear, it whispered so quietly that nobody else could hear: "You're going to get food poisoning from the burgers."

From her purse, she withdrew a tiny spiral-bound notebook and pencil. The front page of the notebook had three columns drawn in it, each labeled in her tiny, immaculate handwriting: *Absurd, Plausible, Likely.*

Absurd already had two entries from that morning: that she was going to be abducted by aliens, and that she was going to be murdered by communists. *Likely* had only one entry, that her welcome-back party was going to suck. So, she crossed out "Welcome Back Party Sucks," as it was evidently not true, and underneath *Plausible* filled in, "Food poisoning from burgers."

Then, she updated the tally at the bottom of the page. 4/100 so far that day.

"Actually," she said, as she put the notebook away. "I know this place has great burgers, but could I get the salad instead? I'm feeling like something light."

None of her coworkers got sick, so that one was evidently incorrect as well, but the salad was good and so the effort had cost her little. Over the course of the day, she continued to update her little notebook, both the entries and the tally.

The tally was key. The tally told her the collective probability that the true event of the day was already written in her notebook. At one hundred predictions for the day, she could be certain that one of the fears on her list was valid. By extension, at one hundred predictions, it was possible to be safe. The lower the count, the lower her certainty.

For example, prediction forty-seven for the day was, "Your cast is going to slip on the bathroom tile, and you'll hit your head on the sink and die." Such a danger was easily negated—she used the porta-potty at the construction site across the street and then washed her hands in the employee kitchen—but she couldn't even claim 50/50 odds that that warning was the right one.

By contrast, as she was packing up for the day, prediction eighty-nine was, "Traffic on the drive home will be horrible." Such a prediction not only merited an entry in the *Likely* column, but as a late-day *Likely*, had more than a 50% chance of being true. More than a 50% chance that a little traffic would be the worst thing to happen to her that day.

It was a comforting thought. So comforting that when traffic did indeed turn out to be horrible, Sarah found a great smile playing across her face. She made it home alive, and cheerfully ignored predictions ninety, ninety-one, ninety-two, ninety-three, ninety-four, ninety-five, ninety-six, ninety-seven, ninety-eight, and ninety-nine.

As she turned off her apartment lights to go to sleep, the thought occurred to her that she had only ninety-nine tallies in her little notebook. But, she imagined that she must have forgotten to record an entry, and thought nothing of it.

At 11:59 PM exactly, the box woke her.

"Today," it said, "two predictions come true."

But did they? Is "Two predictions come true" itself a prediction? And if so, is it true? Or, is "two predictions come true" false, because only one predicted event actually happened? It was a logic puzzle, of the sort Sarah hated in school.

Except in school, the penalty for getting the answer wrong wasn't potentially death.

At midnight, she got out of bed and spent an hour googling the problem on her laptop. When that failed to produce a definitive answer, she ordered textbooks off the internet, guides to logic and math, PDFs for instant delivery. She had detested such books when she was a student and certainly didn't want to read them as a free adult, but the alternative was too dangerous. All night she read them, and when she wasn't able to finish her reading by the time she had to leave for work, she called in sick, claiming her leg needed to be looked at.

Her box spoke twelve times over the course of the morning. In her notebook, she made eight entries in the *Absurd* column (mostly relating to dying in spectacular ways), three entries in the *Plausible* column (mostly relating to her friends secretly hating her), and one entry in the *Likely* column.

"Your research is wrong; you have no idea what you're doing."

But she'd expected that, and after an entire night and morning reading *An Introduction to Logic Puzzles* and *The Basics of Set Theory*, she was fairly certain she knew the answer, that "two predictions come true," was not a valid prediction and was therefore false. The box was only messing with her.

Probably.

"If you don't get something done today," the box said, "your co-workers will think you're lazy." That was prediction thirteen for the day, *Plausible*. But when she pulled out her laptop, it said, "If you get too much done today, they'll know you faked calling in sick." Prediction fourteen, also *Plausible*.

It took her nearly an hour to decide how to avoid both dangers: she would get exactly two-and-a-half hours of work done, and send several emails apologizing for being behind due to her injury. That way, people would see her working and know she was industrious, but nobody would question that she didn't put in a full day. She was quite proud of that plan.

Plus, it gave her plenty of time to deal with other dangers, like prediction twenty-nine, "The food truck up the street has contaminated meat," and prediction forty-four, "You're going to be mugged on the way to the grocery store." She paid extra to have groceries delivered, and spent all afternoon cooking for herself.

Later, prediction thirty-seven came true: "You will feel a brief but intense sadness regarding Mr. Scruffles."

Mr. Scruffles, her cat, had died when she was fourteen. So it wasn't the worst thing that could have happened to her in a day.

"Your productivity will suffer due to stress," her box predicted. But that one wasn't true. Quite the opposite.

Every warning that her coworkers doubted her competence made her double and triple-check her work. Every prediction that her skills were beginning to atrophy drove her to study in her spare time. Every tally in a notebook that foretold of a coworker who secretly despised her heralded the birth of a new friendship. She went so out of her way to be nice to the people who might otherwise plot against her.

People joked that the crash must have knocked the fluff out of her head. She was always so prepared, so focused, so *there* in the moment, with a clarity that only adrenaline could provide.

And her newfound focus was not restricted to the office. The box with the seahorse on the top helped her in all sorts of ways. She was eating healthier, being aware of the sheer number of takeout places with tainted food or staff that wanted her dead. She was exercising more, given the number of acquaintances who could potentially whisper that she was fat and lazy. And she almost never got sick, due to a three part plan of scrupulously avoiding all germs, being up to date on all her inoculations, and turning up at her doctor's office roughly once every-other week.

Felix even asked her out. Felix, the cute guy from IT. He was tall, handsome, charming, well-educated, and from what everyone said, crushing on her.

"He roofies your drink," her box said, prediction ninety-seven for the day.

Ninety-seven was too high. Much too high. No other predictions had come true yet that day. Possibly because she avoided them, but possibly because Felix was a rapist, and she could hardly take that chance. So she canceled their date, and didn't return his calls after that. It was safer that way.

But, she was still happy he asked her out. Cute guys didn't usually give her the time of day. Maybe, she thought, all the exercise was working for her. It was good.

"Do you like the Safety Box?" her parents asked, calling her a week after her cast finally came off.

"It's great," she said, "I love it. Really helped me get my life in order."

Then her hand started to shake, and she didn't know why, a tremble that started in her fingertips and worked its way up to her wrist, her arm. Like she was shivering.

"I'm so glad," her father said. "I carved the top myself. You *loved* seahorses so much when you were little."

"That shaking is the onset of a seizure," the box said. "You're having a stroke."

"I gotta go," Sarah said, hanging up the phone. She immediately called 911, and had an ambulance sent to her house. As she waited for them to arrive, she pulled out her notebook, and added the prediction to her log.

It went under *Plausible*. People in their twenties rarely had seizures, but it could happen.

Her insurance had very little sympathy for her calling an ambulance because she had a shiver. They declined to pay for any of it, and the hospital was cruel. Including her CAT scan for possible stroke, the bill came to over $25,000.

But she had the money the company had given her from the car crash. So it was fine. She didn't panic, or scream, or rant. She paid the bill, and then looked for an insurance plan that *would* cover her in every eventuality.

Such a plan was, of course, much more expensive than her current one, but that was fine; she didn't need to eat out or go to the movies or fritter away her money on other things. Frugality was key. And, she needed to be closer to the hospital in case something happened, and in a low-crime area, and somewhere she could add extra locks to her doors in case of home invasion.

So she left her comfortable three-bedroom in the downtown, and moved to a studio apartment near the hospital. It was much cheaper. The difference paid for extra insurance, extra security, extra peace of mind, and when the box whispered, "This place is full of lead-based paint." She took the time to test every wall herself.

The test for lead came back negative. She repainted the walls anyway.

Her shivering got worse, and a dozen trips to the hospital in a dozen days did not reveal the cause. She shook when nobody was around, and when others were around, she locked her eyes on them like a frightened animal. She tried meditation, medication, mindfulness, until she was reminded that meditation was bullshit, medication could poison her, and she was already pretty damn mindful.

She was more mindful than most, she thought. She saw to every detail of her life.

Of course, driving to work presented its own problems: carjackers, mass shootings, muggings, car accidents, natural disasters. Her company's office was quite old. What if it wasn't up to code, and there was an earthquake? It could collapse and kill her. She looked up the office with the County Registrar, and all its inspections did appear up to date, but those forms were so easy to fake.

"Today you will be exposed to asbestos due to your employer faking a safety inspection of the office." Prediction eighty-seven, *Likely*.

She didn't blunder into her boss's office, shouting that she had to work from home or she'd die. "Your coworkers will become convinced you've gone crazy," was prediction twelve that day, and a prediction several days before that. No; she planned, she prepared. She invented a story about caring for an elderly relative, with tragic implications and reasonable supporting evidence. She assembled an unimpeachable case that working from home would improve both her life and her job performance.

"Well," her boss said, "normally I'd say no, but you are one of our best employees. So as long as your productivity doesn't drop, I suppose it's okay."

Months of hard work paid off in that moment. She said her goodbyes, left the office for the last time, and returned to her apartment. Her apartment in one of the safest buildings in the city, where all possible toxic chemicals had been identified and removed, where there were a dozen locks on the door. Two months worth of food was in storage in case of natural disaster, along with several safety kits. She had her work laptop for talking with her coworkers, and for talking with everyone else, a burner phone and a high-security machine, devices that ensured no criminal on the internet could identify her real location or steal her banking information.

The day she came home, her box said, "You're going to be hit by a car," and with a smile, she wrote it under *Absurd*.

She slept soundly that night, for the first time in so long.

The next morning, her box said, "Today, the world comes to an end." She started a new page in her notebook, added her three columns, and under *Absurd* wrote "Apocalypse." Then she made a tally at the bottom, *1/100*, and got up to start the day. She had to check for spiders, check for mold, check for spoiled food, eat a perfectly balanced breakfast, and start work an hour early before anyone could think ill of her for working from home.

She was examining her bananas when the box said, "Today, the world comes to an end."

It was the first time she had ever heard the box make the same prediction twice. Hesitantly, she made another tally in her notebook, but overall thought it a good thing. "Right," she said aloud, "but only one prediction comes true. So if you predict the same thing twice, that prediction must be wrong."

In reply, the box made its third prediction for the day. "Today, the world comes to an end."

Sarah's shaking returned. She sat at her table, fingers trembling, and waited for the box to tell her she was having a seizure, or had diabetes, or needed to rush to the hospital.

"Today, the world comes to an end."

She hyperventilated, clutching her face, breathing in her hands, whispering profanities to herself over and over. Opening all the locks on her door revealed the building hallway, and she threw a wad of cash halfway through the open doorframe, so it would be visible to anyone passing by. Money, a nice apartment, an unlocked door. She waited for the box to tell her she was going to be robbed.

"Today, the world comes to an end."

She did not go to work. She did not exercise or cook or do any of the other things she meant to do. She spent the whole day research-ing ways the world could potentially come to an end before midnight that night. Predictions the box made were not predestined. Perhaps she could avert what was to come.

Her conclusions did not inspire her: asteroid impact, nuclear war, a black hole passing through the solar system, supervolcano erup-tion. None of the ways the world might abruptly end seemed within her power to change.

But didn't she have to try?

She called NASA, and when their general helpline blew her off, she put her considerable research skills to use finding the personal cell-phone number of a mid-level director. He picked up his phone, and she argued and screamed and ranted about imminent danger from the stars. But he called her crazy, and hung up.

Two more NASA staff blocked her calls, and by mid-afternoon, she couldn't find any more numbers. That left two possibilities she could theoretically do something about: nuclear war, and a supervolcano.

She couldn't find any numbers for anyone at the DoD—not surprising, really—but a nuclear war wouldn't be instant death for everyone on the planet. Remote areas would survive. Likewise, a supervolcano would not be instantly fatal for the entire population, and she might ride it out if she was lucky and had enough food.

"Today, the world comes to an end."

By four o'clock, it was up to prediction fifty-two, all of them the same. Her car tore out of the parking lot for her apartment, headed first to the bank, then to the nearest shopping center. The car she filled with food, clean water, iodine tablets, filter masks, bullets, a gun, and everything else she thought she might need to survive the apocalypse. Stuffed into the glove compartment was a printout from her research.

Likely targets of nuclear strikes, supervolcanos in the western hemisphere, safest places to ride out the above. She'd found a farmhouse in the middle of nowhere, that was somehow listed on AirBnB.

"Today, the world comes to an end."

She drove all night across the country, watching the clock tick by, the box with the seahorse on the top resting on her dashboard.

"Today, the world comes to an end."

When she found the farmhouse, navigating by GPS, she drove through the picket fence that surrounded it. Perhaps because it was hard to see, or perhaps because she simply didn't see it. Either way, she didn't care. It was too close to midnight.

"Today, the world comes to an end."

She threw all her supplies into the basement, and took shelter under the strongest part of the structure.

"Today, the world comes to an end."

Her hands shook uncontrollably, and it was only with considerable effort that she took out her notebook and little pencil, and made another entry on the tally. When she finally came to rest in the farmhouse, she was up to ninety-one.

With the notebook to her right, the light of her cellphone to her left, she watched both the tally and the time advance. To her, the room felt as a furnace, and she broke out in a hot sweat. Drops ran down her face and fell from her nose, staining the paper.

Prediction ninety-two came at 11:12 PM. Still the same. Ninety-three came at 11:22, and so forth. Ninety-nine came at 11:59 PM. "Today, the world comes to an end."

One prediction left. One which had to come true.

Her phone didn't display seconds, so she counted them down aloud: sixty, fifty-nine, fifty-eight, and so forth. Tears ran down her face, and her vision blurred as she began to sob. The trembling in her hands was so violent that she clawed at her own flesh, digging long and bloody scratches down her arms.

Then the last prediction came, at the very stroke of midnight.

"Today's the day you finally snap."

Fog Net

~ Sarah Day

Oleg stole my fucking ICCA grant.

Okay, he didn't steal it. That's not accurate. He was awarded my fucking ICCA grant.

Okay, it wasn't my fucking ICCA grant.

But it *would* have been mine, if not for Oleg.

I'm the best grad student in the department. First author on three papers. Four patents. Senior editor of that stupid journal only a dozen people read. I haven't been on vacation in two years. Sasha's always saying he never sees me anymore. And why? Because I'm the best grad student in the department. Everyone says I'm headed for the Oceanology Institute. Everyone says I'll be a full RAS member before I'm thirty.

Unless fucking Oleg puts a shiv in my career by taking my fucking ICCA grant!

And to do what? Burn some reindeer shit? They want to give a boatful of money to someone studying REINDEER SHIT?!

Okay, Vika, calming breath. Do that synapse breathing you heard about in that podcast. This isn't good for your blood pressure.

List the things you still need to do today:

• Email Vitaly about re-running the neohydrolysis test with those new meteorain magnets. Space magnets = more H20 faster?

• Get to the bug peddler *before* 7pm today—the line's been awful since no one can afford quadruped anymore and the hen flu wiped out all the poultry.

• Buy a pregnancy test. Stress is one thing, but three months is maybe too long.

. . .

. . .

. . .

It's because alternative energy is sexy right now, is why. Everyone wants to be the one to outrun the oil shortages. Failing that, they want to be the ones who funded the person who outruns the oil shortages. So here comes Oleg with some barely-plausible idea about waste reconstitution, can't they see he's just reinventing the omniprocessor? The Gates Foundation already did this, but he went on about how Russia has the best chance to develop the biofuel that saves us because of the unique environmental factors in the taiga and the grant committee just dropped to their knees. Their *knees*. Over *reindeer shit.*

I suppose if I'm going to be completely honest, his research position does paint a slightly more hopeful picture of the future (tldr: we can maintain our current population and living standards if we're all willing to smell burning reindeer shit every time we go outdoors) than mine does (tldr: we're fucked into the seventh generation, and we should accept it and get moving, because our septly-fucked descendents are going to need *water*). I get why that's attractive. But still.

I am medicated to prevent me from feeling feelings EXACTLY LIKE THIS.

OLEG!

☉

Dear journal,

Another day, another dollar. Or another thirty thousand dollars because (surprise!) it turns out the seawall still isn't fixed. Almost a quarter-mile of wall gave way overnight. Found one of the condensers on Jake Willet's front lawn. It's okay—neohydrolysis gel is pretty durable (thanks Mom!). With no rain in four months and the sea advancing on us like the indecisive hand of God, losing a condenser would be a disaster. We're already timing our showers.

Speaking of water, the high school gym is sunk in two feet of it, thanks to the wall breach. I went down there this morning. Smelled like fish shit and feet.

I thought Mox would be freaked out, but nope. Stood there watching the ocean eat the only school in town, like "At least the greenhouse is dry, we can still save the sprouts." Remarkably chill little person I have there. No idea where that came from. Not me, that's for certain. I just had to up my blood pressure meds.

I *told* Public Infra putting a second layer of concrete on top of the first layer of concrete would just make the wall erode faster. But why would they listen to me? I'm just the mayor. Just the person they elected based on the strength of my environmental agenda, my fresh ideas. Just the son of Dr. Viktoriya Aleksandrova, Russia's Nobel-prize winning climate oceanologist, the woman who invented neohydrolysis. My name's on the darn doorplate, right? IVAN ALEXANDER. Sheesh.

And I have fresh ideas! They just take humanpower, which we have, and money, which we don't, and time, which we're running out of.

No one wants to abandon the coastlines, reestablish the topsoil with trees that can tolerate more water (cypress, zelkova, I have a whole list!), pull away from the sea, regroup uphill. Everyone is so focused on maintaining what we have, they're not interested in what we could do.

There are the bad guys outside of town, too. That's what Mox calls them, but I shouldn't even write that down, probably. Some of them are technically my constituents, not that any of them are registered to vote.

~~Bad guys~~ Racists ~~Bad guys~~ Psychos ~~Bad guys~~ Christian death cultists

I'll just stick with bad guys.

I think people in town find them as abhorrent as I do and want to avoid moving inland. I hope that's true. I want it to be true—I want to be safe here as we were in Seattle. Constituency be damned, I can't shake the hand of a man with me-colored skin and a cross tattooed on his neck and then go home and confront Zara's eyes staring at me out of our kid's face. Our half-Black kid.

I miss her every day.

I can see the wall from here. My desk faces a window and on clear days I can see the fleet of condensers bobbing behind the upper lip of the concrete slab. At high tide, water slops over the top like beer over the rim of a glass.

Thank God hops have such high heat tolerance. We may be sinking like Atlantis, but at least we still have beer.

- I

☉

Spring, 1 year after the fall
No idea how to keep an almanac.
No idea how to do anything.

Spring

No one knows what they're doing. Everyone would rather be back in town, but the flooding's so bad it's not safe anymore. The buildings are dissolving, except for the housing shells we moved the condensers into last year when the seas got too rough.

Everyone coming to me for suggestions on seedlings and planting schedules and square footage, like having a botany degree means I'm Mox Alexander, Farmer. Pff. I can't even keep an almanac right.

Still, you do what you can do. I might not be a farmer, but I can make a green thing grow.

Mox Alexander, Grower.

Spring

Planting season. Dog-ass tired every day. Hoping everything roots soon enough that it can survive the summer. It's early spring, but everything's gotta go in the ground as soon as it thaws.

I miss cheeseburgers.

Spring

Bad guys came to the farm today. They wanted our food. Enough of us here to warn them off with just numbers.

Elli wants to move us back into town, maybe see if we can fix up some of the old buildings. Something secure, she says, for winter, but I can tell it's not just that. I saw how the bad guys looked at me. This is a pretty pale population, and I stick out.

Spring

Cherry blossoms!

Summer, 1y ATF

Lost Patrick today. Tiller threw a rock, hit him in the face. Popped his eye. Total surprise. Patrick was our doctor. Kirsten's brother. Fuck.

I can hear Elli crying in the next room. Want to comfort her, but not sure what to say.

Not sure what to say.

Rock whipped him around in a circle like he was dancing, like the news he was dead had to catch up to the rest of his body.

Summer

Hop harvest. Condensers still working, thank God. Every couple days a crew goes into town, lets themselves into the shells, taps the condensers, and comes back with carts of fresh water. That and the catchments off the barn mean there's plenty of water to go around. Gonna make beer.

Miss Dad a lot.

Sept 21?

Sun calendar I keep on the kitchen floor says it's probably the equinox.

October 1ish

Elli's fixing up one of the housing shells in town. Lots of the panels are damaged or missing, but she's starting to repair them, put flexiplas sheeting over the holes. She says if we can scrounge enough material from the dead buildings in town, maybe we can build up a whole network of domes, use them as greenhouses, maybe get the solar working again, maybe live in them, maybe maybe maybe.

Madness. She's always got a big dream. I love her.

November???

Small group came to the farm. They looked rough. Hungry. Faces I thought I recognized—some of the bad guys from the spring? But there were little kids with them. Never imagined the bad guys having kids, but that feels stupid, writing it out. Of course they do.

Don't know what they'd come here for anyway. Barely enough for us to eat.

Winter, 1y ATF

Cold AF.

Winter

One of the condensers died this morning. Not sure if it's a problem with the fans, or with something electric in the box itself? Elli's as close as we have to an electrical engineer but she couldn't make the thing work.

We peeled the neohydro gel from inside the casing, at least. Might be we can add it to the gel in an existing condenser, or save it in case something goes wrong with another.

Fuck it, I'm tired of trying to solve problems.

Bad day.

Winter

Moved into the domes today. They're not all done, still a couple gaps in the upper panels, but the wind got too bad to stay on the farm. Trees going down everywhere. Was worried about the sprouting shed blowing over, taking all the seeds and cuttings with it. In here they'll be warmer, better protected.

Nice to be in a modern building again. The farmhouse leaked like a gassy husband.

Spring, 2y ATF

Planting season. Every day we trek out to the farm before dawn. Walking home in the evening, I can see the domes going up against the sky. Four already and more to come. Don't want Elli up on the ladders much longer—belly's getting too big. Kid should be here by midsummer.

Spring

Blight in the cherry orchard.

Spring

Bad guys came again. Smaller crew than last year, but meaner looking. Had to plead with Elli not to meet them at the farmstead with the rest of the crew. Length of rebar in her hands like she was gonna whack someone.

"It's my home too, Mox," she says, "I can fight."

She's my home, though, and the baby. I talked her out of it.

Spring

Losing the cherry trees a big blow; fruit, yeah, but also morale. No more branches floating on the breeze. No more blossom season. Feels like nothing good can last, sometimes, like we're unspooling the last of our thread.

Enough of that.

Summer

One of the condensers broke today. Down to three now. If we lose those, we're fucked, we'll have to move uphill and that's where the bad guys are and . . .

Be cool. Be cool.

Rainy season was good. Catchments are full. Gonna build a cistern. We can get through this. We've gotten through everything else.

Summer

Baby's coming.

☉

- Log start -

They arrived at dusk yesterday and camped outside the domes. Probably forty of them. I went up on the upper walkway and looked through the panels at their camp. Little fires. All the people dirty and scraggle-haired and stooped. They look so hungry.

Tersa went out to greet them and didn't come back. My baby.

She's so smart, nothing can have happened to her. Nothing has happened to her. I know it.

- Log start -

They want the condenser. One of them, a big man wearing armor made of old tires, came to the antedome today and said so, speaking through a two-inch slit Timor opened in the external door. They know we have a means of making fresh water. He said give it to them and they leave us in peace.

I don't know what they'll do if we tell them the condenser fell silent ten days ago and has yet to wake.

It's not exactly dead—water coalesces on the transparent fleshy lining inside the box, weeps down the walls like sap. You can press a cup to it and come away with enough to drink. But it won't suffice to quench the dozen of us inside the domes, much less the people clustered outside.

Still no sign of Tersa.

- Log start -

They'd like to get in. The doors are holding.

I understand why they'd want to. I remember how the domes looked the last time I was under the open sky. Like soap bubbles full of treasure. The plant dome looks like a green jewel from the outside, and the solar cells gleam in the daylight. It's clear we have power in here, real power like they did in the Old Times . . . although nothing so fine as then. Even with all the cells running, harvesting the light, we have to ration. No one under fifty is even allowed to touch the terminals, leave logs like this one. Guess they figure that's how us old folks can still contribute, ha ha, by sharing our memories.

Did Momma and Moxda plan for this, when they rebuilt the domes? That we could use them not only as a resource, but as a refuge? They must have. The plant dome, sleeping domes, the gathering dome—they're only connected to each other, not to the outside. You have to go through the vestibule dome to get into the world, and all the ground-level panels are reinforced with metal and concrete. We could shelter in here for a very long time.

– Log start –

The condenser continues to sleep. Its six twisters should be running together, giving off the quiet hum that became the background to everything in the plant dome. Aurel says the box was powered by a phantom, and now it's escaped. I think Aurel is a superstitious idiot, but I haven't a better explanation than that.

– Log start –

I saw Tersa! She clambered up the panels and peeked in through the flexiglass. She looked annoyed, but she always does. I wish I could crack the exterior door and let her slip back in, but until those strangers outside are gone, she'll have to make do outdoors. She's clever. She'll be all right.

I spent extra time at the sprouting altar, talking to the seedlings and thanking the earth for its providence. My heart. To see my daughter alive, I, I can't describe it.

– Log start –

They're trying something new today. They've felled a tree and are trying to ram it into the exterior door. When I hold my breath, I can hear the muffled thuds against the metal.

I wish the condenser was working. Maybe if we could give them some water, they would go away.

– Log start –

They took Timor. He wanted to speak with them, the stupid child, and as soon as he had the antedome door cracked an inch, they had branches and spears wedged in, trying to pry it open. They seized him and pulled him out, and two of their own slipped in.

I was in the plant dome when I heard the commotion, and by the time I got to the pressure door, Aurel had sealed it, and used the control panel to lock all the other doors. The two outsiders are trapped in the antedome now, prowling like wildcats. They're holding spears, faces swabbed with mud. They look angry. They look hungry.

I don't know what happened to Timor. I think Horvel does, but from his face I don't want to ask.

- Log start -

The outsiders changed their approach overnight. They sent a dozen young people up onto the smaller domes, so when we awoke bodies were stretched across the panels like spiders. Even as I speak they're trying to prise up the capstones, peel away the roof panels.

Aurel and Brillia took the little ones out of the school dome and into the plant dome, just to be safe. They said it was because the strangers' shadows were distracting, but I can tell they're worried.

Fortunately the bigger domes are too round to climb easily. Now we're all clustered together in the plant, sleeping, and gathering domes. Even if the strangers can make it into the little domes, the pressure doors should keep us safe. Eventually they'll give up, go away.

- Log start -

I went up on the observation walk this morning and saw the outsiders have erected some kind of structure outside the doors. It's like a T with an extra growth on top, or an X tipped on one point. There was a group gathered around it, one of them standing in front of it waving his arms. I couldn't hear anything, but they looked like they were chanting, or singing.

I don't understand anything anymore.

- Log start -

They destroyed the storage dome today. Idiots took too many panels out of the top, and it came down almost atop them. I think one of them got trapped beneath.

We've never lost a dome before. At least it was one of the small ones. If the outsiders go away, perhaps we can rebuild it.

If they go away.

I hate them.

- Log start -

In my dream last night, the domes cracked open like eggs. We all tumbled out in a spurt of saltwater and stale air, each coated in a gel skin like the inside of the condenser. I was bloody and wet and I rolled over on the ground, trying to identify my limbs. That sleeping state where you know you have a body but don't know how it's composed. I flopped onto my belly and worked my mouth, searching for air. I looked up and saw Tersa standing at the waterline, bright clean and new.

Momma told me that that's how people came to the Earth, that long ago we arrived on the shore as fish.

- Log start -

They're at the pressure door.

☉

". . .What are—? Holy crap. You're kidding. What are you doing here?

"Who would leave a baby out in the dirt? Guess they thought they were coming back, didn't they. Idiots. Pulled the whole dome down on top of them. And on top of my people too. Obviously. No survivors . . . Present company excepted."

". . . Fuck. Okay. Come on, Tersa. Breathe. Stop crying."

. . .

"I can't just leave you here, can I?

"At least you fit in my backpack."

. . .

"They killed my family. Our seeds. Everything. I'm alone now—except for you, I guess. You're basically a seedling yourself. A person-sprout.

"I wonder what your name was.

"I'll tell you one thing, sprout, we're gonna have plenty of fresh water. Those idiots—your people, sorry, no disrespect—they broke all the way into the domes, killed Timor, killed my family, didn't even know what they were looking for.

"Aurel thought the condenser was some kind of magical house, that a baby god or something lived inside it, but Aurel's—fuck, Aurel *was* a loony.

"It's not the box. It's the *gel*, the snot coating the inside of the box. It sucks water out of the air, somehow. So once the haze cleared from the collapse, I went in, found the condenser. Lucky I got there when I did—the sea's hungry to eat what remains of the domes. Got the box open, scraped out the gel, found a jar to put it in. Like a big blue loogie. Gross, right? But it still works—see? I take the lid off and it makes a little puddle on top!

"Nonono, don't touch it! Don't—ugh."

. . .

"Okay sprout, how's about we get away from the coast? There's probably more food inland. I don't know about you, but I don't want to live on seagulls and shellfish. If I could catch any seagulls. Or find any shellfish.

"Anyway, I figure we head east and see what's on the other side of the mountains. You in?

". . .You're in."

. . .

"Hang on. Hold still. Let me get this tarp around you. Dust storms aren't gonna be great for your tiny eyes. Hold still. Hold still. Shhhhh. There we go."

. . .

"You like that? That's rabbit. Thinking it over? Hah! Great face.

"Good, right? Here's another little shred. Get that in you, help you grow up real big.

"Glad you're old enough to have real food. No idea what I would have done with an infant."

. . .

"Ohfuckohfuckohfuckohfuck are you okay? I'm so sorry. I'm *so* sorry. I would never drop you on purpose. I just slipped. I'm so sorry. Fuck. Are you okay?

". . .I think you're okay."

. . .

"Ughhhh you're *heavy*. We're only halfway there. I'm hoping that the world is greener on the other side of this hill, because summer's coming out here and I don't know about you, but I'm tired of the dust.

"*Bigass* hill. Basically a mountain."

. . .

"PLEASE STOP CRYING."

. . .

"Wowwww. Look at that view! Not as green as it could be, I guess, but it's still awfully pretty. All those rock formations! Wish I knew anything about rocks!

". . .All this natural wonder is lost on you, isn't it, kid? Jeez.

". . .Wait, what is that? Do you see that?"

. . .

"Okay, so what did we learn? There's people down there. People with what I guess are probably guns. Never seen a gun before. One of them took a potshot at us, I dunno if you noticed that. Thanks to my quick thinking, I fell on my ass, so hopefully they think they got me. Fuck, who shoots at a single person up on a hill? Why do they have those red tattoos?

"Oh. Oh *no*. Oh *fuck*. They broke the fucking condenser jar! Or I did, I guess, when I fell on it! You okay? No glass on you, right?

"Uggggh, this is a disaster, how the fuck am I supposed to carry a gallon of mostly-liquid gel without a container? There's goo all over the inside of my pack! UGH.

"Okay Tersa. Silver lining. Silver lining. At least they didn't hit *you*. And the jar's somewhat intact. It'll still work for a little while, I'll just have to be careful not to cut myself.

"And also? In those rock structures on the other side of the valley? I think I saw the land in rows, like they were planting. Plumes of smoke. Maybe a town."

. . .

"Okay sprout, I've got this idea. Aurel told me that back in the Old Times, people used to catch water with nets, really fine-woven fabric on frames that would wick the condensation out of the air. Fog nets.

"Honestly I think it might be made up, but it's also kinda how the condenser goo works. If we stretch it over something, we can produce more water; if there's regular airflow over it, even more. We gotta carry it somehow, we might as well carry it on us. At least it's sticky.

"See, what I'm thinking is, if we can make it to that village, they might let us in, keep us safe from those red-tattoo people, if I had something to trade. Fresh water's a pretty good thing to trade. So we spread the goo over ourselves like a big blanket, our own fog net, and show up on their doorstep just absolutely dripping. Impressive, right? What do you think? Sprout?

". . .Are you falling asleep?"

. . .

"Okay, first things first. We gotta get around the valley basin. I got most of the goo back in what's left of the jar, and I'm thinking as soon as the sun starts coming up, we head out around the southern edge of the valley."

. . .

"Look, sprout. We were right—it's a village. Wow, it's built *into* the side of that big rock formation. How did they do that? That's nuts. Oop—watch your step. Watch my step, I guess. Slippery. Goodbye, rock. Jeez that made a lot of noise. Yikes."

. . .

"Hsssss okay. Oh fuck. Oh no. Fuck that hurts. Fuck.

"You okay sprout? Please be okay.

"They shot my fucking arm!

"Okay Tersa. Deep breath. Get moving. Your feet aren't broken. Just your arm. My arm . . .

"Stop crying! Move it!"

. . .

"I know, I know, it's cold. I'd cry too if I was you. Let's get this goo over us. Man, we smell bad, don't we? Been out here for awhile. I'm shaky. Not long now, though. Not far. Just another couple hundred feet. We can make it.

"Yikes, that *is* cold. Okay. You ready? It's you and me, sprout. You and me all the way."

. . .

"HELLO! Hello in there!

"Sprout, shh. Someone's coming out."

"What—who's out there? What are you wearing?"

"Please let us in. We have water. I'm hurt. We need help."

". . .Who are you?"

"I'm Tersa. Tersa Adlar. And this is Sprout."

☉

A DL E
AD LA R
ADLAR
Sprout Adlar
Lucee teach me how to write.
My name is Sprout Adlar.
Lucee ses says write abot war because I was there. I don't have all the words to write abot war.

We won but we lost. The redsky people took some of us, our dead. That's their way. But we keep the ones of them we ~~capch~~ captured. And we keep the fog net, which is why they came here to start.

Happy Tersa didn't have to see our dead go with them in the wagons. She would cry a lot.

I miss Tersa.

Better at war than words.

Tomorrow they will come again and we will talk. Maybe there will be no more war. Maybe we give their captured for our dead. Maybe a lot of things.

⊙

Today I raised the fog net and my people's hands bore it.

There's no predicting the rainy season anymore; some years, spring is just a handmaiden for a dry, blazing, tower-cloud summer. Others, the winter skulks off like a coyote, with rain the sound of the brush closing behind its tail.

I am the cloudwatcher, and I declare the harvest, so when the darkness crackled over the west horizon I summoned the eight attendants and carried the fog net to the circle altar atop the mesa.

When the bottom fell out of the clouds, sixteen hands pulled the fleshy membrane wide, until it was thin as a whisper and jittering with the impact of raindrops. I darted beneath the net and lifted the point of my staff.

Rain hit the sloping net and multiplied itself as it ran. Far more water than the clouds provided sobbed off the edges of the net and into the basins set beneath the altar. Each basin drains into the tile-lined cisterns we've hollowed out of the mesa's stone heart. When full, they can sustain us for months.

This is the blessing of the fog net, to give as much water as we're strong enough to hold.

Standing underneath, I watched the net marble. Faint shadows sluiced down my limbs, the ghosts of rainwater. The scent of the storm rioted in my nose; ozone, wet dust, the sweet exhalations of desert plants opening to receive the rain. The net began to weigh heavy. I shoved the staff up against it, working the muscles in my back and shoulders.

Lightning fluttered across the bruised sky. Beneath the altar, the basins glugged and laughed. Being under the fog net was like returning to the womb; dark, stifled, more sound than sight. The world outside the net melted into a blur of grays and blues, the attendants hovering just beyond like eight midwives, ushering in the future of the mesa.

Two of my spouses were among those holding the net. I watched their fingers twist tightly as the weight of water belled it out. Water ran in sloppy sheets off the edges, splashing around their feet. The other six attendants come from the mesa villages. Three of them bore the red-inked knuckles and nails of the Red Sky tribes, who until a generation ago had been our enemies. Perhaps we would be at war still, had my father, the first cloudwatcher, not brought members of the Red Sky atop the mesa, inviting them to hold the net and share the harvest with us. I have reason to be grateful for that—the first Red Sky woman to take up the net later became my mother.

The air inside the net dimmed as the rain thickened. I shouted to hold fast, hoping to be heard over the roar. Water cascaded off the net in such abundance I could no longer see the attendants' feet. I wondered if this would be the time someone's hand slipped, or the net tore, or there was some other catastrophe—but my spouses were strong, and the other six were strong, and the net held. In my heart I felt we could hold until the bottomless cisterns filled, until the pipes backed up and the top of the mesa was ankle-deep in the womb waters of the fog net.

My father says that when he was small, the fog net made water from the air passing over it, that a child's breath could render its blue-silver skin damp like the underside of a stone in the early morning. I don't know if that was ever true, or if he's telling me a fable, trying to keep my idea of magic in the world alive, trying to keep my heart hopeful, like a child's.

He doesn't understand that I don't need hope.

All things are temporary. I know the net may fail. I know my people did not spring up here on the mesa but arrived, and that someday we may depart. I know death swallows each of us.

But not today.

I am Anat, daughter of Sprout, son of Tersa, daughter of Steff, daughter of Mox, child of Ivan, son of Viktoriya, and today I raised the fog net and my people's hands bore it.

CONTRIBUTORS

Forrest Aguirre

Forrest Aguirre's work has appeared in over fifty venues, most recently *Vastarien*, *Infra-Noir*, and *Synth*. He has also written several roleplaying game supplements including B*eyond the Silver Scream* and *Killer of Giants*. He is a World Fantasy Award-recipient for his editorial work on the *Leviathan 3* anthology. His novel, *Heraclix and Pomp*, is available from Underland Press.

He hosts the blog "Forrest for The Trees" at forrestaguirre.blogspot. com and can be found on Twitter @ForrestAguirre.

Forrest no longer lives in Madison, Wisconsin.

Michael Barsa

Michael Barsa grew up in a German-Syrian household in New Jersey and spoke no English until he went to school. So began an epic struggle to master the American "R" and a lifelong fascination with language. He now teaches environmental and natural resources law, and his scholarly articles have appeared in several major law reviews, *The Chicago Tribune*, and *The Chicago Sun-Times*.

His first novel, *The Garden of Blue Roses* (released through Underland Press), made the Preliminary Ballot for the Bram Stoker Award for First Novel and received praise from Alice Sebold, Paul Tremblay, *Kirkus Reviews*, and *Library Journal*.

Nathan Batchelor

Nathan lives in and writes fiction from Columbus, Ohio. He has sold more than a dozen stories to magazines across the world. He is currently in a creative writing MFA program at Ashland University.

You can find him on twitter @NateBatchelor.

Breanna Bright

Breanna Bright is the author of *In The End*. She works as a tech-nical writer in southeast Missouri, and uses her free time travel-ing, reading, and looking for new adventures.

Elou Carroll

Elou Carroll is a graphic designer and freelance photographer who writes. Her work appears or is forthcoming in *Aloe, Emerge Literary Journal, 101 Words, Apparition Lit, Walled Women,* and *perhappened* mag. She is the editor-in-chief of *Crow & Cross Keys*, and she spends far too much time on Twitter (@keychild).

Brandon Crilly

An Ottawa teacher by day, Brandon Crilly has been previously published by *Daily Science Fiction, Abyss & Apex, PULP Literature, On Spec,* Flame Tree Publishing, and other markets. He received an Honorable Mention in the 2016 Writer's Digest Popular Fiction Awards, reviews fiction for Black-Gate.com and serves as a Programming Lead for Can*Con in Ottawa. With Evan May, he's the co-host of the podcast *Broadcasts from the Wasteland,* described as "eavesdropping on a bunch of writers at the hotel bar."

You can find Brandon at brandoncrilly.wordpress.com or on Twitter: @B_Crilly.

Sarah Day

Sarah Day lives in the SF Bay Area with her cat and a large collection of LED lights. Her interests include creature films, festival culture, and doing things on purpose. Find her at sarahday.org or on Twitter @scribblingfox.

Jetse de Vries

Jetse de Vries—@upbeatfuture—is a technical specialist for a propulsion company by day, and a science fiction reader, editor and writer by night. He's also an avid bicyclist, total solar eclipse chaser, single malt aficiona-do, Mexican food lover, metalhead and intelligent optimist.

On March 28th, 2021, he posted the world's first NFT SF novel on Ethere-um's Mintable. The landing page on his website "The Future Upbeat" lists where his debut novel *Forever Curious* is available. https://www.the-fu-ture-upbeat.com/

Eric Del Carlo

Eric Del Carlo's short fiction has appeared in *Asimov's, Analog, Clarkesworld* and many other publications. He co-wrote the urban fantasy novel *The Golden Gate Is Empty* with his father, Victor Del Carlo.

Find him on Facebook for questions and comments.

Louis Evans

Louis Evans is a Jewish writer living and working in New York City, on land once inhabited by the Munsee Lenape. It was good land: fertile slash-and-burn fields, fish and shellfish in the river. Lots of beaver, which was popular in Europe . . . you know what happened next.

Louis's work has appeared in *Nature: Futures, Analog SF&F, Interzone,* and more. He's online at evanslouis.com and tweets @ louisevanswrite

Tori Fredrick

Tori Fredrick is a librarian specializing in reader services, a northern transplant to North Carolina, and a lifetime horror fan (with an incredibly strong stomach). By enthusiast standards she has a moderately sized Tarot collection and is very honored that her second fiction publication is appearing in *Underland Arcana.*

H. L. Fullerton

H. L. Fullerton writes fiction—mostly speculative, occasionally about being haunted—which can be found in more than 50 anthologies and magazines including *Mysterion, Translunar Travelers Lounge,* and *Lackington's,* and is the author of the somewhat haunting novella: *The Boy Who Was Mistaken for a Fairy King.*

You may follow them on Twitter at @ByHLFullerton

Manfred Gabriel

Manfred Gabriel's short stories have appeared in over two dozen publications, most recently *Liquid Imagination*, James Gunn's *Ad Astra,* and *Crimson Streets.* He lives and writes in Western Wisconsin, where he spends his days dealing with people and writes at night to keep his sanity.

Vera Hadzic

Vera Hadzic is a writer from Ottawa, Ontario. Recently, her work has appeared in *Hexagon Magazine*, *Idle Ink*, *Okay Donkey Magazine*, and elsewhere.

She can be found on Twitter @HadzicVera or through her website, www.vera-hadzic.com.

Catherine Hansen

Catherine Hansen lives with her family and teaches literature in Tokyo. She grew up between rural South Carolina and urban Japan. A book with Strange Attractor Press, titled *In Search of the Third Bird*, represents—at the same time—her latest creative work and her latest scholarly work. One day, you may well find her on Twitter.

Christopher Hawkins

Christopher Hawkins is an award-winning horror author, with short stories appearing in over a dozen magazine and antholo-gies. He is a former editor of the *One Buck Horror* anthology series, as well as an avid gamer and collector of curiosities. When he's not writing, he spends his time exploring old cemeteries, lurking in museums, and searching for a decent cup of tea.

For free stories and news about upcoming projects, visit his web-site, www.christopher-hawkins.com, or follow him on Twitter @ chrishawkins.

David Hewitt

David A. Hewitt was born in Germany, grew up near Chicago, and spent eight years in Japan, where he studied classical Japanese martial arts and grew up some more. A graduate of the University of Southern Maine's Stonecoast MFA program in Popular Fiction, he currently teaches English at the Community College of Baltimore County, but has at various times worked as a Japanese translator, an instructor of martial arts, a cabinetmaker's assistant, a pizza/subs/beer delivery guy, and a pet shop boy.

His hobbies include skiing, writing, meditation, writing, disc golf, travel, and writing.

His short fiction has appeared in *Kaleidotrope*, *Metaphorosis,* and *Mithila Review*; his novelette "The Great Wall of America" is also available from Mithila Press as a standalone book. As a translator of Japanese, his credits include the anime series *Gilgamesh, Kingdom,* and *Kochoki: Young Nobunaga*.

Nina Kiriki Hoffman

Over the past four decades, Nina Kiriki Hoffman has sold adult and young adult novels and more than 350 short stories. Her works have been finalists for the World Fantasy, Mythopoeic, Sturgeon, Philip K. Dick, and Endeavour awards. Her novel *The Thread that Binds the Bones* won a Horror Writers Association Stoker Award, and her short story "Trophy Wives" won a Science Fiction & Fantasy Writers of America Nebula Award.

Nina does production work for the *The Magazine of Fantasy & Science Fiction*. She teaches short story classes through Lane Community College, Wordcrafters in Eugene, and Fairfield County Writers' Studio. She lives in Eugene, Oregon.

For a list of Nina's publications, check out: http://ofearna.us/books/hoffman.html.

A. P. Howell

A. P. Howell lives with her spouse, kids, and dog, sometimes near a lake and always near trees. Her stories have appeared in *Daily Science Fiction, Little Blue Marble*, and *XVIII: Stories of Mischief & Mayhem*.

She tweets @APHowell and her website is aphowell.com.

Selah Janel

Selah Janel has written many e-books, including *Mooner, The Ruins of St. Louis, The Inheritance,* and *Candles*. Her work has appeared in anthologies including *The Grotesquerie* and *The Big Bad volumes 1 & 2*, as well as publications such as *Electric Spec* and *Siren's Call*. An unrepentant theater geek, she worked for over twenty years in theater and entertainment building and designing costumes in regional theater, holiday events, amusement parks, and haunted events.

Keep up with her and her work at www.selahjanel.com, www.facebook.com/authorSJ, or @SelahJanel on Twitter.

Nikoline Kaiser

Nikoline Kaiser is the author of several poems and short stories, including "ode to an asexual" published with *Strange Horizons* and "Last Year's Water" with Pole to Pole Publishing. Her work focuses on family, feminism and queer themes. She lives in Den-mark and has a Masters degree in Comparative Literature from Aarhus University.

When not writing, Kaiser works on a project communicating knowledge about women authors around the world and haunts the halls of museums in the hopes of getting to stay among the relics. Visit her at www.nikolinekaiser.wordpress.com.

Jessie Kwak

Jessie Kwak has always lived in imaginary lands, from Arrakis and Ankh-Morpork to Earthsea, Tatooine, and now Portland, Oregon. As a writer, she sends readers on their own journeys to immersive worlds filled with fascinating characters, gunfights, explosions, and dinner parties. She is the author of supernatural thriller *From Earth and Bone*, the Bulari Saga series of gangster sci-fi novels, and productivity guide *From Chaos to Creativity*.

You can learn more about her at www.jessiekwak.com, or follow her on Twitter (@jkwak).

Jon Lasser

Jon Lasser lives in Seattle, WA with his wife and two children. His stories have appeared in *Galaxy's Edge, Little Blue Marble, Untethered: A Magic iPhone Anthology*, and elsewhere. He's a graduate of the Clarion West writers workshop.

Jon McGoran

Jon McGoran is the award-winning author of ten novels for adults and young adults including the YA science fiction thrillers *Spliced, Splintered*, and *Spiked* (Holiday House Books), as well as the acclaimed ecological thrillers *Drift, Deadout*, and *Dust Up* (Tor/Forge). Both *Spliced* and *Splintered* have been honored by American Bookseller's Association as ABC Best Books for Young Readers. His other books include the D. H. Dublin forensic thrillers *Body Trace, Blood Poison*, and *Freezer Burn* (Berkley/Penguin) and *The Dead Ring* (Titan Books), based on the TV show, *The Blacklist*.

He has published numerous short stories, including "Bad Debt," which won an honorable mention in *Best American Mystery Stories 2014*. He is a freelance writer, developmental editor, writing coach, and cohost of The *Liars Club Oddcast*, a podcast about writing and creativity.

For more, visit www.jonmcgoran.com.

J. A. W. McCarthy

J.A.W. McCarthy's short fiction has appeared in numerous publications, including *Vastarien, LampLight, Apparition Lit, Tales to Terrify*, and *The Best Horror of the Year Vol 13* (ed. Ellen Datlow). Her debut collection *Sometimes We're Cruel and Other Stories* was published by Cemetery Gates Media. She lives with her husband and assistant cats in the Pacific Northwest, where she gets most of her ideas late at night, while she's trying to sleep.

You can call her Jen on Twitter and Instagram @JAWMcCarthy, and find out more at www.jawmccarthy.com.

Tristan Morris

Tristan Morris has authored or co-authored four books, but "Seahorses and Other Gifts" is his first publication in *Underland Arcana*. He organizes the Quills and Sofas writing society, a creative writing association based in the San Francisco Bay area, where he lives with his wife.

Linda McMullen

Linda McMullen is a wife, mother, diplomat, and homesick Wisconsinite. Her short stories and the occasional poem have appeared in over ninety literary magazines. She received Pushcart and Best of the Net nominations in 2020.

She may be found on Twitter: @LindaCMcMullen.

Christi Nogle

Christi Nogle's fiction has appeared in over thirty-five publications including *PseudoPod*, *Vastarien*, and Flame Tree's *American Gothic* anthology. Christi teaches English at Boise State University and lives in Boise with her partner Jim and their gorgeous dogs.

Follow her at christinogle.com or on Twitter @christinogle.

Stephen O'Donnell

Stephen O'Donnell is a writer, living in Dublin, Ireland. His short stories have appeared most recently in *Strange Horizons, Short Edition,* and *Typehouse.*

His website is: http://bit.ly/stizzle0dizzle

W. T. Paterson

W. T. Paterson is a three-time Pushcart Prize nominee, holds an MFA in Fiction Writing from the University of New Hampshire, and is a graduate of Second City Chicago. His work has appeared in over 90 publications worldwide including *The Saturday Evening Post, The Forge Literary Magazine, The Delhousie Review, Brilliant Flash Fiction,* and *Fresh Ink.* A semi-finalist in the Aura Estra short story contest, his work has also received notable accolades from Lycan Valley, North 2 South Press, and Lumberloft. He spends most nights yelling for his cat to "Get down from there!"

Visit his website at www.wtpaterson.com.

Lexi Pérez

Lexi Perez is a junkie of all genres, but will always find a home in the dark and twisty. She is inspired by authors like Neil Gaiman and Stephen King, and loves finding cool rocks on hikes. Her hobbies include crochet, knitting, embroidery, and needle felting. Lexi lives in Denver with her partner and cat.

Jennifer Quail

Jennifer Quail is a writer of fantasy, horror, and mystery, a wine-tasting consultant, trivia geek, and owner of two of the world's cutest dogs. In December 2019 she achieved a lifelong dream of appearing on *Jeopardy!* without embarrassing herself in the process. She enjoys travel, art, and excessive amounts of coffee.

Find more at authorjenniferquail.com.

Jonathan Raab

Jonathan Raab is the author of numerous short stories, veteran advocacy essays, and novels including *Camp Ghoul Mountain Part VI: The Official Novelization* and *The Hillbilly Moonshine Massacre.* He is the editor of several anthologies from Muzzleland Press, including *Behold the Undead of Dracula: Lurid Tales of Cinematic Gothic Horror* and *Terror in 16-bits.* He lives in Colorado with his wife Jess, their son, and a dog named Egon.

You can find him on Twitter @jonathanraab1.

Josh Rountree

Josh Rountree writes fantasy, horror, science fiction, and a lot of weird nonsense. His short fiction has appeared in numerous magazines and anthologies, including *Beneath Ceaseless Skies, Realms of Fantasy,* and *A Punk Rock Future.* A new collection of his short fiction, *Fantastic Americana: Stories,* is available from Fairwood Press.

Josh lives in Texas and tweets about movies, books, and guitars @josh_rountree.

Rebecca Ruvinsky

Rebecca Ruvinsky is a student, poet, and emerging writer in Orlando, Florida. She has kept a streak of writing a poem every day since 2016, with work published or forthcoming in *Wizards in Space, Prospectus Literary, Sylvia Magazine, From the Farther Trees,* and others. She loves watching rocket launches, reading late into the night, and finding the magical in the mundane.

She can be found on Twitter @writeruvinsky.

Lorraine Schein

Lorraine Schein is a New York writer. Her work has appeared in *VICE Terraform, Strange Horizons, NewMyths,* and *Mermaids Monthly,* and in the anthology *Tragedy Queens: Stories Inspired by Lana del Rey & Sylvia Plath.*

The Futurist's Mistress, her poetry book, is available from Mayapple Press (www.mayapplepress.com).

Ro Smith

Ro Smith writes fantasy and science fiction that challenges our assumptions about reality through the veil of fiction. Ro has a doctorate in epistemology and metaphysics from the University of York and her short stories have been published by Distant Shore Publishing, Fox Spirit Books, and *Hub Magazine.* As an non-binary author it means a lot to her to represent a diversity of identities in her fiction.

You can find Ro on Twitter @Rhube.

Subscriptions

Underland Arcana is supported by our kind Patreons, who receive quarterly issues of the Arcana in a nifty pocket-sized edition. Consider joining today!

www.patreon.com/underlandpress

Made in the USA
Monee, IL
07 February 2022

89941972R00198